All Aboard for Paradise

Other Five Star Titles
by Dee Marvine:

Sweet Grass

All Aboard for Paradise

Dee Marvine

Five Star • Waterville, Maine

Copyright © 2004 by Dee Marvine

3 1257 01495 1890

This novel is a work of fiction. Names, characters, places and incidents are either the product of the author's imagination, or, if real, used fictitiously.

First Edition
First Printing: February 2004

Set in 11 pt. Plantin by Ramona Watson.

Printed in the United States on permanent paper.

Library of Congress Cataloging-in-Publication Data

Marvine, Dee.
    All aboard for paradise / by Dee Marvine.—1st ed.
      p. cm.
    "Five Star first edition titles"—T.p. verso.
    ISBN 1-59414-114-2 (hc : alk. paper)
    1. Los Angeles (Calif.)—Fiction.   2. Mothers and daughters—Fiction.   3. Women immigrants—Fiction. 4. Railroad travel—Fiction.   5. Businesswomen— Fiction.   I. Title.
PS3563.A7433A78 2004
    813′.54—dc22   2003064710

To my husband Don,
who has made our journey an adventure.

AUTHOR'S NOTE

A fare war between the Southern Pacific and the Santa Fe Railroads took place in March 1886. In two years, 200,000 people flooded into the little town of Los Angeles, producing a land boom that spilled across the surrounding desert. Most of the newcomers were bitterly disappointed by the parched and inhospitable land, and when prices collapsed in 1888, only 50,000 determined immigrants remained to build the city. All this is fact, as are the details of the platting of various Los Angeles suburbs and nearby towns. This book is a work of fiction set in the ambiance of those two momentous years.

PART ONE

CHAPTER ONE

Opportunity seldom knocked at Claire Chadwick's door. But this time she had heard a distinct and fortuitous rap. Determined to respond, she pushed through the crowd in the West Bottoms station and found a place in the line of would-be travelers in front of the ticket window. She held her head high and the flush of indignation on her cheeks prompted a few curious glances, but most of the ticket buyers remained intent on their mission—to take advantage of the bargain fare that seemed too good to be true.

A farmer, his boots still muddied with barnyard soil, counted and recounted the few bills from his pocket while his wife and children hovered near. A drummer of kitchenware retied his battered sample case with a bit of rope as he edged forward in line. Two women of questionable reputation patted their plumed hats and tittered like schoolgirls on a holiday. Having heard the incredible news, all had rushed to the station to seize this chance at a new life. And, heaven help her, Claire was about to do the same.

It all began two weeks before on the night Randy Plank caught up with her as she waited to cross the tracks in front of the station while a monster locomotive, bell clanging, steam hissing, chugged its cars into motion. The raw beam of its headlight silhouetted her tall form and illuminated the anxious planes of her face as the engineer blew two final blasts of the whistle and the train began to roll. Flickering light from the yardman's swinging lantern played over the names on the weathered sides of the freight cars—Atcheson and Topeka, Denver and Rio Grande, Texas Pacific, Southern Pacific, Santa Fe. Claire knew only too well the faded colors and lettering of the rail lines that connected in the Missouri bottomland town of Westport.

Recent snow had melted, leaving a hint of spring in the air, but as she hurried across the tracks behind the departing train, the late February wind tugged at her cloak and whipped fiercely at her skirts. A short distance down the moonlit street, a yellow glow at the window of one of the cottages told her Joanna was already home.

"Mrs. Chadwick, wait up." Frigid gusts reddened the ears and smooth-shaven face of the young man hurrying to catch up with her. Bending toward her to be heard above the train noise, Randy Plank indicated the towel-covered bowl he carried in his farm-strong arms. "Axel said to give this to you."

"Not more kraut and sausages!" Claire sighed through her fatigue. "Thanks, Randy." She would have taken the bowl, but he cradled it against his coat and walked beside her with a jaunty gait, oblivious to the cold wind ruffling his auburn hair. Doing odd jobs around the café while looking for steady work, the amiable Plank had told Claire about having grown up on a hardscrabble farm, the late-born child of aging parents who had both passed on. No longer obligated to them, he said he aimed to find a better way to make a living. His dark serious eyes revealed his vexation at having nothing much to show for his twenty-five years and his impatience with washing dishes, fetching supplies, and sweeping up.

"I'm much obliged to you, Mrs. Chadwick, for lendin' me the books." The open smile he flashed at her hinted that his interest lay not only in the books. "I 'specially liked the essay on self-reliance. I did a good bit of readin' on the farm, but this is my first acquaintance with Mr. Emerson."

"He's a favorite of mine," Claire said.

They had reached the cottage. "Come in and have some supper with us," she offered impulsively, thinking it might be good having Randy there if Axel Kohl came by. Axel had treated her with respect, even showed a generous concern for her welfare by sending leftovers home with her when they closed up at night. She had not encouraged this, lest it place her under some obligation, but he persisted and she was grateful.

But over the past few weeks, Axel had begun to show a more personal interest, and that evening he had asked if he could call on her. What should she do? Even if she could endure the café owner's oafish personality and dull conversation, agreeing would only encourage him. She had been through it all before. First he would ask to stroll out with her, then it would be just a matter of time before he would insist on certain familiarities and, when she refused him, her job would be on the line. Decent jobs for single women were not easy to come by, and she desperately needed this one. It took almost every penny of her wages just to keep her daughter with her, and she would not abandon her hope of sending Joanna to high school in the fall.

The cottage offered relief from the wind, but its two sparsely furnished rooms were icy cold. Joanna sat huddled in a quilt at the table, pencil in hand, studying in the dim light of the kerosene lamp.

Claire hung her cloak on a peg behind the door, the lamplight playing against the copper color of her hair as she tucked stray wisps into the bun at the back of her neck. She crossed to the stove and lifted the lid to the cold firebox. "Joanna, you haven't built the fire?"

"Just got back from my lesson," the girl answered without looking up from her work. "Almost froze to death walking home."

Randy set the bowl on the table and hurried to take the empty coal scuttle from Claire's hand. "Here, let me do that for you."

Joanna looked up in surprise at the sound of a male voice. She was a pretty girl of fifteen, her unusual hyacinth-blue eyes like her mother's, and her hair, a somewhat darker shade of the copper tresses they had inherited from Claire's mother, curled softly at the ends of her heavy braids. "The coal shed's out back," she said, tossing the quilt aside and jumping to her feet. Though she was not as tall as her mother, even in her school jumper her figure promised the same attractive curves.

Randy Plank saw the resemblance between them, but his gaze remained on Claire. "I'll have it warm in here for you in no time." His smile alone would warm the room. He took the scuttle and hurried out the door.

Joanna stared after him. "Who's he?"

"His name is Randy Plank. He works at the café."

"Randy Plank?" Joanna giggled at the name. "Stiff as a board?"

"Now, Joanna, he's a very nice young man." She took a kettle and poured the contents of the bowl into it. "Axel sent us some sausage and kraut."

"Again?" Joanna's rosy lips turned down in a mock pout.

"Yes, again. And I've asked Randy to have supper with us."

"Oh . . ." The girl ran to peer into the small mirror above the washstand.

When Randy had the fire going, Claire warmed their meal and served it.

"Where you from, Randy?" Joanna asked as they ate.

"A farm over yonder," he gestured toward the growing cattle-shipping town called Kansas City strewn over the bluffs above Westport, "but I'm hankerin' to try my luck out west." He speared a forkful of kraut. "California, maybe."

"California?" Claire had seen the recent leaflets promoting California real estate.

Randy nodded. "Land of milk and honey, they say."

"Don't believe everything you read in those leaflets," she cautioned. "Land agents promise anything."

"Some folks made good out there during the gold rush." He helped himself to another sausage.

"Yes, forty years ago," Claire scoffed. "Most of those prospectors squandered what they found and came straggling back dead-broke."

"But some got rich," Joanna interjected, enjoying the novelty of having a guest at the table.

"Only a few, I'm afraid."

"But those who did became important men in San Francisco, didn't they?" Joanna challenged.

"Yes, I suppose some did." Claire was glad to see that her daughter knew something about history. Working such long hours made it difficult to keep up with everything Joanna was thinking and doing.

"California's where I see my future," Randy continued. "Settlers need things. Things I could provide if I had a business out there."

Claire could imagine Randy successful at most anything he tried. He was energetic. Congenial. Smart. She got up to bring the coffeepot from the stove. "You mean you'd like to set up some kind of store in San Francisco?"

"No, someplace farther south where things ain't already grabbed up."

15

"Why don't we all go to Wyoming?" Joanna said. "Women can vote there."

Randy snorted. "There's nothin' in Wyoming."

"Nor in Southern California?" Claire countered.

"Someday there will be," Randy insisted. "You wait and see."

"Life can be hard in a raw, unsettled place like that."

"Maybe. But what's the point in sticking around Westport? Westport's losin' out. It had its day as a jump-off for the old trails, but now that we got railroads these old river ports are dyin'."

"You're right about that." Joanna rolled her eyes to express her boredom with things in general.

"Before long there'll be nothin' but seedy businesses and saloons left here. Mud and mosquitoes. Ain't we seein' it already? Anyone who can will move up yonder to Kansas City."

"And that doesn't appeal to you, Randy?"

"I'm not interested in stockyards and meatpackin'." He turned to Joanna as if convincing her might convince both the Chadwicks. "And I hate these cold winters. They say it's so balmy out there in Southern California you never even need a coat. Sun always shinin'. It's a regular paradise." He rapped his knuckles on the table. "Yes, ma'am. That's where I'm headin'."

"Some paradise! There's nothing down there but barren desert."

"Not according to the land pamphlets. See here . . ." He pulled a tattered flyer from his pocket and unfolded it in the lamplight. "See, it says this place called Los Angeles is a Garden of Eden situated on a clear flowing river." He followed the type with his forefinger as he read aloud. "Warm tropical climate. Soft breezes from the ocean. Acres of orange trees offerin' up their fruit." He thrust the paper toward them. "It says you can't hardly stop those orange trees from growin'."

Claire and Joanna leaned forward to study the illustration of a steamboat carried on the rippling current of a river flanked with orange groves.

"Says eleven thousand people have settled there since the Mexican war," Randy pointed out. "That's a good-sized town."

Joanna studied the sketch. "Golly, Mother, look! Oranges right on the trees."

"I haven't told this to anyone else, but that's where I'm headin'. I made up my mind when I read that essay on self-reliance." Randy leaned back in his chair, thumbs in his pockets, and rakishly raised one dark eyebrow. "It's a whole new country out there, and I aim to take a crack at it."

"I'm sure Emerson knew the difference between self-reliance and foolhardiness," Claire quipped.

"Maybe so. But all I need is ninety-five dollars for the railroad fare and I'm on my way. The Southern Pacific just reduced their price to get passengers for their new line that runs east from Los Angeles and connects with the Santa Fe at the California border, a place called Needles."

"Ninety-five dollars?" Claire exclaimed.

Joanna's eyes widened. "Where would anyone get that much money?"

"That's the problem." Randy slumped back in his chair.

"Don't you have something you could sell?" Joanna remembered the times her mother had sold household items to eke out the rent.

"Sell! I don't have a pot to pee in . . . er . . . sorry, ladies . . . but it's the truth. My folks didn't have nothin'. Pa worked shares all his life. Ma was sick a lot. They never managed to get ahead any." Then he flashed his usual grin. "But I'm young yet. So are you, Mrs. Chadwick. And Joanna sure is. Maybe you two should think about makin' changes, too."

"I never stop thinking about it," Claire confessed wistfully. "There's nothing I'd rather do than find a new and better place for Joanna and me."

"Now's the time," Randy emphasized. "This is 1886. The West is fillin' up fast, and folks with any gumption will be gettin' a toehold out there."

They talked long after the meal was cleared. About sunny California and its promise. About orange groves and accommodating rivers. About the railroads and how they were shrinking the country. About greedy railroad owners who controlled shipping prices, influencing the rise and fall of whole industries and thus the national economy. About dying river towns. About cold Midwest winters and late springs. About self-reliance and its rewards.

Claire liked Randy Plank. A young man with a future, she thought. Just the kind of man she hoped Joanna might someday choose for a husband once he got himself established. Heaven forbid her daughter would ever make the same kind of rash decision she had made. The thought jogged her awareness of the late hour.

"Time for bed, young lady. You have school tomorrow."

"Oh, bother. I'm fifteen, and you still treat me like a baby."

"I treat you like a student who has school tomorrow."

Joanna sighed as she got up from her chair. "Come back and see us again, Randy Plank."

"Thanks, I will." He sat for a moment gazing after her, then turned to Claire, his dark eyes bright in the lamplight. "I suppose I'd better hit the hay, too." He got up and retrieved his coat. "I'm much obliged to you for the supper."

"Thank Axel Kohl. He sent the sausages and kraut." Claire was almost sorry to see Randy leave. His cheerful disposition and new ideas had enlivened the evening.

"Just the same," he said earnestly as they moved toward the door, "I don't know when I've had a better time."

"You're welcome any time, Randy."

"Mrs. Chadwick," he blurted suddenly. "How old are you?"

"Thirty-four. Why?"

"Well, I was just thinkin' that you're very good-lookin', Mrs. Chadwick, for an older woman."

He pulled on his coat and walked into the night, his soft whistling drowned out by the rumble and clang of an arriving locomotive.

CHAPTER TWO

When he had gone, Claire sat down again at the table, took the pins from her hair, and began to brush the long tresses. Suddenly she felt foolish at having been caught up in Randy's enthusiasm for California. Supporting herself and Joanna was difficult enough without entertaining such a crazy notion as making a risky move, especially to such a far-off place.

Yet the idea intrigued her. Was such a thing possible? How could she earn a living there? Open her own café? She had once worked for a milliner, and women everywhere needed hats. She could always do domestic work—she winced at the repugnant thought. Or work as a governess. But was she good with children? She hardly remembered her own mother, and her father had given her little guidance in such matters.

Claire had toughened in the years since she left her father's house on Chicago's fashionable lakeshore, yet a sadness swept over her when she allowed the memories to flow in. Her father, Elsworth Newell, respected financier. Her mother, Caitlin Donovan Newell. Those bittersweet years after her mother's tragic death from pneumonia, years when Claire became her papa's darling. Her private tutoring in the humanities, Miss Palmer's finishing school for well-bred young ladies, her coming-out party on her eighteenth birthday. It all seemed a lifetime ago, as did the subsequent calamity of her father's financial ruin during a sudden recession that caught him overextended, a black season when many banks failed and even some of the oldest established firms toppled.

Of course she never should have married when she did, but in her desolation after her father's suicide, there was Carter Chadwick offering to take care of her. "My beautiful, beautiful girl," he called her. He promised her everything but, after they were married, delivered nothing but abuse and neglect. Her demands that he mend his ways prompted him to distance himself by leaving town for extended trips, and when she found herself in the family way she followed him to Westport. Claire winced with the painful memory of the night she told him about the baby. That was the last time she saw him.

Left penniless in the frontier town, she paid for her confinement by working at a home for unwed mothers, a converted boardinghouse run by nuns. Somewhat older than most of the "unfortunates," and considered trustworthy because, unlike most of the others, she was legally married, Claire served as house mother, confidant, and advisor to the girls, even assisting the doctor at some of the births and helping with adoption arrangements in Kansas City and St. Louis, until she could no longer bear the heartbreak she saw every day.

Her hairbrush moved tenaciously through her customary fifty strokes.

She had raised her daughter alone. She often longed for those brief happy days when she had given herself so eagerly to Carter, but since his betrayal of her girlish dreams, men had no place in her life, and certainly not in her bed. Many she met were thick-witted, others importune or dictatorial, a few clever but arrogant. Even the best of them saw women as inferiors. She preferred being alone.

But it did no good to regret the past. The question now was, could she build a future for herself and Joanna out west? Prospects would have to be much more promising than she now envisioned to give up her steady job at the café. But what if Axel Kohl persisted in his growing infatuation with her and she was forced to leave in order to maintain her dignity? In any case, going to California was a preposterous idea. Her meager savings weren't nearly enough to make such a trip.

The whistle of the 10:15 train interrupted her thoughts. She had grown so accustomed to it that she rarely paid any attention, but now the haunting sound took on new meaning. She had always thought of the big locomotives and their strings of passenger or freight cars as coming *from* someplace—Chicago, St. Louis, Omaha—now she suddenly saw them as going *to* someplace. Perhaps a place where she would find her future.

As the shrill whistle faded, she heard someone knocking. She parted the window curtain and looked out. Axel Kohl stood at the door. For a moment, she considered not answering. Maybe he would think she was asleep. But the light from her lamp denied any such pretense. He knocked again more insistently.

She opened the door a crack. "Hello, Axel."

The stocky man swept his hat from his thinning hair. "Saw your light." His large pale eyes, rimmed by nearly invisible lashes, showed his pleasure at seeing her with her hair hanging loose. "Hope you don't mind." He held out a towel-wrapped parcel that felt warm to her touch. "Had some strudel left tonight."

"You're very kind, Axel." They stood in the doorway for an awkward moment.

"I shouldn't bother you this time of night," he mumbled.

"But I . . . I need to talk to you, Claire."

"It's rather late."

"It won't take more'n a minute." He smelled of bacon grease and stale cigar smoke as he brushed past her and stepped inside. She closed the door but didn't invite him to sit down.

He looked around the room while attempting to swallow his ineptness. "Well, uh . . . you know I appreciate your work," he began. Then, seizing that line of attack, "Never had such good help around the place."

She waited through his discomfort.

"I thought . . ." He cleared his throat, his moon-like face reddening. "Jehoshaphat, Claire! This ain't comin' out right. A man can't say his feelings right off the bat." His voice fluttered. "I only wanted to ask if you'd stroll out with me on Sunday."

"I don't think that's a good idea, Axel."

His eyes popped wide open. "Why not?"

"Working together as we do, I think things should remain strictly business between us. Besides, I have no time for strolling. I have a child to look out for."

"That's just it. Claire, you're a pretty woman, too fine to be buryin' yourself like you do. You need help raisin' your girl."

"Working for you has been very satisfactory, Axel, and I want to keep it that way." Respect for him as a tolerable boss was all she felt or could ever feel for this man. "I hope you understand. Now I must say good night."

"No, I don't understand, Claire. I'm forty years old and all alone. You're alone, too, and not gettin' any younger. We get along good at the café. So why can't we . . ." He reached out and touched her hair with his big paw.

She pulled away. "Please, Axel."

23

"All right . . . whatever you say." He moved toward the door, then glanced back at her. "I'm a patient man."

But Claire put little faith in Axel's patience. Nor her own forbearance. The next morning on her way to work, she stopped by the Santa Fe ticket window to inquire about the cost of travel to California.

"We got a little competition goin'," the agent told her. "Soon as we pushed our line on into Los Angeles, the Southern Pacific cut their own freight charges to the bone." He peered at her over his spectacles. "Tryin' to take business away from the Santa Fe is what they're doin'. Now they're cuttin' passenger rates, too, but we're gonna meet 'em head-on. Yes, ma'am, we're declarin' war. Anyone thinkin' of goin' west, now's the time to do it. Fare to Los Angeles is down to eighty dollars."

"That's still a lot of money," Claire said.

"When you plannin' on goin'?"

"I was only inquiring . . . for a friend." She turned away from the ticket window. California was just a foolish dream.

And yet she could not stop thinking about it as she continued on to the small dingy café. She found Axel scurrying back and forth behind the counter taking the breakfast orders of the men seated there. A heavy aroma of bacon and sausage, flapjacks, and coffee wafted from a pass-through to the kitchen, which offered a glimpse of the white-aproned cook, Monahan, standing at the stove. The few tables in the café were occupied or showed signs of having been, and Claire immediately put on her apron. Axel greeted her with his usual "Mornin', Claire," and his eyes followed her as she cleared the empty tables.

When she had finished serving a group of railroad yardmen, Randy Plank appeared in the doorway of the

24

smoky kitchen, crooking his finger to get her attention, and she went back to where he sat on a stool peeling potatoes.

"Guess what, Mrs. Chadwick." He kept his voice secretively low. "I checked the Southern Pacific again this morning. They've lowered their fares again. A ticket to Los Angeles is down to sixty dollars." He raised an eyebrow in the disarming way he had.

"Why, that's twenty dollars less than the Santa Fe is charging," she said. "I did some checking myself. And please call me Claire."

"Well, Claire"—saying her name held his eagerness for a moment—"the way I see it, their tussle to offer the lowest fare could work to our advantage."

"Randy, I told you . . ." She lowered her voice to remain unheard among the sizzle and clatter of Monahan's culinary performance at the stove. "I can't leave this place right now."

"Could be the chance of a lifetime." Eyes merry, he quickly reached for another potato as Axel Kohl entered the kitchen.

"I don't pay you two to lollygag," the café owner said. Then softening his voice, "Claire, that crew needs more coffee."

Claire promptly left the kitchen, though having just served the railroad men she knew their cups were full. However, with Axel's hungry eyes on her, she circled their table with the coffeepot.

She heard one of the men say, "Ol' Collis Huntington couldn't wait to get his Southern Pacific down the coast to sop up those shipping profits. Now he's doin' the same thing on the southern route." The speaker wore a Santa Fe conductor's cap and jacket along with a savvy look on his weathered face. "Looks to me like President Cleveland could do somethin' about Huntington gougin' the shippers."

"Maybe some of it's justified. They had a hell of a time layin' that track down the coast."

"Yup," another agreed. "Took eighteen tunnels through Tehachapi Pass to build that road. Twists through those mountains like a bowl of night crawlers." He wiped crumbs from his mustache with the back of his hand. "Couldn't have done it without them Chinamen. The poor devils are workin' fools."

The men chuckled.

"Might as well have saved the effort." The conductor swabbed syrup from his plate with a flapjack. "Los Angeles ain't nothin' but a wide place in the road since the silver played out up at Cerro Gordo and they quit freightin' ore out of San Pedro harbor. Can't pay folks to go there now."

"Who'd want to?" A third man in overalls joined in. "Most settlers take a liking to what they see up around Sacramento and decide not to chance it down on that godforsaken desert."

"That's right. I hear the drouth down there killed off all the sheep—and that was after the ranchos couldn't make a go of it with cattle."

"Yup. Anyone with a lick of sense packed up and went back where they come from."

The conductor snorted. "Tell that to Huntington. He fought tooth and nail to keep other roads out of Southern California. He's spendin' a fortune advertisin' all that railroad land."

"He ain't the only one," said the man in overalls. "Every two-bit promoter in the West is ballyhooing land out there. You seen them pamphlets. 'Come to Los Angeles and find paradise.' Claim it's the best farmin' in the whole country.

To hear them tell it, you gotta get on horseback to pick a watermelon." More laughter.

"And the climate's 'sposed to cure consumption or rheumatism or practically anything else that ails you. They say there's over ten thousand people there now."

"They do, huh?" The mustached man chuckled. "Far as I know, anyone who's tried to grow anything has gone belly-up."

"I don't know about that," another said. "Had a letter from my cousin sayin' he's doin' okay out there in a place called Riverside. They're irrigatin' and growin' fruit. He says you can buy a good town acre for only twenty dollars, but not many are buyin'."

"I'm sure as hell not." The conductor shook his head.

Claire followed the conversation with interest. If things were that uncertain in California, she wanted no part of it.

"Well, good morning, Warren." She was surprised to see Warren Stanfield slide onto a stool at the counter. "How are you?" A husky, dark-haired man who worked at Gibson's blacksmith shop around the corner, Stanfield rarely took time from his sweaty tasks to come into Kohl's. With a wife and four kids to support, his meager, hard-earned wages did not allow such a luxury.

"Truth is, I could be better." He sounded downhearted. Claire had met the quiet smithy four years before when he came into the café pleading urgently for someone to help his wife who was giving birth. The doctor could not be located, so Claire, calling on her experience at the maternity home, had gone to deliver Birdie Stanfield of her fourth child, a little girl. Though the delivery was routine, Birdie's convalescence lagged, and Claire continued to stop by to see how she was, often taking some leftovers from the café.

"How's Birdie doing?" Claire set a cup in front of him

and filled it with coffee. The Stanfields had come from Kentucky where the rocky acreage belonging to Warren's father proved to be too small for the two generations.

"She's pretty fair," he said, glumly adding cream and sugar to the coffee. "It's me that ain't doin' too good. Truth is, I just lost my job." He pressed his lips together to quell his emotion. "After four years I'm out on my ear."

"What happened? I thought you were getting on well with Mr. Gibson." A good honest worker and capable smithy, Warren had nearly doubled Gibson's business in the years he'd worked there.

"His girl's marryin', and her man's comin' to work at the shop." Warren's big hands trembled as he lifted the steaming cup of coffee to his lips. "No need for the both of us."

Of everyone Claire knew, Warren Stanfield was the most deserving. "You'll find other work, Warren. A man like you . . ."

"I don't know. Jobs is scarce." He turned and gazed out at the railroad yard. "Westport's not where we want to be anyhow," he said. "We want to get us some land. I'm partial to workin' the land. Trouble is, I just ain't got the money. We've saved a little, but the kids been needin' things and with Birdie sickly . . ."

"Claire." Axel Kohl, observing her conversation with Warren Stanfield, inclined his head to call her attention to two more customers who had just entered the café and taken a table.

Claire flushed. It irked her that Axel kept track of her every move.

"I'll keep my ears open, Warren," she said, refilling his cup before she went to take the new order. "I'm sure something will turn up."

28

CHAPTER THREE

Two weeks out of work and out of hope, Warren Stanfield broke down and cried in the arms of his wife, Birdie. Having looked for work ceaselessly, he found nothing that would support his family.

"Seems like I just can't make things come out right." He raised his face from Birdie's flannel-clad breast and looked into her eyes, those luminous amber eyes that had gone all hollow since baby Stella was born.

"Warren, it ain't no fault of yours that Mr. Gibson's girl married a blacksmith." She stroked his forehead and smoothed his thick dark curls.

"Maybe we was wrong to come here, Birdie." Warren lay back on his pillow, searching the faded wallpaper as if it held the answer. "Leastwise back in Kentucky we had family. And Pa had the land."

"No, Warren. That broken-down place weren't big enough to support your ma and pa, let alone us and the kids." She smiled across the tiny bedroom at the sleeping form of their rosy, dark-haired four-year-old. "Stella eats 'most as much as the boys do now."

But Warren was out of smiles. The two-room cottage behind the rail yards, with attic space where the children slept, was hardly a decent roof over their heads. He worried about the boys hanging around the depot, even though twelve-year-old Tucker and ten-year-old Daniel had begun earning a few pennies there running errands. Six-year-old Eddie liked to play in the cinder piles along the tracks making pretend farms and roads. Warren regretted he could not give his sons the happy, carefree days of his own youth on the farm, where he could take off across the meadow to hunt squirrels, fish in the creek, or pull a carrot right out of the garden when he got hungry. No place for a garden here. Summertime was just heat and noise, bricks and cinders underfoot, anvils clanging, trains screeching.

"Birdie," he murmured. "What would you think of movin' on from here? They say there's cheap land in California."

Her brows knit over the hollow eyes. "California?"

"The railroads are havin' what's called a fare war. It's the damnedest thing. You can go clear to California now for twenty-five dollars. Kids even cheaper."

Birdie sat stunned. "But that's most of our savings." She hesitated before continuing. "Ninety-seven dollars is what we got."

"Ninety-seven dollars? You saved that much?"

Birdie grinned shyly. "Well, I been addin' to what we had. The boys been givin' me what little they make runnin' errands. My sewin' and mendin' has been bringin' in some. Mrs. Woods paid me for helpin' her with her cannin' last summer. Besides, I been tryin' to put away twenty-five cents a week from the grocery money." She gave her husband a proud and adoring look. "Ain't you been noticin' all the grits we been eatin'?"

"Birdie, you're a wonder for sure." Warren gazed at his wife's drawn face. "That might be enough."

"But we'd have nothin' to live on while you was findin' work."

"Los Angeles is a fair-size town. Should be work there for a good smithy. But that's not what I want in the long run. I'd aim to get me some land out in the countryside and

30

raise fruit. Oranges grow there. Think of going out and pickin' 'em right off the tree for Stella and the boys."

"Warren Stanfield, all this worry's made you crazy. Where would we get the money to do all that?"

"I don't know."

Birdie tried to sound cheerful as she always did when he was downhearted. She, too, could see those beautiful trees full of oranges. "Maybe I could take in some washin' or somethin'."

It was then that Warren found a faint smile and passed it on to his wife. "Take in washin'? Why, Birdie, you ain't hardly strong enough to do your own." He reached for her hand. "Now, don't you worry. Somethin' will come up."

March brought more moderate weather, and while looking for work, Warren often stopped by Kohl's Café. Claire could see his discouragement grow day by day when nothing turned up except a few odd jobs that paid very little. He took anything, whatever the pay, but with the persistent talk of opportunity in California, he also kept track of the continuing feud between the Southern Pacific and the Santa Fe.

He learned that until 1880, Collis P. Huntington's Southern Pacific had held absolute control of California railroads and had blocked all other lines from entering Southern California at Needles, hoping to extend his own line east from there. The Southern Pacific had already built a line through Yuma, the only other passage across the mountains, but Huntington was unhappy with the greater distance involved in reaching Midwestern destinations through the more southerly Yuma to New Orleans route.

At the same time, financier Jay Gould, who held controlling interest in the Santa Fe, wished to extend his line west through Needles into California. To remedy the situation, Gould negotiated a series of agreements that joined his Santa Fe track with that of Huntington's Southern Pacific. A connecting bridge was built across the Colorado River at Needles, and by sharing track the two railroads opened a direct route from Kansas City to Los Angeles.

Thus began a fierce competition between the two for traffic on the line, primarily for control of shipping rates, but also for the potential profit in the sale of adjoining land allotted by the government to encourage settlement. Each railroad vowed to meet any reduced passenger rate offered by the other, and travelers scurried back and forth between the two to obtain the lowest fare.

The crucial day came on March 6 when the Southern Pacific announced a twelve-dollar fare from Kansas City to Los Angeles. The Santa Fe promptly cut theirs to ten, and was, in turn, undercut by the Southern Pacific's announcement of an eight-dollar fare—all duly reported by telegraph to eager passengers in Westport.

That morning Randy Plank arrived at the café out of breath. "Look, everybody! I'm goin' to California." He waved a railroad ticket. "Eight dollars!"

A man sitting at the counter jumped up. "Well, now, that's gettin' down to my size." Pulling on his coat and hat, he hurried from the café.

Claire stared at Randy's ticket. Was it possible that she and Joanna could go all the way to California for just eight dollars each? She glanced at Warren Stanfield, whose face showed the same emotion she was feeling.

"By God, Claire," Warren Stanfield said, "maybe this is the answer for me and Birdie and the kids." He chuckled. "If I'm gonna be out of work, it might as well be where I can pick oranges off the trees." He slid his stocky body from the stool. "I'm gonna talk to Birdie."

The café buzzed with news of the unprecedented travel bonanza. Everyone knew someone who had been tempted by newspaper advertisements or railroad-land pamphlets, and many had entertained the idea of going west themselves. There began a steady stream of pedestrian traffic between the café and the ticket offices, along with commentary on the pros and cons of taking advantage of the unusual opportunity.

Shortly before noon a Santa Fe brakeman ran into the café with still more news. "Folks, you'll never believe this," he shouted to the gaping diners. "It's down to a dollar! Southern Pacific just lowered the price of a one-way ticket to one dollar."

Claire, carrying a tray of dirty dishes, stopped in her tracks.

"That's right. One dollar! Only a dollar from here to California! Old man Huntington can't stand to see anyone else gettin' his passengers. He was afraid the Santa Fe would match his eight-dollar fare, so he dropped the Southern Pacific to a dollar. But Santa Fe ain't goin' no lower."

"Next thing you know, they'll be payin' folks to go," someone quipped.

"Mark this day," another shouted, doing a kind of merry jig as he dashed for the door. "March 6, 1886. The day I shucked my misery and headed west."

Randy appeared beside Claire. "Guess I got my ticket a little too soon."

Axel Kohl stood at her other side. "Now, Claire, don't you get any fool ideas. California sure as hell ain't no place for a woman like you."

Suddenly a fresh new start was what Claire wanted more than anything in the world.

Later that afternoon, Warren Stanfield hurried into the café. "Claire, I've done it. Birdie said okay, so I went down there and got the tickets. Only a dollar apiece! Ain't that somethin'? The whole family for a dollar apiece." He held up a fistful of tickets. "We go next week."

"I . . . I'm glad for you, Warren."

"Why don't you come along, Claire?" His grin faded to seriousness. "I'll look out for you and Joanna. You know I will. You've done a lot for Birdie and me. Let me help you out some."

"Joanna would like to go, I know," she said. "But what about her education? Are there schools there?"

"If there ain't, we'll start one. I got young'uns, too, you know."

Of course Warren didn't understand the kind of education she wanted for Joanna. It was clear there would be no finishing school, as she herself had enjoyed, to teach Joanna poise and give her an appreciation of the finer things. Even the dancing lessons put a serious strain on the budget, but they represented an artistic discipline, a refinement that Claire wanted for her daughter, and Joanna's teacher, a Russian immigrant woman, insisted she showed remarkable talent.

Still, unless Claire found a better living, something that would enable her to attain the kind of life she wanted, Joanna would have few advantages. She was growing up so fast. And she was headstrong. Perhaps in California things would be better. At least it would be different there.

She squared her shoulders. "All right, Warren." Her heart began to pound. "We'll go. Joanna and I will go with you."

"That's the spirit." He clamped his big hands around hers. "But you better hurry before they change their minds and raise the price back up."

She hesitated. She couldn't just doff her apron and rush out to buy tickets for California. Such a move needed careful planning.

Axel's critical voice interrupted. "Claire, am I payin' you to loaf?"

Claire turned to see him standing near the kitchen, arms folded, scowling at the jubilant ticket holders. A dispiriting sight.

"Axel, I have some urgent business," she blurted as she strode toward the door. "I'll be back . . . well, when I get back."

Axel sputtered, "You can't leave me with this noon crowd."

"Randy can wait tables for me."

To Claire's astonishment, Axel grabbed her by the arm. "Now wait just a minute, Claire. We need to talk." She allowed him to lead her into the kitchen.

"Claire, don't do this. If you stay, I'll . . ." His pale eyes bulged with something akin to desperation. "Well, we can get married." He looked so wretched that she pitied him.

"I'm sorry, Axel, but I must do what's best for me."

"That's what I'm sayin'," he argued. "It'll be best for you right here. You'll see."

"No, my mind is made up. I'm going."

"Claire, you don't know what you're doin'." He tried to embrace her. "Let me take care of you."

"I said no!" She pushed him away. "Now, please, Axel, don't spoil things."

He clutched her tighter. "But, you . . . you can't go. I need you!"

Her sudden swing found its mark. Axel lurched backward, his big hand covering his offended jaw. Claire ran from the kitchen. Pulling off her apron, she tossed it to Randy. "Fill in for me for a few minutes, will you?"

"Sure, Claire." Randy grinned as she hurried out the door and Axel Kohl emerged from the kitchen, sputtering and blinking, his hand cupped over his left jaw.

Claire's aggravation changed to excitement as she made her way toward the station, her desire to go to California suddenly eclipsing all that had gone before. She pushed through the throng of travelers eager to purchase tickets—young husbands with pregnant wives, railroaders, farmers, well-dressed merchants, extended families with bonneted grandmothers and restless children—all embarking on a hastily conceived journey into an unknown future.

As Claire took her place in line, a tall, distinguished gentleman in a fur-collared coat and expensive-looking homburg stepped up behind her. "What's all the excitement?" he asked.

"The railroads are competing for passengers," Claire said. "They've reduced the price of a ticket to Los Angeles to only a dollar."

He looked quizzically at the radiant young woman. "One dollar? You must be mistaken."

"No, I have friends who've already bought tickets." Elated now, she had dismissed any lingering doubts. "And I intend to do the same."

"You're going to Los Angeles?"

"Yes, are you?" The excitement of the moment made her forget her manners.

"No. I'm on my way home. To Chicago."

Chicago. For an instant Claire felt a pang of nostalgia. Maybe if they were offering bargain fares to Chicago . . .

"You're going out there by yourself?"

"With friends," Claire said.

"You're very brave, Miss . . ."

"Claire Chadwick."

"Harry Graham." He tipped his homburg, revealing soft brown hair trimmed to complement his mustache and beard. He had the sharp, irregular features of a New Englander, Claire thought. She seldom saw such an attractive, well-groomed man around Westport.

"I've been reading about Southern California," he said. "This could create a real boom there."

"I hope so."

His gaze swept from her flushed face, startlingly blue eyes, and spun-copper hair to her plain gingham dress, roughened hands, and worn shoes.

"And what do you plan to do there, Miss Chadwick?" The unusual straight line of his brows lent intensity to his eyes.

But Claire had learned to be wary of forward men who felt they had the right to pry into a woman's affairs. "It's Mrs. Chadwick."

Graham grinned. "Of course. Mrs. Chadwick. Sorry. I just thought if people like you are rushing out there, maybe it's a place my bank should be looking into."

CHAPTER FOUR

A week later, dwarfed by the huge locomotive and its affronting huff and squeal, Claire and Joanna huddled under a single umbrella in the cold morning rain. A pudgy uniformed conductor, irritated by the increased number of clamoring passengers, ambled back and forth along the train making little effort to assist them.

The box-like cars had small windows along each side and a door at either end, different from regular passenger cars that had skylights in a raised portion of the roof to let in light and air. To make up the special train, the flat-roofed cars had been added to a string of freight cars, now standing with wide-open doors on either side to accommodate baggage and other cargo. Some men were attempting to lead a balky Holstein and her calf into one, while the anxious voices of a group of Italian-speaking travelers rose above the general din.

Claire scanned the platform for a glimpse of Randy and the Stanfields among the profusion of umbrellas. She had slept badly. Noise from the railroad yard had begun before dawn with the chugging of engines switching cars from track to track, brakes scraping, and yardmen shouting instructions as the train was made up. Toward dawn, horse-pulled drays crunched along the cinder-bed tracks, then waited in line to unload their cargoes.

Claire's two trunks containing her meager household necessities, bedding, dishes and utensils, books, her clothing and Joanna's, had been picked up the previous evening by

Randy Plank. He had borrowed a handcart to take the trunks to the depot, where they were to be loaded early that morning into a baggage car. Having been reassured by the depot agent that her things had indeed been placed on the train, Claire and Joanna, their hand luggage at their feet, peered about, wondering which car to board.

Claire tried to put on a brave face for her daughter and to quell her own anxiety over committing their lives to such uncertainty. Taking Joanna out of school, interrupting her education just two months short of her receiving an eighth-grade diploma, had been the hardest decision. She had no guarantee there would be adequate schools in Los Angeles, perhaps no high schools at all. But the bargain fare had demanded a hasty decision. Already the ticket price was back up to twenty-five dollars.

Joanna's energy knew no bounds. Eager to board, she stood on tiptoe, trying to glimpse the inside of one of the cars, then peered along the platform taking in the variety of people going to California. "Can we eat soon?" she asked. "I'm starving."

"I've brought plenty of sandwiches." Claire indicated the covered basket beside her small valise. "And there's cheese, apples, sugar cookies, and a jar of water. We'll eat as soon as the train gets under way." She had planned for them to have a hearty breakfast at the café, to say an amiable good-bye to Axel, who had withdrawn to gloomy silence during her last few days of work, but checking on the whereabouts of the trunks had taken too much time. The train would depart, they were told, as soon as everything was loaded and ready. Already after nine, it seemed to be taking hours. Joanna shifted the hatbox containing personal belongings, too precious, she insisted, to entrust to the baggage car.

"Claire. Mornin'." The cheery voice belonged to Randy, who appeared from nowhere carrying under one arm a large cardboard box strapped with a worn leather belt. "I been lookin' all over for you two. Mornin', Joanna."

Joanna brightened at the sight of the tall, good-looking young man in the rain-soaked coat and stocking cap.

"Ain't this some train?" he shouted over a warning huff from the smokestack. "I counted twenty-three cars besides the engine and coal tender. The first fifteen are freight cars and baggage wagons, then these eight flattops for passengers. Emigrant cars, they call 'em. Not too fancy, but they'll do."

Randy's good humor and relaxed manner did little to ease Claire's apprehension. "There are all kinds of folks goin'," he continued. "Some brought seed and farm tools. Some have chickens and pigs. The brakeman told me that one group from some little town in Illinois hired a whole boxcar to bring everything from a barber chair to a forge, even stuff to outfit a pharmacy and a mercantile." His smiling eyes locked on Claire's as he conveyed this evidence that his promise of opportunity in California had not been overstated.

"The Stanfields are in that last car in front of the caboose. They're keepin' seats for us." He pointed out the long, box-like car in which they were to spend the next four days and three nights. The two-and-a-half-day journey on a luxury passenger train nearly doubled on the slower-moving freight carriers, which, on the upgrades, had to make a water stop nearly every twenty miles in order to maintain enough steam pressure to pull the heavy loads.

Picking up Claire's food basket with his free hand, Randy led the way to where the impatient conductor, his bushy muttonchops flaring over a worn, gold-buttoned uniform, stood next to a portable step stool that enabled access to the entrance platform at the front of the car. An ornamental brass strip on his hat read "conductor," which he seemed to take as a license for arrogance.

"Let's get a move on." He pulled the fobbed chain that secured his pocket watch, checked the time, and snapped the cover shut. "Watch where you step." He scowled as two flamboyantly dressed ladies stepped up into the car. Claire had seen the women in the depot the day she got her tickets, and she remembered their big fancy hats whose rain-dampened plumes now drooped woefully.

"They look like a couple of wet turkeys," Joanna whispered, merry in Randy's presence. Claire smiled at Joanna's humor. Both she and Joanna were wearing small plain bonnets and, under their cloaks, their best woolen dresses with high collars and leg-of-mutton sleeves, Claire in gray, Joanna in blue.

"Hurry it up," the conductor urged again, his expression stony. Instead of giving a helping hand to Claire and Joanna, or to Randy struggling with his cardboard box and Claire's food basket, he moved off toward the next car where he yelled at a group of Italians who were attempting to board with an assortment of boxes and bundles. "Hey! You! Luigi!" he barked. A flurry of questions from the group, mostly in Italian, irritated the conductor, who growled, "Talk English. Nobody understands that gibberish."

Inside the boxy plank-floored car, Claire assessed the rows of wooden seats down each side of the aisle. The backrests, she noted, could be flopped forward or backward to convert them to booth-like seating. Above the seats, supported by a post at the end of every other seat, was a shallow shelf-like arrangement, divided into cubbyholes, some with curtains that could be drawn across, apparently for sleeping compartments. Several children, hurriedly consigned to these spaces, peeped out upon the bustle below as their parents stashed food containers and hand luggage beneath the seats or in any other vacant spot. Two kerosene lamps hung from the ceiling, one at either end, and at the front of the car, near the enclosed "convenience," stood a potbelly stove, its isinglass panels glowing red, its stovepipe angling out through a vent high on the side wall. A few men stood holding their wet coats toward its heat, and the smell of burning coal and damp woolens permeated the crowded car. This was nothing like the luxurious coach Claire remembered from her journey to Westport nearly sixteen years earlier.

She closed her umbrella and brushed at the moisture on her coat. Then she saw the Stanfield family waving from the far end of the car, where they had converted the last two seats on each side of the aisle. Birdie held the lively Stella on her lap, while Warren made space for Eddie among their bundles and settled the two older boys, Tucker and Daniel, across the aisle.

As Randy led the way through the crowded car, the two women in plumed hats shed their wet coats and took the seat in front of the Stanfields, sitting opposite each other next to the window. "Claire, you and Joanna can sit with Tucker and Daniel," Randy directed. "I'll sit with these ladies." He nodded cordially to the women as he stowed his cardboard box under the seat.

"Our pleasure." Responding with a husky voice, the dark-haired woman removed her hat, shook moisture from it into the aisle, then put it under her seat atop her handbag. She said to her younger companion, "Take off your hat, Peach. It's dripping on the seat."

"I told you to call me Priscilla." The younger woman pursed her painted lips prettily and did as she was told, smoothing her hand over her high-piled blonde curls as she settled into her seat.

"The conductor and the crew have quarters in the caboose and will be using this back door," Randy said to Claire. "I hope they won't disturb you."

"This will do just fine." Claire and Joanna greeted the Stanfields, and Tucker jumped up to help Randy stow their valises. They settled onto the hard wooden seats, and Joanna slipped off her wet cloak.

"Better leave it on," Birdie advised. "It's chilly down here at this end."

Warren took off his work jacket and hung it over the end of the seat to dry. "I swear, Birdie, you made us wear enough clothes to survive a blizzard." He partially unbuttoned his heavy wool shirt to reveal a second shirt over a union suit buttoned to the neck. He winked at Claire. "I told her it'll be hot in California."

"We ain't in California yet," Birdie cautioned.

"The trunks hold so little, it's hard to know what to take and what to leave behind," Claire said.

"We brought 'bout everything we had," Birdie told her. "Warren built two big wooden chests that are plumb full, and they let us put what little furniture and tools we have in with the baggage."

"I brung my slingshot," Eddie piped up, proudly pulling the weapon from his back pocket. "Gonna shoot me some squirrels." Eddie was the only Stanfield child who had his mother's fair coloring, and the curly blonde halo around his face gave him a particularly angelic appearance. The two older boys and little Stella were dark-haired and brown-eyed like their father.

43

"Put that slingshot away," Warren said gently.

Eddie obeyed his father, but remained in perpetual motion, peering from the window at the boarding passengers, then touring the car, silently assessing each traveler in turn with an open blue-eyed stare, including the two women seated next to Randy.

The whistle sounded two short blasts, and the conductor shouted, "All aboard." One last passenger, warding off the rain by holding his scruffy suitcase above his bowler hat, clambered aboard, and the conductor took up the portable step. The car lurched and began to move, chugging slowly at first, spasmodic, then the cars tightened and the train began to roll. An excited murmur went up from the eager travelers.

The latecomer squinted to get his bearings in the dimly lit car, then made his way unsteadily down the aisle to the only remaining seat—beside Randy and the two ladies. Randy jumped up in surprise when he recognized the ruddy-faced café owner. "Axel!"

Claire tensed, and Warren turned in his seat to verify Axel Kohl's unexpected appearance. "Axel Kohl. You, too?"

"Yup. You folks got me thinkin'." He glanced at Claire. "So I sold out to Monahan, lock, stock, and barrel." Seeing no place to stow the suitcase, he set it down in the aisle and settled gingerly onto the end of the empty seat across from Randy. "I been wantin' to do it," he explained, "sell out, I mean. Runnin' the place was gettin' to be a handful." He grinned at Warren. "Those California orange groves got to soundin' better by the minute, and I said to myself, I gotta get me a taste of one of them oranges."

Warren chuckled. "Glad to have you along, Axel. Reckon we'll take a gander at those orange groves together."

44

"You two grow 'em, I'll sell 'em." Randy seemed pleased to be on equal footing with the older men. Pulling off his rain-soaked coat and cap, he undid the top button of his collarless shirt, which he wore with shapeless trousers tucked into heavy work boots.

The young blonde woman studied his handsome profile. "What business you in?" she asked sweetly.

Randy's happy expression did not change as he turned his attention to her. Her wide blue eyes and rouged cheeks, her tight-fitting, rose velvet gown trimmed with gold fringe at the shoulders and hips, usually changed not only a man's expression but his behavior as well. Randy's smile remained warm and friendly. "I'm not sure yet," he said. "I only know I'm gonna build me a enterprise. My name's Randy Plank."

"Randy Plank." The other woman's keen dark eyes seemed to find amusement in the name as her husky voice played with the sound of it. "I'm Blanche Oliver." She offered a hand that bore a large, glittering ring on the middle finger atop the glove. A big-boned woman with pouffed dark hair, she wore a dress of a dark blue, shiny material that exactly matched the gloves. Her pointy lips were painted red. "And this is my sister Peach . . . I mean, Priscilla."

"It's nice to meet you both." Randy's earnest gaze from one to the other seemed to question their plans for California.

"We're going to visit an uncle in Los Angeles," Blanche offered.

"You're lucky," Randy said. "I don't know a soul out there . . . except these friends. This here's Axel Kohl."

Axel Kohl's expression did change—to one of embarrassment—as he awkwardly touched the brim of his bowler to acknowledge his female seatmates.

The relaxed rhythm as the train picked up speed turned their attention to the dwindling outskirts of Westport. The train puffed around a long curve, then climbed a slow grade onto the gently rolling prairie stretching away from the hills along the river.

"Can't we have the sandwiches now?" Joanna pleaded.

Claire opened the food basket and, as the train crossed into Kansas, they ate. Uncomfortable with Axel's unexpected arrival, Claire stared out the rain-streaked window at the misty, greening landscape. She had embarked on this uncertain journey at least in part to get away from Axel. What on earth was he doing here? And in a seat hardly an arm's length from hers. Was she to be plagued by him all the way to California?

CHAPTER FIVE

The train settled into a steady speed of eighteen miles per hour, the maximum allowed freight cars. The conductor came through demanding tickets, eyeing each ticket-holder suspiciously as he applied his metal punch, and responding to questions with a barely intelligible grunt that indicated he didn't intend to waste time in unnecessary gab with third-class riffraff and foreigners.

Adult passengers relaxed into quiet conversation or, exhausted from hurried preparations for the journey and lack of sleep the previous night, tried to nap, folding their coats for cushions, while the children, charged with seemingly limitless energy, explored up and down the aisle, climbing in and out of the sleeping cubbies, inventing games, and making friends with other children. Tucker and Daniel exchanged riddles with an asthmatic youth who had frequent spells of wheezing and coughing. Eddie demonstrated his slingshot to a small German boy in the private sanctuary they had made of one of the cubbyholes.

Joanna busied herself with combing out her braids and arranging her hair in cascades of copper curls on either side of her face, peering into a small mirror propped against a corner of the window, until another stop to take on water dislodged it onto the seat. Already she was growing impatient with the frequent delays.

Some of the water towers were situated next to depots, but many of the tall bulky wooden tanks stood alone on the prairie, lonely sentinels existing solely to service the big steam engines. Each water stop produced a great deal of lurching and joggling as the long train braked and slowed, then an uncertain creeping forward brought the engine into position beside the elevated tank, followed by a tedious ten- or fifteen-minute halt while water was taken on.

Claire, fighting weariness, began to wonder how she could endure the long days and nights in the crowded car. The seats were too short to stretch out on, except for children, and so hard that already her back and legs were aching.

The rain had stopped, and gradually the car warmed with the spring sunlight streaming through the window glass, and the body heat of the passengers. Gazing out at the vast, rolling prairie, Claire saw an occasional farmstead or a small herd of dairy cattle. The countryside offered a lovely panorama in its greening mantle, and she was eager to see the great mountains and deserts yet to come in the more than 2,000 miles before they would reach the Pacific Ocean. What an education for Joanna . . . and for herself. Worth the discomfort, she decided.

When little Stella Stanfield fell asleep across the seat after clinging to her mother most of the morning, Birdie eased out from under her and came to sit opposite Claire. It was then that Claire noticed how ill Birdie looked.

"Are you all right, Birdie?" she asked.

Birdie offered a weak smile. "It's just all the strain of gettin' ready. Trying to make the money stretch. The kids all needed shoes. With four, it's hard."

Claire nodded knowingly. "I can hardly manage with one. Would you like a little air, Birdie?" She leaned over Joanna and pushed up the window a few inches. Immediately they were pelted with bits of flying ash and choked by heavy smoke from the stack. "Sorry," she apologized, quickly closing the sash. This would be a long, stuffy trip indeed if windows could not be opened.

Birdie leaned her head back against the seat, wearily studying the passing panorama.

Claire heard Blanche Oliver ask, "Do you play poker, Mr. Plank?"

"No, ma'am," Randy responded politely.

Blanche took a deck of playing cards from her handbag. "You, Mr. Kohl? How about a game of five-card stud?"

Axel watched her remove her ring and gloves, put them into her handbag, and begin to shuffle the deck. He loosened the black silk four-in-hand anchoring the high stiff collar he wore with his suit. His new bowler remained in place. "Come on, Randy. I'll give you some pointers." Axel slid Randy's cardboard box between the seats and hoisted his own suitcase on top to make a table.

"Maybe your friend wants in," Blanche said, indicating Warren Stanfield who was returning to his seat after a check on Eddie's whereabouts and a warning to the boys not to get too near the stove. Blanche handled the cards expertly, saying, "Peach, you're the banker." Peach dug through her valise and came up with a velvet pouch filled with coins. She began counting out small stacks of coins on the makeshift table.

"I'll take a dollar's worth." A big, coarse-looking man across the aisle dug into his pocket and came up with a silver dollar. "I'm Isaac Jacobs," he announced in a booming baritone. "Isaac J. Jacobs, carpenter, bricklayer, and well-digger." He sat with three other stocky men whose rotund bellies and solid thighs seemed to fill every square inch of their seat space. Bewhiskered and wearing rough work clothing, they slept soundly in various upright postures. Though his snoring companions seemed dead to the world, Jacobs presented a jolly, wide-awake grin that echoed the arc of his curly red beard. He put the dollar on the table, pushed his battered derby back on his head, and rubbed his hands together as Peach counted out a dollar's worth of change.

"Warren, you want to join us in a few hands?" Axel placed his dollar on the table.

"I'm not much of a card player," Warren said. "I'll watch." He perched on the end of his seat, turning so he could observe the card game.

Isaac Jacobs eyed Warren's massive shoulders and muscular arms. "You do carpentry?" he asked, putting a cigar in his mouth and scratching a kitchen match against the sole of his boot to light it.

"Blacksmithing mostly. But I'm open to most anything."

"There'll be plenty of building where we're goin'," Jacobs said. "I aim to get me some of that cheap land and put up some houses. Folks'll need places to live."

"They sure will," Randy interjected. "They'll be pouring in by the trainload." He chuckled with the implication that they themselves were part of these trainloads.

Blanche waited. "Mr. Plank, are you in or out?"

Randy's attention returned to the card game as he checked the coins in his pocket. He did not intend to touch the contents of a money pouch strapped to his waist beneath his shirt.

"A nickel gets you in," Blanche said, deftly dealing cards to each player.

"Reckon I can afford a couple of rounds," Randy said, adding five cents to the ante of Axel, Peach, and Isaac Jacobs. But after winning the first two pots, Randy decided to risk a bit more, and after an hour of play, his winnings had multiplied enough to impress him with the idea that money might be made in a card game. Peach and Blanche, both careful bettors, were about even. Axel and Jacobs continued to ante up, hoping to recoup their losses, which, though less than a dollar each, were enough to hurt their pride.

Claire ignored the proceedings until Joanna woke and, after a few minutes of watching over the shoulders of the players, begged Randy to teach her the game. Blanche invited Joanna to sit in.

"Joanna!" Claire recoiled at the thought of her daughter engaging in such a public exhibition.

"No need to get in an uproar," Blanche said, obviously amused. "It's just a friendly little game. Something to pass the time away."

"Yes, Mother, it's just to pass the time," Joanna echoed.

Was this how it would be the entire journey? Didn't Randy realize that these women were not fit companions for him, let alone Joanna?

"Come on, Mother," Joanna urged. "Let's both play." The sparkle in her eyes, along with the attractive curls she had taken great care to arrange that morning, made her appear more mature, and Claire resolved at that moment to keep her daughter's hair in childish pigtails during the rest of the trip. There were too many eager, unattached men aboard, including Axel Kohl, not to mention Isaac J. Jacobs and his burly companions.

"Here, Claire," Axel said, getting up to offer his seat. "I can sit on the floor." Randy slid down beside him to make room for Joanna.

Against her better judgment, Claire seated herself with the group. "I'm Claire Chadwick," she said to Blanche. "And this is my daughter, Joanna."

"Pleased to make your acquaintance," Blanche responded, dealing them both in. "My name's Blanche Oliver, and this is my sister Peach."

"Priscilla," the younger woman corrected, smiling at Claire and Joanna. "Peach is my nickname." The heightened color of her cheeks combined with her fair complexion, light hair and eyes gave credence to her nickname.

"Priscilla," Joanna repeated. "That's beautiful. Just like you."

"Are you girls in or out?" Blanche said impatiently, and while the betting progressed, she explained the game to the newcomers.

The day passed pleasantly enough as the train puffed across Kansas. Toward sundown the heavy-jowled conductor, his paunch bulging under his seedy uniform, came through the door from the caboose. Scowling at Axel and Randy who were blocking the aisle, he announced that there would be a thirty-minute supper stop in Newton, that it would be thirty minutes only, no waiting for stragglers to reboard. He snorted when Birdie asked about facilities for washing up at the stop.

"Lady, you should have washed up before you came."

"Don't you have a dining car on the train?" Peach Oliver asked.

"How about a smoker?" Blanche rolled her eyes toward Jacobs's cigar.

"Not on this one there ain't." The conductor turned away, muttering under his breath.

Axel grumbled, "What's eatin' him?"

Immediately the poker game broke up so that the ladies could freshen themselves for the meal stop. Claire placed the coins she had won in her reticule, commenting happily, "This will buy our supper." She had won forty-five cents, Joanna had lost twenty cents, but the afternoon had passed pleasantly despite the noisy children, the coughing and wheezing of the asthmatic youth, and the car's stuffiness, which had increased as the day warmed, even though the stove had long since gone cold.

"Newton! Restaurant facilities!" the conductor bellowed as he came through the train again. "Thirty minutes. Thirty minutes only." The train began to slow, then ground to a stop in front of a small depot. "Open your windows," the conductor barked. "Let in some air while we're stopped."

"Thank heavens," Joanna said, lifting the sash. "It smells awful in here."

The bricklayers awoke and joined the other passengers pouring from the exit doors, pausing momentarily to assess the tiny railroad settlement, which consisted mostly of the depot and a few wooden shacks. The Stanfields allowed the children a brief run along the platform during the stop, as did many of the travelers who had brought food baskets and would not be going into the restaurant.

Next to the depot stood a large board-and-batten building with broad steps leading up to a covered porch running the length of the front and adorned with a painted sign that read "Harvey House." Inside, a lively crew of white-aproned young women bustled about to assist the hungry passengers at the long counter or at tables set with attractive dishes and real silverware on white tablecloths. Thanks to the telegraph wire that paralleled the track, a message had been sent during their water stop in Topeka, alerting the restaurant so that the staff had a well-prepared assortment of foods ready and waiting.

Randy and Axel, accompanying Claire and Joanna, selected food from the buffet table and lost no time in consuming a meal of piping-hot roast chicken with mashed potatoes and gravy, biscuits, lemon pie, and coffee. Mindful of the thirty-minute time limit on their meal, they ate hastily, nodding their enjoyment. Randy and Axel looked about the restaurant as they downed their meal, as much in awe of the operation as the tasty food.

"I'd no more expect to see a place like this way out here than I would a rhinoceros trompin' through a pea patch," Randy commented.

"Five minutes!" the conductor bellowed from a spot near the door.

"What a grump," Joanna said, determined to finish her pie. "I wonder when he eats." She wrapped her biscuit in her handkerchief and slipped it into her reticule. Claire did the same.

A bell began to clang, and the conductor impatiently urged the straggling diners to hurry. When the passengers had clambered aboard, two short whistles sounded, and the conductor lifted the step. At that moment, Isaac Jacobs came sprinting from the restaurant. "Wait!" he shouted. He scrambled aboard without benefit of the step which the conductor, glaring at him with disdain, refused to reposition.

Jacobs's usual grin faded, and his cheeks flushed almost as red as his beard. "That's one rude sonofabitch," he muttered as he returned to his seat.

"Sure was a mighty fine meal, though," Axel commented, hand on his belly. "I've heard about Frederick Harvey and his Harvey Girls. He's 'sposed to be settin' up those restaurants all across the Southwest just to feed railroad travelers. Don't see how he can manage it out here in the middle of nowhere. Must give the help board and room right on the premises."

"Candy. Tabacca. *Gazette*." The voice belonged to a young vendor who came into the car carrying a wooden box suspended from his shoulder by a leather strap. "Git yer candy here. Tabacca." He was a homely boy of stunted growth, hardly bigger than a ten-year-old, and dressed in well-worn knickers and tattered shirt, his boots missing portions of their laces. His pimpled face sloped down a misshapen nose to protruding front teeth that centered his wide grin.

There seemed to be considerable demand for his wares, and by the time he reached the back of the car, he had little left. Randy, peering into the box, saw only a few squares of chewing tobacco, a small bag of peppermint candies, a *Police Gazette*, and a Deadwood Dick dime novel—one he had already read. Blanche bought the bag of peppermints. Isaac Jacobs bought tobacco. Axel flipped through the *Police Gazette*, then changed his mind and put it back.

"I can git more stuff," the boy told Randy, "if there's somethin' ya want."

"A newspaper," Randy replied.

The boy winked acknowledgment and continued on into the caboose, whistling an unmelodious tune through his buckteeth.

As twilight descended, Isaac Jacobs took a harmonica from his pocket and began to play "My Wild Irish Rose," whereupon his three companions, wide awake after the strong Harvey House coffee, joined in singing harmony parts. The passengers immediately quieted, grateful for the diversion, and some added their voices to the song. Soon Claire and Joanna, Randy, and the Stanfields, too, sang with the rest through a succession of tunes.

They had just finished "The Daring Young Man on the Flying Trapeze" when the conductor came through the car to light the two kerosene lamps suspended from the ceiling. He carried a wide board that he offered as a sleeping aid. For a two-dollar fee he would supply such boards to fill the space between the seats, which, with straw-filled cushions included in the price, would convert the two seats into a sleeping platform. He demonstrated the procedure on one pair of seats while the occupants stood aside. Unfortunately, such a conversion would displace two of the four passengers in each pair of seats.

Protests rumbled through the car, while the conductor offered curt suggestions as to how four seatmates could pair up—two of them getting a few hours' sleep on the converted "bed," then retiring to the floor while the other two slept. Recruiting the Stanfield boys to fetch these accessories from storage in the caboose, he supervised the disbursement of boards and cushions for those who wanted them and collected the two-dollar fees. Happily the fees were payable only once; passengers could keep these luxury items for the entire trip, storing them under the seats when not in use.

Isaac Jacobs leaned across the aisle. "I hear them conductors keep most of the money they collect." When Axel gave him a quizzical glance, Jacobs added, "At the end of a run they throw the money up in the air. What sticks to the bell rope they give to the railroad, the rest they keep for themselves." His red-bearded mouth parted in a throaty laugh. Peach, seeing his humor, giggled merrily.

Randy and Axel relinquished their seats to the Oliver women for the night, Randy climbing up to test the overhead cubby, his long legs and feet sticking out at an angle. Axel prepared to bed down in the aisle, while Isaac Jacobs joined his once again comatose companions dozing upright in their seats.

"You and Joanna can make up your seat," Warren advised Claire. "The boys can sleep in the cubby above you, and we'll put Stella and Eddie above us. I want Birdie to get some rest."

Darkness had fallen across the prairie. The two kerosene lamps were turned low, and Claire lay curled beside Joanna on the torturous sleeping platform, watching the eerie shadows cast about the car as the lamps swung with the steady rock and pitch of the train. They had removed their shoes, loosened their clothing as best they could, and covered themselves with their coats for warmth, but every bump, every lurch, every dip and rise of the tracks was keenly felt as the cars lumbered along behind the chugging locomotive. The sporadic coughing of the asthmatic youth heightened the suffocating atmosphere.

An occasional shower of sparks streaked past the window, fireworks apparently less visible during daylight hours, and Claire braced herself against the squeak and grind of the brakes at each water stop. She studied Joanna's slim shoulder silhouetted against the window. What would this trek into the desert wilderness mean for a young girl on the brink of womanhood? Would it coarsen her? Prevent her from finding a suitable marriage partner? Or, worse yet, make her the prey of women-starved hooligans and adventurers? No, Claire wouldn't let that happen. Surely there would be young men of good family in California. Perhaps Randy Plank . . . But he was too old for Joanna. At least for now.

Throughout the night a steady traffic stumbled among the sleepers on the floor to the "convenience" at the front, and Claire began to appreciate their spot at the back of the car. Several times the conductor passed through, slamming doors, but finally his meandering ceased, and Claire fell into a fitful sleep.

She dreamed she was on a train. A train from Chicago to Westport. Desperate to find Carter Chadwick, she hugged her swollen belly to protect the child. But Carter hovered over her, his hand raised in fury. "Your old man killed him-self," he snarled, "and you came crawling to me." . . . *No, Carter!* . . . "You got me to marry you, then got yourself in the family way." . . . *Carter, this is your child, too. I haven't been with anyone else. Ever* . . . "You're only after my money." . . . *No!* . . . "Get out of my sight, you cheap gold digger!" . . . *But where can I go? What can I do?* . . .

CHAPTER SIX

A sudden squeal of brakes, and Claire bolted upright to find dawn breaking over the prairie. Carter Chadwick vanished with the nightmare.

Joanna stirred in her sleep and turned toward the window. Warren and Birdie appeared to still be asleep across the aisle. The wide-eyed faces of Stella and Eddie peered down from their cubby, and when Stella's soft little voice called, "Mama," Birdie awakened instantly. With one finger to her lips, she helped the children down and led them toward the convenience.

Randy, also awake, extricated himself from his cubby. "Worst bed I ever slept in," he groaned, arching his back to ease the kinks.

"At least you slept," Blanche Oliver grumbled as she slid into the aisle, avoiding stepping on the still sleeping Axel who lay spread-eagled on the floor next to her seat, his hat over his face. She brushed at her disheveled clothing. Everything seemed to be covered with gritty dust. Then seeing Claire awake, she quipped, "These accommodations ain't exactly deluxe."

Soon the entire car bustled with travelers stowing sleeping boards under the seats and repositioning luggage. Food parcels were opened and the travelers ate a cold breakfast. Claire and Joanna each savored an apple with their Harvey House biscuits, washing them down with water from their nearly empty jar.

Little Stella, clutching a tattered rag doll, came across

the aisle to talk to Claire. "I got new shoes," she said, raising one foot to show the shiny high-button shoes beneath her faded pinafore. "I'm gonna see the orange trees," she said soberly. "That's where Santa Claus gets his oranges."

"I know," Claire responded warmly.

The little girl nodded. "And I'm gonna have one any time I want." Tossing the dark ringlets that framed her rosy cheeks, she stomped down the aisle chanting, "Any time I want. Any time I want."

The train began to slow. "Water stop!" the conductor called. "Fill your jugs." When the train finally jerked to a halt, those eager to stretch their legs after the uncomfortable night spilled out onto the roadbed that stretched in each direction across an endless prairie. Under the wide-open sky the fresh morning air seemed a magical tonic to be ingested in great gulps.

A high wooden water tank stood alone next to the tracks, surrounded by an ocean of dried grasses nearly three feet tall. While the engineer engaged the chute to take on water, passengers strolled along the track, and children, delighted with their brief freedom, ran through the tangled grass laughing and shouting. A Negro baggage handler carried two buckets of water into a boxcar for the cow and calf, pigs and chickens, then released three little black-and-white dogs that came yapping from the car, crazed with joy at escaping their confinement. They raced through the grass, marking several spots as their own, while their owner called to them, "Stay now, Two! Come on, Three. Good girl. One, ah say stay here now."

Randy assumed command of the hand pump on the well platform, working the iron handle up and down as the travelers waited in line, each with a jug, bottle, or jar to fill. But before half of them had succeeded, the engineer sounded two short toots of the whistle and the conductor hollered, "All aboard." The three yapping dogs bounded back into the baggage car at the Negro's command, and passengers ran for their cars, the last few scrambling aboard as the train began to move.

"Why is the conductor so mean?" Joanna clutched her jar of fresh water as passengers taking seats jostled her in the crowded aisle.

"Ain't no need for him to be in such a hurry," agreed Birdie, who hadn't left the train. The Stanfield boys, out of breath from their wild run along the track, flung themselves into their seats.

Warren chuckled as he seated himself. "They have to keep to a schedule, or we'd never get there." Then, scanning the car, "Tucker, where's Stella?"

Tucker looked startled. "She was with Eddie."

Eddie shrugged.

"My God!" Birdie shrieked, flying to her feet. "Where is she?"

Warren stepped into the aisle and confronted the conductor. "Our little girl!" He clutched the man's sleeve. "I think she got left back there by the water tank. You got to stop the train."

The conductor scowled. "I didn't see anyone when I took up the step. She's on board somewhere."

"No!" Warren pleaded. "We got to go back."

Birdie clutched the conductor's arm. "Please! You must stop!"

"Now don't get excited. Look through the train. She's probably in the next car." He pushed past Birdie, calling out, "Food stop at noon."

Warren sprang after him like a cannonball, pinning him

61

against the car door with the bulk of his weight. He gripped the lapel of the man's uniform in one powerful fist. "You're stoppin' this train!"

"Okay. Okay. Keep your shirt on." The conductor freed himself from Warren's threatening grasp and reached for the emergency cord. Immediately the engine braked, the train lurched, and the wheels skidded and squealed to a stop. A puzzled brakeman appeared from the caboose.

"Some kid is missing," the conductor growled. "We'll back up to the water tank and take a look. Tell Herb." The brakeman went out through the caboose and ran along the track toward the engine.

Isaac Jacobs now stepped forward. "What's your name, mister?" he demanded of the conductor.

"Barnes." The train lurched again as it began slowly backing.

"Well, Barnes, let's you and me round up a crew to look for that little girl."

"I'll check through the train," Randy offered, and quickly moved forward through the cars, explaining to passengers why they were backing up. Sympathetic murmurs of "Poor little girl," along with a few critical comments such as "Wasn't anyone watching her?" and "Where were her folks?" filtered through the cars.

"Don't worry," Warren comforted Birdie. "We'll find her."

"Nothing could have happened to her there on the flat prairie," Axel said, ". . . if she stayed away from the well."

"There could be snakes in that grass." Peach's worried comment received a withering glance from Blanche.

When the train rolled to a stop, after backing up a quarter of a mile, eager searchers poured from every car. Birdie nearly collapsed when she stepped from the train and scanned the vacant prairie. Warren, Randy, and Joanna waded into the tall grass, followed by Axel, Isaac Jacobs, the three bricklayers, and others who fanned out for a thorough search.

"Stella!" Warren called. "Stella, where are you?"

Other voices joined in, calling her name.

While Peach and Blanche hurried along the track to scan the prairie, Claire searched around the water tank, reassuring herself that the well platform was solidly intact.

"Want some water, Claire?" The male voice startled her. She whirled to see that Axel had followed her. He took hold of the pump handle. "I brought my cup."

"No. I mean . . . it's thoughtful of you, but . . ."

"I just thought . . . well, we haven't had a chance to talk. I guess you know why I came on this trip."

"No, Axel, frankly I don't."

"I couldn't let you go off all by yourself. A woman alone. That's not right."

"Axel, really . . . I think that's for me to decide." Then, impatiently, "Can't this wait? Warren's little girl is lost."

"I . . . I just want you to know there's no hard feelings," he said.

"Hard feelings?" Claire stood, hands on hips. "No, Axel, there are no hard feelings. I have no feelings for you at all. Please understand that." And she strode away, leaving him more puzzled than discouraged.

Just then, a shout went up from one of the Italians. *"Trovato! Aqui! Trovato!"* The eyes of the searchers focused on a swarthy man standing waist-deep in the grass several yards from the track, waving his arms to get their attention. *"Filia e aqui! Trovato!"*

Warren raced to the spot. There, lying in the tangled grass, was little Stella, still clutching her doll. The Italian crouched over her, stroking her hand, murmuring to her. She stared up at the stranger's face, her eyes wide, her mouth puckering as she tried to hold back her tears.

"*Signore.*" The man grinned broadly, revealing a gold front tooth, as he relinquished his place to Warren.

"Stella!" Warren fell to his knees to clasp his little daughter in his arms. Then he saw that her foot was caught in a hole of some sort. "It's all right, honey," he murmured as he grasped her ankle and gently angled the foot so it slipped past the thick root that was holding it fast. "Papa's got you." He lifted her into his arms.

Birdie uttered a muffled cry and stumbled forward as Warren appeared above the tall grass with Stella in his arms. She clasped the child to her breast and kissed her tear-smudged face.

"I fell down," Stella said solemnly, wincing as Warren examined her foot.

"She stepped in a badger hole," he said. "Somehow her shoe got caught."

Stella's chin trembled as she continued to hold back her tears. "I got my new shoes all dirty."

"That's all right," Birdie soothed. "They'll clean up just fine."

The engine bell clanged insistently as the other searchers gathered around to express their delight in Stella's recovery before scrambling back onto the train.

Warren spoke earnestly to the conductor as they re-boarded: "I'm much obliged, Barnes." Barnes responded with a curt nod, glancing at his watch as he took up the step.

The poker game started almost immediately, absorbing some of the energy generated by the search for little Stella, and Isaac Jacobs introduced his three companions to Axel

and Randy with an eye cocked toward Blanche. "Three of
the best goldarn bricklayers this side of the Alleghenies," he
said, gesturing toward the heavyset trio. "That's O'Grady,
that's Kelly, and this here's Murphy. They'd like you to
deal them in, too, ma'am."

Blanche acknowledged them with a mirthless smile,
while Peach, setting up her bank, barely glanced their way.
Clearly Peach found little to interest her in the beefy trio.
Randy was another thing; she fastened her eyes on his face
every time he spoke. But Randy wasn't there at the mo-
ment. He had discovered an English speaker among the
Italians, and had gotten on their car with them, telling
Claire he wanted to see what other folks were planning.

Claire, exasperated by the encounter with Axel, passed
up the poker game, preferring to read from the small
volume of poetry by an innovative poet, Walt Whitman,
that she carried with her. Joanna slid into Randy's seat opposite Axel, and once again Blanche began the deal.

As the land began its gradual upward slope toward the
Rocky Mountains, the engine needed increasing amounts of
water to keep the boiler pressure sufficient to pull the drag,
and progress was further slowed by more frequent water
stops. Somewhere just over the Colorado border the train
squealed to a stop for the noon meal.

"Fifteen minutes," conductor Barnes bellowed.

"Only fifteen?" Passengers groaned in unison.

"Got to make up the time we lost lookin' for that kid."

There was no fine Harvey House restaurant waiting to
serve their noon meal, only a little hole-in-the-wall depot
café that had set up a long table out front heaped with
cheese sandwiches wrapped in butcher paper and plates of
molasses cookies. Coffee was available to those who consumed it on the premises—a prominent sign warned against

carrying away the tin cups. The number of serving women dispensing the food proved pitifully inadequate, and Claire, Joanna, and others waiting in one of the long lines had barely reached the table when they heard the all-aboard signal. They quickly snatched up two sandwiches each, thrust payment into the hand of the cashier, and made a dash for the hissing train.

"I talked to the engineer," Randy said when they were again underway and nibbling at the stale sandwiches. "He says we'll cross this corner of Colorado, and reach Raton Pass before dark." He craned his neck to watch the passing landscape. "And I visited with that group from Illinois. One of the leaders, a Mr. Bowman, he's a pharmacist, went out a month ago and found a spot for them at a place called Arcadia. He says there's communities sproutin' up all over. Says promoters are clamorin' for settlers, and some of the newcomers are buying up land they ain't even seen."

"I'm lookin' for a café I can buy into," Axel interjected. "One already set up in an established town."

"We're goin' wherever there's construction," Isaac Jacobs offered.

"Maybe that Mr. Bowman would know something about the schools," Claire said.

Randy polished off his second sandwich. "Let's go find out." He tugged Claire up from her seat and led her toward the front of the car. Glad to be able to further stretch her legs, she followed his lanky, broad-shouldered form leading the way. She couldn't help but admire his easy manner. He seemed so able, so resourceful.

As he swung open the heavy car door, the roar of the wheels assailed them and a rush of air pelted them with grit. Claire gasped when she realized there was no enclosed vestibule, only a narrow sill with iron handholds on each of the closely coupled cars. Going from car to car while the train was in motion would be a precarious business.

"Are we supposed to be doing this?" she called above the din, her skirts whipping about her, the wind tugging strands of her hair from its prim bun.

"As long as that pickle-puss Barnes don't see us," Randy answered. "Now wait till I get that other door open, then grab my hand." While the train continued its gentle swaying, Claire, holding fast to the bar and Randy's steadying hand, stepped over the coupling and through the door into the next car. There they were accosted by a different sort of noise, a cacophony of foreign languages. Claire recognized the group of Italians—and the pungent odor of garlic—among the European travelers.

"Got some Germans here, too," Randy said. "Even a few Russians." He smiled and nodded as they picked their way through the aisle, stepping over bedding and around opened boxes and baskets. Claire noticed the man with the gold tooth who had found Stella and gave him a grateful smile.

After another precarious leap into still another car, Randy led her to where the sandy-haired man he introduced as Mr. Bowman was seated reading a book.

"This is Mrs. Chadwick," Randy said. "I was telling her you'd been to California before."

"That's right." Bowman took off his glasses. "Been out to Los Angeles twice already. Finally decided that's where the future lies."

"What about schools?" Claire said. "I have a daughter."

"Well, what schools there are," Bowman said, "are bursting at the seams right now. They're planning new ones, but that takes time and money. Our group will set up our own as soon as we get settled. Brought a teacher with us."

"But are there high schools?"

Bowman nodded. "Some. Even a college. University of Southern California. Out on the west side near Figueroa Street. Not more'n fifty students, but a university bodes well, you know, if you want to buy or sell land."

"I hope to enroll my daughter in high school, then find work and a place to live nearby," Claire said. "Are there any jobs for women?"

"None to speak of, for women or men. Too many coming. But you . . ." he scrutinized her more closely, ". . . you might find someone wanting a hired girl. A nurse-maid or something. Any family with you?"

"Just my daughter."

He shook his head. "Could be tough on you then. A woman alone."

"I'll manage. Thank you, Mr. Bowman."

"Good luck to you, ma'am." He nodded to Claire before resuming his seat.

Claire turned and led the way back through the car, once again stepping out into the noise and blowing grit between cars, while Randy gripped her hand.

"Not very encouraging, is he?" Claire said.

"Don't pay him no mind. He'd hire you himself if he had a spot for you."

"What makes you think that?"

He grinned at her. "Who wouldn't?"

They passed through the foreign immigrants' car and out again onto the platform. As she stepped across the gap, the train suddenly leaned into a curve, and Claire grabbed Randy to keep her balance.

"I got you," he murmured, maintaining his grip on the door handle while holding her securely around the waist with his other arm. Claire, glimpsing the cinder-bed track rushing below them, clung to him, her face pressed against his shoulder. They remained in this embrace for a moment longer than it took for the train to straighten and Claire's fear to pass.

CHAPTER SEVEN

Flustered by her unexpected response to Randy's embrace, Claire led the way down the aisle to their seats. It seemed an eternity since she had felt the comfort and promise of a man's arms about her. Her long-buried feelings overwhelmed her, and she struggled to compose herself.

Joanna, looking up from the poker game, frowned as she fixed her hyacinth gaze on the two of them. "Where were you, Mother?"

"I found out there are high schools in Los Angeles, Joanna," Claire said, hoping to explain the pleasant flush that still lingered.

Joanna, more concerned with Randy's attentiveness to her mother than this bit of information, looked from one to the other.

"If I can find work near a school . . ." Claire continued.

"Now, Claire, don't you worry," Axel interjected. "You know you always have a spot with me."

After a water stop in Trinidad, Colorado, the homely young vendor again came through the car. "Got yer paper for ya," he said, handing a folded newspaper to Randy. "Denver *Rocky Mountain News*. Not hardly a week old. Hope you din't mind I took a look at it."

"No. 'Course not." Randy could see the paper had been previously read by many.

"Twenty-five cents." He held out his hand.

Randy gave him a sharp glance. "Ain't that a little steep?"

"Special order."

Randy raised a skeptical eyebrow. "No wonder you fellas are called news butchers. How long you been workin' this line?"

"I been a news butch three months already. Been all over. New York. Boston. Atlanta. Chicago. St. Louis." Buckteeth centered the boy's grin.

Joanna purchased a ten-cent package of peppermint while Tucker Stanfield waited his turn.

"What you got for a nickel?" Tucker asked, holding out the coin his father had given him. He stood nearly a head taller than the stunted vendor.

"Buy somethin' you can share," Birdie reminded.

The vendor dug down in his box. "Got some licorice."

Tucker took the package of licorice drops, gazing in fascination at this able salesman who was not much older than himself. "My name's Tucker. What's yours?"

"Swifty. Swifty Lydick."

Swifty Lydick. Tucker savored the name. "Where you from anyway?"

"Boonville. Workin' my way up in the railroad business." He winked at his young admirer before moving on. "How 'bout you, ma'am?" he said to Blanche, whom he had tabbed as a potential big spender.

"Can you get me some drinking water, please?"

"Yes, ma'am. Been thinkin' of addin' water to my inventory. The regular trains, they carry an ice-water tank, but this one ain't got one. I'll git some next stop."

Joanna savored a bit of peppermint as the train began the long climb up through the mountains toward Raton Pass. The pass, she learned from Randy who was now seated beside her, offered the only gateway from Colorado onto the high plains of New Mexico Territory. Claire, feeling it best not to linger too close to Randy, chatted with Birdie across

71

the aisle. Little Stella's ankle felt much better after the application of a peppermint to the child's tongue.

"Raton Pass is a hard pull for the fireman," Randy told Joanna. "He says he has to keep shovelin' like a son-of-a-gun to keep up the steam pressure. Says scoopin' coal from tender to firebox has made a hunchback out of him." Randy shook his head. "You'll never catch me settlin' for nothin' like that."

"Me neither," Joanna agreed.

"He has to scatter the coal just right. Has to know exactly when and how much to leave the firebox door open so the draft will keep the fire burning nice and even. All the while keepin' an eye on the gauges so the boiler won't blow."

Joanna listened with admiration. "Where did you learn all this stuff?"

"At the Trinidad stop. The fireman—Ezra, his name is—told me he catches holy heck if he can't make enough steam to get the train in on time. And sometimes he has to do it with poor-burnin' coal, leaky valves and pistons. Ain't that somethin'?"

Joanna found Randy's stories fascinating and, after offering him some of her peppermint, they engaged in an animated discussion about whether or not they might witness one of the infamous skirmishes between Indians and United States soldiers in the territories of New Mexico and Arizona. Randy had read that though the Navajo, Hopi, and Comanche had settled into a new way of life more than ten years earlier, and Geronimo, the much-publicized Apache renegade, had surrendered the previous September, a few small bands of hostiles still roamed those areas.

The locomotive attained the top of Raton Pass just as the sunset sky displayed a glorious panorama of golds streaked with orange, pink, and lavender over the far mesas. The train braked to a stop a little beyond the summit to take on water after the long climb, and passengers scrambled off to fully enjoy the spectacle.

"Look at that," Warren said, pointing out the broad vistas of undulating mountaintops, wooded with ponderosa and pinyon pine and mottled here and there with luminous pale-green clusters of budding deciduous trees. He stood with his arm around Birdie, who held tight to Stella's hand. "That's New Mexico Territory down there."

"It sure is pretty," Birdie said.

Claire continued to avoid Randy. It was clear that something had been kindled between them. It was also clear that Joanna sensed it. Claire knew she would have to conceal her conflicted feelings, not only to avoid giving Randy further encouragement, but to avoid Joanna's scrutiny. The upheaval of this hasty move would be enough for Joanna to cope with. Besides, Claire flatly dismissed the idea of any liaison with Randy Plank.

Randy was only twenty-five years old, far too young. A fully mature man, yes. Intelligent, able, and obviously destined for a fine future, but much too inexperienced in the ways of the world. A Missouri farm boy really. Why had his touch stirred her so? Surely it was simply his concern and the support he offered on this difficult journey. She had longed for a man in her life, but through the years none had materialized. Maybe that was her fault, too. There had been several who pursued her. The problem was that she had never wanted any of them. She could never settle for someone like Axel Kohl. Marriage had to offer more than mere security.

While the fireman tended to the water chute, the engineer climbed down, took a chaw of tobacco, and stood enjoying the pine-scented mountain breeze on his flushed face. Randy, seeing that a new crew had come aboard in Trinidad, went over to chat.

"It'll be downhill for a while now," the engineer said. "Should make some time tonight and be in Albuquerque before noon tomorrow."

"How fast can we go on a down slope?" Randy wanted to know.

" 'Sposed to keep it down to eighteen miles an hour, but with this drag I could open 'er up to twice that on a straightaway. I don't push 'er too far. Don't want no surprises when I hit the outer rail on one of them curves." He spat a stream of tobacco juice between his teeth onto the rocky ground. "Safety first, you know." It was then that Randy noticed the two missing fingers on his right hand.

"Ever been wrecked?"

"Came close. Had some cars break loose at the top of a six-mile grade once." The engineer savored the recollection. "Chased me to the bottom and pretty near caught me, too." He glanced at Randy to gauge the effect of his story. "Didn't dare brake with those runaways barrelin' down behind me, so I hung on the throttle, blastin' the whistle like a crazy man to signal a broken train."

"Gosh, what happened?"

"That's the amazing part. A switchman at the bottom was able to throw the switch just after I passed. Headed the loose cars that were chasin' me onto a sidetrack. They piled up like kindling, but no one got hurt." The engineer chuckled. "Except the switchman. When that runaway flew by like a hurricane, he was blown down a forty-foot bank by the rush of air." Eyes twinkling, he pulled his watch from his pocket and flipped the cover open.

"I could tell you some good ones about those old hand

brakes," he continued, slipping the watch back into his pocket. "Used to lose a lot of brakemen, you know. Cat-footed they was, up there on top of them cars on snowy nights, twistin' the brake wheels to slow those heavy drags."

Randy scanned the top line of the cars, imagining the dangerous maneuver.

"Air brakes are changin' all that." The engineer gestured toward the air hose running from car to car beneath the train. "Got a tank of air on each car now, you know. With the air pressure off, the brakes are off. Put the squeeze on the pressure and the brakes start takin' hold. But dump it all at once and they can lock up on you."

"A pretty responsible job you fellas got."

"Yup, a good hogger's been at it a while. I 'bout done it all—brakeman, tallow pot, switchman." He held up his dismembered hand. "Lost these in the yards puttin' a pin in a coupling link."

Randy nodded knowingly. "Carry much freight to California these days?"

"Quite a lot. Both ways. But the big bosses got the rates so high it squeezes out lots of shippers."

"Ain't that a little shortsighted?"

"To my way of thinkin', it's just plain greedy." Again the engineer spat tobacco juice onto the ground. "You plannin' on goin' into business?"

Randy nodded. "Don't know what kind just yet."

"Well, good luck to you." The engineer glanced at the fireman who, having completed the water intake, began yanking the bell rope.

Joanna came up to Randy as they hurried back toward their car. "I admire someone who can talk with strangers like you do."

"I'm tryin' to learn what I can about the railroads so if

my business needs to ship, I won't be so ignorant of what's involved."

"Randy, when you get your business, will you let me work for you? I could learn to operate one of those type-writers or something."

"Your ma wants you to go to school. And she's right. Everyone needs an education these days." Then, teasing, "Even women."

Joanna stopped, arms akimbo. "Randy Plank. Women are smarter than men any day."

"Could be, but you still need an education. I tried to get one on my own, from books and newspapers, but that ain't enough. You'll get yours in a fine school, maybe even a uni-versity."

"Well, maybe. But after that will you give me a job?"

"Don't you worry. I'll have jobs for everybody," he promised.

"Even Peach and Blanche?" She flashed a flirtatious smile as they hurried to board the train.

Across Kansas and Colorado the view had gradually changed from flat Midwestern terrain to the rugged peaks of the Rockies, and as they dropped down from the moun-tains, the New Mexico Territory assumed yet another to-pography, arid and rugged, with cactus, sagebrush, and mesquite competing for nutrients in the rocky soils.

Darkness again swept over the land. The lamps were lit, and preparations for the night began once more. There were no songs that night. The bed boards and cushions were put in place and children bedded down, leaving little for adults to do but to try to get some sleep themselves. Claire's eyes, nose, and throat burned from smoke leaking in through partially open windows. Her skin felt gritty to the touch. She ached in every muscle. And she longed for a bath and a nice warm supper.

From her reclining position, she could see through the window the incredible canopy of stars that hung over the mountains, mixed with the occasional shower of sparks from the smokestack. Joanna was already asleep.

"You know what they say," Isaac Jacobs, stretched out in the aisle, mused aloud. "First night in a strange bed, no sleep; second night, better; third night, sleep like a baby."

Axel yawned, adjusting his bowler under his head for a pillow. "Guess you can get used to anything."

Randy, cramped in the cubby above them, lay awake listening to the wheels against the rails, sensing the smoother passage of the downhill ride, and feeling the presence of Claire Chadwick lying one seat away. So near, and yet so far. If he were to have a chance with her, he would need to get established in Los Angeles right away. He knew now for sure that he loved her. He wanted to take care of her. And only when he was able to do that could he ask her to be his wife. He lay awake devising a plan.

The gentle sway of the car, the rhythmic click-clack of the wheels, the increased rush of the wind on the downgrades heightened the drowsy ambiance. Brief snatches of conversation drifting among the seats soon gave way to snores as the travelers, covered with coats against the welcome cool of the night, fell into exhausted sleep.

A child whimpered. A man coughed. And the chugging of the locomotive came into Claire's consciousness. She opened her eyes. All around her, across from her, above her, on the floor below her, lay men, women, and children in various stages of sleep. The car smelled of unwashed bodies and half-smoked cigars. Her stomach felt queasy.

She sat up and reached over Joanna to open the window a few inches. Smoke and ash be damned, she had to have air. In the gray dawn light she could make out a high mesa in the distance, and sagebrush, mesquite, and huge cactus plants dotted the landscape as the train puffed steadily along. A few low willows trailed along dry creek beds, and a herd of antelope standing beside the tracks suddenly bolted, their white rumps flashing in the dawn light as they bounded away. Claire felt an intriguing newness to it all as she breathed in the rush of fresh desert air.

Then she realized Axel was awake and watching her. He lay with his shirttail out, trousers askew, his thinning hair standing out every which way. He grinned at her.

Claire lay back on her pillow, denying him a response. She hadn't dreamed the trip would be so primitive. So disturbingly intimate. She would have to endure just one more day, one more disgusting night, before they would arrive in Los Angeles and she could begin her new life. Next to her, Joanna still slept, her lashes dark against skin as fine as porcelain, silky copper braids flung out across the pillow. With such youthful promise as Claire saw in her daughter's face, who could doubt the future?

Axel got to his feet, put on his hat, and lumbered down the aisle poking his shirttail into his trousers. In the privacy of his absence, Claire straightened her clothing, combed out her hair, and was pinning it into a bun high on her head when the door to the caboose banged open and the conductor came through.

"Breakfast stop in Albuquerque!" he bellowed, waking those not already stirring. "Albuquerque in twenty minutes!"

"How long do we stop this time?" someone asked.

"One hour! One-hour stop in Albuquerque! Got a

Harvey House there." The announcement was met with enthusiastic shouts, grateful sighs, and immediate joyful dismantling of the beds.

"That will be heaven itself." Joanna, awake now, reached for her shoes.

The village of Albuquerque drowsed lazily under the warm morning sun. A few harnessed teams and saddled ponies stood at hitching posts in front of the adobe buildings or moved along the dusty street fronting the railroad tracks. Men wearing high-heeled boots and ornate sombreros clustered in small groups to chat, while dark-haired women in colorful long skirts and embroidered shawls went in and out of the stores carrying parcels. A few poorly clad Indians squatted in the shade in front of the depot.

Again the restaurant had prepared for the onslaught of passengers with its standard menu of fruit, melon, ham and eggs, bacon, sausage, beefsteak, potatoes, pork chops, hot cakes, oatmeal, grits, biscuits and gravy, muffins, pies, and cakes, along with tortillas, jalapenos, and refried beans for local flavor. The deprived travelers were overwhelmed—all you could eat for fifty cents, plus the railroad's gift of a whole hour in which to feast. There was no milk, the Stanfield children were told by their smiling, crisply aproned Harvey Girl, because dairy cows did not do well in New Mexico or Arizona, though Fred Harvey was trying to develop a herd in each state to service his restaurants.

"Develop something people need and want," Randy mused. "That's the secret to success." Then pointing his fork, "Warren, I been thinkin'. Neither one of us can afford to waste time when we get to Los Angeles. What if we put together what little we got and set it working for us right from the start?"

Warren continued his breakfast. "Got somethin' in mind?"

"Well, you're a blacksmith. And all these people coming in will need horses, buggies, and other means to move their goods. I figure if you and me could each put in fifty dollars—that's all I got—that should be enough to open a livery stable."

"I don't know, Randy. Birdie and me are fixin' to farm."

"You'll get your farm, Warren. Eventually. I'm talkin' about next week, how we can survive while we're workin' up to what we really want."

"Well, I s'pose it wouldn't hurt none to get a little comin' in right away."

"Look at it this way. If we can find an old shed or barn to rent and get hold of a forge, we're in business. We'll advertise that we can supply whatever they need. Then I'll go find whatever they ask for."

Slowly Warren absorbed Randy's enthusiasm. "By God, you might have an idea." Then, hesitating, "But what about competition? We won't be the only ones tryin' this."

"Maybe not. But we can sure be the best at it."

"Should be plenty of call for a good livery," Warren mused.

"Never greater than right now with all these folks comin' in."

Birdie seemed skeptical. "Warren, I want a good place for the kids. Not another noisy place by the tracks."

"I know, Bird. This wouldn't be for long. It'd just be so we don't go under while we're findin' our land and waitin' on our first crop."

"I can get at it as soon as we get there," Randy explained. "Find out who's selling good horses, who's making wagons. They'll know of a shed somewhere we can rent. Do you think we can get hold of a forge?"

"If we can't, I'll build one." Warren extended his hand. "Randy, you got yourself a partner. And I reckon fifty dollars is about all I can invest, too." He finished his coffee and leaned back in his chair. "By God, a good meal sure puts the starch back in a man. How about you, Bird? You feelin' better?"

Birdie's smile softened her drawn, narrow face and brightened her eyes. "Everything tastes so good. I didn't know there was places like this."

"Maybe we should stay right here in Albuquerque," Joanna said, savoring a large cinnamon roll.

"Not me," young Eddie chimed in. "I'm goin' to California."

"Me, too," Stella said. "I'm gonna see the orange trees."

Claire laughed with the others. "That's right, Stella. We're all going to see the orange trees."

CHAPTER EIGHT

Harry Graham responded quickly when summoned to the office of his boss, Phineas B. Mossburg, president of Illinois Security Bank. Lately P.B. had been more testy than usual as news of the railroad wars continued to filter in. Competition for shipping profits had affected the whole nation. Companies saw their profits being wiped out by excessive rates, leaving them unable to repay loans—a troubling situation for bankers like P. B. Mossburg—and a spate of mergers between the different railroads left considerable uncertainty as to which lines would survive and prosper.

Harry tried to stay on top of these developments. Newly promoted to vice president of commercial loans, he had earned the board's trust with his prudent dealings. Thus far the loans he approved—the Blackstone buyout, the Chicago Grain financing, and the Midwest Meat Packing loans, for example—had kept him in good standing with Mossburg, but he remained ever mindful of what an error in judgment could cost the bank.

Harry didn't intend to make such an error. He had worked hard to earn his place as Mossburg's right-hand man, the trusted new blood in the old hierarchy. The Mossburg family had controlled Illinois Security Bank for more than twenty-five years. Old Mordechai Mossburg had arrived in Chicago in 1864 just at the time the National Bank Act chartered independent banks to issue national bank notes. As the city grew and prospered, so did Mossburg's bank, and on his death ten years ago, his son

Phineas B. had assumed the presidency. P. B. Mossburg, having no sons, favored the energetic new vice president Harry Graham—for his intelligence and good manners as well as his banking savvy—for P.B. had three daughters of marriageable age, one of whom, Daisy, had already set her cap for the highly eligible, thirty-five-year-old Harry Graham.

"Sit down, Harry." Balding and portly with a gray handlebar mustache, Mossburg dressed impeccably in a black cutaway and striped cravat. He dropped his monocle to his chest and ceremoniously lit a cigar from his private stock. "Harry, I've been thinking about your proposal. Southern California does indeed appear to need banking services."

"I did some more checking, P.B." Harry produced a small packet of newspaper clippings and notes from his vest pocket. "Last October, the *Los Angeles Tribune*, reporting on individual fortunes in that city, claimed fourteen millionaires, twenty-seven with a half-million, forty-nine with a quarter-million. The article states there are at least two hundred citizens with more than ten thousand. That's a lot of money."

Mossburg exhaled a controlled stream of the aromatic cigar smoke. "A lot of potential business."

Harry shuffled through his clippings. "According to this, thirty-two acres at the corner of Vernon and Central Avenues, purchased for twelve thousand dollars just four years ago and sold at a loss two years later, just resold for forty thousand."

"Hmm." Mossburg twirled the cigar between his lips while an idea formed behind his broad, bald pate. "Harry, why don't you go out there and see what's going on. Find out where we might be able to fit in."

"All right, P.B."

"How long would it take you to tie up loose ends here?"

"Not long. A week or so."

"Excellent! Plan to spend two or three months out there to get a clear picture. If investors pour into Los Angeles the way you predict, those with big ideas and limited cash will need to borrow. Your job will be to pick the winners." He inserted his monocle and looked earnestly at Harry. "And you better come to the house for dinner Saturday evening. I'm sure Daisy and the rest of the family will want to see you before you go."

Harry dreaded the long evening with the Mossburgs. Black tie, flowers for Mrs. Mossburg, chocolates for Daisy and her sisters. All part of the job, and how tedious it had become. Actually, the California assignment had come just at the right time to save him from having to break it off with Daisy. She was nice enough, intelligent, pretty, and would make a fine catch for an up-and-coming financier, but somehow, for Harry, bells just weren't ringing.

Harry Graham and Daisy Mossburg had been matched up almost from the day Harry went to work at Illinois Security. They met at the annual soiree P.B. held for the bank's employees. Eager to make the right impression, Harry, wearing his new black tailcoat with white satin tie and cummerbund, arrived at the appointed hour to find he was the first. A butler invited him into the marble-floored foyer where a long staircase curved up to the second floor.

"Well, hello." The feminine voice belonged to a young woman descending the stairs. Dark-haired and wearing a pale blue gown most becoming to her nicely rounded figure, she held out her hand to Harry. "I'm Daisy Mossburg." Her lively dark eyes skimmed over the stranger's tall, angular form, his stylish attire, and finally, with disarming boldness, looked directly into his eyes.

He clasped her extended hand. "Harry Graham."

"Mr. Graham! My father speaks highly of you."

He smiled. "I'm glad to hear it."

"Usually he doesn't bother to mention the new employees by name." While her words put him in his place, her gaze seemed to imply she considered him worthy of her attention.

"Well, I hope I can fulfill his expectations," Harry said.

"I think you already have." A mischievous smile brightened her eyes. "He says you're clever as all get-out when it comes to business."

In the four years since that initial meeting, P. B. Mossburg's expectations had been more than fulfilled, but Daisy's had not. Reluctant to get involved with the boss's daughter, Harry kept his distance at first, responding politely to their social invitations, but often feigning other commitments or a heavy workload when asked to join in more intimate family evenings. Daisy showed no such reluctance. She had pursued Harry with every wile she could muster, and gradually he had acquiesced.

Not that Daisy was unappealing. Twenty-two when they met, she had had the best finishing-school education, had traveled abroad, and as the oldest of three daughters, had received the attention her father would have given a son had he had one. Harry found her knowledgeable, even sensible, under all her expensive trappings.

"You never talk about yourself, Harry," she said one hot summer evening as they sat together in the gazebo swing. "Why is that?" She leaned back against the cushions, her fair skin moist in the heat, her eyes mischievous.

"There isn't much to tell, I guess."

"I know you were born on the north side of Chicago, that your father and grandfather were printers who came from Massachusetts, and that your mother died when you were five. What was it like being raised by your grandmother? Did she spoil you?"

"Spoiled me rotten." He grinned, loosening his tie and collar. Then elaborating on the joke, "As a matter of fact, no one has ever said no to me. Until you, that is."

"But I'm not saying no to you." She took hold of his tie and pulled him closer, kissing him lightly on the lips. "It's you who's saying no."

When Harry did not respond with a more passionate kiss, she said, "Harry, it's not a girl's place to pursue, but after all this time . . . Well, you're no spring chicken yourself. Don't you ever think about getting married and settling down?"

Suddenly he knew. He didn't want to marry Daisy Mossburg. Or anyone, for that matter. Family life held no charm for him. His mother's early death left his father bitter and unprepared to care for a young son, so the task fell to his grandmother, who had resented the burden. Over the years, her constant carping aggravated his father's drinking, and Harry had to keep a close watch when his father operated the presses. By Harry's senior year in high school, he could run the printing shop, and his scholarship to the University of Illinois was based in part on his working experience. Harry vaguely remembered his mother's gentle loving ways. After she died he received little emotional comfort from family life, and now he viewed the Mossburg family's easy congeniality with suspicion.

"Daisy, you're wasting yourself with a confirmed old bachelor like me." He tried to make light of it. "You're far too good for me."

"Don't be ridiculous. I've never met anyone finer than you."

"I'm afraid marriage isn't for me, Daisy."

"What nonsense! You're decent, generous, and kind. You'd make a wonderful husband." She turned to nestle in his arms, her body stretched out on the swing.

Her perfume gave off the faint fragrance of flowers, and with the curve of her body inviting his caress, he did feel love for her. Or something as close to love as he had experienced. He kissed her, and with her eager response, an overpowering desire rose in him to take what she was offering. To have it over with one way or the other. If they knew each other fully, completely, the unpleasant tension would end— either they would marry to eliminate the possibility of a premature pregnancy, or they would part. Maybe that's the way other men decided. Marriage had a certain appeal—if they were forced into it. Having to take Daisy as his wife was a fate he could live with. But he couldn't play this game anymore. He wasn't a kid. Thus far he had taken sex where he found it, most often at Madam Opal's salon, but the physical release he found there only left him more emotionally empty.

"Daisy," he murmured against her warm neck. "Daisy . . ."

"Harry, darling . . ." Her slender arms were around him.

The swing was too short. Lifting her, he pulled the cushion onto the gazebo floor and gently eased her onto it. His hand found her bare thigh above her rolled stockings. Her skin had the texture of fine satin. He ached to force himself upon her, but he knew that for all her sophistication Daisy was inexperienced. He unbuttoned her shirtwaist and lifted her camisole. She caught her breath with the pleasure of his touch. But when he kissed her bare breast, she bolted upright.

"Harry, we can't do this."

"Don't worry, Daisy." Harry felt a sudden irritation at her change of mood. "If anything happened . . . if you became . . . you know . . . in the family way . . ."

Her expression contorted. "Oh, why did you have to say that?"

"Daisy, we have to face facts. That's always a possibility. I just wanted you to know that if you did we would get married."

"And if I didn't . . ." Tears welled. "If I didn't, we wouldn't get married?"

"You know that's not the way I meant it."

"Well, what way did you mean it?" Her voice was brittle.

"I'm sorry, Daisy. I guess we're not ready for this yet."

"Obviously, you're not." She stood up, rearranged her clothing, and hurried across the lawn toward the house. Harry left through the garden gate without saying good night to the Mossburgs.

Since that night in the gazebo, Harry had managed to avoid Daisy. P.B. even broached the subject when it became clear to him that something had gone wrong with the budding romance.

"You're not seeing much of Daisy these days," he said. "She's moping around the house like a sick calf."

"Sorry, P.B. I've been rather preoccupied."

"You're working too hard, Harry. Better let up a little."

But Harry hadn't let up. In fact he had increased his workload so that he wouldn't have to deal with the fact that no matter how fine a girl Daisy Mossburg was, nor how good a match her father thought they were, he didn't love her. And he refused to hurt her even more by marrying her anyway. She deserved more than a marriage of convenience.

That may have been the prime reason he began to think about going to California. And now that P. B. Mossburg himself endorsed his proposal of starting a new bank there, it seemed the perfect solution.

CHAPTER NINE

"This heat is unbearable." Stripped to her camisole, Blanche Oliver washed in the cool water at the row of sinks in the Harvey House ladies' lounge, where women were enjoying the luxurious running water and pristine hand towels provided by the management.

Blanche, in her paint and finery, had remained apart from the group during their meal, choosing to sit alone with Peach, thus attracting the stares of some of the Harvey Girls. But now, having scrubbed her face bare of makeup, she looked remarkably fresh, young, and wholesome.

Claire unbuttoned her own dress and pressed a cool, wet towel to her neck. "This wool dress is a bit warm for this weather." She smiled at Blanche.

"Be hotter yet across the desert," Blanche said.

"I'm roasting, too," Joanna said. "Please, Mother, I've got to take off my stockings."

"If you must. But try to keep your bare legs decently covered."

Blanche suppressed a smile at Claire's sense of propriety. "Peach and me took off our stockings back in Emporia. Our corsets, too."

Claire hadn't noticed this breach of decorum, nor had anyone else, she decided. "Well, I'll not be the only one dying of the heat." She turned her back and lifted her skirt to unhook her garters, then deftly whisked off her stockings, banishing them into the reticule dangling from her wrist. Her corset would have to remain in place.

Joanna was more demonstrative. "Ahhh, that feels heavenly," she confessed, wiggling the toes on each foot and fanning her petticoats up and down to cool her legs. Then she pulled her braids up off her neck and wound them around her head, studying herself in the mirror. "I wish I had hair like you, Priscilla. It's so much prettier than mine."

Peach, who stood beside her ratting her blonde locks into a high pouf, returned a surprised smile. "Do you really think so? Yours is such an unusual shade of red, so shiny and thick." She reached over to tuck a stray strand into Joanna's braid.

Until then Claire hadn't realized how young Peach was, but now she saw that she must still be in her teens. Blanche appeared to be closer to Claire's age. Big-boned and tall, she had a nice, well-rounded shape, but as she applied fresh circles of rouge to her cheeks and dabbed on powder, she again set herself apart from the other women.

"Where are you from?" Claire asked, wondering how two women like the Olivers came to be in their apparent profession.

"Kansas City. But there's no future back there in Missouri." Blanche brushed at the wrinkles in her skirt. "Maybe California will give a woman an even chance." Then, as an afterthought, "You must believe that, too, coming on this trip by yourself and all."

"Yes, I'm hoping for a new opportunity. Work in an office maybe."

"In an office?"

"I know it's a little unusual, but I think I would like that kind of work."

"And your daughter?"

"Why, she's going to school. She's only fifteen."

For an instant, sadness fell across Blanche's dark eyes, but then she turned to the mirror, gave a last pat to her teased up-do, and raised her chin haughtily. "Well, good luck to you." She flashed a mirthless smile, and the two Olivers swept out of the room.

The climb from Albuquerque to the Continental Divide, an altitude of nearly 8,000 feet, was a tedious one. The blistering sun beat down on the train as the engine labored up the long grades and across desert terrain cut by arroyos and flanked by broad mesas. In the stifling car, Claire and Joanna, creating privacy for each other with their cloaks, managed to change to the calico shirtwaists and summer skirts Claire had packed in her small valise and, with Claire's banishment of her corset, both felt more comfortable. Other women discreetly pulled off extra petticoats and other dispensable garments, while the male passengers removed vests and rolled up their shirtsleeves. Opening the windows only made things worse, as specks of flying ash irritated their eyes and an occasional hot cinder stung their skin. They compromised by keeping the windows open only a narrow crack at the top. Axel suggested another poker game, but Blanche said she was too hot and the others agreed. Weary children whined.

By mid-afternoon the train had climbed over the divide and into the small settlement of Gallup. The travelers saw a few scattered Indian settlements of dry, sun-baked hogans that blended into the desert on the outskirts, then low, board-front buildings housing a few businesses parallel to the track. The depot included a somewhat questionable café where a few of the travelers consumed an unappetizing fifteen-cent plate of beans and tortillas.

On returning to the train, a group of passengers waited

to cross the street while a team of mules pulling a wagon loaded with chicken crates passed in front of them, an elderly Mexican man wearing a huge sombrero, on the driver's seat. A sudden hiss of steam from the locomotive frightened the team, and they lunged forward along the track. The driver, resolutely gripping the lines, could not hold them back.

Randy sprang from the crowd and caught hold of the near bridle. The mules, eyes wild with fear, reared and Randy fell into the dust. The crowd gasped, afraid he would be trampled. But as the team plunged ahead Randy rolled free, jumped to his feet, and clambered onto the back of the careening wagon. Scrambling forward over the crates, he took the lines from the old man and within moments had tugged the runaway team to a stop.

"You okay?" he asked the driver.

"*Si.*" The old gentleman slumped with relief, breathing hard. "*Muchas gracias.*"

Randy climbed down from the wagon and stroked the mules, making sure they were calm. "They don't like the sound of that engine."

"*Si, senor. Los cabellos* no like loud noise." The driver flicked the lines and the team started off at a docile walk.

"Say," Axel said as Randy rejoined the group, "you're pretty handy with a team."

Randy looked sheepish. "Drove mules on the farm. Stubborn cusses." The locomotive gave two short bursts on the whistle as they joined the others, and the bell clanged its departure warning.

They were scarcely underway when young Swifty Lydick came through the car carrying a gallon jug, a tin cup tied to its handle with a long string. "Water!" he called out. "Fresh water." He sold to several customers before he reached

Blanche. "I din't forget, ma'am, here's your water." He poured a half-cup from the jug. "Five cents."

"That's highway robbery," she protested good-naturedly. "But I'll take some."

Swifty sold out his supply before moving on toward the front of the train.

The train dropped down from Gallup into Arizona Territory, and they rolled past an ancient forest of petrified trees, then a spectacular area of colorful terrain called the "Painted Desert." To the disappointment of Joanna and Randy, they had seen no Indian war parties. The only tribesmen they had encountered were loiterers at the frequent water stops, where lean-to trading posts offered a few meager items for sale and refills for their water jugs.

As the lavender twilight descended, the train chugged on across the vast emptiness of Arizona, past huge saguaro cacti, some as tall as twenty feet, standing like hulking sentinels as they passed. The altitude began to fall off rapidly, and the engine purred its appreciation of the reduced drag as the track slipped smoothly beneath them. When darkness fell, Isaac Jacobs began to play his harmonica, and singing rang out over the desert with a fervency proportionate to the travelers' growing relief that the journey would soon be over.

After the singing, Axel and Randy sat with Claire and Joanna until the last possible moment before they had to set up the beds. Joanna hung on Randy's every word like a lovesick kitten.

"A railroad fireman is called a tallow pot," Randy was saying, "because engine valves used to be oiled with tallow. They use oil now, but the tallow pot still has to climb out the engine window and crawl along the boiler while the train is goin' full speed. When he's all set, the engineer shuts off the throttle, just for a few seconds, and during those few seconds the fireman has to pour oil into the vent in the steam chest. All this while the wind is blasting him full force."

"Why would anyone want to work for the railroad?" Joanna wondered.

"They say it gets in your blood." Randy's glance sought Claire's, and held it for a moment. "When something's in your blood, it's hard to get it out."

CHAPTER TEN

A full moon hung over Arizona Territory as Claire again lay sleepless on her platform bed. Assailed by the chorus of wheezes and snores from the bricklayers, she sat up and gazed out over the passing blue-shadowed landscape. As the train descended a long curving grade, she saw below a ribbon of river glinting silver in the moonlight, and she watched in awe as a cantilevered bridge spanning the broad waterway came into view.

Randy, seeing Claire awake, crept down from his cubby and crouched beside her. "Look," she whispered. "The Colorado."

They gazed at the spectacular sight, their heads together, leaning toward the window for the best view. As the train moved onto the bridge, a different sound engulfed them, and for a spellbinding interlude they were suspended over the glimmering river below. Then as suddenly as they had come upon it, they left the echo of the bridge behind, and the locomotive began its long chuffing climb out of the valley.

"We're in California," Randy whispered, his breath warm against her cheek.

She nodded, but his nearness blocked all thoughts of the long-awaited destination. When she turned her face to his, her eyes questioning in the dim light, his lips brushed hers. For a brief moment she responded and they clung together in a tender kiss that acknowledged their growing feelings.

But then she pulled away, holding her fingertips to his

lips in a restraining gesture neither forbidding nor encouraging. He pressed her hand and quietly climbed back up into his cubby.

She sat stunned by the feelings he aroused in her. And fear that someone had seen. Across the aisle, Warren and Birdie lay curled together facing the window. Blanche and Peach, sleeping with their heads toward the caboose, could not have seen over the seat back, but of course they might have heard Randy climbing down from above. The bricklayers and Axel snored noisily, while Joanna continued to sleep like an angel, her soft breathing undetectable.

Claire lay back on the cushion still feeling Randy's touch. What was happening? She was no giddy schoolgirl. She was a sensible, fully mature, married woman. Well, not actually married—she had been granted a divorce from Carter Chadwick long ago on grounds of desertion though, for Joanna's sake, she still wore her wedding band. Still, people were bound to misunderstand. Randy was considerably younger than she. But he was so fine. And full of surprises. The way he handled that runaway team . . . Strong. Yet gentle. And handsome. His eyes . . . She was aware of the train stopping to take on water at Needles, but after that she slept.

"Lucky we crossed the desert at night," Isaac Jacobs said over their final morning's poker game. "I hear it can get up to a hundred and twenty degrees or more during the heat of the day. That's why they call it Death Valley."

"It's gotta be hotter'n that in here now." Peach blotted her brow with a handkerchief as Blanche shuffled the deck for the next deal. Claire, Joanna, Axel, Peach, and the bricklayers anted up. Randy and Warren had spent the morning making plans for the new livery. The children played noisily up and down the aisle, scaring each other with talk of Death Valley rattlesnakes and Gila monsters.

The conductor, a friendlier fellow who had replaced Barnes in Albuquerque, volunteered information that they would be in Los Angeles by late afternoon. Westport, Missouri, seemed so long ago, as did everything in Claire's past. A fresh start. That's what she wanted. And that's what she surely would have.

When the train screeched to a stop at Barstow, travelers poured from the cars but found little relief from the heat. The small depot with its grim adjoining café boasted one appealing feature. Oranges. Several women surrounded by bushel baskets were selling the fruit for five cents each.

"These oranges sure are a sight for sore eyes." Warren gleefully purchased fruit for his family. Claire and Joanna purchased two oranges each, then hurried into the café where they bought premade sandwiches, two slices of dried-out bread containing a paper-thin piece of questionable ham.

Birdie managed a bright smile as Warren came down the aisle with his hat full of oranges. "It's Christmas in March, Birdie," he beamed. "Here's one more for each of us." He handed her one of the plump fruits. "By God, if we don't get rich in California, at least we'll be healthy."

The locomotive had begun its climb toward the 4,000-foot Cajon Pass, last geographical barrier to the Pacific coast, and the midday heat increased as the sun glared white-hot over the parched terrain.

Blanche and Peach, fanning themselves with portions of Randy's newspaper, argued about whether the window should be open or closed. Birdie, looking pale and weary, tried to get little Stella to nap beside her, while the re-charged Stanfield boys left their seats to banter with their young counterparts toward the front of the car.

But the train seemed to be laboring under an excessive burden. It slowed to a crawl, barely able to pull its drag up the increasingly steep grade. Near the Cajon summit, just when it seemed the engine would stop and perhaps be tugged back down the slope by the weight of the cars, the brakes squealed, and the train came to rest at a water stop on a high plateau. Some of the passengers spilled out along the track, but most immediately got back aboard as they discovered it was even hotter in the blazing sun. Randy went up toward the engine, hoping to learn how far it was to Los Angeles.

"Tank box's gone hot on us," the fireman called out from his perch atop the engine. The engineer nodded.

Randy watched as the fireman lowered the water chute to fill the boiler, then used water from a hose to cool down the hot tank box. The Negro carried buckets of water into the stifling boxcars for the livestock, but soon he appeared with the Holstein calf in his arms. He carried it some distance from the track and laid it on the ground behind some rocks. Randy realized the calf was dead. "Hyuh, now, pups," the man called as the three black-and-white dogs, yapping furiously, frisked around the carcass. "Stay out a' dat!"

With the tank box sufficiently cooled and the water supply replenished, the train once again got underway. Within minutes they were over the Cajon summit and beginning the descent down the other side, picking up such speed that nervous titters of alarm rose from the passengers.

Birdie gripped the edge of her seat, too frightened to speak, but Warren made light of it. "The engineer must be as tired of this trip as we are. He's sure makin' good use of this downgrade. At this rate, we'll be there 'fore we know it." But his hand reached for the window ledge as the train lurched around a curve without reducing speed. "You kids come sit down," he ordered. "Watch the scenery."

Over the next three hours, the oppressive heat seemed to diminish a bit as air fanned through the partially opened windows stirred by the extra downgrade speed through the San Gabriel mountain range. It was clear that the engineer meant to make time while he could. Randy expressed his fascination with the engineering that had built the track over the rugged mountain pass. Peach began to laugh at the sooty smudges on his face until, glancing at Blanche and the others, she realized they all looked like chimney sweeps.

When they rolled into San Bernardino and the train again halted to take on water, the impatient passengers piled from the train to refill water jugs, gazing westward over green rolling mountains, luminous under a morning haze. There they saw another sight that verified they were indeed nearing their destination—an acre of small citrus trees planted in neat, orderly rows on one of the hillsides. An orange grove, someone said. They were too faraway to see whether there were oranges on the trees.

"I don't suppose I'll be seeing you," Peach said wistfully to Joanna, "once we get there, I mean."

"Why not?"

"Well, you know, with you in school and all . . ."

"Have you ever thought of going back to school, Peach?"

"I ain't never been to school much." Peach's long lashes swept her cheeks. "We moved around a lot."

"Never been to school?" Joanna stared in astonishment. "But that's terrible, Peach."

"Priscilla. My name is Priscilla."

"But I saw you reading Randy's newspaper, even the boring parts."

"Blanche taught me to read and write and showed me my numbers."

"Then you'd do fine at school." Joanna pulled her aside. "After that, if we learned how to work those typewriting machines, we could work in an office."

Peach giggled. "Only men do that."

"No. Ladies do it now, too. You'll be my only friend in California and going to school together would really be swell." Joanna led her to where Blanche stood enjoying the San Bernardino vista. "Blanche, do you think Peach could go to high school with me? I know she'd like it."

"High school?" Blanche looked startled. "Why, I . . . I don't think she has the proper preparation for high school."

"She can get prepared. We can get jobs in a café while she studies."

"We'll see," Blanche murmured.

Breathing deeply to fortify herself for the remaining hours on the stuffy train, Claire sensed something different in the air. Something invigorating. "Could that be the ocean air?" she said. They all took long breaths.

"I'm going to run and jump in that ocean," Joanna announced. "I never felt so hot and sweaty in all my life."

Randy grinned. "You better take a mighty long leap. Los Angeles is twenty miles or more from the ocean."

"Oh, piffle," Joanna pouted.

Excitement was high as they hurried back aboard to begin the last leg of their journey. Though they saw occasional clumps of tall sycamore trees, most of the terrain was covered with low jungles of brambles, nettles, yucca, and scrub palms. Then they began to see new settlements along the railway, many of which sported brand-new depots among the cactus and chaparral, fronting totally barren tracts displaying signs announcing land for sale. Sycamore

Grove, Colton, Garvanza, Cucamonga, Ontario, Claremont, San Dimas, Olivewood, Azusa, Duarte, Etiwanda, Monrovia, Arcadia, Sierra Madre, Alosta, Pasadena, Gladstone, Lordsburg, Palomares, Magnolia—such intriguing names.

Finally they topped a shallow rise and saw before them on the rolling, sunburned desert a squat and scattered town cradled by a distant fluting of deepest blue, the Sierra Madre Mountains.

And as the train carried them closer, their expectations held in check like a giant breath waiting to be exhaled, they saw the signpost they had longed for across the tedious 2,000 miles of their journey, a sign that made their hearts and hopes soar.

Los Angeles.

PART TWO

CHAPTER ELEVEN

Los Angeles lay in a wide basin, a sprinkling of two- or three-story brick buildings among small frame structures and low adobes basking in the warm sun. Here and there a church spire asserted itself toward the cloudless sky. The disarray of new construction lay everywhere.

The street in front of the depot teemed with buckboards, drays, and buggies making passage difficult for the bell-clanging horsecars providing public transportation, while teams with wagons for hire stood at the hitching posts ready to haul whatever the travelers had brought with them. Vendors noisily hawking everything from lodgings to land accosted the weary newcomers as they edged their way off the train, and pushcarts laden with fresh vegetables, fruits, and flowers dispensed California's colorful bounty in the heat of the late afternoon.

One enterprising land developer pushed forward with a large sign: *Utopia Town! Land of your dreams. Twenty easy miles from Los Angeles. Thirty dollars per lot. Easy terms. Two excursions daily, 9 a.m. and 2 p.m. Don't miss this chance of a lifetime.*

Another placard urged, *HO! FOR THE CORSON TRACT. For the accommodation of all desiring to examine these Lots, A FREE CARRIAGE DAILY (except Sunday) will leave the Santa Fe Station at 1:36 p.m.*

Another stated simply, *E. H. Lockwood, Cor. Colorado St. and Fairoaks Ave. Dealer in GILT EDGE REAL ESTATE.*

Still another announced *Night excursions!*

Claire and Joanna had barely found footing on the platform when a disheveled man carrying a sign reading *Welcome Hotel* accosted them.

"Lodging, ma'am? Best in town. Two dollars." His breath smelled of whiskey, and Claire politely refused the offer. Isaac Jacobs inquired as to whether workingmen stayed there and were told that they did.

"Sounds like it might be a place where we could find us some construction work." Jacobs turned to Claire and tipped his hat. "It's been a real pleasure, ma'am."

"Good luck, Jacobs." Randy and Warren, in turn, shook his hand, and they watched the bricklayers start off along the crowded sidewalk.

Men in starched collars and derby hats, identifying themselves as attorneys, approached the more prosperous-looking travelers and urged them to employ the services of a "reliable counsel" if they planned to buy land. Axel, finding himself squeezed with one on either side, was forced to shake them off with gruff denials of any intention to become a property owner.

"My word!" Claire, affronted by the audacious sales pitches and disoriented by the strange sensation of being on solid ground after days on the lurching train, took Joanna's arm so they wouldn't become separated in the hubbub.

"This is it, Claire. City of the Angels!" Randy's wide grin and sharp eyes took in the astounding panorama.

Joanna caught her breath. "It's wonderful!"

Amid the noise and confusion, a sleek team of black horses pulling a fancy gold-fringed surrey edged in among the other carriages at the curb, and a swarthy man in a Mexican sombrero stepped down from the driver's seat. When he spotted Blanche Oliver he approached her. "Senorita Oliver?" His gaze strayed from Blanche to Peach.

"*Por favor,* Senor Lorenzo send me."

Blanche nodded her good-bye to the others and started for the carriage. Peach turned to Joanna, and they clasped hands. Peach flashed a hesitant smile, then turned and followed Blanche through the crowd.

"Their uncle must be rich," Joanna mused as the carriage pulled away.

The beat of a bass drum penetrated the din, then the blare of cornets as a marching band came down the street, a drum major in a brass-buttoned, red-and-gold uniform and a high furry hat, leading the procession. The crowd gasped as a huge elephant lumbered into sight behind the band, a dark-skinned man in a turban perched atop the spangled adornments.

Scarcely taking his eyes from the clowns, midgets, and acrobats strutting and tumbling in the street, followed by several bareback riders on white ponies, Randy questioned a man in the crowd, "What is this?"

"A circus went broke here a while back so the whole troupe found work promoting real-estate sales. Got a tent set up on down a ways, where they put on a performance every day after the parade."

"You mean this sort of thing sells land?" Randy was dazzled both by the spectacle and its apparent purpose.

"You bet." The man handed Randy a flyer that read, *WHERE IS LINDA ROSA? WE GIVE YOU THE PARTICULARS NOW. Situated in San Diego County on the line of the California Southern Railroad and offering direct outlet with the port of San Diego.*

"And this is the way they do business in the city?"

"This ain't just a city," the man said. "This is paradise." He winked at Randy. "All things are possible in paradise."

Randy stuffed the flyer into his pocket and edged in behind Claire and Joanna for a better view of the gilded cages passing before them. A heavy animal odor hung in the air from the tigers and lions lying in the shady corners of their cages, their tongues lolling in the heat. Claire's attention focused on a troop of costumed monkeys making their way along the fringes of the crowd, passing their little hats for coins.

"This beats anything I ever saw," Randy enthused. "I think I'm gonna like California."

After the parade passed and the sound of the band drifted on down the street, the noisy bustle of activity resumed.

"Folks, I got a fine lot for sale in Cucamonga," a woman said to them. She looked much like some of the immigrant women from the train, her round weathered face topped with a plain, flattened hat. "Only forty dollars for a quarter of an acre." She held up an official-looking paper. "It's a bargain, mister."

"I'm lookin' for farmland," Warren told the woman.

"Got no farmland," she said. "Town lots are what's sellin'."

"Who should I see about farmland?"

"Don't know nothin' about farmland. No one farms 'round here." With a suspicious look at Warren, the woman moved on, calling out, "Cucamonga! Good lot in Cucamonga. Forty dollars for a dandy lot."

As Warren stared after her, a portly man chomping a cigar commented, "I saw that woman this mornin' out in the valley buyin' lots. She'll double her money by nightfall."

"Is that possible?" Warren frowned in amazement.

"That's the way things are now," the man replied. "Folks pourin' in. Land changin' hands faster'n anybody can keep track of."

108

Claire looked each way along the street, trying to see past the signboards, the milling people, and the street traffic. "The first thing we have to do is find a place to stay tonight. Birdie is worn out. And so am I."

They decided to try the Angeleno Boarding House advertised on one of the placards: *Rooms and meals for ladies and gentlemen.* The bearer pointed out that the place was conveniently located not more than a dozen blocks away. Warren arranged for the Stanfield belongings, along with Claire's trunks, to be stored at the depot until they found permanent lodging, and Randy secured a team and wagon to transport the group to the boardinghouse with their hand luggage.

On the way, they skirted a very different-looking part of town—their driver called it Sonoratown—an area of adobe houses overhung with red-berried pepper trees, their crumbling walls sheltered by spear-leafed century plants. An ox-drawn cart loaded with firewood lumbered along the dusty street, and three *caballeros* sporting silver-studded saddles and jingling silver spurs rode by on easy-stepping horses. Mexican women in colorful shawls moved among the handcarts of fruit peddlers conversing in their soft Spanish language, while men lazed in front of a café watching a brown-robed priest scold a group of mischievous children. The visitors were fascinated by the unfamiliar scenes. Clearly there were two distinct cultures thriving side by side in the city of Los Angeles—the bustling, ambitious world of the Americans and the sleepy traditions of Old Mexico.

The sun hung low in the western sky by the time they reached the Angeleno Boarding House, where they saw a line of people waiting to get in the door of the weathered frame building, an assortment of bags, boxes, and bundles at their feet. A weary husband and wife with two small children stepped into the line behind Claire and her group. "We're the Corbins," the gaunt wife said with a soft Southern drawl. "We hear tell there's tents set up on the edge of town, but you gotta have your own tent."

When her turn came, Claire entered the small lobby area. A stairway leading up from the front door was flanked on one side by a reception desk, on the other by an arched doorway into a room containing two long dining tables. Noise of food preparation came from the kitchen beyond. A sharp-featured woman with dark hair coiled over her ears sat on a stool behind the desk.

"Take it or leave it," was her curt reply to Claire's inquiry as to whether there wasn't something available for her and Joanna other than what was offered—a small bed in a room with two other ladies. The Stanfields were to be favored with one bed in a room with another family. Randy and Axel could share a mattress with a third gentleman in the attic. "Three dollars per person including supper and breakfast." Then, glancing at the Stanfield children, "Kids under ten, one dollar."

"We'll take it," Claire said.

"Ain't but one bathroom per floor," snapped the sharp-beaked proprietress. "Don't hog it." Then indicating a stack of small clean towels on the counter, "And only one towel per person. Twenty-five cents deposit. Return the towel, you get your quarter back." Recording their names in a dog-eared ledger, she assigned each a room. Second floor, Room 5, bed 2, for Claire and Joanna. Second floor, Room 12, bed 1, for the Stanfields. Third-floor attic, mattress 10, for Randy and Axel. "Supper at six, breakfast at seven," she concluded, waving her arm toward the arched doorway into the dining room.

"Thanks, Miss . . . uh . . . Miss . . ." Randy hesitated.

"Triffen. Meta Triffen." She offered a stiff smile, then turned to the Corbin family as they stepped up to the desk. "Sorry, we're full for tonight."

Mrs. Corbin, teetering the fussy baby in her arms, looked as if she might faint. "But we got no place to go. We'll take anything."

"Can't give what I don't have."

"Look, miss," Corbin said. "We're wore out. My kids is hungry. Cain't we rest on the floor somewhere? Please, I got money."

Meta Triffen looked sympathetically at the ragged two-year-old clinging to his father's pants leg. "You can bed down in the washhouse out back. But you gotta be up and out of the way by breakfast time."

Corbin took out his shabby wallet. "How much?"

The woman scrutinized the sorry family before her. "How much you got?" Her sharp nose inclined toward the wallet as Corbin counted the bills.

"Seven dollars."

"Well . . ." She appeared to be weighing the plight of the Corbins. "Tell you what. No bed. No charge. Two dollars total for the meals and towels."

"That's good of ya, ma'am. We're much obliged."

"Just keep out of the way . . . and keep them kids quiet."

"Yes, ma'am."

Claire and Joanna toted their valises and the food basket up the stairs and along the second-floor hall to No. 5, and the Stanfields continued on toward the back looking for No. 12. Claire opened the unlocked door and entered a small room containing two beds and a washstand. One of the beds was partially unmade with various items of women's clothing strewn over it. Several suitcases were stacked in a corner.

"I guess our roommates are out." Claire put down her bags and approached the second bed, whose lumpy mattress was covered with a dark patchwork quilt. She pulled back the quilt to scrutinize the sheets, which were dingy and threadbare but clean. "After that train, this will seem like heaven." She sank onto the bed and lay back against the pillow. "I may sleep for days."

Joanna sat on the other side, testing the squeak of the rusty springs, then stretched out beside her mother, her face aglow with excitement. "Didn't you just love the parade?" Unable to contain her renewed energy, she jumped up, ran to the window, and peered across the rooftops toward the distant ridge of mountains. "Everything feels so different here." She took a deep breath. "Look! There's a palm tree. Right in the middle of town. Oh, Mother, isn't California the grandest place?"

Claire sighed as she eased herself up from the bed. "Words cannot express." Then, giddy with relief that their long uncomfortable journey was over, they laughed.

But Joanna held a finger to her lips, inclining her head toward the adjoining bed, saying, "Remember, we're going to have very close neighbors," which produced another round of laughter.

"Suppose we check out the bathing facilities." Claire took clean shirtwaists and underthings from the valise, and by the time they heard the supper bell, each had brushed the dust from her hair, used the big iron tub down the hall, and dressed in fresh clothing.

In the dining room they found the two long tables set up with enough serviceable plates, glasses, and cutlery to feed forty boarders. A steady stream of diners filed into the room and found places around the tables. Claire recognized the Corbin family at one of the tables, and a few others from the train. Randy and the Stanfields, already seated at the second table, had saved seats for her and Joanna.

"Our attic has mattresses wall-to-wall with numbers tacked up above so we don't get the wrong one by mistake," Randy said, brimming with good humor. "The fact that there may be someone else on it is no clue. Axel and me haven't seen our bed partner yet."

"Where is Axel?" Claire asked.

"We went out to buy a newspaper, and he decided to start checking out the cafés right away."

Claire felt more at ease with Axel absent. "Our bed is a bit lumpy," she said, "but at least it's clean."

"And no flying cinders," Joanna quipped.

"We're making do, too," Warren said. "The boys don't mind sleeping on the floor. They'll bed down on our coats."

"It's costin' an awful lot," Birdie murmured. She looked too exhausted to last through supper.

"Now, Birdie," Warren soothed, "we're gettin' meals, too. We'll find somethin' else tomorrow."

"The bathtub alone is worth the price," Claire said. "But I can't afford this for long. I hope to find something more reasonable tomorrow while I look for a job."

Two serving girls appeared from the kitchen carrying large steaming bowls of beans and rice mixed with bits of meat. Cabbage slaw, fresh bread, apple butter, and pitchers of tea were passed around the table, and for a time the only sounds were the clatter and clink of dishes and utensils as the hungry diners ate. When he had finished his lemon pie, Randy pulled out the newspaper and folded it open to the advertisements. Under "Rooms for Rent" he saw only one or two offerings at exorbitant prices.

"Are there any positions for women?" Claire wanted to know.

"Not a one." He handed her the paper. "Several women askin' for work though."

Claire scanned the paper. "I don't see any mention of schools."

"Must I go back so soon?" Joanna groaned. "I want to see everything first."

"Of course you must. You have to get your diploma so you can enroll in high school this fall." Joanna sometimes resented that she was older than others in her grade, due to Claire's having boarded her with the nuns for an extra year and not enrolling her in public school until she was old enough to be alone before and after school while Claire worked.

Joanna poked out her lower lip in the familiar mock pout. "Randy's never been to high school, I bet."

Randy looked at her from under a raised eyebrow. "You bet wrong. Trouble is, my Pa got sick and I had to quit a year short of graduation."

After another glance at the classifieds, Randy held the paper out to Warren, his finger marking one of the ads. "Look here, Warren. Small barn for rent or sale. On Pico Street. I'm gonna find out where that is." He rose from the table and went out to the desk where Meta Triffen, having hung the *No Vacancy* sign in the front window, perched on her stool eating a piece of pie. Randy placed the paper on the desk before her and pointed to the "Barn for Rent" ad. "Could you tell me how I can find this place?"

She peered at the small print. "It's on Pico, out on the west side close to that Electric Railway Homestead. They even got an electric streetcar to get people out there."

"Electric streetcar?"

"Uh-huh. Pretty soon we won't need horses pulling the streetcars, they'll all be electric." Then, scrutinizing him closer, "You lookin' for a house?"

"No, a barn. I'm in the livery business."

"Umm." She tilted her narrow face thoughtfully. "I get lots of folks here asking about hiring rigs or saddle horses. What's the name of your business?"

"Stanfield and Plank." He held out his hand. "I'm Randy Plank."

"Are you dependable?" The question was flirtatious.

"Yes, ma'am. Very dependable. And we offer the best prices in town."

"Then you should do well, Mr. Plank."

He made his way back to the table against the flow of diners leaving the room. "Warren, that barn's on Pico Street. What say we go out there and take a look? There's still time before dark. If it's any kind of a place, it won't be vacant long."

Warren felt revitalized after the meal. "Can we walk there?"

"No, but we can take something called an electric streetcar."

"Electric streetcar, huh? I'd like to see that. Let's go then." Warren got up from his chair. "Birdie, you get some rest. The kids can have my half of the bed till I get back."

CHAPTER TWELVE

The electric streetcar on the Maple Avenue and Pico Street line sped along its narrow rails, powered by current carried through an overhead wire from an electric line strung along the street. Randy learned from the conductor that though a few horseless cars were in operation in the East, this one, intended to promote the new subdivision called the Electric Railway Homestead Tract, was the first in this part of the country. The driver, declaring it a vast improvement over the horse-powered cars, clanged the bell along the way to clear the track of carriages, drays, an ice wagon, and other conveyances. Soon it left the downtown area for the more sparsely settled west side.

The open countryside boasted humble ranch buildings surrounded by small vineyards, family orchards, vegetable gardens, and jungles of brambles. Stretching off beyond the ribbon of settlement along Pico Street lay hay fields and occasional groves of citrus or avocado trees. Parcels of land had been sold off for development into residential or commercial properties, and everywhere raw wood marked the sites of new construction.

Not far from one of the car stops, Randy and Warren found the advertised barn. It stood toward the back of its lot, more a large shed with a small lean-to on the front than a barn. Warped and weathered, windows fuzzy with dust, battered doors hanging askew, the building displayed a sign, *For rent or sale.*

"It's seen better days," Warren commented.

"The location's not too bad." Randy scanned up and down the street at several existing businesses, including a general store and a lumberyard. "We passed a saddlery back a ways, too."

Warren assessed other aspects. "Roof prob'ly leaks."

Twilight was deepening as they pushed open the sagging front door and peered inside. "Anyone here?" Randy called out.

Getting no answer, they walked around back where a hand pump and a horse tank occupied one corner of a small fenced corral. Warren tried the pump, which drew a stream of clear water into the half-full tank. Toward the back of the lot a tumbledown privy surrounded by a heap of rusty cans, broken jars, rotting fence posts, and tangled wire provided the foreground for a row of eucalyptus trees.

"Don't seem to be anyone around," Randy said. "Let's look inside."

Enough light filtered through the grimy windows for them to see the few stalls sectioned off on one side and a broken-down farm wagon, along with other litter.

"You gents lookin' for somethin'?" The gruff voice came from behind them.

"Yes, sir," Randy said, squinting at the shadowy form outlined in the open doorway. "We're here to see about rentin' this barn."

"Fifty dollars a month," the voice intoned.

"Fifteen dollars? For this?" Warren scowled as his eyes scanned the premises.

"Not fifteen. Fifty!"

"Holy . . . !" Warren muttered. "Ain't that pushin' it a little?"

"That's the price," the man said. "Rentals are scarce these days."

117

"We're aimin' to start a blacksmith shop and livery," Randy said. "Any close by?"

"None that I know of. There's mostly new building going up out here, lots of folks moving in. That new subdivision over there just west of Vermont Avenue, the Electric Homestead, has more'n a hundred houses already." He gestured toward the window to point out the general location of the subdivision. "It's two hundred eighty acres cut into twelve hundred lots. New businesses springing up, too. Some of them folks prob'ly could use a smithy close by."

Warren and Randy exchanged glances.

"I'm Ned Godfrey," the man said, and Randy and Warren quickly introduced themselves.

"How much you askin' to buy it?" Randy asked.

"Eight hundred dollars."

Warren fell back as if struck by a sudden gust of wind.

Randy gave a low whistle. "We're lookin' to buy a place," he said, "but not right away. If we rent this barn for a few months, could that rent count toward buyin' it . . . if we decide to buy, I mean?"

Godfrey nodded. "I could maybe give you three months to decide."

Warren tugged Randy's arm. "We need to talk this over."

"Take your time," Godfrey said. "I'll fetch a lantern. It's gettin' dark in here." He disappeared from the doorway.

Warren turned to Randy, his face anxious. "You ain't thinkin' of payin' that kind of money . . ."

"Here's the way I see it, Warren. If it's true that downtown lots are sellin' for eight hundred a frontage foot, and this barn stands on maybe a sixty-foot lot, it won't be long before we can make a good profit on the lot alone. In the meantime, we can use it to get our business started. He said he'd give us three months before we have to decide about buying."

"I don't know, Randy." Warren held his hand protectively over his money belt. "My share—twenty-five a month for three months—is most of what I got left. And I got to find someplace for us to live."

Randy nodded. "We'll get some business comin' in right away to cover the rent." Then, inspired by another idea, "And why couldn't you live right here while the business gets goin'? Sure can't afford that boardinghouse."

"I thought I'd try to get hold of a tent."

"Warren, you could move your family in here tomorrow. And I could bunk in the loft with your boys—if Birdie wouldn't mind, I mean—till we can afford somethin' better."

"I can't ask Birdie to live in a barn, her feelin' so poorly."

"This could be our chance, Warren. There's water here. A corral out back, such as it is. We can board horses. You get your forge set up, and I'll see about getting some horses we can hire out to folks. Eventually we'll get our own stock, and rigs to hire out, too."

"Now how're we gonna afford our own stock and rigs?"

"Don't know yet. But if we get set up, that woman at the boardinghouse said she'd send some business our way. And I'll contact every boardinghouse and hotel around. Your boys can meet trains at the station with an advertising sign. We'll get business, I know we will."

A shaft of lantern light spread across the floor as the owner returned. Its glow illuminated Randy's face, revealing not only his enthusiasm, Warren noted, but his determination. Randy Plank was unquestionably a young man with good prospects. And here he was, offering to share his ideas and energy. This barn might be too hasty a decision—they hadn't looked around, hadn't compared prices—but maybe Randy was right. Maybe they wouldn't find anything better. At least the family would have a roof over their heads.

"All right then," he said. "Let's look the place over." He took the lantern and the two of them inspected the barn thoroughly, from the loft containing a few matted clumps of hay to the broken-down wagon and a greasy workbench they discovered under a clutter of junk near the back door.

"We'll take it," Randy told Godfrey, who still sat in the doorway smoking his pipe. "Three months' rental with the chance to buy."

It was nearly eleven when Warren rapped on the door of Room 12 at the Angeleno Boarding House. Birdie, in her faded wrapper, lifted the flimsy latch and opened the door. "What took so long?" she whispered. "I got worried." She smelled like soap, all clean, and her hair glistened in the lamplight.

"Birdie, I invested in our future." Warren glanced at their four sleeping children in the bed, then at the other side of the room where a family of five lay, some on the bed, others on the floor. When she held her finger to her lips, he took her hand and led her out to the stairs, where they sat down on the top step.

"Invested?" Her brow furrowed with apprehension. She seemed so frightened and fragile that he wished he didn't have to tell her he had handed over twenty-five dollars of their money to rent a tumbledown barn, and that tomorrow they would move into it.

"We're sure to make money when we sell the lot," he said, concluding his explanation. "Till then we can run our business out of the barn, we'll have a little money comin' in, and we'll have a place to live."

"Live in a barn?" Birdie's eyes searched his. "Oh, Warren, is it clean?"

"Well . . . no. Not yet. But it will be." He tried to re-create the enthusiasm Randy had shown when convincing him. "It's a start, Birdie. Only a start." He kissed her forehead. "Now you get into bed. Soon as I have a soak in that bathtub, I'll be there, too. We got a big day tomorrow."

Randy climbed a second flight to the attic dormitory. A low flame in the hanging lamp over the landing allowed scant light for him to find the lavatory at the top of the stairs, give himself a good scrub, and make his way among the boots and piles of clothing to his mattress. He easily recognized Axel's pudgy body spread-eagled in his underwear beside a smaller man sleeping in a shirt, socks, and garters. Neither awoke as Randy stripped to his underwear, sized up his best bet for a sleeping spot next to his two bedmates, and, barely clinging to the edge of the mattress, fell asleep at once.

Waking as others began to stir in the early light, Randy dressed hurriedly amid the grumbles, coughs, and hoarse conversation of the other lodgers. The stranger who had shared the mattress opened his eyes. He was slightly built with a large head defined by a heavy crop of nearly orange hair, with matching muttonchops and handlebar mustache.

"Good morning." He yawned and stretched, then crawled past the snoozing Axel to the foot of the mattress, where he pulled on his trousers and snapped a pair of yellow spats over his shoes. "Hope I didn't crowd you."

"Not that I noticed," Randy said, grinning. "But California's sure a whole lot cozier'n I expected."

The man, who appeared to be in his forties, smoothed his heavy orange thatch with his fingers. "You a first-timer here, too."

Randy nodded. "Westport, Missouri."

"Missouri? I hail from St. Louis originally. Lately Topeka, Kansas. I'm McKenzie Tate. Land promotion."

Randy clasped his hand. "Randy Plank. I'm startin' a livery."

Tate indicated Axel's comatose form. "You know this one?"

"He's in the restaurant business," Randy said. Axel snored on.

Tate smiled. "That's California for you. A cross-section of society right here on one mattress. Takes all kinds to produce boom fever, you know." He flexed the brim of his derby, which had been stashed beside the mattress atop his neatly folded clothing. Whisking off a smudge of dust with his fingers, he set the hat on his head at a rakish angle. "Astute businessmen counting on slow, steady growth. Promoters like myself. Gamblers who plunge in for quick profits. Greedy parasites attracted by the smell of blood."

"Sounds like you been through it before."

"Actually, I am thoroughly schooled in boom behavior. Kansas has been a hotbed of land speculation—railroad-grant sales, mass migrations to newly opened grain areas, prairie homestead activity . . ." He buttoned his shirt and tied his cravat without benefit of a mirror. "I've seen it all, my boy, and, if you're thinking of buying real estate, I caution you to beware. Unscrupulous promoters—Escrow Indians, they call them—will do anything for the almighty dollar." He raised one eyebrow mischievously. "When I heard they were hanging oranges on Joshua trees to sell desert lots as citrus groves, I knew I had to come to California."

The breakfast bell sounded. Folding his brown-and-yellow-checked suitcoat over his arm, Tate said, "Join me for breakfast?"

"I have friends here." Randy pulled on his own wrinkled suit coat. "Why don't you eat with us?"

"I'd like that," Tate responded. And the two new Angelenos started down the stairs.

"Birdie, you look rested this morning," Claire said as she and Joanna found places next to the Stanfields at one of the long dining tables.

Birdie smiled. "I had me a good hot bath last night. You were right, Claire. It was worth the price. Even Stella and the boys took to it."

"I sat in the big boat," Stella echoed, "and Mama washed me." Tucker, Daniel, and Eddie, neatly combed and scrubbed, eyed the platters of sausage and pancakes carried in by two serving girls.

"They got all prettied up for our new place," Warren beamed proudly.

"New place?" Claire exclaimed. "You found something last night?"

"Randy and me rented that barn for our livery," Warren said, "and we'll be livin' there, too, for a while." His grin coaxed a wan smile from Birdie. "We'll have it spruced up in no time."

Randy entered the dining room in the company of an unusual-looking stranger wearing a checkered suit, and they took the seats being saved for Randy and Axel.

McKenzie Tate introduced himself, nodding politely.

"He's in land promotion," Randy said, helping himself to pancakes and sausage from the passing platter. Then to Tate, "And these are the Stanfields, Warren and Birdie, and

123

their kids." Warren extended his hand.

Little Stella pointed at the stranger. "He looks like a orange kitty cat." Tate's green eyes, glinting amidst his heavy brows, mustache, and unruly muttonchops, suddenly became a central focus as everyone saw that he did indeed resemble an orange kitty cat.

Warren cast a stern glance at his daughter. "You'll have to excuse her, Mr. Tate. Four years old, you know."

"I'm Claire Chadwick," Claire interjected. "And this is my daughter Joanna."

"I'm pleased to meet all of you," Tate said. "I'm new in California myself."

Axel, hurrying into the room, saw Tate in his place, scowled, and took a seat on the other side of the Stanfield boys toward the end of the table.

Tate turned to Randy. "This property you found, may I ask where it's located?"

"Out on Pico."

"I'm not familiar yet with the area, but I intend to try Pasadena. The Crown City, they call it." Tate focused on each of his listeners in turn. "Developed from a barren rancho into a prosperous citrus colony, and just in the past year has become one of the fastest-growing little cities around. They say land is changing hands so fast no one has time to tend the groves."

"I'll be gettin' some land myself," Warren said. "The livery is only temporary."

"When you do," Tate said, "perhaps I can help you find something satisfactory in Pasadena. I'll be opening an office. 'Everything on the up and up' is my motto. Whatever you do, be sure to get legal counsel for any transaction."

"It's a little late for that," Randy said. "We already put

down our first month's rent. Plenty of time for lawyers when we buy the place."

"If . . . we buy the place," Warren cautioned.

"Warren, we better get a move on," Randy said, pushing back from the table. "Got to hire a wagon and pick up our stuff at the depot." Then, regretting that Claire would not be coming with them, "Will you be staying here another night, Claire?"

"Until I find something more suitable." She extended her hand to him. Then, wondering how they would keep in touch, she added, "I'll leave my new address here with the woman at the desk when I find a place. Good luck, Randy." Reluctantly she withdrew her hand from his.

Birdie, too, regretted the parting. "You won't be far from us, will you, Claire?"

"I'll let you know, Birdie, when we're settled." Claire clasped the frail woman's hand.

Warren got up from the table. "We'll invite you for supper, Claire, as soon as we get the place set up."

"You can get downtown from almost anywhere on the horsecars," Randy assured them, "then catch the electric car that goes out Pico."

"Six trains a day to Pasadena," Tate announced.

Axel rose from his chair and came toward them, his expression something akin to panic. "But, Claire . . ."

"Good luck, Axel," she said curtly, leading Joanna out to the lobby to get information from Meta Triffen about jobs for women in Los Angeles.

Axel and McKenzie Tate were left alone in the dining room. Tate moved into the chair next to Axel. "I hear you're in the restaurant business," he said.

125

CHAPTER THIRTEEN

Meta Triffen offered little encouragement for Claire's plan to find office work. There weren't enough jobs for the men streaming into town, she said, let alone any left over for women. She herself had gone to business school to learn the typewriter and would much prefer a job that would employ her mastery of the Remington, but just now there were no office jobs for women and, since her uncle happened to own the Angeleno, she was lucky to have her position there as desk clerk. She had no suggestions as to how Claire could find a job except to direct her downtown to the business district.

Claire determined to begin a thorough canvass at once. Leaving Joanna to help Birdie amuse little Eddie and Stella, she started downtown, enjoying the brisk walk in the morning sunshine while keeping an eye out for *Help Wanted* or *For Rent* signs. She saw none. Entering a mercantile store, she found a stout, shirtsleeved man behind the counter.

"I'm looking for work," she began, "and I'm wondering if you might know of something."

The man grinned at her. "There's nothin' but stores and offices around here."

"I know. I'm good with numbers and . . ."

The man looked her up and down. "Lady, there's ten men for every job right now. Ain't you got a husband?"

"No. And I'm new in Los Angeles."

"Then you gotta go where they want waitresses or

nurses, work that needs a woman's touch."

She heard the same arguments at each place she inquired. They didn't hire women. Women couldn't handle the work and were undependable. A woman's place was in the home caring for a husband and family. A woman had no business trying to take a man's job, especially since jobs were scarce and there were so many newcomers out of work. Men had families to support.

"Look, ma'am," a bookkeeper said when she persisted. "Find yourself a man to take care of you. Plenty of 'em around now wantin' housekeepers."

Claire inquired at every likely business without turning up a single possibility. She began to feel anxious. Had she been too caught up in Randy's enthusiasm for California to look at things realistically? Would she have to seek domestic work? Or go back to waiting tables? If it came to that, there were probably hundreds of newly arrived women seeking the same work. What would she do if she couldn't find anything?

" 'Scuse me, missus." The voice addressing her came from a ragged woman huddled in the shade against a building. She held out her open palm. "Can you spare me a nickel? I'm hungry, missus. I got no place to go."

Claire, feeling too weary and discouraged to focus on another's misfortune, turned away, then felt ashamed. The poor woman. What were her troubles? Had she come to California with high hopes only to see them dashed against an unyielding wall of no opportunity? Claire reconsidered, opened her coin purse, and took out a nickel.

"Much obliged, missus." The woman took the coin and shuffled off down a side street.

Claire stared after her, shaken by the encounter. The beggar woman's apparent desperation increased Claire's growing apprehension. By afternoon, her spirits flagging and the heat sapping her energy, she returned to the boardinghouse where she found Joanna waiting on the front steps.

"What took you so long?" Joanna said. "Randy and Warren came with a wagon this morning for Birdie and the kids. They went to get their things from the depot and move into that barn. Mother, do we have to stay in this place again tonight? The food was awful this noon, some kind of Mexican stuff."

"I'm afraid so."

"You didn't find work?" Joanna looked surprised, as if the thought hadn't occurred to her.

"No. There doesn't seem to be much work here for women like me."

"But did you try the cafés?"

"I had hoped I wouldn't have to." Claire sighed wearily. "But I will tomorrow. I thought maybe we could check on a school yet this afternoon. I'll ask the woman at the desk."

"Do we have to? I want to see some of the town, Mother. Maybe I should get a job."

Ignoring Joanna's grumbling, Claire again approached the front desk and asked whether there was a grammar school nearby.

"There's one on Fort Street just a few blocks over that way." Busy fielding questions from the day's new arrivals seeking lodging, Meta pointed in the general direction of Fort Street.

They found the old adobe-stuccoed grammar school and talked with the principal, an intense, scholarly man from Illinois, who enrolled Joanna in the eighth-grade class for the following Monday.

"We do our best to educate the children," he said, "but

things are still a little disorganized here with so many coming in." He provided information on high schools and seemed sympathetic to Claire's newcomer status. "I was in your position myself just a year ago," he said.

She asked about suitable lodging nearby.

"There's the Overland Hotel not far from here," he said. "But that's a bit expensive." He drummed his fingers on the desk while he thought. "There's a boardinghouse over on Eighth, but it's noisy and the food is bad. Once in a while I see *Room for Rent* signs on residential streets, but they're scarce right now."

Joanna nudged her mother. "I don't see how I can study in that awful boardinghouse."

"My brother-in-law owns an apartment house not far from here," the principal added, penciling a few lines on a sheet of paper. "Take this note, and maybe he'll consider you. The town is so full of scalawags and no-good drifters that he has to be careful. But it's a pleasure to see people like you coming into the state."

Responding to their knock, the principal's brother-in-law eyed the two unescorted females suspiciously, but after reading the note, admitted that a second-floor rear had just been vacated. "Couldn't pay their rent," he said pointedly, "and I had to throw 'em out."

Once a two-family duplex, the aging, two-story, frame building had been chopped up into six small apartments to take advantage of the population boom. Leading them up an outside stairway built to access the small upstairs units, he unlocked the door to an apartment that had been converted from two former upstairs bedrooms. The first room served as a parlor, partitioned at one side to form a kitchen area. Overly warm from the intense afternoon sun, the place held the faint smell of kerosene from a small stove jammed between some cupboard shelves and a table and chairs. The room's other noteworthy features included a shabby sofa and a window overlooking the street. The second room, which boasted a double bed, a mirrored chifforobe, and a view of the vegetable garden next door, had been walled off at one end to form a tiny bathroom.

"Eighteen dollars a month including water," the landlord stated. "And I don't rent to fly-by-nights. If you want the place I'll have to have a whole month's rent in advance."

"Yes, of course," Claire said, choking back her dismay. The way things were going, she would be lucky if she could even earn that much. More to the point: What if she couldn't find work at all? How long would her meager savings last, paying such exorbitant rent? What if he asked about her job prospects?

"Good cross ventilation," he said, flinging open the bedroom window and propping it with a stick left there for that purpose. The stifling heat remained unchanged. "Not many places have a private water closet and tub." He went into the bathroom, pulled the chain on the wooden overhead tank to demonstrate the plumbing and turned on the tap in the tiny sink wedged into a corner next to a small claw-footed bathtub.

"It's nice, Mother." Joanna recalled the backyard privy and tin washtub that had served their needs back in Westport.

"Hot water?" Claire hardly dared to hope for such a luxury, but she had already made up her mind. She didn't intend to squander another three dollars on a second night at the boardinghouse.

"Just what you heat on the stove," the landlord said. "Do you want it or not? I got a list of folks waitin' for these choice units."

"Yes," Claire said. "We'll move in tonight."

It was nearly dark by the time she and Joanna had checked out of the boardinghouse, took a streetcar to the depot, and hired a wagon to bring their trunks. Having purchased some eggs and bread on the way, they unpacked a few kitchen things and Claire scrambled eggs for their supper. Joanna filled the teakettle from the tap in the bathroom sink and set it on the stove to boil.

After supper, too weary to unpack anything but a few necessities, Claire donned her nightgown and climbed into bed.

"I'll finish unpacking tomorrow while you're out," Joanna offered.

"All right, dear. And on Sunday we'll do something special before you start school on Monday."

"Oh, could we, Mother? That would be just . . . just swell."

"Joanna, such language."

"I don't care, Mother." Joanna whirled in front of the mirror in her nightdress, happily studying her reflection. "That's the way I feel. Just swell."

"I know." Claire said sleepily. "I feel just swell, too."

Randy and Warren had begun the day by renting a team and wagon near the depot and transporting the Stanfields and their belongings to the Pico barn. If Birdie felt disappointed with their new home, she didn't let on. While the men and boys unloaded the tools, furniture, and other household items, she put on her apron and tied a cloth around her hair. She located the lye soap, rags, and broom she had packed, and while the children swept out the loft and cleared litter from the stalls, she scrubbed the feed bunk in the back stall.

"Warren, you can put the stove in this stall and run the stovepipe out that little window," Birdie called to him. She filled a water bucket at the pump and placed it in the bunk along with a basin for washing up. Warren and Randy set up the small, flat-topped stove to Birdie's satisfaction, then moved the table, benches, and dough tray into place.

"I'm not unpacking a thing till we get rid of some of this dirt," Birdie announced, more to herself than to anyone else. "Tucker, you and Daniel start wiping the cobwebs off the windows. Eddie, you and Stella pick up that stuff in the yard. Looks like a pigpen out there."

The men set up a bed for Warren and Birdie in the stall next to the "kitchen," two beds in the loft for Randy and the boys, and for Stella, a pallet of hay covered with an old blanket. When the little girl declined to sleep on it, Birdie got out her best quilt for the child's coverlet, and Stella promptly changed her mind, putting her doll to bed there while Birdie produced a hot midday meal of canned tomatoes poured over the dry bread left from the journey, followed by fresh coffee with plenty of sugar.

"Thanks, Birdie," Randy said when he had eaten his fill. "That was real tasty."

"I'll set up my tin oven," Birdie replied, "and make some corn bread for supper."

"Make a list of the groceries you need. I'll scout around before we take the horse and wagon back," Warren promised her. "I want to get some firebrick for the forge, first thing. Tucker, you better come along and help."

"Sure, Pa." The twelve-year-old felt privileged to be part of the important work of establishing the blacksmith shop that would provide their living.

Ten-year-old Daniel frowned his disappointment at having been excluded. "Can't I come, too, Pa?"

"No, Dan, you and Eddie stay and help your ma. I want you to take as much of this other junk as you can lift and carry it out behind the privy. Stella, you can help, too."

"I want to play upstairs with my dolly." Stella pursed her rosy lips.

Warren smiled at his little daughter and ruffled her dark curls. "Well, you be careful climbin' up that ladder."

Dusk had fallen when Randy, Warren, and Tucker pulled the team up in front of the barn and unloaded firebrick, horseshoes, nails, and other smithing supplies. After conferring with a blacksmith farther out on Adams Street, they had located a used bellows and anvil, and arranged for the lumberyard to deliver a supply of coal.

"And we brought you some beefsteak, Birdie." Warren looked pleased with the day's accomplishments as he carried in a box of grocery staples. "I got a peach pie here, too, and some fresh butter. That general store down the road has garden seeds and kerosene."

Within minutes Birdie had a hearty meal prepared, and after pleasantly stuffing themselves they lingered around the table in the back stall, their faces illuminated by the kerosene lamp in the middle, until Randy said, "Well, I reckon it's time to take the team and wagon back."

"Tonight?" Birdie glanced out the window at the thick darkness.

"No sense payin' another day's hire on it," Randy said. "I want to talk to the livery man anyway. Find out how his service operates. I'll come back on the streetcar."

Warren, smiling, shook his head in admiration of Randy's youthful energy.

"First thing tomorrow," Randy said, "I'll nose around some other liveries to see what I can learn. And, Warren, if you think you can bring that old wagon back to life, I'll keep an eye out for a horse."

The following morning, Claire slept later than she had intended, but she took time to heat water, refresh herself in the new bathtub, and dress carefully before resuming her search for work. She left a list of things for Joanna to purchase from the grocer down the street.

Yet as she made the rounds of businesses, each inquiry brought more of the same rebuffs and reminders that women need not apply for office work. The relentless heat soon wilted her best efforts at grooming herself, but still she trudged along the teeming streets, inquiring at each likely establishment.

By afternoon she had lowered her requirements and began stopping in cafés and restaurants asking about waitress work. She found one position open for a cook, but the proprietor was adamant in his insistence on an experienced male cook who could handle the heavy workload.

She stopped at a butcher's shop on the way home and purchased a fresh-dressed chicken. She and Joanna hadn't had a decent meal since the Harvey House. If she found work in a café, at least they would have food. Maybe she hadn't fully appreciated Axel Kohl's generous sharing of the daily leftovers.

She found Joanna sitting cross-legged on the sofa, wearing only a camisole and bloomers, looking at the family album. In the midst of unpacking, she had left everything strewn about the small rooms. Various items of outer clothing hung on pegs behind the bedroom door, and the doors and drawers of the chifforobe stood open, festooned with intimate apparel. Kitchen items leaned in precarious stacks on the table, and linens lay on the bed. She had spent the day scrutinizing her own clothing for her new life in California, trying on a few of her mother's things, and practicing dance steps—which hadn't left much time for putting the apartment in order.

When Claire entered, Joanna looked up and smiled brightly. "I didn't know where to put all this stuff," she said. "I thought we could do it together tonight."

"All right." Though perturbed by Joanna's failure to carry out her chores, Claire returned the smile. This was a difficult time for Joanna, too. "But first I'm cooking us a fine dinner," Claire said. "Did you go to the grocery?"

"Oh, I forgot." Joanna jumped up. "I'll go right now." She scurried about looking for her shoes.

"Hurry then. I need that flour and lard to fry the chicken. Do you have the list and the money?"

"Right here in my pocket," Joanna called as she danced out the door and down the steps. Claire sighed. Were all fifteen-year-old girls like Joanna?

The apartment was stifling. She changed into a cool shirtwaist and began arranging things on the kitchen shelves. By the time Joanna returned, she had the table set and the chicken cut up, and soon the dinner was under way. While it cooked, she put Joanna to work arranging her things in drawers assigned to her. Claire continued organizing the kitchen. The kerosene stove intensified the heat, and when the food was ready they moved the table closer to the open door to eat their meal where it was slightly cooler.

"Joanna, I'm worried about getting a job," Claire confessed as they ate. "I guess I was too optimistic about getting work in an office. I applied at cafés and restaurants today but there is nothing available. I may have to look for domestic work, housekeeping maybe."

"Does that pay enough?"

"I'm not sure. But I don't know what else to do."

"Maybe I could get a job," Joanna said. "It's no fun just sticking around here."

"We'll see . . . after you get started in school."

"You promised we could go on an outing to explore Los Angeles before I go back to school."

"We will, Joanna. Just be patient. Tomorrow is Friday, which gives me two days yet this week to look for work. Sunday, we'll do something special."

CHAPTER FOURTEEN

Just past noon on Saturday, near the corner of Sixth and Main, Claire stepped from the curb to avoid two tall ladders propped against a brick office building. The ladders supported two workmen who were installing a sign beneath a second-floor window.

"Excuse me, madam," a voice called to her. She looked up to see a goateed man leaning over the windowsill to direct the sign hanging. He peered down at her through his small round spectacles. "Would you tell me whether the sign looks straight?"

Claire shaded her eyes to better read the fancy lettering: *Farley Foster Dodd, Attorney at Law, Real Estate a Specialty.*

"Have they hung it straight?" he repeated.

"The end against the wall is a bit low," she said.

"Pull it up some," he ordered the two workmen on the ladders. "How's that, ma'am?"

"Now that end is too high," she judged. The workmen made the adjustment. "Yes, that's about right."

"Hold it there," the man told the installers. "I'll come down and make sure." And while they steadied the sign, he hurried down the long flight of stairs and out onto the sidewalk. A smallish man of about forty, he wore a neatly pressed suit, stiff-collared shirt, and silk cravat with stickpin.

"Just when I'm barely moved in, they come with the sign," he grumbled, glancing at Claire. "I have to see a client this afternoon, and . . ." He craned his neck to assess the position of the sign. "Yes, that looks fine." Then, without missing a beat, he turned to Claire, continuing his lament. ". . . I can't find a thing and I have to draft a lease before two o'clock, I haven't any help, and . . ."

"You haven't any help?" Claire repeated.

"I just opened my office yesterday, and already I've gotten two clients. I'm trying to hire a clerk, but who knows how long it will be before I find one qualified to handle the work." He glanced at the sign. "And now that my shingle is up, it's sure to get worse."

"I'm looking for work, Mr. . . . ," she glanced up at the sign, "Mr. Dodd."

"What sort of work?" He scrutinized her through his small wire-rimmed lenses—an attractive, though slightly bedraggled, young woman with a determined look about her.

"Clerical work. Secretarial. I'm good at composition and I can cipher. I have some higher education, plus vicarious experience in the world of business—my father was in stocks and bonds—but I'm willing to consider anything that will pay me enough to support myself and my daughter."

Dodd's eyes narrowed behind his spectacles. "Good handwriting and spelling?"

"Yes."

"Come with me." He led the way up the stairs, scowling as he admitted her to his office, two large sunny rooms across the third-floor front. "I'm desperate for help this afternoon," he said. "Sit here." He indicated a cluttered desk in the middle of the first room, and moved stacks of papers from the chair. "I'll just move these things, and we'll try you out." His voice was unusually resonant and rich for such a slight man. "Now, your name is . . . ?"

"Claire Chadwick. Mrs. Claire Chadwick."

"I need you to copy this contract, Mrs. Chadwick." He

pushed the remaining clutter aside and smoothed out a wrinkled scrap of paper containing a few jotted notes. Then he hurried into his office and returned with several sheets of fresh paper, an inkwell, and pen. "A routine transaction, but we still have to draw up a legal document. Here's a similar one from the files. Just follow the same form, filling in the new information. Can you do that?"

"Yes, I think so." Claire seated herself at the desk.

"The client will pick it up this afternoon at two." He went into his office and busied himself at his big rolltop desk, set perpendicular to the windows for the best light.

Claire studied the note he had given her, comparing the information conveyed in his neat handwriting to that required on the document. She cleared space on the desk, dipped the pen into the inkwell, and began to draft the document. It was a simple one-page sales contract for a small bungalow, but she was determined not to make a mistake that would require copying it over, since it had to be ready in little more than an hour.

"Mrs. Chadwick," Dodd called. "I can't find my accounts-receivable ledger. Do you see a ledger on any of those shelves?"

Claire glanced around at the near-empty shelves. "No, Mr. Dodd."

"If you run across it, please let me know."

"I will, Mr. Dodd."

"Mrs. Chadwick?"

"Yes."

"How are you coming on the contract?"

"Fine. Just fine."

"Good. I admire someone who can get right down to business. The wheels of industry and all that. Isn't that right?" His deep-toned voice rambled on until Claire was uncertain whether she was required to listen, and she continued carefully copying the sales contract, concentrating on her task.

"Are you having any trouble with my notes, Mrs. Chadwick?" He got up from his desk and came to stand behind her, peering over her shoulder at her progress. "Your penmanship is quite satisfactory," he said as his small brisk steps carried him back to his own desk.

When Claire finished the document she took it to him.

"Excellent!" he exclaimed after finding everything correctly done. Leaping up from his chair, he placed the contract on one of the empty shelves. "We'll just put this where we can find it when the client comes." Then facing her, "Mrs. Chadwick, would you consider filling in here for a week or so—just till I can find a clerk?"

"Yes, I would, but . . ."

"Your hours will be from eight in the morning till six in the evening . . . unless we get rushed and I need you to stay later." He forced a smile. "You'll have Sunday off, and your pay will be eight dollars for the week."

"Oh." Claire's voice fell as she weighed the feasibility of the salary.

"You can't expect top wages for a temporary job," Dodd said.

Claire gathered her courage. "What might you be paying a man when you find one?"

"Depends on his qualifications. He may be supporting a family, you see."

"Mr. Dodd, I am the sole support of my daughter. I'm dependable and thorough. I'll work hard for you. And if I do a satisfactory job, what difference does it make that I'm a woman?"

Dodd blinked behind his spectacles. "Why, it makes a

great deal of difference. Some of your work may involve talking with clients when I'm not available, and you must agree that is risky for any business."

"Risky?"

"I could lose business if it were thought that a woman . . . Well, you wouldn't be making decisions, of course, but your very presence in the office would be suspect."

"Mr. Dodd, I've just come all the way from Missouri to make a new life. I need this job. I'll do good work for you. And I insist on a salary of at least twelve dollars for the week."

Dodd choked back a cough, took off his spectacles, polished them, then peered at Claire through the wire-rimmed lenses. He wasn't keen on hiring a brash woman, but, on the other hand, such forward behavior often accompanied a capable mind. He had learned that much after ten years with his wife Tibby. "Very well, Mrs. Chadwick. Twelve dollars. But I'll expect you to earn every penny." His expression was not entirely disapproving.

"Thank you, Mr. Dodd." Claire smiled then, feeling a surge of confidence. "I'll be here first thing tomorrow morning."

"But what about this afternoon? Can't you stay?" He gestured toward the papers and books stacked everywhere. "Look at this mess."

"I'll stay until your client comes, in case there are corrections to the contract, but then I must go. I've only last night moved into a new apartment, and I have yet to make it livable. I can come in first thing tomorrow morning."

Dodd cleared his throat. "Very well then. Eight o'clock sharp. I prefer getting an early start."

CHAPTER FIFTEEN

"That's right, my friend." McKenzie Tate gazed earnestly into the bulging eyes of would-be restaurateur Axel Kohl as they lingered at the breakfast table in the Angeleno Boarding House. "It's foolish to put your money into a greasy little café when you can double or even triple it in real estate."

"I don't know nothin' about real estate." Axel wished the pushy land promoter would leave him alone, yet he liked the idea of being able to increase his modest nest egg enough to establish a good restaurant.

Tate talked expansively. "Do you realize, this very minute, right here in southern California, we're sitting on an opportunity that may not come again in our lifetimes."

Axel nodded. "But I have to put what little I have into what I know about."

"You're just the kind of fella I like to deal with, Axel. You know the value of a dollar, and that's the way I like to operate." Tate touched his napkin to his lips. "You're looking to invest, and I can get you into the right properties."

"But I thought you just got here, too."

"I've been here three days. That's long enough to get the lay of the land. I've been in land promotion for some time. Illinois and Kansas. Now California. The San Gabriel Valley is where things are happening out here. Forty miles of fertility between Pasadena and San Bernardino, and all served by the railway lines. Good soil, good climate, and ample water supply. If you don't want citrus groves and grape lands, you can sell the land off in residential lots and make a handsome profit."

"But I don't have that kind of money."

"There's something for every pocketbook. You can make money on just one lot. Axel, my friend, if we could get our hands on some of that good foothill property, we could unload it overnight."

"You should talk to Warren Stanfield. He wants growin' land."

"I will. I will. But, Axel," Tate draped his arm across Axel's shoulders, "don't you see? You could be the one to sell to Warren Stanfield—if you had the right property."

"Naw, I wouldn't feel right about making money off Warren."

Tate sighed. "But why not? Warren would be getting the deal of his life. You've heard about Rancho Santa Anita?"

Axel shook his head.

"A fella named Baldwin bought a big chunk of land a while back, and recently he sold off portions for the towns of Arcadia and Monrovia. He's made a fortune."

Axel couldn't fathom why Tate was throwing all this big talk at him.

"Monrovia's probably the most successful town around right now." Tate turned on a warm smile. "I wouldn't be telling this to just anybody, you understand."

"I s'pose it wouldn't hurt to take a look at it," Axel said.

Tate continued without missing a beat. "Monrovia was laid out last year on sixty acres bought from Baldwin by a railroad engineer named Monroe and some partners. Now they're running excursions to attract buyers."

"You know," Axel mused, lost in his own vision, "with

all those folks comin' in, they're gonna need good places to eat."

"Good places to eat?"

"You're damn right!" Axel's face lit up as if he finally understood what Tate was trying to tell him. "I'm goin' out there and see if they got any cafés."

On the first morning of her employment, Claire had to wait a few minutes until Farley Dodd arrived to open the door. "I'll see about getting a key for you," he said, peering at her through his round eyeglasses as if surprised to see such an attractive yet crisply businesslike young woman standing at his door. "I trust you got your living quarters in order." Claire had forgotten the rich resonance of his voice, which gave him a commanding presence despite his slight stature. His goatee neatly groomed, he wore a pressed dark suit, pristine stiff collar, and silk cravat, as he had the day before.

"Almost." Claire surveyed the array of papers, books, and folders strewn about.

"I've made a beginning here," he said. "I want you to finish unpacking these boxes and put the books on the shelves, the law books here next to my office, the rest you can use your own judgment. Just remember where you put things."

"All right." Claire took off her hat and hung it on the hall tree.

"I'd like you to begin by answering this letter," he said. "Tell him I'll look into it."

The morning passed quickly as she did her best to absorb Dodd's further instructions, making notes in order to remember all that he told her. Toward noon, Dodd left for a brief visit to the recorder's office, and she spent her half-hour lunch break putting the law books on the shelves while eating the egg sandwich she had brought.

As Dodd predicted, the new sign attracted passersby. Two brothers came in for advice on a store they hoped to purchase in the neighborhood, and by late afternoon three more potential clients had been drawn into the office. Greeting visitors, along with copying documents and following Dodd's instructions to post invoice amounts in the accounts-payable ledger left little time to finish unpacking, sort things, and arrange the shelves.

When six o'clock came, Dodd reminded her that the day was over. "We'll get an early start again tomorrow," he said, putting on his suit coat. "I live just down the street at the Overland Hotel, and I do enjoy my morning walk to the office."

The low afternoon sun still felt quite warm as she walked the few blocks to the apartment. She still didn't feel fully rested from the long journey, and her hands were scratched and sore from digging in Farley Dodd's packing boxes, but the colorful flower beds along the street seemed to nod encouragement as she passed. Back in Westport it might be snowing. She felt a deep contentment with her good fortune. She had made the move to California, had found work and a place to live. It truly is a land of milk and honey, she thought. A paradise.

That morning she had left Joanna to straighten the apartment. Now she found the parlor and the kitchen still in disarray. She checked the bedroom and bathroom. No Joanna. Maybe she had gone to the grocery to get something for supper. Claire decided to go and meet her, leaving a note in case she had guessed wrong about Joanna's destination.

She had. Joanna was not at the grocery, nor was there a

trace of her along the way. Claire quickly purchased a few food items and hurried back to the apartment. Joanna was not there. And it was getting late.

Twilight hung at the windows. Claire lit a burner under the teakettle and sat down at the kitchen table. What could Joanna be thinking of, going off without leaving a note? Especially in a teeming city she knew nothing about. Surely she wouldn't have gone to the boardinghouse so late in the day. Never before had there been reason to worry about her daughter's safety. But now . . . Her throat tightened with growing concern.

Claire was well acquainted with loss. Left motherless during most of her growing-up years, her father's suicide further heightened her feelings of loss and abandonment. Carter's desertion had been the final devastating blow. Surely fate could not be so cruel as to take Joanna from her, too.

She cast aside such morbid thoughts. Her long day at the office was distorting her perspective. There must be a simple explanation. But what could it be? What if Joanna had been hurt? Claire remembered the runaway team that Randy had stopped at the Gallup depot. Should she try to get in touch with Randy? Always resourceful, he might know what to do.

Or perhaps she should get in touch with Farley Dodd. He mentioned he was living at the Overland Hotel. Yes. If Joanna didn't come home soon, she would go to the Overland and ask his advice.

CHAPTER SIXTEEN

Randy Plank began his second full day in Los Angeles by visiting a carriage maker. After looking at several carriages at the livery barn the night before and weighing the rental information he had gleaned, he realized that his plan would take more than enthusiasm to succeed. Without rigs and horses to hire out, the fortunes of Stanfield and Plank would depend entirely on Warren's blacksmithing.

Randy introduced himself to the man in charge, then added in a matter-of-fact manner, "I'm in the livery business."

"Bud Hawkins." The muscular Hawkins had an iron grip. "Me and my brothers own Hawkins Carriages."

"I have connections in real estate," Randy continued, borrowing a line from McKenzie Tate, "and I hope to represent a line of carriages to land buyers."

Hawkins eyed the young visitor, who appeared to be one of those immigrant bumpkins whose clothes didn't fit right. But there was a serious, even trustworthy, look in his eyes, a certain pride in the way he presented himself. "How many do you think you can sell?"

"Don't know yet. Me and my partner are settin' up in business over on Pico. Stanfield and Plank. We'll be hirin' out horses, offerin' rentals on rigs, things like that, and we'll be needin' carriages. How much of a discount could you allow me on each one I order? I'm lookin' to pick out a rig today."

"We might be able to give you, say, ten percent off . . .

starting with your second order."

Second order? That didn't help much now. "I had in mind fifteen percent," Randy countered.

"Let's make it twelve," Hawkins said. "I'll show you what we have."

Randy followed him toward the back of the huge barn where several men were working on vehicles in various stages of completion. A number of finished carriages stood on display. After looking over the available rigs, Randy settled on a small buggy.

"If you need a horse to pull it," Hawkins suggested, "our stable is just around the corner."

Randy nodded and the two walked out to a small grassy pasture behind the stable where a fine team of Morgans, a work team, and a few saddle horses were grazing.

"I can give you only a twenty-dollar down payment," Randy confessed. "The rest I'll pay off at ten dollars a month."

Hawkins frowned. "For the buggy *and* a horse?"

"That's right."

"Well . . . uh . . . I'd have to come over and look at your setup."

"We need the rig now," Randy urged. And while he related the details of his business venture with Warren Stanfield, his plans and hopes for the future, Hawkins saw a determination in him that inspired confidence. Randy Plank didn't seem the type to pull a fast one. Besides, there was potential for a good profit later if Stanfield and Plank succeeded as Plank envisioned. "I reckon I could let you have that mule over there on those terms." Hawkins pointed out a small gray jenny at the back of the corral. "Three years old and strong as an ox."

Randy studied the expression on Hawkins's face to see

how much truth he could ascribe to his claim. He walked over to the mule and inspected her teeth, legs, and hoofs. The animal seemed sound, even appealing, as she nosed up to Randy.

"Her name's Sugar," Hawkins said. "I give her sugar sometimes—if she decides to get a little balky."

"Let's try her on the buggy," Randy said. "Got a harness that'll fit her?"

"There's an old one that needs a little repair. It'll cost you extra." Randy agreed to the price, and they hitched the mule to the buggy. Hawkins made out a bill of sale, and Randy paid him twenty dollars, the last of his money, signing a note for the balance.

"We'll discount your next purchase twelve percent," Hawkins verified. He took a small, nearly empty paper sack from his pocket and gave it to Randy. "Don't hurt to have some sugar along in case she gets a sweet tooth."

"Thanks." Randy climbed into the new rig and, with a flick of the lines, the little jenny stepped out with a jaunty gait. The shabby harness had been poorly maintained, its collar padding was worn thin, and one broken line was held together by an uncertain knot. But Randy felt proud. He had his own rig, a brand-new buggy and a small gray mule that he had managed to get for only a modest cash investment.

As he pulled into the yard in front of the barn, he saw Warren and Tucker under the lean-to, finishing work on a forge of firebrick framed up with old fence posts from behind the barn. They turned to stare at the neat little buggy pulled by the perky gray jenny.

"I bought us a rig," Randy called, jumping down to pat Sugar's neck. The other children came running, toting bits of junk they were clearing out of the barn. Birdie, in her cleaning kerchief, followed.

"This is Sugar," Randy said. "She's the sweetest little trotter you ever did see. And . . ." he turned to Warren, "I got a real bargain. Buggy, mule, and harness for twenty dollars down and ten dollars a month."

Warren's mouth gaped open. "Twenty dollars down and ten a month? For how long?"

"Four months," Randy said. "We'll make it back easy. I'm planning to offer private tours."

"Good God! You're thinkin' of buying this old barn for eight hundred, and now we owe for this . . ." Warren frowned as he ran his hand down along Sugar's knee and ankle joins, scarcely daring to look at the shiny new buggy. Tucker climbed onto the seat and picked up the lines, pretending to drive.

"We coulda made a down payment on a farm for that," Warren fretted.

"Not out here you couldn't," Randy said. "This boom has inflated the price of everything."

"I don't know, Randy. Seems like we're gettin' in too deep."

"Now just keep your shirt on, we'll pay it all off in no time."

Sugar nosed Randy's pocket. "The only thing is . . . this little lady has a sweet tooth. Had to give her a couple licks of sugar on the way over. But she's sure a dandy." He took the near-empty sack from his pocket and poured some into Daniel's hand. Sugar eagerly licked it from the boy's palm. "Let's take her for a spin, Warren. You'll see."

Warren and Randy climbed up into the buggy with Tucker, who took the lines, and Sugar set off again at a pleasant trot.

"I just hope you know what you're doin', Randy." Warren felt keenly the expenditure of his hard-earned money. "Couldn't you have found a horse? One a little bigger, maybe?"

"The deal didn't allow for a horse." Randy grinned. "Now don't make Sugar feel bad. Look how she loves her work." The little jenny did indeed seem to revel in pulling the new buggy through the streets of Los Angeles.

"Not much of a harness," Warren muttered. But smiling then at his son manning the lines, he settled back on the comfortable seat, breathing in the smell of new leather.

McKenzie Tate learned on the train to Pasadena that a tract of land was being promoted as a new town called Azusa, a name derived by taking the first and last letters of the alphabet and adding USA. Though earlier attempts to colonize the area had been unsuccessful, new owners calling themselves the Azusa Land and Water Company were making a renewed effort. They had platted the town on 4,000 rocky upland acres near the San Gabriel River, saving the better land surrounding it for agricultural purposes.

Tate's informant was a weathered, bandy-legged cowhand named Slim.

"I'd had a bellyful of cattle drives," Slim confessed. "The day I got my last pay was when I headed for Cal-ee-forn-eye-ay."

"And you say this Azusa is opening up tomorrow?"

"For a fact. Saw it in the paper." Slim eyed the orange-whiskered man beside him. "I'm lookin' to get a piece of it, then turn it over, same as was done in Monrovia. Plots of ground that sold last Fourth of July for a hundred and fifty brought five to eight thousand by Christmas." He grinned, showing more teeth missing than present.

"And you expect lots in Azusa to do the same?"

"Dang tootin'. But the word's out, and we'll more'n

151

likely have to wait in line overnight." He patted the bedroll beside him.

"Are there that many buyers?"

"On a deal like this there are."

"All right, Slim." McKenzie Tate had stumbled onto just the opportunity he had hoped for. "Let's you and me go on out there and buy us some land."

When they arrived at the Azusa land office, a small shack on a wide expanse of barren terrain, they found several would-be buyers ahead of them. The office didn't open until seven o'clock the following morning, yet there was a line of men—and one woman, Tate noted—standing, sitting on chairs, or napping on bedrolls ahead of them.

Hardly had they taken their place in line when an anxious-looking businessman, wearing a homburg and starched collar despite the heat, approached the first person in line, a man of Italian descent whose swarthy good looks were shaded by a straw skimmer.

"I'll give you a hundred dollars for your place in line," the businessman said.

The Italian laughed heartily. "A hundred dollar no buy dis place."

"All right then. A hundred and ten."

"*Mama mia!* You crazy."

The homburg moved to the next in line. "How about you?"

"Not on your life. See me after the sale. I might have something for you then."

The fifth person in line, the woman, to whom the price offered seemed a fair exchange, gave up her place to the man in the homburg. She then went to the end of the line, which by now had expanded to more than a hundred people.

The night passed uncomfortably for Tate, who, having no bedding, sat huddled on the dusty ground much of the night, finally rolling his jacket to make a pillow and catching a few winks. At dawn, an enterprising vendor with a pushcart sold sandwiches and tepid coffee to the waiting line, which had grown considerably longer during the night.

When the land sale began, Tate and Slim gradually moved up in line until each was able to buy, sight unseen, four lots at $175 apiece in the as-yet-nonexistent town of Azusa.

"Guess it don't have much to recommend it but the publicity," Tate mused as he stepped from the office with the deeds to his property.

By now a crowd of what seemed like hundreds had gathered. A band began to play, clowns and other acts hired by the promoters were entertaining the throng, food and beverage concessions had been set up, and those who had purchased lots were now offering to resell them.

Tate heard offers of $200, $300, and $400 per lot. He sold two of his for $500 each, and by mid-afternoon his other two went for $750 each. He lost track of Slim in the crowd, but the last he saw of him, the determined cowboy was holding out for $1,000 a lot.

CHAPTER SEVENTEEN

Earlier that day, after Claire left for her first full day at her new job, Joanna began straightening up the apartment. She found a calendar showing a picture of a pretty young woman in a flower garden, and after some consideration hung it on a nail in the bedroom. She unpacked the trunks and shoved them into place as bed tables, putting dresser scarves atop each one. Then, glimpsing herself in the chifforobe mirror, she struck a few poses she had learned in ballet class and danced through the two rooms practicing her steps. Frowning at her pigtails and wrinkled pinafore, she decided to take a bath in the new tub, after which she dressed in her prettiest summer shirtwaist and arranged her hair atop her head with a fashionable curl hanging on either side. Tucking two dollars into her reticule, she started for the grocery.

Outside in the pleasant sunshine, she marveled at the incredibly warm weather for this time of year. Perfect for a nice walk. Why not walk to the Angeleno, as her mother had suggested, and leave their new address for Randy. She wanted to see everything there was to see in her newly adopted town. Los Angeles, California. Just saying the words was thrilling.

Emerging from the Angeleno, Joanna heard the faint beat of drums and march music coming from the direction of downtown. It sounded like the circus parade they had seen at the depot the day they arrived, and she hurried toward the music, remembering with delight the lumbering elephants, the acrobats, and the adorable monkeys collecting coins.

She overtook the parade in front of the depot, where, as usual, it coincided with the arrival of the Southern Pacific's afternoon train. Intrigued by the procession of exotic animals and circus performers, the toe-tapping sounds of cornets and trombones, tubas and fifes, the thump of the bass drum, she stood and watched, feeling the excitement of it wash over her. Again she was caught up in the throng of arriving passengers, the hiss and squeal of the locomotive drowning out barkers touting lodgings and land, vendors hawking flowers and food. Though it took her breath away, this time it didn't seem quite so foreign. After all, this was Los Angeles. Her new home.

She admired the bareback riders in spangled tights pirouetting on white ponies, and a dashing Wild West cowboy riding a black stallion. One of the clowns carried a sign announcing an afternoon circus performance that would begin immediately after the parade and, as the procession passed by, Joanna fell in with the crowd following the marchers.

Had her attention not been on the broad-shouldered cowboy, she might have noticed a distinguished-looking gentleman who had just arrived on the afternoon train. The man's well-tailored, brown pinstripe suit, handsome with his brown hair and mustache, set him apart from most men in the crowd. But Joanna hurried after the parade without noticing Harry Graham as he signaled a waiting hack.

The circus tent stood in the middle of a vacant block not far from the depot, and Joanna took her place in line to buy a ticket. Fifty cents was not too high a price, she thought, for all the incredibly interesting and wonderful sights she would see. Inside the big tent, she found a seat on the wooden bleachers.

Immediately her attention focused on the center of the ring where a clown was putting several small poodles through a series of tricks to open the performance. Simultaneously, the bareback riders rode into the ring on their white ponies, only to be replaced on the second round by monkeys in plumed hats and little jackets leaping from pony to pony. The crowd applauded happily for each act—the lion tamer, the elephant tricks, and finally the trapeze artists who took her breath away with their daredevil performance. The band played throughout, and when it was over Joanna applauded wildly. She had never imagined such fine entertainment.

As the crowd filed out of the tent, she stopped at a concession stand to buy one of the bright red taffy apples displayed. Standing nearby were two young women also waiting to purchase the treat. One had blonde hair and a flawless complexion, and Joanna recognized her former traveling companion.

"Peach!"

"Joanna!" Peach seemed stunned to see her.

"Only two days since we came," Joanna exclaimed, "and yet it seems like years. Have you gotten settled?"

An evasive look swept over Peach's pretty face. "Yes, we're settled. And you? Where are you living?"

"We found an apartment just a few blocks from my school. I start on Monday."

"Oh." Peach's voice fell. "That's nice." She glanced at her companion, who looked a bit older than Peach, dark-haired and taller, but with poor posture which made her chin jut out unattractively, emphasizing her long narrow face and pinched features. "This is Tess," she said. "My . . . uh . . . cousin."

"Pleased to meet you, Tess," Joanna said merrily. "Did

you see the circus? Wasn't it swell?" Joanna's turn in line came and the girls each ordered a taffy apple, then walked on together, nibbling the sticky confection.

"Wouldn't you love to be a bareback rider?" Joanna continued. "They're so graceful."

"It looks dangerous," Peach said.

"I could do the poses," Joanna said, "but staying on the horse might be a little tricky." She laughed as she contemplated the potential for taking an undignified fall from one of the ponies. "I guess it's better if I do my dancing on solid ground."

"You're a dancer?" Tess eyed her with interest.

"Well, yes. I guess you could say so."

"Peach, we should take her to talk to Lorenzo," Tess said. "He's looking for dancers. With that red hair . . ."

Peach shook her head. "No. I don't think so."

"Why, she'd be perfect." Tess turned to Joanna. "You're pretty darn good-looking, you know. You could make some money in your spare time."

"I could?" Joanna wanted to hear more.

"No, Joanna," Peach insisted. "You wouldn't want this."

"Why not? Getting paid for dancing would really be swell."

"Come on home with us," Tess suggested. "It's not far from here, and you can talk to Lorenzo."

"All right," Joanna agreed, thinking how pleased her mother would be if she actually found a part-time job and could pay some of their expenses. Peach said nothing more.

They left the dispersing crowd and turned down a side street, treeless and unpaved, lined with plain, two-story houses. Unlike other Los Angeles streets, Joanna noted, there were no carefully tended flower beds in the dusty front yards.

157

Tess led the way to the front door of one of the houses and into a cool, darkened vestibule. Floral carpeting flowed up the open staircase and into open parlors on either side, where green brocade draperies covered the windows and several sofas upholstered in red velvet lined the walls.

"This is real elegant, Peach," Joanna said.

"You two wait in there." Tess gestured toward the parlor on the right. "I'll get Lorenzo."

A lamp on the ornately carved table in the center of the room cast eerie shadows as Joanna perched uneasily on one of the velvet sofas. Smaller marble-topped tables holding humidors and ashtrays flanked the sofas, and an upright piano, draped with a gold-tasseled velvet cloth, stood against one wall. Before Joanna had finished scanning details in the unusual room, Tess returned with a big, hulking man, whose rolled shirtsleeves revealed beefy arms. Broad-shouldered and potbellied, his upper body was so fleshy his shirt would barely button, while his lower body was so slim-hipped his trousers seemed to have difficulty staying up. He waved a smelly, half-chewed cigar at Joanna.

"So you're a dancer?" he began without customary niceties, the creases of his brow echoing the line of his pencil-thin mustache.

Joanna stood to show respect for elders. "Well, I . . . I've studied dancing."

"Show me what you can do."

"What?" Joanna thought it a strange request, without music, without a costume.

"Show me some dancing. Come on, hike up your skirt a little." He took hold of her skirt and tugged it up enough to show her knees.

Joanna pulled away. "But I don't have my costume with me."

"We're not fussy here. Tess, let's have a little music." Tess sat down at the piano and immediately began to thump out a lively ragtime tune. "Come on, kid," Lorenzo urged. "Give it a little pizzazz."

"Go ahead," Peach whispered. "He'll get around to the money part in a minute."

"Well, all right," Joanna said. "But you'll have to imagine my costume." She struck a few ballet poses, holding them in near perfect form as she had been taught. Then she went into her *barre* routine of modest *pliés* and *arabesques*, concentrating on her arm and hand movements.

"You call that dancing," Lorenzo said. "Put some life into it." He began to clap his hands in time to Tess's music.

Having no idea what he meant but hoping to please, Joanna began to dance around the room in a freestyle of her own invention, much as she had done that morning in the front of the chifforobe mirror. She rather liked the ragtime beat.

"That's more like it," Lorenzo said, nodding at her nicely rounded figure. "But you gotta take off that dress so I can see your legs." He stepped forward and began to unbutton her shirtwaist.

"No." Joanna jerked away abruptly and the buttons on her shirtwaist went flying. She cried out as she looked down at the gaping bodice and the revealing outline of her nipples through her thin camisole.

"What's going on here?" The angry voice belonged to Blanche Oliver, who stood in the doorway.

Joanna clutched at her dress to cover her embarrassment.

"What are *you* doing here?" Blanche's harsh tone brought tears to Joanna's eyes. Blanche turned to Peach. "Have you lost your wits? Why did you bring her here?"

159

"She wants a job."

Blanche strode over to Joanna, took her by the arm, and propelled her from the room. "Not here she doesn't."

"What's eatin' you?" Lorenzo growled. "The kid can dance . . ."

"Go home, Joanna." Blanche held open the front door. "And don't come back!"

Joanna ran out into the gathering twilight, her cheeks burning. At the corner she hesitated for an instant while she tried to remember which way led back to the circus tent. Then the depot. If she could find the depot, she knew the way from there.

Oh, why had she gone off with Peach and Tess? And what kind of place was that? How could they live with such a vulgar and offensive uncle? He had taken indecent liberties, that's what he had done. Her mother had warned her there were such men. She should have had better sense than to go there.

She quickened her step as she passed the depot. The streets were quieter now with occasional passing carriages and a few pedestrians strolling in the warm evening air. She took a wrong turn and had to backtrack before finally asking directions to the depot. It was a much longer walk than she remembered, and with darkness coming on everything looked different. But she managed to find her street, and finally the familiar-looking duplex with an outside staircase leading up to their second-floor apartment came into view. She fairly flew up the steps, pausing at the top to smooth her hair and to make sure her shirtwaist was closed. Perhaps her mother wouldn't notice the missing buttons.

Claire met her at the door. "Where on earth have you been?" Her tone was more worried than angry. "I was about to go and get Mr. Dodd to help me look for you."

"I'm sorry, Mother." Safe in her mother's embrace, Joanna burst into tears, her sobs releasing some of the humiliation of her encounter with Lorenzo.

"Joanna, what's wrong? Are you all right?"

She clung for a moment longer, while she made up her mind not to tell what had happened. It was too shameful, and she felt too guilty about having brought it on herself. How naive, thinking Peach's uncle would have a job for her. A job dancing.

"I'm all right." She brushed away her tears. "I went to the Angeleno to leave our new address for Randy and the Stanfields, and then I heard the circus parade and walked down to the depot to see it. They were giving a performance in a tent and I decided to go. I thought I'd be home before you, but it got late and I couldn't find my way."

"Joanna! You must *never* go off like that without telling me. Not in a strange town." Realizing that something unfortunate could have happened but that Joanna now stood before her safe and sound, she softened. "You're home now, and no harm done." She kissed Joanna's tear-streaked face.

Then she saw that buttons were missing from Joanna's shirtwaist, the fabric torn slightly in places where they had been ripped off.

"I . . . I fell, Mother," Joanna hurried to explain. "At the circus. I tripped over a . . . a monkey . . . and he grabbed my dress and wouldn't let go till the buttons came off."

"A monkey?"

"I startled him and he was so strong." Tears again glistened. "I was so scared, Mother."

"You poor dear. No wonder you're shaken. Did the trainers see what happened?"

"Yes. They said sometimes the monkeys do that." She

161

hated being dishonest, but once she started she couldn't seem to stop.

"Good heavens!" Claire gasped. "They should warn people. Did he scratch you?"

"No, nothing like that."

"Did you find the buttons?"

Joanna shook her head. "I was too scared to think about the buttons."

CHAPTER EIGHTEEN

As the parade moved on down the street, Harry Graham tossed his bags into the waiting hack. "Can you recommend a good hotel?" he asked the driver.

The driver scrutinized the well-dressed fare. "Some put up at the Overland."

"Let's have a look at it," Harry said, stepping into the buggy and settling back for the last brief leg of his journey. He had come all the way from Chicago in a luxurious Pullman car, the fast passenger train making the trip in two and a half days. His immediate assignment from his boss, P. B. Mossburg, was to determine the feasibility of opening a bank in booming Los Angeles. California Security Bank, it would be called. To be capitalized by Illinois Security Bank, the venture seemed certain to produce a good return on investment.

Banking in southern California was yet in its infancy. Harry knew that during the War Between the States California had supplied millions and millions in gold, the "hard money" that backed the North's credit in Europe and enabled the Union Army to persevere to victory. Yet for nearly three years following the war, not a single bank existed in Los Angeles. He had heard that shrewd money changers stood on street corners handling the exchange of different coin from all corners of the world, profiting when they could. Paper money was suspect. Businesses kept small iron safes on their premises, and customers sometimes got permission to safeguard cash in them rather than risk the hazardous eighty-hour trip by stage to banks in San Francisco. The Wells Fargo coaches were frequently robbed, and the county treasurer of Los Angeles faced the perilous assignment every six months of delivering accumulated county funds to the state capital at Sacramento. Even making the journey up the coast by ship still left a considerable perilous distance to be covered over bandit-controlled land.

Banks came to the rescue in 1868, Harry had learned, when Hayward & Company, founded by a wealthy San Franciscan, opened its doors with $100,000 in capital, followed shortly by Hellman, Temple & Company with $125,000. With credit available to new business, expansion in the area proceeded. But in 1869 the national bank panic—after the disastrous Black Friday when Jay Gould and James Fisk attempted to corner the gold market—had caused three Los Angeles banks to close, two permanently, and a dozen merchants to go bankrupt. Mindful of that calamity, along with two additional banking crises, in 1873 and 1883, Harry doubted that the current boom could continue indefinitely. Obviously, caution was the watchword for any significant deployment of Illinois Security's funds.

The Overland Hotel offered a comfortable room with bath, and after settling in, Harry went down to the lobby where he bought copies of the Los Angeles newspapers— the *Times, Express, Herald,* and *Tribune*—which he perused after dinner in the dining room. He had done considerable research on the train, studying financial statements of existing banks, population statistics, records of real estate sales, reports and maps on further development of the city's gas, water, and sewers, even projections for outlying communities, and he felt ready to begin his work.

Harry's final visit with Daisy Mossburg, on a cold and rainy March evening in Chicago, had been strained. In the presence of her family, she had assumed a forced gaiety, praising his charging off to California to slay the financial dragons and predicting he would return triumphant with the commercial grail he sought. At the end of the evening, her parents and sisters wished him well then left the two alone together in the parlor.

For a while they sat silently on the divan before a warm and crackling fire in the fireplace.

"You're not coming back, are you?" Daisy said finally.

He answered honestly: "I don't know."

"I love you, Harry. You know that." She turned to him, her welling tears glistening in the firelight. "The fact that you don't love me is the hardest thing I've ever had to bear."

"Daisy . . ."

"Please. There's no way you can make it easier for me." She looked earnestly at him. "So it's up to me to try to make it easy for *you*, I guess. It's the least I can do for you." She tried a feeble smile. "Sort of a farewell gift."

A lump came to Harry's throat. She was unselfish and strong, even brave, and he was turning her down. Was he crazy . . . or just heartless? At that moment, he almost took her in his arms to reassure her that he would be back, that they could build a life together after all. But he couldn't bring himself to do it.

"You truly are too good for me, Daisy." He clasped her hands and kissed them. Then he got up and left the house.

He walked for some time, hardly noticing the cold wind swirling through the empty streets. He and Daisy had at least one thing in common—walking away from what otherwise might have been the perfect match was one of the hardest things he, too, had ever had to do. Work was the treatment he prescribed for himself, along with the resolve never again to become so entangled.

Harry Graham was not the only Los Angeles newcomer who threw himself into his work. Birdie Stanfield painted a sign, *Stanfield and Plank*, in large letters flanked by smaller words, *Blacksmith* and *Livery*, at either side. She had some help on the spelling of "Livery" from her son Tucker, who, standing on a barrel, nailed the finished sign above the barn door while Warren took time out from his work at the new forge to hold it in place for him.

The forge, fired with the newly delivered coal, conducted air up to the glowing coals through gaps in the masonry near the bottom, providing more than adequate heat to reshape the wheel rim of the abandoned wagon. As soon as he could also repair the tongue, they would have another conveyance at their disposal. He smiled to himself at the satisfying red glow of the hot metal and the special clang of his hammer as it struck.

While he worked, a man drove up in a buggy pulled by a horse that had lost a shoe. Warren quickly remedied the situation and chalked up his first California income.

Randy, too, had been productive. He talked Warren into the extravagant idea of spending a few dollars to have cards printed advertising their business—*Stanfield and Plank Livery, Rigs for rent or sale, Blacksmithing, No order too big or too small*—then made the rounds of hotels and boardinghouses talking to desk clerks, and pinning cards up on bulletin boards at the depot and on trees or fence posts at streetcar stops. He also placed a small notice in the newspaper, and spent the late afternoon contacting livestock dealers in order to look over their horses.

★ ★ ★ ★ ★

Claire's second day at work in the office of Farley Foster Dodd began with her posting his recent expenditures in the ledger while responding to his frequent interruptive comments and instructions. Then she worked on unpacking boxes and arranging the shelves and cupboards while Dodd talked with the few curious passersby who drifted up from the street to meet the new attorney.

One, a gentleman wearing a light summery suit with a string tie and a wide-brimmed plantation hat, introduced himself as Mercer Albright. His deep Southern drawl confirmed his statement that he was visiting from Louisiana. Seating himself with his hat on his lap, he wanted to know about the legality of the Azusa land sales. "My brother-in-law's just out here for his rheumatism," the Southerner explained, "but he went over there yesterday and bought a piece of ground for three hundred dollars from a lady who had waited in line all night to get it for a hundred. I'm wondering if that's all legal and aboveboard?"

Dodd assured him that it was.

"But shouldn't such proceedings be registered somewhere?"

"Anyone intending to hold a property will have the deed recorded."

"My brother-in-law says folks are buyin' sight unseen. Barren, rocky tracts that won't grow nothin' but scorpions. That don't sound too sensible to me."

"When people get land fever," Dodd said, "they don't behave rationally."

"But if there's that kind of profit to be made, I suppose a man's a fool not to take advantage of it," Albright mused.

"Who's to say?" Dodd, too, seemed to be weighing the idea.

"Do you have any interest in checking into it, Mr.

167

Dodd? There's a train to Azusa in an hour. Why don't we go out there and see for ourselves? I'd appreciate your opinion and I'm willing to pay for that advice—if I should decide to buy."

"I wouldn't mind getting a firsthand look at those new towns." Dodd got up and went into the other room where Claire was busy arranging shelves.

"Claire, I'll be out of the office the rest of the day. Tell anyone who stops in to come back on Monday." He reached into his pocket. "Here's your new key. Lock up the place when you leave at six. I'll see you here bright and early Monday morning." Almost before she could respond, he was gone.

Claire liked being alone in the quiet office, working without the constant interruptions of her loquacious employer. By late afternoon, she had the boxes unpacked, books and folders organized alphabetically, office supplies out of sight in the cupboard, and her own desk arranged efficiently. She planned to leave promptly at six. Joanna's escapade the day before had been somewhat unnerving, and Claire hadn't been able to dispel the nagging realization that while she was working, she could not watch over her daughter as closely as she would like.

Only one potential client came to the office that afternoon, a middle-aged Polish woman who wanted to know if ladies could buy property. Poorly attired in a faded dress, her graying hair pulled back into an untidy bun, she told Claire in halting English that she wanted to own her own house—if such a thing were allowed. She said that she was recently widowed, and had been shocked to learn that her husband had left her some money.

"Mr. Dodd isn't here," Claire said. "Can you come back another time?"

But the woman wanted to talk. "I never had nothing," she confided. "All my life I wash, I clean, I cook. My man sick from the mines. He come here to get well, but too late. He never tell me about the money. After he die, I find it."

"Are you alone in California?" Claire asked. "No relatives?"

"No one."

"If you'll give me your name, I'll . . ."

"Vanda Kolinski."

"I'm sure Mr. Dodd can advise you, Mrs. Kolinski."

At that moment, footsteps were heard coming up the stairs, and Randy Plank burst into the room. Seeing Claire with the woman, he swept off his hat and stood gripping the brim. "Oh, I see you're busy."

"Hello, Randy." Claire rose from her desk.

The neck of his shirt was open, his sleeves rolled, and he was tanned from two days' exposure to the California sun. His warm dark eyes fixed on Claire.

The woman, seeing what passed between them, got to her feet. "I come back another time." She shuffled across the room, looking back at Claire, then Randy, before starting down the stairs.

When she was gone, Randy stepped forward and took Claire's hand. "Golly, Claire, it's good to see you." He looked as if he wanted to embrace her, but hesitated, glancing toward the other room. "Your boss here?"

"He's out right now. And I'm in charge," she said merrily. "What can I do for you? Is it legal advice you want?"

"It's you I want," he said. "I've missed you, Claire."

"I've missed you, too," she confessed as she put away her ledger. "But so much is happening. We found an apartment, Joanna starts school Monday, and, Randy, I like my job here with Mr. Dodd. What about you? And the

169

Stanfields? Is the barn working out all right?"

"It's okay for now. Warren has the forge fired up, and I've been leavin' our cards around where they'll be seen. Come and see our new rig. A brand-new buggy and a mule named Sugar."

She laughed. "That's wonderful, Randy." Then, glancing at the wall clock, "I can leave at six. You can give me a ride home."

"With pleasure."

"Did you see our new sign?" She led the way into Dodd's office, and both inspected the new sign projecting from the window ledge. "It's bringing in clients." The street below, still crowded with Saturday commerce, enlivened the view across the rooftops of the expanding city.

"Just look at us," Randy said. "You workin' in a fancy lawyer's office, and me with my own business." He pointed out the shiny, black rig hitched to a small gray mule. "Now tell me you're sorry you came west," he teased, looping his arms around her waist.

Their lips touched lightly. But when he pressed for more, she hesitated. This was not a proper place—or time. She slipped from his grasp on the pretense of closing the windows before they left.

"I couldn't ask for a better job," she said. "Mr. Dodd is teaching me so much."

Randy frowned. "This Dodd . . . Is he married?"

"Yes, but his wife is still in Chicago. He lives at the Overland Hotel."

"Well, someday we'll all be livin' at the Overland." Then, offering his arm, "Come on, Claire, it's six o'clock. Let's go for a buggy ride."

CHAPTER NINETEEN

Claire felt like Cinderella riding beside Randy Plank in the new buggy through the bustling streets of Los Angeles. Sugar trotted along, ears and nostrils alert as if she, too, were savoring every fascinating sight, sound, and smell. To Claire, it seemed a magic coach carrying her from the discouragement of her job at Axel Kohl's café to the pride she felt in establishing herself, however precariously, in the business world. It was a transition few women ever experienced, and Claire owed much of her good fortune to the resourcefulness of the young man seated beside her.

She had disappointed him, she knew, by avoiding his kiss when they were alone in the office. But how could she allow herself to fall in love just when things were turning around for her? Her tenuous hold on independence could be jeopardized if she succumbed to such conventional solutions. Besides, a thirty-four-year-old woman could make a spectacle of herself allowing a twenty-five-year-old man to court her. And yet Randy took charge of things in a way uncommon to men much older and more experienced. Now, close to him in the buggy, his strong, capable arms gripping the lines, Claire was keenly aware of his masculine presence.

"Well, what do you think of the new buggy? It's available for hire, you know." He took one of his business cards from his pocket and handed it to her. "No order too big or too small."

They laughed easily, and Randy put his free arm across

the back of the seat as they rode along.

"I've finished the Emerson book," he said. "Do you have any others he's written?"

"You might like *The Conduct of Life*, which gives his thoughts on wealth and power, on culture, and even fate."

"I think I'm beginning to believe in fate." He hardly took his eyes from her face, but she kept her gaze on the passing scene lest she reveal more of her feelings than she intended.

When they reached the apartment, she invited him to supper, which she hoped Joanna would have at least partially prepared, but he declined, saying it would be dark by the time he drove back to the Pico barn. "Warren may need some help fixin' that old wagon," he explained. "I've rented it out for tomorrow to a family I met at the depot." He looped the lines around the brake handle and stepped to the ground. "I need to get hold of a team for them so they can move their things to a tent town out near Inglewood."

Randy helped Claire from the buggy, his gaze lingering in a caress as real as if their lips had touched. But then, dutifully, he got back into the buggy and picked up the lines. "Oh, I almost forgot," he said. "Birdie wants you and Joanna to come over for dinner a week from Sunday. You can bring me that book then."

She stood looking after him as he urged Sugar into a trot. She would have to wait more than a week before she would see him again.

Joanna met her at the door. "Was that Randy? Why didn't he come in?"

"He drove me home from the office," Claire said, hoping the glow she felt from his touch didn't show on her face. "But he had to go and help Warren. Birdie has asked us for dinner next Sunday, and . . ."

She stopped in her tracks. Seated at the kitchen table was Axel Kohl.

"Hello, Claire." His sunburned face seemed ruddier than ever, emphasizing his pale lashes and protruding eyes.

"Axel! How did you find us?"

"The boardinghouse. That woman told me where you were, so I came on over." He took a deep breath as if fortifying himself for what he had to say. "Claire, I went out to Pasadena yesterday. Tate said it was a good place to settle and he's right. The town is swarmin' with folks. I'm gonna get me a café there."

"You found one?"

"Not yet, but I talked with a real-estate fella. He told me if I intend to get a place I better do it quick. He says just seven years ago there was nothin' but a general store and a post office in the whole town. A stage to Los Angeles only twice a week. Five-acre plots were only fifty or sixty dollars, and even as recent as four years ago you could still get good land for a hundred an acre. Can you believe that?" He arched his pale eyebrows in disbelief. "Now land's up to a thousand an acre, and there's more'n fifty real-estate companies all tryin' to raise prices. They're choppin' down the orchards to make more building lots."

"Then you intend to buy a place?"

Axel shrugged. "Not much there to rent. The town's only been incorporated for a year, but there's a town hall and a library and they've built some hotels just to put up the speculators—they're all over the place. Twenty-two trains a day runnin' regular to and from Los Angeles." He paused to gauge the effect his words had on her. "Claire, we could have a real good life in Pasadena."

"Axel, I think I've made it clear that . . ."

"Now don't say nothin' hasty. I know you're not one to

173

rush into anything. Wait till you see it. Must be four or five hundred new homes goin' up, even an opera house. Next year there'll be a gas plant."

Claire sighed, exasperated. "Axel, I have a job now. In an office."

"An office?"

"I'm working for an attorney named Farley Dodd."

Her announcement gave Axel pause. "But, Claire, you're not that kind of woman. To have to work in an office, I mean. I can take care of you."

"Axel . . ." How could she make it plain enough for him to grasp? "I will never marry you, Axel. Please try to understand that."

He offered a patronizing smile. "You may see things different after you work a while in that office. Think on it. It'll be a few weeks before I'm set up."

"Axel, my answer is no." Claire opened the door and stood glaring at him, waiting for him to walk through it.

Axel glanced at Joanna as if to enlist her help in convincing her mother. Getting no encouragement, he picked up his hat. "Well, I guess I better be on my way before I wear out my welcome." He tipped his hat to Claire. She snapped the latch after he left and leaned against the door as if to shut him out by physical force alone.

"No wonder you wanted to get away from Westport," Joanna said. "Is he always like that?"

Claire nodded. "I certainly didn't expect him to follow us here."

Joanna slumped onto a kitchen chair. "Men are such a pain." Her shocking introduction to Lorenzo still troubled her.

"Not all men, Joanna." Claire sat down across from her. "There are good men, too."

Joanna's clear eyes searched Claire's. "Mother, tell me about my papa. Was he a good man?"

"In some ways, I suppose he was." Over the years, on the rare occasions when she couldn't avoid speaking of him, Claire had tried to give Joanna a neutral view of her father. "I've told you about everything there is to tell. We met at a party. Your grandfather had just died, and our home and all our things had been sold to pay his debts. I was feeling very much alone. Carter Chadwick was one of the young men about town. Handsome. Charming. When he began to pay attention to me, I fell in love with him."

"But what happened? Did you fall out of love?"

"Joanna, love is not always what it seems. Initial attraction seldom lasts—at least it didn't in the case of your father."

"But why?"

"For some reason, he began to resent me. Called me 'redheaded riffraff.' Once he grabbed a scissors and cut off a hunk of my hair. Right here." She held her hand to her temple. "I tried, but nothing I did seemed to make any difference." She couldn't reveal that he hadn't wanted his daughter, and that his rage when he learned of the pregnancy had wounded Claire almost more than the physical abuse. Carter Chadwick III with all his arrogance, his selfish cruelty, his pompous family who had clung so desperately to their waning social position long after their money was squandered—she had vowed Joanna would never know how awful it was.

"But if you were good to him, why did he resent you?"

"He felt I was a burden, I guess. He had never learned responsibility."

"But his family, the Chadwicks?" Joanna said. "Didn't they ever want to see me?"

Tears came to Claire's eyes. "They returned my letters unopened."

"I'm sorry, Mother. I didn't mean to make you sad."

Claire placed her hand lovingly on Joanna's beautiful hair, the deep copper that, in the eyes of the Chadwicks, had been the telltale mark of tainted blood. "If I hadn't gone through it, I wouldn't have you, Joanna. You've always been my joy."

"Life is strange," Joanna mused.

Claire smiled wistfully. "Our good times are coming, dear. Now let's stop all this gloomy talk. Tomorrow we'll go out and see some of the sights. Would you like to visit the old pueblo and ride the electric streetcar? Or how about taking a picnic out to the tar pits on Rancho LaBrea? They've actually found skeletons of prehistoric beasts there."

At that moment, not far away in the Overland Hotel, Harry Graham entered the dining room to take his dinner alone at a quiet corner table. After a day of appointments with members of the banking community, he was convinced he should go full speed ahead with the new bank and had sent a wire to P. B. Mossburg to that effect. While he perused the newspapers for tidbits of information about the workings of the city, he took critical note, from force of habit, of each paper's journalistic and printing savvy or lack thereof.

As the dining room filled to capacity, he noticed a dapper-looking gentleman waiting nearby to be seated. "Would you care to join me?" Harry asked, folding the papers. "Looks like it may be quite a wait for a table."

"Why, yes, thank you," the man answered, easing his small frame onto the chair opposite Harry and extending his hand. "I'm Farley Dodd. Attorney."

"Harry Graham. Banking. Just got in yesterday from Chicago."

"I'm from Chicago, too," Dodd said. "What bank were you with?"

"Illinois Security."

"That so? I banked at First National. Just opened my law office here." Dodd scanned the menu. "I specialize in real estate."

"Land fever is rampant just now." Harry gave his dinner order to the waiter. "I may be interested in some commercial property myself," he said. "Illinois Security plans to open a new bank out here. Any advice on the most promising areas?"

"Hard to tell which direction the city will grow," Dodd mused. "The new City Hall on Fort Street and the Buena Vista Street Bridge could take it east, and right now there's some movement toward the southwest, but my guess is it will grow toward the ocean."

Harry nodded, and Dodd continued, "I went to look over the Azusa development today. A bit dusty out there. Nothing much to recommend it. However, a gentleman of my acquaintance purchased quite a sizable tract . . ."— Dodd readjusted his spectacles on the bridge of his narrow nose—". . . which he plans to subdivide when the time is right."

"Timing's important, all right."

"When things are new and malleable, Mr. Graham, that's when you find the best opportunities, whether it's in real estate, business, politics, or . . . well, I'm sure the world of finance is the same." Their soup came and Dodd tucked a napkin over his cravat.

"That's what I'm here to find out."

The two enjoyed their conversation enough to linger over glasses of port. "Are you planning to settle out here?" Dodd asked as each signed for his meal. "Is there a Mrs. Graham?"

"I'm not sure how long I'll be here, and no, I'm not married. You?"

"Twelve years already. Tibby will be coming out as soon as I get things organized."

"Well, Mr. Dodd, I hope to run into you again." Harry extended his hand. "Are you living here at the Overland, too?"

"Yes. Good to know you, Mr. Graham. And I'll keep an eye open for that commercial property."

When Randy got back to the barn, he found Warren still at work, setting the newly rimmed wagon wheel into place. The broken tongue stood fully repaired. "Glad you got it fixed," Randy said. "I've rented it out for tomorrow. I'll go over to the stable first thing in the morning and get a team." The two worked by lantern light to grease the axles before making their way to bed.

Next morning Randy got up at dawn, hitched Sugar to the buggy, and drove to the Hawkins stable where he rented a team and harness, working out a twelve percent discount on the rental. He would charge his own customers enough over his costs to show some profit. Hardly a satisfactory arrangement, he knew, but it would have to do until they could afford to buy their own.

Leading the hired team behind the buggy, Randy made it back to the barn in time to tackle one of Birdie's hearty breakfasts before the immigrant family came to get the team and wagon to move their belongings to Inglewood.

CHAPTER TWENTY

The month of April brought one beautiful day after another. While encouraging Joanna's progress at school and enjoying Sunday visits with Randy and the Stanfields, Claire concentrated on her work with Farley Dodd. Increasingly engaged outside the office, he allowed her to take on more of his tasks, and she began to wonder if he had given up the idea of hiring a man to replace her. Each day seemed to bring in additional transactions with more and more legal documents to prepare—bills of sale, transfers, payment contracts, mortgages, liens, leases, partnerships—there was no end to it.

Late one afternoon when Dodd left the office to take care of some business at the new City Hall, Claire seized the opportunity to catch up on her bookkeeping. Suddenly a dapper man with abundant orange whiskers, having entered as if on padded feet, appeared before her desk, his straw skimmer in hand. He beamed as he recognized her.

"Aren't you the woman I met at the boardinghouse?" he said cordially. "Remember me? McKenzie Tate?"

"Yes, of course. I'm Claire Chadwick. I work for Mr. Dodd."

"Well now, isn't that fine? Is he in?"

"I'm sorry, he isn't."

"Drat! I have some title papers I'd like him to file for me at the recorder's office. Some property I intend to subdivide. When will he be back?"

"Eight o'clock tomorrow morning. He's always prompt."

"I'll come then." Tate tipped his skimmer. "Thank you, Mrs. Chadwick."

Hardly had he gotten out the door when Vanda Kolinski, the gray-haired Polish woman who had stopped by before, came in. She seemed distressed to learn that again Mr. Dodd was out. "But I got to buy house. They give me this paper. I got to know if it says right thing."

Claire looked at the sale contract, which described a ten-year-old brick home with carriage house, built during the real-estate flurry of the mid-seventies. The price seemed exorbitant to Claire.

"I'm sorry, Mrs. Kolinski, but Mr. Dodd is not available until tomorrow."

"They say I got to tell them tonight. They say they got other buyer." She tapped the paper with her finger. "Just tell me if it says right thing."

Claire studied the contract. "Well, it appears to be properly made out, but without seeing the property . . ."

"You come then," the woman said, extending her hand as if to drag Claire from the office. "You come see."

"Mrs. Kolinski, can you afford this property?" It was an improper question, but the woman's shabby dress and ill-fitting shoes certainly created doubt.

"I got money. This house I want real bad. You come help me, missus, or they cheat me."

Her distress touched Claire. She recalled the woman's earlier visit, when she revealed she had lost her husband after years of living in poverty, then discovered he had somehow accumulated some money—apparently quite a lot, judging from the expensive house she intended to purchase. But Claire was hesitant. What little she knew about appraising property she had learned from copying contracts.

"We go on streetcar," Mrs. Kolinski urged.

Claire wondered what Farley Dodd would say if she took this upon herself? What if she made a terrible blunder and Mrs. Kolinski got into a bad investment?

"Please, missus."

"All right," Claire agreed. "I'm not sure what help I can be, but . . ." She glanced at the clock. "I can go with you when I close the office at six o'clock."

"Oh, thank you, missus." The woman took Claire's hand in both of hers and shook it gratefully. "I wait." She seated herself in a chair, where she remained until the clock struck six, then she stood. "We go now, ya?"

The house Mrs. Kolinski had chosen was an attractive two-story brick, and her eyes shown with delight as she pointed out the well-kept yard where geraniums, roses, verbena, hibiscus, and other plants formed a lacy pattern around the open porch. The realtor, on the premises to show the home, admitted them, and the two women looked through the house. Claire was impressed with its quality. "It's a fine house, Mrs. Kolinski. I see no reason not to buy it . . . if it's what you want and you can afford it."

A smile crept across the woman's ruddy cheeks. "Ya. I can pay." She opened her shabby handbag and held it out for Claire to see. It was stuffed with currency.

"Mrs. Kolinski, you're not carrying your money around with you . . . ?"

"Not all. The rest I got safe place. The man say he only need part today."

Vanda Kolinski's bag contained $5,000, only $1,000 of which, Claire pointed out, was needed to secure the sale. The balance of the selling price could be paid at the time of the deed transfer the following week.

"You come home with me," the new homeowner said to

181

Claire when they finished securing the purchase. "I make you *golabkis*. You too thin."

"I'm sorry, Mrs. Kolinski, but I must go home to my daughter."

"My name Vanda," she said, grinning happily.

"I'm very glad you got your house, Vanda." Claire folded the signed contract. "I'll show this to Mr. Dodd, and he'll help you with the closing."

Vanda shook her head. "I want you to help me. You smart lady, missus."

Claire smiled, indulging the woman's whim. "We'll see when the time comes. Now I really must go."

Again Vanda seized her hand. "I bring you some *golabkis*."

Joanna sat at the kitchen table trying to concentrate on her lessons. After nearly a month of school, she didn't feel the same enthusiasm for learning as she had before the move. Many of the eighth-graders in her class were older teenagers whose schooling had been interrupted during relocation from other states. Often having to work periodically to help their parents, their focus on scholarship was difficult to maintain. Joanna, with the same conflicting changes in her life, tolerated her own role as schoolgirl, knowing that in another few weeks she would have her eighth-grade diploma.

But she couldn't forget the strange and frightening world she had glimpsed at Lorenzo's. Men. Everywhere they seemed to intrude their coarseness and power on an otherwise beautiful world. Joanna's own father had deserted them, heartless in his apparent indifference to them. Axel Kohl had followed them all the way to California, obnoxious in his refusal to stop pestering them. Randy was the only man who seemed to fit into Joanna's scheme of things. He always seemed to do what was right. He was intelligent and kind. And very good-looking. But he seemed smitten with . . . with her own mother. Joanna couldn't bear to think about it.

Obsessed with increasing his business and tired of having to waste time and money renting a team and harness for use by customers, Randy spent the last of Warren's nest egg, plus what they had taken in during the month, for an underfed, long-in-the-tooth pair of bay geldings. The team, Pat and Mike, had seen some hard times, but they fattened with good care and became useful additions to the Stanfield and Plank stable, faithfully performing their duties when hired out and politely vying for Sugar's attention in the corral.

Birdie, who had painted the additional words *Horses for Hire* at the bottom of their sign, seemed to thrive in her new surroundings. Daily work in her garden brought color to her cheeks and improved her strength. She worked from dawn till dark keeping their quarters in the barn clean and livable, cooking on the small stove, washing clothes on a washboard, and still finding time to make new shirts for the boys and to see that they got off to school on time in the mornings, clean, combed, and toting jelly sandwiches. Most noticeable of all was her cheerful optimism.

"The kids is gettin' brown as Indians," she murmured to Warren one night in the privacy of their bedchamber, which she had curtained off in one of the stalls with an old worn sheet. Randy and the children had long since fallen asleep in the loft.

Warren smoothed her faded hair. "Birdie, I sure never thought we'd be spendin' so long in this flea-bitten barn."

"I don't mind." She gently touched his face. "We're eatin'. The kids is happy."

"Randy's sure bringin' in the customers," he said. "We made all the payments this month, and soon as we can see our way clear, I'll look around for a better place for us to live." In the dark he couldn't see her soft amber eyes welling up at his thoughtfulness. He could only feel the warmth of her slender body as he enclosed her in one powerful arm and pulled her to him. They had not made love since coming to California.

"Sweetheart." Her neck smelled of homemade soap. "Do you feel well enough?"

She answered by raising her lips to his. She still seemed so frail and weary that he hesitated. But with her arms around him saying it was all right, he made love to her with all the passion he had stored up since they left Missouri.

The next morning at eight, Claire ushered McKenzie Tate into Farley Dodd's office and introduced the two men. Dodd, peering through his round eyeglasses, smiled at Tate's lavish orange mustache and muttonchops. "How can I help you, Mr. Tate?"

"I've been buying property the past few days. Waited in line all night for the Azusa sale and picked up some lots that I turned over the same day. Made enough profit to secure a five-acre tract in Pasadena." He took a folded document from his pocket and shoved it across the desk. "I'm going to subdivide into business lots, and I need to file the proper papers."

Dodd studied the deed. The land Tate had purchased came from the same larger tract as that purchased by the gentleman from Louisiana, Mercer Albright. "It may take a few days," Dodd said. "The recorder's office is swamped."

"I'd appreciate anything you can do to speed things up so I can get the lots listed." He stood to leave. "I'm going over west of the city today to look over those new Palisade developments, Beverly Hills, Westwood, and Bel Air."

"I hear some are hoping to make that area the new high-rent district," Dodd said. "But as far as I can tell, there's nothing out there but wild mustard and sunflowers—useless for anything but grazing sheep."

"Miracles happen when land fever sets in." Tate's smile revealed a row of tiny sharp teeth.

Dodd chuckled. "Let me know what you find out. If you stop back in a week, I should have your title papers ready."

Tate nodded his farewell and eased himself out of the office.

"Mrs. Chadwick," Dodd called when he was gone, "I need you to go to the recorder's office and file some papers."

"All right. And I have a contract for you to look over," Claire said. "A Mrs. Kolinski came by yesterday. She had to make a decision on a house, and she was afraid she would be cheated. When you weren't here she begged me to go with her. I hope you don't mind."

Dodd scowled at her as if trying to understand what she was saying.

"After I closed the office at six," Claire explained, "I did go with her to see the house and be sure the contract was in order." She frowned at the recollection of Mrs. Kolinski's money-stuffed bag. "She had five thousand dollars in cash with her and would have given all of it to them, but I pointed out that the contract called for only a thousand earnest money."

"Good. Good." Dodd resumed his absorption in the deed to Tate's five Pasadena acres.

"Then you don't mind?"

"Mind? Why should I mind?" He pondered the question. "A woman's eye. Yes. I'm sure that appeals to some buyers. My Tibby tells me she even prefers going to a lady doctor. Imagine that! There's only one in Chicago, but leave it to Tibby to sniff her out." He snorted at the idea. "As a matter of fact, Mrs. Chadwick, I've decided not to replace you."

Claire caught her breath.

"Actually, I don't have time to look for a replacement right now, with the campaign about to start."

"Campaign?"

"I'm appalled by the politics in this town. We need a competent city government to cope with this boom, and I don't see it happening, so I've decided to run for mayor myself. Farley Foster Dodd, mayor of Los Angeles. How does that sound to you?"

"Very impressive."

"This town needs conscientious leadership," he continued. "It's been hobbling along for thirty-seven years now, since it first incorporated, a hopeless morass of political demagoguery." His eyes narrowed behind his lenses as if peering into the future. "I feel I can render a real public service."

"I'm sure you can, Mr. Dodd."

"At any rate, Mrs. Chadwick, in the coming months I'll be increasingly involved with politics. I'm going to need someone to manage things here in the office. I'm afraid I'm going to have to rely on you for a little while longer."

The full implication of her expanding duties began to sink in. "I assume I'll receive an increase in salary commensurate with my new duties," she blurted.

The color rose in Dodd's thin cheeks. "Well, actually, no. You're only a temporary employee . . . and, as you well know, my accounts receivable are modest at this point, very modest."

Claire pulled herself to her full height. "The kind of responsibility you're talking about deserves a pay increase, Mr. Dodd."

He sputtered, his indignation focused more on her outspoken manner than her request. "Well, perhaps we can scrape up a slight increase for you. Say to . . . uh . . . fifteen dollars a week?"

Fifteen dollars a week came to more than sixty dollars a month, a fortune. But Claire pushed her advantage, countering firmly, "Sixteen."

Dodd's mouth dropped open.

Claire waited, her gaze steady.

"Oh, very well," Dodd muttered. "But you'll have to earn it."

"Mr. Dodd, I assure you, I will."

CHAPTER TWENTY-ONE

Farley Foster Dodd immersed himself in city politics. His outspoken concern for remaking city government, his legal reputation, and his orator's voice began to impress important political players, and he was appointed to a vacated position on the city council.

Harry Graham, implementing his plan to establish California Security Bank, leased a ground-floor location in the Temple Block, which he felt would be adequate until the fledgling bank attained solid enough footing to justify constructing its own building. He then set about acquiring furnishings and personnel.

McKenzie Tate, developer of a city block in Pasadena, proved to be one of Farley Dodd's best clients. Having secured his land title, Tate sold only to solid buyers, advising them in the planning and construction of their buildings. In the course of three months, he had earned enough return on his investment to forge ahead with other projects, and his frequent visits to Dodd's office provided occasion for conversations with Claire Chadwick.

"Mr. Tate," Claire ventured on one such visit. "I've been admiring your real estate expertise, and I'm wondering if you might have some advice for me. I'd like to make a small investment in a good property myself." She paused in her preparation of the transfer papers for Tate's latest acquisition, a row of two-flats in Pasadena near his business block. "I've watched properties double and even triple in value in just a short time, and I see no reason why I should let such opportunity pass me by."

"No. Of course not." His bushy brows knit over his keen, narrowed eyes as if he were seeing her for the first time. "It never occurred to me that you, a lone woman . . ."

"A lone woman with a daughter to support," she reminded him, smiling as she quoted his own often-stated remark, "I'd be foolish not to take advantage of these unusual times, don't you think?"

Tate stroked his muttonchops with a manicured hand. "You're absolutely right, Mrs. Chadwick. Who's in a better position to pluck a few plums from this thorny brush than you, working with a property lawyer as you do."

"I've been thinking I could put a small amount down on a property," Claire said, "then resell it before I had to make too many of the payments. From what I've observed, properties are more than holding their value. They just keep going up."

"So far, they have." He studied her face as if trying to determine whether her plan could pay off for him as well as for her. "But the fact is, Mrs. Chadwick, I've worked like a crazy man to build up my holdings, stood in line all night to get the opening price, shamelessly hustled buyers, and haggled with stubborn sellers till I'm blue in the face. I don't believe a woman like you would want to do that."

"No, I have something a little less vigorous in mind. Just a small investment that can be turned over for a modest profit. I'm afraid that's all I can afford."

"I'll tell you what, Mrs. Chadwick." He leaned closer to her desk. "You've done a fine job keeping Dodd on top of all my business dealings, you've worked late when I needed you, and you're discreet, too. Let me do you a favor." He tapped his finger on the papers she was preparing. "These two-flats. I'm putting them back on the market as soon as I

189

close the deal. I could let you have one for ten percent over my costs. Roscoe Longworth, one of our leading real-estate magnates and a new acquaintance of mine, thinks they'll sell for fifty percent over cost."

Claire reread the papers she had just copied. Four frame buildings, each two stories with a five-room flat on each floor. Tate had contracted to purchase each building for $4,000. His new selling price could be $6,000 each.

"These properties are solid gold," he said. "All you need is a five-hundred-dollar down payment to buy one of the buildings. When you sell it, you pay me my ten percent and you'll have leveraged your five hundred into a very nice profit."

"That's generous of you, but I'm afraid I don't have five hundred."

"Oh." His voice fell.

"I do have two hundred." She dismissed the inner voice of reason that told her it was all that kept her and Joanna from the poorhouse. "Is there any chance you could loan me the rest till the sale goes through?"

Tate shook his head. "Unfortunately, I myself am leveraged up to my last penny on this deal. In fact, I don't know how I'm going to come up with that last five hundred. I may have to let one of the buildings go." Then, reluctant to accept that alternative, "Perhaps you could borrow the money from someone else?"

Claire considered possible benefactors. Warren and Randy certainly had no money to loan. Axel? Never. Farley Dodd might have money to spare, but she wouldn't want to become beholden to her employer in that way. A bank loan would be much more businesslike. Yes, she would get a loan from a bank just as others financed real-estate ventures.

"I'll try to get the money, Mr. Tate. I'd like very much to be part of this."

"Very well then." He moved toward the door. "We're set to close right here in Dodd's office Thursday morning. You'll need five hundred cash or a certified cash voucher." He winked at her. "I'm counting on you."

As soon as he was gone, Claire put on her hat and told Farley Dodd she was taking her lunch break. She hoped McKenzie Tate's "solid gold opportunity" would convince a banker to lend her three hundred dollars.

After stating her business at the front desk of the new California Security Bank, Claire was ushered into the presence of the loan officer. Distinguished-looking with sharp features, stylish beard and mustache, he wore a well-tailored suit and, Claire thought, resembled the young financiers who worked for her father during her early years in Chicago. In fact, he looked somehow familiar as he extended his hand across the desk.

"Good morning. I'm Harry Graham."

Then Claire remembered where she had seen him before. "Well, hello."

His sudden smile showed he recognized her, too. "It's Miss . . ."

"Mrs. Chadwick," Claire said. "We met, briefly, at the depot in Westport."

"Of course. The day of the stampede."

"Some of us *were* a bit eager," she said.

"I'm glad to see you made it out here." He motioned toward the sturdy oak chair in front of the desk. "And how do you like our City of the Angels?"

"I like it very much. I have a position as assistant to an attorney who specializes in real estate."

He assessed the attractive woman with copper-hued hair

and earnest blue eyes. "How can I help you, Mrs. Chadwick?"

"I've been presented with a real-estate investment opportunity. For a five-hundred-dollar down payment I can buy a two-flat building." She gathered her courage. "I have two hundred dollars. I need to borrow the other three. And I plan to resell the property immediately. It could return a fifty percent profit in just a few weeks."

"And what is your husband's business?"

"I'm divorced."

His eyes widened slightly. "What collateral can you offer?"

"I have none."

He raised a skeptical eyebrow. "None? No other real estate? Stocks or bonds? Jewelry?"

She shook her head. "Nothing."

"Hmmm." The straight line of his brow remained impassive. "That complicates things some."

"I assure you, Mr. Graham, I don't undertake such a step frivolously. I've learned quite a lot from my employer about buying property. I've worked with others who have parlayed a small investment into a substantial nest egg. This is my opportunity to do the same." She took a packet of papers from her reticule. "Here, I've listed all the particulars. And this is a copy of Mr. Tate's contract on the buildings."

He nodded knowingly as he scanned the papers. "This is all well and good, Mrs. Chadwick, but California Security can't help you if you have nothing to secure the loan." He handed the papers back to her. "I'm sorry, Mrs. Chadwick."

"But there must be some way. If I signed a six-month note . . ."

"Believe me, I'd like to help you, Mrs. Chadwick. I have

no doubt that any well-chosen property in this area will increase in value over the next few months—if not weeks—but California Security can't do business on mere speculation." He paused, considering whether to continue, then said, "Perhaps there's someone who could give you a *personal* loan—payable with interest when you resell the property."

A personal loan? He had emphasized the word "personal." Was he patronizing her? "No, Mr. Graham," she said pointedly. "There isn't." She rose to leave.

"I'm sorry," he said. "If I can be of some help in the future . . ."

But Claire was already out of his office. She had been foolish to think she could get a bank loan without collateral. Her recent successes must have warped her judgment.

Returning to her office, she found Vanda Kolinski waiting.

"I make some *golabkis* for you." The woman held out a small roasting pan that emitted a tantalizing aroma. "You take home to your girl, ya?"

"That's kind of you, Vanda. It smells wonderful." Claire lifted the lid to view enough meat-filled cabbage rolls to last her a week. "But you shouldn't have . . ."

"No trouble. You my friend. I got fine house now, with thanks to you."

"Come home with me for supper then," Claire said. "Joanna and I will never eat all this by ourselves."

"I like to meet your girl." Her eyes shown with grandmotherly concern and Claire sensed that she must be lonely here in California, so far from all she had known before, and with no family.

Women without children would never experience the joys of raising children, but they also could never compre-

193

hend the anxieties. Claire worried about Joanna. Since school let out for the summer, she moped around the apartment or, worse yet, went out without telling Claire where she was going or when she would be back. She balked when asked to help with the cleaning or cooking, and for the first time in her young life she grew belligerent when Claire tried to talk to her.

"I'm sure Joanna would enjoy meeting you, too," Claire said. "If you come back at six, we can walk to my place together."

"Ya, I come back."

Shortly before six o'clock, Vanda reappeared in Claire's office toting several parcels. "I buy some things," she explained.

Claire locked the office door and, carrying the pan of *golabkis,* accompanied Vanda down the stairs to the street. To make conversation as they walked along, Claire asked, "So you're happy with your new home?"

"I happy more than whole life," Vanda said, her round face a study in contentment. "I never live such nice place."

"I'm glad for you, Vanda."

The evening took on the festive spirit of a holiday. The parcels Vanda brought contained bakery goods to round out the dinner, a lace-trimmed scarf for Claire, and a small oval locket for Joanna. "For your graduation." Vanda beamed as Joanna put on the locket.

"It's very pretty. Thank you, Mrs. Kolinski."

"You welcome," she beamed. "Now I show you what I buy for me." She unwrapped parcels that held several yards of blue pongee for a dress and nainsook for a petticoat and camisole. "I find a nice dressmaker." The last package contained a pair of white high-button shoes with dainty one-inch heels. "Lady shoes," she said. "They fit good. I show

194

you." She sat down to take off her old shoes and step into the fashionable footwear.

"Here, let me help you." Joanna, caught up in the woman's delight with her new finery, knelt before her and wielded the buttonhook. When the shoes were securely buttoned, Joanna exclaimed, "They're beautiful."

"They fit good!" Vanda got up and walked around the room with a springy gait.

"I wish I had a pair like that," Joanna said, half-joking.

Immediately Vanda offered, "I buy you some."

"Oh, no, I didn't mean . . ." Joanna blushed.

"You good people." Vanda smiled lovingly at them. "I like to help."

Prompted by Vanda's kindness, an idea hit Claire with such a jolt she wondered why she hadn't thought of it sooner.

"Vanda," she said, "there is a way you can help us."

CHAPTER TWENTY-TWO

The Stanfield and Plank livery made considerable progress in its first three months of operation. Randy's advertising efforts brought in customers, and Meta Triffen sent business nearly every day as did other boardinghouses and hotels. The little mule, Sugar, reveled in her trips about town pulling the shiny new buggy, while the team, Pat and Mike, stalwart now, proved to be dependable with all kinds of drivers, pulling load after load in the repaired wagon to destinations near and far. When extra horsepower and conveyances were needed, Randy provided them through his rental arrangement with the Hawkins stable, utilizing the two older Stanfield boys, Tucker and Daniel, as messengers, stable boys, and grooms.

Warren's smithing skills and his growing reputation for fair dealing brought in an increasing number of regulars, and he often worked by lantern light late into the evening, his hammer clanging against the red glow of the iron. The family had settled into a reasonably comfortable routine in the barn, though not once in the three months they'd been there had Warren gone out looking at land. There hadn't been time. Besides, his nest egg had long since been spent.

One day a customer, pointing at their sign, inquired as to where he could have one painted. Warren explained that he didn't know since his wife had painted theirs, wherein the customer asked if she would consider painting one for him. The sign turned out so well that Randy suggested she advertise.

"Me?" Pleased with Randy's compliment, Birdie grinned modestly. "Why, I used to draw things when I was a girl back home, but I weren't that good."

"You're good enough to make a nice sign," Randy said. "If you want me to, I'll have some cards printed up for you, too, and Tucker can take them around."

"I'd like that just fine." Birdie seemed to smile a lot lately, and her lightly tanned face emphasized her even white teeth.

But Warren worried. Rent on the barn was due again in a few days, and they had to make a decision whether to simply go on renting, or to try to find the money to buy it, taking a credit for the three months' rent toward the purchase price. Randy favored buying the place—it served their needs and wasn't a bad location—but if they did, Warren felt, he was drifting further and further from that orange grove.

"Warren," Randy said one evening as he rubbed saddle soap on a worn saddle purchased from an itinerant peddler, "the only way we can get ahead in this business is to expand. We need another location closer to the depot."

"How could we afford that?" Warren, accustomed now to Randy's sudden ideas, had learned not to reject them too hastily. "We have to come up with another two hundred down payment just to buy this place."

"I know. But once we own it we should be able to borrow on it. It takes money to make money, Warren," Randy said. "I've learned that much."

"Can't argue with you there." Warren looked around, assessing their small holdings. "But if we had a second place we'd need to hire another smithy. Get more stock. More carriages. We can't hardly make our payments now."

★ ★ ★ ★ ★

The following evening Randy came for Claire after work and drove her home again in the new buggy. "We've got to make up our minds about buying the barn," he told her. "The three-month trial rental is almost up."

"Of course you should buy it," Claire said.

"I don't know. Warren's got his family to think about . . ."

"Almost any property is a good buy right now, Randy. You should buy the barn and, if you need more capital, turn right around and sell it."

"You think so?"

"Property keeps going up. Those new businesses closer in on Pico are paying up to five thousand dollars for the lots alone."

"Five thousand?"

"Yes. You'll soon be able to sell that lot by the frontage foot. You could make more than enough profit to start up in a new location."

"But I can't see how we can scrape up the down payment. In addition to the hundred and fifty we've already paid in rent, the owner wants another two hundred down."

"Go to a bank and borrow it." Claire felt confident of the potential in Randy's venture. "Try the new California Security. The loan officer there is Harry Graham. I'm sure he would lend you what you need. You have your business as collateral. You have your horses and equipment. He wouldn't lend me money for my property because I had no collateral."

"You bought some property?"

"I'm in the process of buying a two-flat building. Then I'm going to resell it. It's the way things are done now. Keep reinvesting the profit."

"Claire, you're a surprising woman."

"These are surprising times, Randy. You were right about opportunity here in California. It seems there's more than oranges waiting to be plucked. You have only to seize the moment."

"Seize the moment. Sure wish I could." His gaze lovingly held hers, and she knew he wasn't talking about business opportunity.

Axel Kohl stood waiting at the bottom of the stairs when they arrived at the apartment. As they drew up, he came to meet them, waving happily.

"Claire! Good news!" His pasty complexion under his bowler hat had failed to acquire the customary California tan.

"What is it, Axel?" He was the last person Claire wanted to see right then.

"I got my place. My restaurant. In Pasadena. Right near the depot." He took her by the arm and began leading her toward the stairs. "Come on inside. I want to tell you all about it. You, too, Plank. Maybe you'd like to come to work for me, too."

Claire pulled her arm free. "Really, Axel, I . . . I'm busy right now. I . . ."

Axel turned to Randy. "Remember what we was talkin' about back at that Harvey House in Albuquerque? Well, that's what I'm gonna have. A place like Fred Harvey's. Good food. Good service."

"Did you buy out an existing restaurant?" Claire asked, not at all certain that Axel could establish a Harvey House atmosphere and menu.

"Yup. But I intend to remodel the whole place. Everything new and fresh. All new people. That's where you come in."

Claire stiffened. "Axel, I won't be coming to work for you. I have a fine job now with Mr. Dodd and I wouldn't dream of leaving it."

Axel smiled with pride. "But I'm offering to make you a hostess. Manager. Anything you want. Keep it all in the family, so to speak."

Claire sighed, exasperated. "The answer is no."

Axel seemed surprised by her abruptness. "But you ain't heard all my plans yet."

Claire started up the stairs. "Joanna will be waiting supper."

"Ain't no one home," Axel said. "I knocked. Got no answer." He, too, started up the stairs. "I'll help you with supper, Claire."

But Randy caught hold of his sleeve. "The lady don't appreciate your attentions, Axel."

"She don't, huh?" Axel's puzzled look changed to an indignant glare. "Well, she'll feel different when I'm a big success and the rest of you are still a bunch of bums." He tapped his bowler to make sure it was in place and stomped off down the street.

"Thanks, Randy. I'm afraid I couldn't have gotten rid of him." Claire continued on up the stairs and stepped into the silent apartment. The bed was unmade, dirty breakfast dishes remained on the table, and, as Axel had foretold, Joanna was not there.

"I'm worried about Joanna," Claire confessed as she cleared the table. "Since her graduation, she seems preoccupied about something. She mopes around the apartment and doesn't confide in me like she used to. Just seems to think she can do as she pleases."

"She's showing her independence." Randy pulled out a chair from the table and sat down.

"I hope that's all it is," Claire mused. "I've encouraged her to get together with some of the girls from her school, but she hasn't formed any close friendships yet. I'm thinking of inviting them to a little celebration for her. She'll be sixteen in two weeks."

"Good idea. Who doesn't like a birthday party?" As Claire moved around the table, Randy playfully pulled her onto his lap. "Will I be invited?"

"Of course." Claire's lighthearted reply was stilled by Randy's kiss. A gentle meeting of the lips at first, then Claire's arm stole around his neck and she relaxed in his embrace, returning his passion.

Suddenly the door opened and Joanna burst into the room. Her carefree expression faded when she saw her mother on Randy's lap, her eyes wide with horror at their kiss. She turned and fled.

"Joanna!" Claire jumped up and ran to the door, but Joanna's flight echoed down the stairs and she was gone. Claire came back into the kitchen. "Oh, Randy. What have we done?"

"We've done nothin' wrong." He came to her and put his arms around her. "I love you, Claire. I want to marry you."

"But everything is so unsettled. And Joanna . . ."

"She'll get used to the idea."

"We must go after her, Randy." Claire started down the stairs.

When they reached the street, Joanna was nowhere in sight. Randy helped Claire into the buggy and coaxed Sugar into motion. They drove up and down the neighborhood streets, checking the horsecar stops, but there was no sign of Joanna. It was getting dark, and Claire began to worry in earnest. "Oh, where could she have gone?"

"You wait here in case she comes back," Randy said as they again pulled up in front of the apartment. "I'll make a loop downtown. When she comes back, talk to her," he said, helping her from the buggy. "Make her understand how it is with us."

But Claire herself wasn't sure how it was with them.

"Joanna! What are you doing here?" Peach Oliver greeted her friend in the vestibule at Lorenzo's. Joanna carried a small valise. After fleeing from the apartment, she had hidden herself until her mother and Randy had driven away in the buggy looking for her. Then, on impulse, she went back upstairs, quickly packed a small bag, and took a streetcar to Lorenzo's.

"I'm running away," Joanna said.

"Running away?" Peach led her up the stairs and into her room, closing the door behind them. "Where to?"

"I don't know. I just know I don't want to live at home anymore. You need to leave this place, too, Peach."

"I couldn't, Joanna. Blanche would come after me."

"We'll go where no one can find us."

"Where would that be?" A flush of excitement rose in Peach's fair cheeks.

"I want to be a dancer," Joanna announced. "Not for Lorenzo. On the stage, where nice people can see me. We can both get jobs in the theater."

"You're crazy, Joanna. What about your mother?"

Joanna sighed. "Mother is . . . She and Randy Plank . . ."

"Randy Plank?" Peach looked incredulous. "Your mother and Randy?"

Joanna nodded.

"Pish posh. I don't believe it."

"I saw them," Joanna said. "With my own eyes. They

were . . . well, you know."

Peach wrinkled her nose. "But why is he going for someone as old as your mother? Randy's more our age."

"I don't know." Joanna's eyes filled with tears.

"And you have an itch for him yourself. Is that it?"

Joanna lowered her dark lashes.

"Well, why not?" Peach quipped. "I could go for him, too."

"Come with me," Joanna urged. "You don't belong in this place. Lorenzo's a terrible man . . . even if he is your uncle."

"Don't be silly. He's not my uncle."

"He's not?"

"And you're right, he's awful." She tossed her blonde curls. "But Blanche won't let him touch me."

"I should hope not." Joanna felt indignant at the very idea. "Peach, I didn't come to California just to see the orange trees. I want to do something important with my life. Don't you?"

"I suppose."

"Then let's do it. Let's go to San Francisco." Joanna reached into the reticule hanging at her wrist and pulled out the folded bills. "I have a hundred dollars. That should last us a while."

"Saint Agatha!" The money seemed to convince Peach. She rummaged in a bureau drawer and produced a small purse containing coins and bills. "It's my poker money. Over a hundred last time I counted it. Blanche sometimes lets me win when she sets up a game."

"You mean she cheats?" Joanna remembered that Peach was one of the poker winners on the train.

"Joanna, you're so naive."

Joanna thought for a moment. Having Peach along

would be good protection against any unscrupulous persons she was likely to encounter. She seemed to know almost everything. "Will you come with me?"

Peach sighed. "I guess I better. You need someone to look after you."

"I do not!" Joanna straightened to her full height. "I'll soon be sixteen. How old are you?"

"Old enough to know a dumb kid like you could get into a lot of trouble on her own." Peach packed a few things in a small bag and put on her rose and gold traveling suit and plumed hat. Scribbling a brief note for Blanche, she propped it on her pillow, and the girls crept down the stairs and out of the house.

"There's a night train to San Francisco," Joanna said as they walked toward the depot, valises in hand. "I checked the schedules."

"Why waste money going to San Francisco when there's places you can dance right here?"

Joanna turned to her friend. "Do you know of one, Peach?"

"Maybe. Let's get a room for the night and think about it."

CHAPTER TWENTY-THREE

Waiting for Joanna's return, Claire paced the small apartment, peering anxiously every few minutes out the front windows into the darkness. Then she heard someone on the stairs.

"Joanna?" She ran to the door and flung it open. Before her stood Blanche Oliver, whose flamboyant style was unmistakable even on the darkened landing.

"Forgive me for coming." Her husky voice remained as distinctive as her appearance. "I must talk to you about Joanna." Her nervous manner further alarmed Claire.

"Please. Come in."

"She came to Lorenzo's tonight to see Peach," Blanche continued. "One of the girls said they talked for a while in Peach's room, then they were gone." She held out a note with a few words scribbled on it. "Peach left this."

Joanna and I are going to find where we belong. Someday you'll be proud of us. Priscilla.

"But how did Joanna know where to find you?"

"Sometime ago she ran into Peach at the circus. She's been to see her several times since. She didn't tell you?"

"No."

"I told her she shouldn't come. But when she did . . . well, I felt it was harmless, since they usually went out for walks—in the afternoon, of course—just around town. Peach has grown fond of Joanna, and Joanna wanted her to

Dee Marvine

go back to school. Peach hasn't had a lot of formal schooling."

Claire felt faint. Joanna friendly with Peach and Blanche Oliver? "Blanche, Joanna's a young impressionable girl . . ."

"All young girls are impressionable."

"But Joanna is . . . well, yours is not her kind of life."

Blanche glared at Claire. "You think I don't want the same for mine as you do for yours?"

Claire regretted having made such an insensitive remark.

Blanche began pacing about the room. "I've spent my life looking out for her. And I can tell you it hasn't been easy."

"Please, Blanche, won't you sit down?"

"I never had any little-girl dreams," Blanche said bitterly. "My daddy saw to that. I had no place to go but the streets. But I been luckier than some—I always had my pride. That's one thing I could give to Peach."

Claire realized that Blanche's struggle, in some ways, may have been similar to her own.

"When I got into the better houses," Blanche said, "I learned proper manners and how to talk right. I sent Peach to school now and then, but with moving around a lot . . ."

"Have you any idea where they've gone?"

Blanche shook her head. "I thought maybe you would."

"What about Lorenzo? Could he be behind this? I mean, would he help them run away? Take them someplace?" This was difficult to discuss.

"Not a chance. Peach hates Lorenzo."

"Oh, Blanche." Claire wrung her hands. "Joanna's not even sixteen yet. How old is Peach?"

"Eighteen. I've done the best I could for her. Kept her with me. Watched out for her." She seemed to soften as she talked, revealing her tender feelings for Peach. "I protected

206

her from the business—if you know what I mean."

Claire could recognize a mother's concern. "Raising a child alone is hard."

A silence fell between the two women. Then Claire said, "Randy Plank has gone downtown to look for Joanna. If he doesn't find her, I think we should notify the police."

"Good Lord, no! No need to bring the law into this. That'd be asking for trouble. Won't Joanna get in touch with you?"

"Ordinarily, she would. But she was angry with me when she left." Claire remembered the shock on Joanna's face when she saw her and Randy together.

"I thought you two got along good. What was she mad about?"

A knock at the door saved Claire from having to answer that. She jumped up and went to the door. Randy stepped in.

"I looked everywhere I could think of," he reported. "Asked at several places. No one's seen her."

"Hello, Plank." Blanche's presence left Randy gaping.

Claire hurried to explain, "Randy, Joanna's run away with Peach Oliver."

"What! How? Did she have some money with her?"

Claire's heart leapt into her throat. She had hidden in her trunk the $500 she planned to deliver the next day as down payment on the two-flat building—$300 she had borrowed from Vanda Kolinski, plus her savings of $200. She hurried into the bedroom where she probed deep into the trunk for the handkerchief box in which she had secreted the money.

One hundred dollars was missing. Claire sank onto the bed. How could Joanna do such a thing? Then she noticed that some of Joanna's clothing was missing from the pegs. A quick inspection revealed that her drawer was empty, her valise gone. Claire put the remaining money back into the trunk.

"Joanna must have come back to get some clothes while we were out searching for her," she said, returning to the parlor. "She took some money, too."

"Enough to keep her for a while?" Randy wanted to know.

Claire could hardly bring herself to say it. "One hundred dollars."

The full implication of Joanna's departure hung in the air.

"Well," Blanche said, "I'm glad they didn't run off stone broke. Money in the pocket can keep a young girl out of trouble."

"But what can we do?" Claire felt herself trembling. "We must find them."

"They don't want to be found just yet," Blanche said.

Randy agreed. "Blanche is right. Give them time to realize what it's like to be out there on their own."

"But I can't just sit here and do nothing." Tears welled in Claire's eyes.

"If it's any comfort," Blanche offered, "I know Peach. She's not as wayward as you may think. She's actually quite sensible . . . most of the time."

Claire looked from one to the other. "And I know Joanna. She's headstrong, but she's not reckless. Maybe it is best to let the girls carry out their little adventure. If they don't come home in a day or two, then we can notify the authorities."

"No police," Blanche repeated. She took a small notepad from her bag and scribbled an address. "You'll find me here," she said, getting up to leave. "Get a message to me if you hear anything. I'll do the same."

When the door closed behind the visitor, Claire fell into Randy's arms, weeping. "I've driven Joanna away."

"You've done no such thing."

"But we shouldn't have . . ."

"You've given her fifteen years of devotion, Claire. You have a right to live your own life, too." His strong arms were convincing. "She'll be all right."

"But she took some of the money I need to buy the two-flat. What can I do now?"

"Why not take your own advice? Go to a bank and borrow the hundred."

"I can't. I tried."

"Then where did you get the money?"

"I had saved part of it. The rest I borrowed from a friend. A woman I met at the office. Her name is Vanda Kolinski."

"Could you get another hundred from her?"

"I'd rather die than ask."

"I thought you said you'd rather die than lose out on this two-flat deal."

Claire sniffed back her tears. "You're right. I can't let Joanna's silly schoolgirl escapade keep me from this opportunity. Randy, would you drive me to see Vanda tonight?"

Vanda, wearing a tattered dressing gown, her graying hair undone and hanging down her back, welcomed Claire and Randy into her parlor, which she had furnished in ornately carved furniture with horsehair upholstery. It wasn't often that she had visitors, she said, but she did love company. Before they could protest, she was serving them strawberry cookies she called *mazurkis* and strong coffee with cream and sugar.

"Vanda," Claire began when finally their hostess seated herself on one of the parlor chairs, balancing a cup and saucer in her work-worn hands. "I don't know how to say this, but I'm afraid I must ask for your help again."

"Ya, I glad to help."

"Something very upsetting has happened."

Vanda's brow furrowed with concern.

"It's my Joanna. She's run away."

Vanda's gaze softened in sympathy. "She come back soon."

"Maybe she will, but . . ." It hurt Claire to say it. "She took some of the money you loaned me, and I have to close the deal on my property tomorrow. Vanda, if you could loan me another hundred dollars, I'll pay everything back to you as soon as the property is sold."

"It's one hundred you need?" Vanda seemed to understand that much of Claire's explanation.

"Just until I sell the property. I hate to have to ask you again."

Vanda put her cup down on the library table and left the room. Almost before Randy and Claire could exchange glances, she was back. "One hundred," she announced, placing the bills in Claire's hand.

"I've made out a note for that amount." Claire handed her a folded paper. "Just like I did for the other money you loaned me. It's your proof of what I owe you." Vanda stuffed the paper into the pocket of her dressing gown.

"You've been so kind," Claire continued. "I don't know how to thank you."

A grin crinkled Vanda's cheeks. "You the kind one. I not have my house if you not help." Then sobering, "But your girl . . . she in trouble?"

"Not really. She's just . . ."

"She run away before?"

"No. Never. It's not like her. And she has never taken anything that didn't belong to her."

"Maybe she have good reason."

"I'm afraid she's angry with me."

Vanda glanced at Randy, then back to Claire. "At the both of you?"

Claire nodded. "Yes, that may be part of it."

"Maybe she afraid he take you away from her."

"Whatever it is," Randy said, "she's got us mighty worried."

"If she not happy with you, she can stay here," Vanda said. "My house too big for one old lady."

"She needs to be with me," Claire said.

"Maybe not."

Was this woman a babbling old fool . . . or a very wise woman? Claire wasn't sure she wanted to know the answer. "Vanda, it's good of you to offer. I appreciate your kindness more than I can say. But we must go now."

Randy sprang to his feet. "Yes, thanks for the coffee."

"You like my *mazurkis?*"

Randy nodded. "Yes, ma'am."

"Then you come see me again."

"We will," Claire said. "And Vanda," she pressed the woman's hand, "thank you so very much for the loan."

Vanda smiled. "You save my house, I save yours. It's good to have friend."

"Yes." Claire clasped Vanda's hand in both of hers. "Very good."

When Claire and Randy were in the buggy, rolling through the dark streets behind the perky little mule, Randy said, "That's some lady."

"It doesn't seem right somehow to take advantage of her generosity."

211

"You heard what she said. She feels indebted to you for helping her get her place."

"Just the same, I hope I can resell the property quickly so I can repay her. She's loaned me four hundred dollars, Randy. And all just on my signature."

"She trusts you." He grinned at her as they passed under a streetlamp. "Maybe I should have asked her for the money I need."

They laughed briefly. But Claire felt too upset over Joanna's disappearance to find much humor in anything.

CHAPTER TWENTY-FOUR

Suit pressed and shoes shined, Randy entered the offices of California Security Bank, where he introduced himself to vice president and loan officer Harry Graham. Well-dressed and well-spoken, Graham seemed to fit his station in life with ease, and Randy instantly disliked him. Why was it that some lucky devils had everything all laid out for them, while others had to hardscrabble it every step of the way? It must be easy to sit behind that mahogany desk all day passing judgment on the poor saps who came in desperate for money.

"What can I do for you, Mr. Plank?" Graham seemed cordial enough.

Randy explained his situation, then summed up, "We have to come up with the down payment on the barn right away, and if we're to expand, we need to buy more horses and equipment."

"How much do you think it will take?"

Randy steeled himself. "A thousand dollars would set us up with the essentials. But it has to be a long-term loan so the payments won't bust us."

Graham studied the Stanfield and Plank financial statement and the inventory of their equipment and livestock that Claire had helped Randy prepare.

"You seem to have a good start here," Graham commented. "And you show good steady growth for the three months you've been operating."

"Yes, sir." At those hopeful words, Randy's enthusiasm

bubbled over. "There's more customers out there than you can shake a stick at. And I can bring 'em in if we just have the stock and the rigs. We plan to hire another smithy, but Warren's boys can take a lot of the load off—they're good workers—so we can get by without payin' much in wages. We ain't takin' hardly nothin' for ourselves."

"How are you living, if you're not paying yourselves salaries?" Graham's expression registered moderate curiosity, but Randy felt an implied criticism.

"We're livin' in the barn right now . . . to save on expenses."

"In the barn? You and the Stanfield family?"

What was Graham so damn surprised about? Obviously he had never had to resort to such a humbling situation.

"Warren's a good, honest man," Randy said, defensively. "A fine blacksmith. As you can see on that statement, he's making a living on the forge alone. I'm a hard worker, too, and a pretty fair salesman. We'll make this business into a lot more'n you see on those pages . . . whether or not you give us a loan. It'll just take longer if you don't, that's all."

Graham raised his hand to temper Randy's outburst. "Your plan seems sound, but I can't act on your word alone. I'll need some references. Can you give me the names of three people you're doing business with, people who know you well and can vouch for your character and abilities."

"Sure, I guess so. There's Bud Hawkins at Hawkins Carriage Company. I'm dealin' with him. And Ned Godfrey that we're renting the barn from." Randy thought of giving Claire's name as a character reference, but she probably wasn't high enough on the hog to impress the bank. Still, there was no one who knew him better. "Mrs. Chadwick can vouch for my character."

"Mrs. Chadwick? You mean Claire Chadwick?" The memory of his meeting with the intriguing Mrs. Chadwick remained fresh.

"We're friends," Randy said. "She works for that lawyer, Farley Dodd."

"She does?" A frown dented Graham's brow as he mulled this bit of information. "I'm acquainted with Mrs. Chadwick, but I didn't know she worked for Dodd. Very well, Mr. Plank. This should be enough to go on. If you'll sign this, I'll send someone out to look over your setup." He pushed an application form across the desk and Randy scratched his name at the bottom. "I should have an answer for you by next week."

Randy hated being dismissed in such a perfunctory manner. If he had to grovel to men like Harry Graham he might as well do it for a sum that meant something. "You know, Mr. Graham, that thousand dollars is barely enough to keep us afloat. I'd like to change this application to two thousand. With that much breathin' room, there'd be no stoppin' us." He gave the banker his most ingenuous grin. "It takes money to make money, ain't that right?"

"Confidence and hard work are important, too, Mr. Plank." Harry stood and offered a handshake. "If your references check out, I think maybe we can do business."

McKenzie Tate arrived at Farley Dodd's office with a Mr. Harris, owner of the buildings he intended to purchase. After introductions all around, Tate said, "We're still missing one of the parties to this transaction. Won't you join us, Mrs. Chadwick?"

Dodd blinked at Tate. "What's she got to do with it?"

"She's buying one of the two-flats," Tate explained,

pulling up a chair for her. "I trust you are prepared, Mrs. Chadwick?"

"I am." She clutched an envelope containing $500 cash along with the title papers she had prepared.

Farley Dodd cleared his throat. "Well, now, this is a bit irregular. Bringing in a third party at the last minute. A mystery party, as it were. Is that satisfactory with you, Mr. Harris?" Dodd's pointed remark did not mask the unsettling effect Claire's involvement had on him, and he continued to stare at her incredulously as she sat before him like any other client.

"The property's for sale," Harris said, "to anyone who comes up with the money."

"Very well, then," Dodd said, "if Mr. Harris has no objection, we have only to sign the papers and transfer the money."

Presenting the documents for Tate's three buildings and for the one she would soon own, Claire took her cash from its envelope. Tate produced a bank draft in the amount he owed. The contracts were read and signed. Gathering up the money and documents and placing them in his briefcase, Harris shook hands with the men, tipped his hat to Claire, and left.

Claire sat tingling with the realization that she now actually owned a two-flat building—the beginning of financial security for her and Joanna.

"I'll see that the documents are recorded promptly," Dodd said.

"Thanks, Farley." McKenzie Tate rose from his chair. "And thank you, Mrs. Chadwick." He bowed in polite acknowledgment of Claire's contribution to the deal. "I trust that you'll want to turn over this investment as quickly as I do."

"Yes, I'd like that very much."

"Then I'll include yours in the package. Longworth may find the buildings more salable as a group."

"Thank you, Mr. Tate." She stood and extended her hand.

"Not at all. Not at all. Always glad to help a friend." He padded toward the door. "Farley, I'll be in touch."

When he had gone, Claire offered the explanation she felt was owed. "Mr. Tate told me he was short the necessary cash, and offered me the opportunity to purchase one of the buildings if I could contribute five hundred of the down payment he needed."

Dodd flew into a fury. "But why didn't you tell me? You might have gotten into a bad investment."

"I didn't know until last night whether or not I could come up with the money," Claire said. "I had to borrow part of it."

"And you intend to repay it when the building sells."

"Yes."

"God almighty, woman!" His face reddened. "Don't you realize this boom could go bust? What if you can't resell the building?"

"I'll just have to take that chance."

Dodd dropped into his chair. "Well, you apparently got yourself a good Pasadena property." Changing his tone, he leveled his gaze at her. "You've become quite astute in handling my business, and now it seems you've put some of that know-how to work on your own behalf."

"Yes, Mr. Dodd, and I'm most grateful for your tutoring."

Dodd smiled ever so slightly. "Well, I'm pleased, Mrs. Chadwick. I'm quite pleased."

Was this the right moment to bring up her new idea?

"Mr. Dodd," she began. "I have something else I'd like to discuss with you."

"What now?" He moaned as if the surprises she offered were endless.

"I've been watching how McKenzie Tate and others operate, and since I've taken the plunge into real estate, I think I'd like to carry it even further."

"Don't tell me you want to become a broker?"

"No, I'm afraid that might take me away from Joanna too much." With the mention of Joanna's name, the full impact of her daughter's absence returned. She wanted to confide in him about Joanna's running away, but she felt a woman in business should keep domestic problems to herself, lest she appear incapable of handling home and family along with her job. It was best that he not know the turmoil she was going through. Anyway, Joanna would surely be home soon.

"I'd like your permission to utilize information that may come through this office," Claire said. "I may want to buy a few more properties to resell . . . on a modest scale, of course. Would you have any objection to that?"

His lips pursed pensively. "I suppose not . . . as long as you don't take advantage of any of my clients . . . and don't neglect your duties here." He leaned toward her. "I've come to depend on you, Mrs. Chadwick. You know that. And with the campaign soon to get under way, I'll need your full concentration more than ever."

"Of course."

"Tibby may need some help, too, with her campaign duties. She'll be first lady of the city, you know, if I'm elected mayor. Did I mention that she's coming out here? Arrives Saturday. She's finally decided Los Angeles is adequately civilized, and I'm sure your presence here in the office will help to affirm her opinion."

"I'm looking forward to meeting your Tibby. She must be a very special woman."

"Yes, she is. A very special woman."

CHAPTER TWENTY-FIVE

Arriving next week. Harry Graham let the telegram drop to his desk. Damn. Phineas B. Mossburg was coming to Los Angeles to check on the new bank—and Daisy was coming with him. Harry welcomed P.B.'s firsthand input on the new enterprise, but having to deal with Daisy again would be difficult. He had not written her since coming to California, nor had he heard from her, except through P.B.'s occasional businesslike "greetings from the family." Harry had been too busy the past few weeks to even think about Daisy Mossburg, and that's the way he preferred to keep it.

That evening he mentioned over dinner with City Councilman Farley Dodd that the Mossburgs would be coming out, and was surprised to learn that Dodd's wife Tibby would be coming on the same train.

"Perhaps they'll get acquainted," Dodd said. "Tibby will be eager to make suitable friends."

A sick feeling settled in the pit of Harry's stomach. If the Mossburgs stayed at the Overland, there'd be no escaping Daisy's attentions.

"I'm looking for a house for Tibby and me," Dodd commented. "I hope to get us settled before it's time to start planning my mayoral campaign."

"Then you're going ahead with it?"

"I'm willing to give it a try. Los Angeles has a strong city council but a weak mayor. Maybe I can even it up a bit, that is, if I can get any support from the newspapers. You interested in politics, Harry?"

"Running for office, you mean? Not in the least. I may take more interest as a voter, however, if I decide to stay out here. We certainly need some legislative attention paid to this phenomenal growth."

"If you plan to buy property here, now's the time to get in on the boom, invest in something that will appreciate fast. Tibby and I will buy as soon as possible."

"I'm comfortable here at the hotel."

"If you change your mind, I'd be happy to do the legal work for you."

Harry wished Dodd would back off, but you couldn't blame a man for trying to drum up business for himself.

Joanna and Peach decided to spend the night at the Del Rio, a first-rate hotel, reasoning that the luxury of a good dinner and a comfortable night's rest would give them the proper frame of mind to look for work in the theater the next day. They slept late, then, delighted with the fragrant soaps and immaculate towels in their private bath, bathed, dressed, and lingered longer than they intended over a sumptuous breakfast in the dining room.

"Let's do this again as soon as we find work." Peach spread sweet butter and marmalade on her toast.

"It's rather expensive." Joanna felt a twinge of remorse at having spent some of the money she took from the trunk. "As soon as I pay my mother back, I intend to save my wages for dancing lessons. If I'm going to be a dancer, I want to be the best." She stirred another sugar cube into her coffee, her little finger extended daintily. "Peach, why don't we both take dancing lessons? You could be a dancer, too."

"Lorenzo says I'm clumsy."

"You are not. You're as graceful as can be. And beautiful, too."

221

"Depends on who's looking." Peach batted her eyelashes provocatively.

"Oh, Peach, you don't take anything seriously," Joanna scolded. "We've got to decide what we're going to do."

"Yes, ma'am." Peach straightened primly in her chair. "First, we'll go to the Barbary Theater and get you a job in the chorus line. I know a couple of girls who worked there."

"Really, Peach? Is it decent? I mean, is it respectable?"

"It's legitimate. I don't know how respectable. What is respectable anyway?" Her answer was a bit snippy. "Something your mother approves of?"

Joanna frowned, realizing her mother was probably frantic with worry at this very moment. But maybe not. The image of Claire sitting on Randy's lap, actually kissing him, overpowered any regret she felt at having left without telling them. When she was established on her own, she would contact her mother with the good news: she was no longer in the way.

"Let's go then." Joanna picked up her valise. "Mother has no hold on me now." Tossing her curls haughtily, she led the way from the dining room.

The Barbary Theater in downtown Los Angeles was locked and looked deserted, but Peach led the way into the alley and around to a back door which stood open to let in the fresh morning air. As the girls peered into the semidark interior, a gruff voice barked, "You girls lookin' for somethin'?"

Joanna stepped forward into a cramped backstage area. "Yes, we're looking for work."

A burly man came from the shadows. "What kind of work?" Through a cloud of cigar smoke his gaze slid from the pretty young girl with bright copperish hair to her attractive blonde friend.

Joanna cleared her throat. "I'm a dancer."

"Hey, Bernie!" the burly man called out. "Couple'a dancers here." His gaze lingered on the applicants. "Couple'a lookers, too."

A muffled voice responded from somewhere among the backdrops, and a short, stocky man appeared, sleeves rolled, rumpled trousers held up with suspenders. He scrutinized the two girls standing in the light from the doorway. "Where you danced before?"

"I've studied dancing and . . . and I've danced in recitals," Joanna said.

"How about you?" He stepped closer to Peach, studying her natural blonde hair and flawless face in the light. "Any experience?"

"She's the one who wants to dance." Peach pointed at Joanna. "I don't know beans about dancing."

"With your looks, you can fake it," he said. "Fact is, I could use a couple of fresh faces right now to spark up the show." He took a watch from his pocket and noted the time, 11:30. "We're havin' a run-through at noon. Let's see what you can do." He waved off her reluctance. "I'll get Sophie to dig up a costume for you. You won't be the first to learn on the job."

Bernie led the way up a narrow stairway to a room toward the back where a woman sat at a sewing machine beneath a row of dingy windows.

"Sophie, got anything these two can wear for a run-through?" he asked.

Sophie was a plump little bird-like woman, her jet black hair slicked back from her sharp-beaked face into a feathery bun. Sighing wearily, she assessed the two girls. Then, pawing through the disarray of garments hanging on a rack against the far wall, she came up with two sleeveless, knee-length bloomer costumes, more suitable, Joanna thought, for bathing than for dancing.

Gingerly, Joanna picked up one of the garments to look it over. Peach shrugged and took the other.

"Go ahead. See if they fit." Sophie indicated a screen set up in the corner.

"Get a move on," Bernie urged, indicating a dingy clock on the wall. "And be on stage at twelve sharp."

The cramped space behind the screen was barely big enough for one at a time to change. Peach went first, handing her dress, petticoat, and stockings out to Joanna, who hung them over a nearby chair. When she appeared in the costume, her pale arms and legs jutting shockingly from the shapeless costume, Joanna burst out laughing.

Peach, too, giggled as she surveyed herself in the wall mirror. "It ain't elegant."

When Joanna appeared in hers, it was Peach's turn to convulse with laughter. Joanna felt indecently exposed and clasped her bare arms across her chest as they started down the steps to the stage, where they found a piano player warming up at a battered upright while six girls in skimpy, mismatched togs engaged in a variety of kicks, shuffles, and turns.

"Okay, girls," Bernie yelled. "We got two new ones with us today, so I want you to go through the routine slow and easy so's they can catch on." The six girls took assigned places across the stage, and Bernie put Joanna and Peach at either end with instructions to watch the others.

The piano player began a lively rhythm. Joanna watched the other girls and soon began to pick up the simple steps along with exaggerated hand and arm movements that she thought quite silly.

Peach was another case. She tried to copy the move-

ments of the girl beside her, but was always hopelessly behind the beat, kicking when the others were turning, and
turning when the others were kicking. But instead of getting
flustered, Peach giggled, and when her feet got tangled up and
she came down hard on her backside she mugged comically.
The piano player snickered.

"Hey," Bernie called out, "that's funny! What's your
name?"

"Priscilla." Unperturbed by her ineptness as a
dancer, she blurted out the first surname that came to
mind. ". . . Plank."

"Priscilla Plank." Bernie grinned. "You got some talent,
kid. As a comic."

"A comic?"

"Yeah. A looker like you, all peaches and cream, takin'
pratfalls. What an act! With the right material, you could
become a headliner."

Peach glanced along the row of dancers at Joanna, who
stood beaming at her, obviously pleased.

"What about it?" Bernie snapped. "You interested in
tryin' some comic material?"

"Got nothing better to do," Peach said.

"Morry," he addressed the piano player, "work out some
funny stuff for her, will you?"

He walked over to Joanna. "You're okay, too. Handled
the steps real good. Lottie here can polish you up a little."
He indicated the jaded trouper standing next in line.
"Okay, Lottie?"

"Sure, Bernie." Lottie had a long narrow face and feet to
match. "What's your name, kid?"

"Jo . . ." Joanna stopped short. "Josephine," she said.
Then, as she groped for another name, her father's given
name came to mind. "Josephine Carter."

"Okay, Josie," Bernie said. "Get together with Lottie this afternoon to brush up on the routines, and you can start tonight. Sophie!" When the bird-like woman appeared on the stairs, Bernie told her to come up with a dancer's costume for Josephine and a comic outfit for Priscilla.

"Why did you call yourself Priscilla Plank?" Joanna asked Peach as they climbed the stairs toward Sophie's wardrobe room. "That's Randy's name."

"Why not? You got some kind of claim to it?"

"No," Joanna answered, then added glumly, "not anymore, I guess."

CHAPTER TWENTY-SIX

Two days went by, and McKenzie Tate again appeared in Farley Dodd's law office.

"Mrs. Chadwick! Good news! We have a buyer for the two-flat buildings."

"Already?" Claire hadn't dared to hope for such a quick turnover.

"He'll be here this afternoon to close the deal." Tate, obviously pleased with himself, perched on the edge of Claire's desk. "You'll be happy to know I was able to get sixty-five hundred for each building."

Claire sat stunned.

"Twenty-five hundred profit on each building." He cocked his head to one side and then the other to emphasize each numeral. "You'll receive your share this afternoon when the check is turned over to me. Naturally, I'll deduct my ten percent commission for having sold your property for you."

"Yes, of course." She could hardly believe her ears. Even after the commission and repaying the $400 she had borrowed from Vanda, she would have more than $1,800. If only Joanna knew about this, and the financial freedom it could buy for them, perhaps she would come home.

"I want Farley to look over the contract," Tate said. "Is he in?"

"He's at City Hall this morning," Claire said. "He'll be in around three."

"I'll leave it and come back then."

"I can't thank you enough, Mr. Tate." She walked toward the door with him, nearly bumping into Axel Kohl, who was entering.

"Well, hello, Kohl," Tate said. "How is your search coming along?"

"I found a place! In Pasadena. Right next to the depot. I'm callin' it Kohl's Kafeteria, spelled with a 'k.' "

"That's a fine idea!" Tate savored the name for a moment. "Kafeteria with a 'k.' Good luck with it." He nodded a farewell to Claire and moved on down the stairs.

Axel grinned happily. "Claire, I wanted you to be the first to know."

"I hope it does well for you," Claire said. "You say it's near the depot?"

"Yup. Twenty trains a day to and from Los Angeles alone. Not to mention the foot traffic right there in downtown Pasadena. Claire, it's a dandy." He grinned at her. "And I want you to be my hostess."

"Axel, I thought I made it clear. I'm not interested in restaurant work."

"But, Claire . . ." He seemed bewildered. "I'll pay you good wages. I'll look out for you. I'll help you take care of your girl."

"My answer is no!"

Axel blinked as if hearing the word for the first time. "Why so all-fired testy?"

Was the man deaf and blind? "Axel, I want no part of you or your restaurant."

He moved toward her. "But, can't we just . . . ?"

"Get out of here!" Teeth clenched, she picked up a book from the desk and threw it at him. It struck his shoulder and fell to the floor with a startling thud. "Don't say another word," she demanded. "Just go!"

Axel's eyes bulged with incomprehension as he rubbed his shoulder.

"Go!" She heaved another book and he raised his arms to shield his head, but the book missed its mark and knocked over the coat tree.

"Now, Claire, you don't mean . . ."

When Claire reached for another book, Axel fled down the stairs. She went into Dodd's office and watched from the front window as he climbed into a one-horse rig and drove off down the street. Her anger drained, she stood at the window till he was out of sight. Then she grinned. Maybe losing her temper had finally convinced him she meant what she said.

Returning to her office, she righted the coat tree and picked up the books, smoothing their rumpled pages as if to soothe her own ruffled feelings. She knew only too well what attracted most men, and she was careful never to flaunt her natural attributes. But what was she to do? Wear a Mother Hubbard and shave off her hair? Or did Axel think her a poor helpless woman who needed protection and guidance? Perhaps that was it. Her financial vulnerability made him feel strong and important. Well, sorry, Axel, but as of this afternoon she would no longer be without means.

She sat down at the desk and picked up the contract McKenzie Tate had left. It documented the sale of four two-flat buildings in Pasadena—one of which was her ticket to independence. All she need do was invest her share of the proceeds wisely and prudently, but with enough courage and imagination to make it pay off. Compensation for all the indignities she had suffered since the day her father died. The day she became that freak of nature, a woman alone.

★ ★ ★ ★ ★

When the newly drawn papers were signed that afternoon, McKenzie Tate turned over to Claire a bank draft in the amount of $2,250. Once she repaid Vanda's $400, she would have $1,850 free and clear. Farley Dodd observed the proceedings, and after Tate and the sellers had gone, he asked Claire to remain in his office.

"You've made quite an impressive profit for yourself," he said.

Claire smiled. "I hope to turn it into a series of profitable investments."

Dodd frowned. "Mrs. Chadwick, I'm sure you're aware that I won't tolerate any neglect of your duties here. Especially since I'll be out of the office a bit more when Tibby gets here. We'll be looking for a house."

Claire considered his comment. Would she be confined even more closely to running the office just when she needed time to search for her daughter? Nothing was more important than finding Joanna and bringing her home. "Mr. Dodd, there's something I must tell you." And she related the essential facts of Joanna's absence.

Dodd listened with concern, commenting, "Children can be quite troublesome."

"No, Joanna's not like that. She's . . . well, I'm not sure why she left. But she's been gone two days now and I've got to find her."

"You should have told me sooner." Dodd got up and put on his hat. "This city isn't so big that a young girl can just disappear without a trace. Let's go and talk with my friends in the district attorney's office."

At that very moment, Joanna was prancing through her second afternoon of rehearsal at the Barbary Theater. She

had joined the dancers on stage the night before and managed to bluff her way through the performance on Lottie's
basic instruction, but afterward Bernie had suggested she
might pay closer attention to the finer points.

Joanna saw no reason for finer points, since the audience
hooted and hollered and seemed more interested in the
amount of leg and bosom revealed by a girl's costume than
any refinement of her movement. Sophie had supplied a
somewhat tawdry, bright green Southern-belle costume for
her, identical to those worn by the other dancers, taking a
few tucks here and there to make it fit. Not only was the
bodice cut embarrassingly low in front, but the skirt was
hiked up in back so that the ruffled pantaloons produced a
barrage of whistles and vulgar shouts each time the dancers
turned their backs to the audience.

From somewhere backstage, Joanna could hear Peach
going through her lines with Morry, the piano player turned
comedy coach. Bernie planned to put Priscilla Plank into
the show on Saturday night.

Peach: *"What kind of husband would you advise me
to get?"*
Morry: *"I'd advise you to get a single man and let the
husbands alone."*

Peach: *"George is just crazy about me."*
Morry: *"He was crazy before he ever met you."*

Morry: *"I will say that George dresses like a gentleman."*
Peach: *"Really? I never saw him dressing."*

Lottie made a sour face as she led Joanna through the

dance routine. "Those old gags died before I was born."

Joanna, breathing hard to keep up, kicked her right leg—one, two—then took two steps to the left—three, and four. "I've never heard them before," she panted.

> *Morry: "That's an unusual pair of stockings you got on, one red and one green."*
>
> *Peach: "I know, and I got another pair just like them at home."*

When the girls finished their rehearsal, they went back to the room they had rented in a boardinghouse that catered to theater people. Peach seemed amused by the quirk of fate that had made her a comedienne.

"Can you imagine me doing those cornball jokes?" She took off her dress and stretched out on the bed to rest before they had to eat supper and go back to the theater. "How about it, Joanna? Do you like being a dancer?"

"I think I will, once I'm comfortable with the steps." She grimaced. "The crowd seems sort of . . . crude."

Peach laughed. "What did you expect?"

"I don't know. Something more like the ballet, I guess."

"The ballet? When did you ever see a ballet?"

"Well, I haven't actually, but I guess I expected dancing to be more like that."

"Piffle!" Peach rolled her eyes at Joanna. "You're so green you're pitiful, Joanna. It's a good thing you have me to look after you."

On Saturday night the Barbary Theater was packed as Joanna and Peach, faces bright with makeup, peeked through a slit in the curtain at the crowd, mostly men waiting impatiently for the show to begin. Peach seemed cavalier about her few lines and the three pratfalls she would take at appropriate times in the show.

"What's there to be nervous about?" she taunted. Peach's costume, an abbreviated version of the green satin worn by the other dancers, had no skirt at all to cover the skimpy ruffled pantaloons and the lavender and yellow polka-dot stockings. "I could do this stuff in my sleep." She batted the spiky false lashes Lottie had helped her apply along with a crop of huge freckles painted across her nose.

"Maybe you could," Joanna whispered, "but you don't have Bernie and Lottie and the others glaring at you for missing the steps."

"I thought you had it almost perfect now."

"I do, but . . . I'm not sure Mother will like me working in this place."

"Pish posh. She'll be proud of you." Peach draped her arm around Joanna's bare shoulders. "We get paid after to-night's show. Let's go to the Del Rio and have us a real nice dinner."

Joanna felt good about her performance that night. Growing more certain of the steps, her natural grace began to show. She enjoyed the ragtime rhythms and began, within the structure of the routine, to put some of her own feeling into the dance. But it was Peach's clowning that attracted the most attention. Her sense of timing and, Joanna thought, absolute shamelessness, produced exactly the kind of comedy Bernie had hoped for.

"What an act!" he said after the show. "Priscilla, you had 'em rollin' in the aisles. You're outrageous!" And he gave her a little kiss right on her painted freckles.

He liked Joanna's dancing, too. "Good work, kid," he called to her as she brushed past him in leaving the stage.

The backstage area was crowded with an assortment of

men—gentlemen, Lottie called them—eager to make the acquaintance of the dancers. Joanna's fresh face had not gone unnoticed, and she was deluged with compliments on her performance along with invitations to supper.

"I have other plans," she insisted, looking toward Peach for reinforcement.

But Peach seemed flattered by the attention she was getting. She mugged and joked with her admirers, finally selecting two of the younger ones and leading them toward Joanna. "Josephine, we've been invited to supper by these two gentlemen, Mr. Jones and Mr. Smythe. S-m-y-t-h-e." She dissolved into merry laughter at the phony names.

Joanna protested, "But I thought you and I . . ."

Peach nudged her in the ribs, whispering, "Don't be a dope. They'll buy."

"Pleased to meet you, Miss . . ." said the stocky Jones.

"Miss Carter." Peach beamed at Joanna. "Her name is Josephine Carter."

"How do you do, Miss Carter." Jones tipped his derby. In his early twenties, he had a rough, coarsely groomed appearance, his dull hair plastered down on either side of a center part.

"Hello," Joanna said glumly.

Smythe was taller, more gangly, with dark hair and a forward manner that immediately irritated Joanna. "You damsels look like you need a night on the town." He swaggered as he moved to take Peach's arm. "Come on, Priscilla."

"We still have to change," Peach protested coyly.

"Sure thing. We'll wait," Smythe said.

The girls, using the communal dressing room shared by all the dancers, hurried to take off their makeup and get into street clothes. "Peach, I don't like those two fellas," Joanna confided.

"It's Priscilla, remember? And you don't have to *like* them." Peach applied her usual circles of rouge. Joanna sat unconvinced.

"You look much too pale, *Josephine*," Peach chided. And while Joanna frowned at her image in the mirror, Peach applied the rouge puff to her cheeks, too.

CHAPTER TWENTY-SEVEN

Claire left the office a few minutes early to deposit her profit in the bank. As she finished her business at the teller's window, Harry Graham, leaving his office for the day, saw her there. "Why, Mrs. Chadwick. Have you been helped to your satisfaction?"

"Yes. As a matter of fact, I just opened an account." She tucked the receipt into her reticule.

He looked pleased. "I'm glad to hear I didn't sour you entirely on California Security."

"Of course not." Claire returned his smile. "It's very convenient to my office."

"I trust you found the financing you needed."

"I did. In fact, I've already resold the property."

"So soon?" His eyes reflected his approval, if not of her business acumen then certainly of her person.

"So if you had given me the loan you would have been promptly repaid."

"Mrs. Chadwick," he said impulsively. "If you're not busy this evening . . . would you join me for dinner?"

Harry Graham was an exceedingly appealing man, and if she weren't in such turmoil over Joanna she would certainly welcome such an invitation.

"It's Saturday night, Mrs. Chadwick, and I haven't had a relaxing evening since I came to Los Angeles. I'll bet you haven't either."

"I'm sorry, Mr. Graham. But I have a daughter . . ."

"Bring her along."

"I don't know where she is." Tears she had been holding back since Joanna's disappearance threatened to well up. "Two days ago . . . she left home."

Concern shadowed his brow. "Have you contacted the authorities?"

"I talked with District Attorney Haycroft. He's alerted the police department, but . . . well, I hated to do that. Joanna isn't a wayward girl. She's gone off with a friend is all, another young girl." Claire regretted having revealed so much. "I'm sure she'll come home soon. But till she does . . ."

"Is there any chance she may have come home this afternoon? Maybe she's there right now."

"I'm hoping."

"Then let's go to your place and see." He offered his arm and led her out of the bank. "If she isn't there, we'll figure out what to do over a bite of supper."

Claire smiled wistfully. "You're very kind, Mr. Graham. But this is no concern of yours."

"Of course it is." He grinned then. "As one of California Security's customers, you're entitled to our full complement of services." He signaled a passing hack.

"Well, all right," Claire said. "But I'm afraid I'm not very good company right now."

Harry helped her into the hack and climbed in beside her as she gave her address to the driver.

"Has your daughter been unhappy since you came to California?" he asked.

"No, not really. But girls that age can be moody. Do you have children, Mr. Graham?"

"I've never married. What went wrong with *your* marriage, Mrs. Chadwick?" It was a startlingly frank question, but his obvious concern prompted Claire to answer.

"He left me before Joanna was born. He was . . . irresponsible."

"And you've raised your daughter by yourself all this time?"

Claire nodded. "She's a wonderful girl, Mr. Graham."

"I don't doubt that for a moment."

"I'm afraid she feels neglected because I'm working such long hours."

"Apparently with a great deal of success." His relaxed manner reflected the ease Claire felt in his company.

But that ease was short-lived. Joanna was not at the apartment. Harry Graham led Claire back down the stairs to the waiting hack, and they went to a small café where they were ushered to a corner table. Claire told him the whole story—their meeting with the Olivers on the train, Joanna running into Peach at the circus and her subsequent visits to Lorenzo's, then Blanche informing her that the girls had run away together.

"I see why you're worried."

Claire hadn't mentioned Randy Plank or the part his involvement in their lives may have played in Joanna's behavior.

"Do you think they might have gone back to this Lorenzo's place?"

"Blanche said she would contact me if the girls showed up there." Claire picked at the well-prepared food that was placed before her. "There is one thing," she said. "Joanna thought she wanted to be a dancer. I plan to talk with the dance teachers around town. And if there's a ballet school . . . I don't suppose the theaters would hire an inexperienced young girl like Joanna no matter how well she danced."

"Was she good at it?"

"Yes, quite good. Her teacher back in Westport was giving her special instruction."

"That might be the place to start then. There are a couple of theaters in town that have chorus lines. Let's go check them out."

"Mr. Graham, I can't thank you enough for your help."

"It's Harry," he said. "Mr. Graham is that fella who works at the bank."

"Thank you, Harry." She savored the last of her dessert, relieved at having confided in someone.

The streetlamps cast a soft glow as they left the restaurant, and the cool breeze carried the faint smell of the ocean. Declining Harry's offer to get a hack, Claire took his arm and they strolled along the downtown streets to a theater, the Granada, whose marquee announced a number of vaudeville acts. The evening performance was about to begin.

"Would you like to see the show?" he asked. "We can inquire backstage afterward." The program was a mix of comedians, singers, dancers, and variety acts, including a juggler and a talking dog. Claire hadn't been to a theater since Chicago, and she found the lighthearted performances most entertaining.

When it was over, Claire and Harry went backstage where they were stopped by the stage door keeper, who sat at a desk to eject uninvited visitors. After explaining their mission, Claire was permitted to go up the stairs to the dressing rooms where she talked with several performers as they changed clothes. She described Joanna and Peach, asking if anyone had seen them. None had, but she learned the name of a dance teacher and a rehearsal group, and someone mentioned that the Barbary burlesque theater often hired hopeful young dancers.

Claire came away disappointed. "I can't see Joanna working there. Those girls seem so brazen. Joanna is just a child."

Harry nodded knowingly. "Shall we check out that other theater?"

Claire reluctantly agreed.

In front of the Barbary Theater they paused to read the posters. On one, a hand-lettered card had been tacked: *Introducing Priscilla Plank, comedienne.*

"I know someone named Plank," Claire mused. "I wonder if they could be related."

"Randy Plank? He was in my office just this morning. As a matter of fact, he gave your name as a reference."

"Randy's a good friend. I suggested he see you about a loan."

Harry seemed amused. "Would you approve him for the financing?"

"I would indeed. He's most reliable. Capable and enterprising, too."

"He mentioned that you work with Farley Dodd . . ."

"Yes, Mr. Dodd is my boss."

"I've become quite friendly with Farley. We both live at the Overland. Funny he's never mentioned you. He did say he has an assistant." Harry reached for her hand and held it in both of his. "If you were working for me, I'd shout it from the housetops."

They stood, their hands clasped between them, held fast by the emotion each felt in their closeness.

"Claire . . ." He seemed to want to say something that was not easy to verbalize, but they were on a public street, standing in the garish light from the theater marquee, and passersby were beginning to glance their way.

Claire gently withdrew her hands from his. "Let's go talk

to this Priscilla Plank. Maybe she's seen Joanna and Peach."

But at that moment, Priscilla Plank and her friend Josephine Carter emerged with their escorts, Smythe and Jones, from the stage door at the back of the theater,

"You girls sure put on a show tonight," Smythe said. "I 'bout split a gut, Priscilla, when you tripped and fell flat on your face with your heinie stickin' up in the air." He gave his knee a slap to punctuate his boisterous laugh.

The stocky Jones put his arm around Joanna's shoulders and led her down the alley toward the street. "Now where would you girls like to go for a nightcap, huh?"

Joanna, revolted by the stench of liquor already on his breath, looked back to make sure Peach was following. "I'd like something to eat."

"First we got to get loosened up a little," Smythe said. "You girls must be tense after all that dancin' around."

Peach giggled. "Did you really think my part was funny?"

"Heck, yeah. You're a barrel of laughs, especially in them drawers and polka-dot socks and them freckles. Ain't she, Josephine?"

"I guess so," Joanna said glumly.

"What's the matter, Red?" Jones chucked her under the chin. "You don't seem like you're up for a good time."

"She's fine," Peach interrupted. "We're just hungry is all."

"Then let's get these dainty damsels something to eat," Smythe said in a loud voice calculated to attract attention, "so's they can enjoy theirselves."

Once backstage, Claire and Harry found that nearly everyone had already left the theater, but the stage door keeper did not object as they made their way up the narrow staircase to the dressing rooms. Hearing voices, they looked through the open door of one of the rooms and saw a balding man wearing a washerwoman costume standing before the mirror. He peeled off his fuzzy gray wig and tossed it onto the dressing table, then lit a cigarette and took a deep drag.

Harry tapped on the door frame.

"Everybody's gone." The man gave them a cursory glance as he stripped off the outer layers of his costume. "I should be out of here, too, only I got held up arguing with wardrobe." He unbuckled the straps supporting the heavy padding shaped like an old woman's sagging breasts and hips, dropped it onto a chair, and stood there in his underwear rubbing his belly. "That Sophie's got me gussied up so tight I can't breathe. Next season I'm doin' a bicycle act."

Claire blushed. "Is there anyone working here by the name of Joanna Chadwick?"

"Nah. No one by that name."

"Would you know if two young girls were here recently, inquiring for work?"

"They're all young, lady. And they all want work. There's a big turnover."

"Oh."

"Is your manager around?" Harry asked. Then to Claire, "We could ask him to keep an eye out."

"Bernie's gone, too," the man said, taking another drag on his cigar. "You can catch him here any night next week."

Outside, the balmy night air seemed wonderfully fresh after the stale theater. "It's all right," Claire said when Harry expressed his disappointment at not turning up any clues. "I'd hate to think I'd find Joanna in a place like that."

★ ★ ★ ★ ★

In the darkened beer garden where Joanna and her companions found a booth and ordered sandwiches and a pitcher of beer, Jones became more intoxicated.

"Let's have us a little kiss, huh, Josie?" He thrust his face into the curve of Joanna's neck.

"Stop it!" She pushed him away.

"Hey, you're a feisty little pony."

Repulsed and frightened, Joanna looked at Peach for a clue as to what to do, but Peach remained focused on Smythe's witless conversation. "I think it's time to go, *Priscilla*," Joanna said pointedly, pushing aside her half-finished sandwich.

"What's your hurry?" Jones pawed at her, trying to kiss her.

"I said stop it!" She grabbed hold of his ear and tugged as hard as she could. He howled in pain and lurched back, his elbow knocking his beer glass off the table. Joanna seized the opportunity to brace her foot against his thigh and shove him from the seat. He hit the floor with a thud, a startled look on his face.

Joanna slipped out of the booth. "Are you coming, Peach?" Not waiting for an answer, she ran out into the street.

"What's wrong with you?" Peach scolded as she hurried to catch up. "Don't you know anything about men?"

"I know those two are awful."

Peach giggled. "Guess they *didn't* have much to recommend them."

"If you want someone to take *me* to supper," Joanna said, "you'll have to find someone a little more classy than . . ."—Joanna saw the humor then, too—". . . than Jones and Smythe."

Both girls convulsed with laughter under the streetlamp.

243

CHAPTER TWENTY-EIGHT

A shiny rig pulled by a small gray mule stood in front of Claire's apartment when she and Harry returned from the theater. Randy jumped down from the buggy and came toward them. "Claire, where were you? I got worried."

"I'm sorry, Randy. You remember Harry Graham, from the bank."

"Hello, Plank," Harry said cordially.

Randy extended his hand. "I didn't recognize you in the dark, Mr. Graham." He hesitated, puzzled as to why Claire would be with the banker.

"We've been looking for Joanna," Claire explained. "We went to the theaters. I thought she might have applied for a job as a dancer."

There was an awkward moment before Harry said abruptly, "I'll say good night then, Claire. If there's anything I can do . . ."

"You've been very helpful," Claire said. "Thank you. For everything."

After watching him get back into the hack and drive away, Claire and Randy started toward the apartment.

"How come Graham's in on this?" he asked.

"McKenzie Tate sold my building for me." The excitement of her recent venture spilled over. "And so quickly. I never imagined such a thing. And, Randy, I came out with a nice profit. When I went to the bank to open an account, Harry was very kind. He offered to help find Joanna."

Randy stopped in his tracks. "So it's Harry, is it?"

"He asked me to call him Harry. He's just being nice to a bank client. Oh, Randy, that money in the bank is going to buy financial independence for me someday. I intend to make it grow until . . . until I have so much money I won't know what to do with it all." When she spread her arms to illustrate the scope of her ambition, he clasped her around her waist and lifted her onto the bottom step of the apartment stairs.

"You're not the only one who's gonna be rich," he teased. "I asked Graham for *two* thousand, and he's gonna loan it to me, I know he is."

"*Two* thousand?"

"With two thousand, we'll have enough to expand just the way I'd hoped. Warren may be a little nervous about borrowin' so much, but he'll go along when he sees the kind of business we can build with it. I've been out all afternoon lookin' at locations."

"Would you like some coffee before you start back?" she asked.

"I better not. Got to be up early to deliver this rig to a customer comin' in from Denver."

"I'm very proud of you, Randy."

"You ain't seen nothin' yet, my dear lady." He kissed her lightly on the lips. "That's to hold you till we have time to do it proper."

She watched his long stride carry him out to the buggy. He swung aboard, and the little jenny trotted off, harness jingling.

Claire climbed the stairs still feeling Randy's kiss on her lips. How could she be thrilled by his touch, when only moments before she had felt so comfortable with Harry Graham? Someone she hardly knew. The attentions of a man like Harry Graham could make a woman forget her vow of independence, so it certainly didn't seem practical to get to know him better. Then again, maybe she should, since she felt that most men became less desirable the better she knew them. Except Randy. His good qualities constantly surprised her. She still felt a pleasant glow as she opened the door to the apartment.

But Joanna's absence hit her like a physical blow. The apartment was tomb-like without her. Claire walked into the darkened bedroom, sat down on the bed, and wept.

Early the next morning, Randy and Warren delivered Sugar and the buggy to the Denver customer, then spent the morning canvassing the downtown area for a possible location for their second livery. Just a block behind the depot they saw a sign on an old adobe warehouse: *For Sale, Inquire Within.*

"Sure would be handy for travelers wantin' rigs," Warren commented.

"It's plenty big, too," Randy said as they walked in through the wide double doors. Threading their way between stacks of stored lumber, they came to a small office where a watchman was dozing in his chair, feet on the desk. Randy soon had him awake and explaining that the building was owned by a lumber company that had moved out to Monrovia, closer to the new subdivisions. He pointed out the advantages: thick sturdy walls and floor, plenty of space, water piped in to a sink, even a small, fenced yard in back with a horse tank. They discovered at least two of the disadvantages themselves: small windows limiting the light, which could be remedied somewhat by opening the large double doors front and back, plus discoloration on the rafters indicating a leaky roof.

"It'll do," they agreed.

After their inspection of the premises they stopped at the depot to check out the trains going to Monrovia. If the loan came through from the bank, Randy planned to call on the warehouse owner. As they stood before the big chalkboard trying to decipher departure times, someone tugged Randy's sleeve. He turned to see a boy, small for his adolescent years, with a long face and misshapen nose.

"Hey, 'member me?" The homely youth flashed a broad grin that showed protruding front teeth. "On the train." He wore the same shabby knickers, his high-topped shoes still missing portions of their laces. "I'm Swifty," he said, holding out a grubby hand. "Swifty Lydick."

"I remember you." Randy shook hands. "Still working the trains?"

"Yeah, but I'm fixin' to settle in Los Angeles. Know of any work around here?"

"Can't say that I do."

"What work you fellas doin'? I could help you out with that." Swifty would never be accused of shyness.

"We started a livery. My sons work with us," Warren said, hoping to gently ease the boy from his determined course.

"I could get the word out for ya," Swifty persisted, "get customers in, supply 'em with the little necessities." He stood expectantly. "I got the power of persuasion."

"I'd like to help you, Swifty, but we can't afford to hire anyone just yet." Randy saw the disappointment on the boy's face. "How come you're out here by yourself? Don't you have any folks?"

"Naw. None to mention. I din't take to the ones that was keepin' me. Din't much like Boonville either. I aim to make a go of it out here." He screwed up his face in thought. "Tell you what. If I don't bring in customers, I

247

don't get paid. Whadaya say?"

Randy glanced at Warren, who could only shrug at the bantam youth's persistence. "Swifty, we're lookin' into a warehouse building behind the depot here. If we move in there, you stop by and we'll talk about this some more. Stanfield and Plank, that's our name. Livery and smithing."

"Gee, thanks. I'll keep an eye out." He scooted across the lobby and out the door, apparently to check out the warehouse.

After a hearty roast beef dinner with pie and coffee at a café, an indulgence that gave each of them a pang of guilt, Randy and Warren took a horse-drawn streetcar out toward Glendale to talk with a livery owner they had heard was selling out. But they didn't like his setup, and it was poorly located. Randy went back to talking about the warehouse behind the depot.

"I don't know, Randy," Warren said on the way back. "Maybe we should stick with the operation we got. Pico's a good location and my smithing is goin' good. We could lose what customers we got if we spread ourselves too thin."

"Look, I been bustin' a gut tryin' to find us a place downtown," Randy snapped. "We won't find a better spot than that warehouse."

Warren had never seen Randy out of sorts, but anyone who worked so hard was bound to lose patience once in a while. "You been doin' more'n your share, Randy. Maybe you should let up a little."

"I'll let up when I get that loan," Randy groused.

Harry Graham, too, was out of sorts that day, having awakened early with a knot in the pit of his stomach. P.B. and Daisy Mossburg would be arriving that afternoon. He wasn't concerned with his boss's scrutiny—the bank was functioning well—but Daisy's presence in Los Angeles was certain to complicate things. And just when his growing feelings for Claire Chadwick could not be ignored.

There was something special about Claire. Not just her beauty—she could certainly hold her own with the best of them—but the way she conducted herself, with a kind of independent pride and integrity uncommon in a woman. She was intelligent and sensible, and, according to Farley Dodd, a capable businesswoman. Now that was quite a package.

For a moment there in front of the Granada Theater, he had longed to take her in his arms, to further discover what it was about her that intrigued him. But she wasn't the sort of woman who could be charmed with a few soft words and a meaningful look. She deserved something solid and true. A woman of her quality made a man want to refurbish his soul and hold it out to her.

Daisy had never affected him like that. In fact no woman had. But now at thirty-five, casual flirtation, sexual games of any sort, no longer interested him. He had grown more and more impatient with meaningless liaisons. Daisy, anything but casual in her pursuit of him, did have a certain strength of character, but . . . well, the whole thing made his head ache.

After breakfast and the Saturday morning papers in the Overland dining room, Harry went to the bank to make certain that everything was ready for his boss's visit. He had been working on a plan to expand California Security to branches in Pasadena and Inglewood, which, along with the present location, would provide financial services to people over a wide area. He knew the plan was sound, but he was equally certain that P.B. would do his best to find flaws in it.

With everything at the office in readiness, Harry walked

to the depot and stood waiting on the platform amid the crowd gathering to meet the afternoon train. Farley Dodd appeared, dressed in his most dapper attire but anxiously adjusting his cravat and smoothing his goatee in anticipation of his wife's arrival.

They didn't have long to wait. As the train huffed into the station, stopped at the platform, and began to disperse passengers, the vendors and hawkers began their spiels. Harry spotted P. B. Mossburg, distinguished in his pearl-gray suit and Panama hat, followed by Daisy, looking as fresh as her name in a natural linen travel suit. They stood momentarily confused by the pandemonium.

"Tibby!" Farley ran to embrace his wife, an attractive brunette in navy blue, directly behind the Mossburgs.

P.B. caught sight of Harry and waved. But it was Daisy who hurried to him.

"Oh, Harry." She threw her arms around him. "I thought we'd never get here."

"Hello, Daisy." He returned her embrace awkwardly. Hadn't she accepted the fact that their little romance was over? His leaving her that night, deliberately and cruelly, should have discouraged her. He hadn't written her. Yet here she was, entangling herself in his arms and in his life again as if nothing had changed.

P.B. pushed through the crowd. "What a trip!" he shouted above the din. "Luxury Pullman. Fine dining car. Beautiful scenery. Great way to travel."

"When word gets around," Harry agreed, shaking P.B.'s hand, "you won't be able to stop folks from coming out here."

"And we'll be ready for them, won't we, Harry?"

"I want you to meet a new friend," Daisy said, pulling him toward Farley's wife. "Harry, this is Tibby Dodd."

"Mr. Graham, Farley wrote me about you." Tibby extended her hand, her direct gaze and warm smile justifying Farley's pride in her. "Farley, dear, this is Daisy Mossburg and her father, Phineas Mossburg."

After greetings all around and much excited talk about train trips, cross-country travel, and what they had seen of California so far, Harry engaged a three-seated buckboard to carry the new arrivals and their luggage to the Overland Hotel where P.B. had reserved rooms for himself and Daisy.

"I hope my quarters aren't too cramped," Farley told his wife as they sat together on the backseat. "As soon as we find a house, we'll have the rest of our things shipped."

"Oh, Farley, I like it here already."

Holding her close, he kissed her temple. "I like it even more now that you're here, my dear."

P.B., sitting with the driver on the front seat, struck up a conversation about the burgeoning population in Los Angeles and the prospects for further growth, while Daisy occupied the middle seat with Harry, her arm looped with his.

"Is California everything you had hoped, Harry?" she asked earnestly.

"Yes, I think it may be."

"And you don't miss Chicago?"

"I've been too busy to notice," he said.

Her voice softened. "I've missed you. Terribly."

Harry turned to her. "Daisy, I . . ."

She touched her fingertips to his lips. "You needn't explain, Harry. I don't expect a miracle."

PART THREE

CHAPTER TWENTY-NINE

Days passed, and Claire began to doubt the wisdom of simply waiting for Joanna and Peach to return home. She used her Sunday off to visit the dance teacher whose name she was given at the theater. Setting out early, wearing a gingham dress suitable for the warm June weather and a wide-brimmed hat she had purchased to ward off the sun, she would have relished the walk had she not been filled with anxiety. Her spirits were further dampened by the dance teacher's statement that she had never seen or heard of Joanna Chadwick, and that her rehearsal group had had no recent inquiries for membership.

To quell her disappointment, Claire turned her attention to a realty office whose front window displayed placards announcing the availability of both residential and commercial properties.

"Yes, ma'am," the brusque salesman replied when she inquired about investment possibilities. "I have one property here, a fine brick home just offered for sale." He pushed a flyer across the desk. "Part of the Los Feliz tract. An outstanding property. We're showing it today, and in this market I guarantee it won't last long. If you and your husband are interested, I suggest you take a look." Claire recognized the address as being only a few blocks from the home of Vanda Kolinski, and she decided to visit Vanda before looking at the house.

Vanda clucked with delight to see Claire on her doorstep. "Come in. Come in." She swung the door open, smiling a warm welcome. "Your girl, she come back?"

"No, not yet. I just came to see how you are doing."

Vanda gestured toward the dining room, where one place was set at the table. "Look, I eat by myself." She whisked another place setting from the sideboard, and before Claire could protest Vanda was dishing up *golabkis*.

Claire explained that she had the money to repay the $400 Vanda had loaned her, and that she would deposit it for her at California Security if Vanda would go to the bank and open an account. With that agreed upon, Claire invited her to go along to see the house for sale. Vanda took only a few minutes to put on her white high-button shoes, the new pongee dress, and a perky summer hat trimmed with forget-me-nots.

The house for sale was a stately colonial built of ochre brick with a terra-cotta tile roof and two yucca plants standing like sentinels on either side of the heavy front door. Claire was impressed with the attractive design of the leaded windows and the fine carpentry work on the open staircase, moldings, and woodwork. Of course it was much too expensive, but the salesman insisted that $1,000 would secure the deal until the closing. Then the balance would be due.

"Buy this house," Vanda said. "I like you for neighbor."

"I can't afford to live in a place like this, Vanda. If I bought it, it would be only for an investment to be resold as soon as possible."

"I will loan you the money."

"What!" The idea was so preposterous that a brief laugh caught in Claire's throat. Then her brow furrowed and she stared at her friend. "Are you saying that you would loan me the entire cost of the house?"

Vanda nodded happily. "And I charge you big interest."

Claire pondered the outrageous offer. "I'll think about it tonight. If I decide to do it, I'll withdraw the earnest money from the bank tomorrow."

"No, it be sold by then. You pay now." Vanda opened her bag and took out a roll of bills. "One t'ousand, ya?"

"Vanda!" Claire lowered her voice so she wouldn't be overheard. "You mustn't carry so much around with you."

"I know." She grinned impishly. "But lucky I do, ya?"

Claire left with a preliminary bill of sale for the property and a promise from Vanda to go to California Security Bank the next morning and deposit every penny of her remaining cash—a large part of which she was willing to loan to Claire so that Claire could purchase the elegant Los Feliz home. In return, Claire would make up a contract between them that would spell out regular payments to Vanda until the home was resold and the entire loan balance paid.

Feeling some trepidation about her deeper venture into real estate, Claire decided to make one more Sunday call. She hadn't seen the Stanfields for a few weeks, and she wanted to tell Warren about some farmland Farley Dodd had mentioned. The barn looked much the same as she approached from the streetcar line, except for an additional sign on the door that read, *Signs Painted*.

She peered in through the open door. At a worktable near the front window, surrounded by bits of lumber, cans of paint and turpentine, drawing tools, and paintbrushes, a young woman was tracing letters on a large oval sign.

"Birdie?"

Claire hardly recognized her. Gone were the sallow skin, hollow eyes, and thin frame sagging with fatigue. This woman, tanned and strong, her fair hair streaked by the sun, looked at her through clear amber eyes. "Claire!" She broke into a vibrant smile and hurried to welcome her friend.

"Birdie, you . . . you look wonderful."

"California does it to folks, I guess." She seemed pleased by Claire's compliment. "I'm feelin' real good now. I'm paintin' signs."

Claire glanced at several of the finished products. "You're good at it."

"I am, ain't I?" Then, with concern, "Randy told us about Joanna. Any word?"

"Nothing yet."

Birdie gently touched Claire's arm. "She'll be back. I know she will."

"I'm sure you're right," Claire said without conviction. Then, sensing the unusual quiet, "Where is everybody?"

"Warren and Randy are out lookin' for another place, the boys are playin' baseball on the vacant lot down the road, and Stella's taggin' after 'em." She grinned happily. "The kids like it here real good. And so do I. Even livin' in this barn. We started goin' to a little church not far from here." Her voice held a note of pride. "I joined the Ladies Aid."

While the women chatted, Birdie continued working on a sign due to be delivered the next day. "I'm bringin' in a little money now, so we may be gettin' us a better place real soon," she said.

By the time Warren and Randy got back the children were home, and Birdie had invited Claire to stay for supper.

"We found an old adobe warehouse that will work for us," Randy reported. "It's right behind the depot, but we'll have to wait and see if the bank gives us the loan." Then, turning his attention to Claire, he announced to the others, "Claire's bought some property, too."

"Bought and *sold*," she corrected. "And I'm afraid I took the plunge again this afternoon. I'm buying a house out near Vanda Kolinski's."

"You sure don't waste any time."

"Just keep your fingers crossed for me that prices continue to go up till I can sell it for a profit."

"You will," young Eddie piped up.

"What a dope," Daniel chided. "You don't know nothin' 'bout buyin' stuff."

Eddie defended himself with a grimace aimed at his brother. "Do, too. Leastwise, I will when I'm growed up."

"You're growed up now, Eddie," little Stella said earnestly.

Birdie laughed. "I hope before then we'll have us a house."

"I don't like houses," Eddie said. "I like it here in the barn with Sugar."

"That mule's Eddie's pet," Warren explained. "Follows him around beggin' for sugar, then lets him climb on at that old stump and ride around the yard bareback." He tousled the boy's blonde curls.

Randy turned to Claire. "Guess who we ran into at the depot. Remember that newsboy on the train? Swifty Lydick?"

"I do," spouted twelve-year-old Tucker. "He was swell." They all laughed at Tucker's admiration for the streetwise youth.

"He's quit the railroad and wants to stay in Los Angeles," Randy continued, "so we told him when we get the warehouse set up, he could help us around the place, meet the trains, that sort of stuff."

"But I thought I was gonna do that," Tucker protested.

"There'll be plenty to do for both of you when we get the new livery open."

"Incidentally, Warren," Claire said, "Mr. Dodd mentioned some farmland out in what's called Cahuenga Valley. He said north of Foothills Road there's farmland that's frost-free even during the coldest winters. I thought maybe you'd like to go out there and take a look at it."

"Good for growing oranges?"

"He said there's a strip of land a mile and a half wide that gets moderating ocean breezes. Farmers are starting to raise oranges and lemons, avocados, even tropical fruits like bananas and pineapple, on what was once just rangeland for sheep."

Warren looked at her wistfully. "Sure wish we could afford somethin' like that."

"Don't take no money to look," Birdie prompted.

"No, I s'pose it don't." He touched her hand affectionately.

Claire hadn't been fully aware of how much she missed all of them, and Birdie's concern for Joanna made her realize the importance of good friends, especially women friends. Only a woman, she thought, a mother, could fully understand what another mother felt. When the time came to leave, she reluctantly prepared to do so.

"I'll drive you," Randy offered.

She shook her head. "Thank you, Randy, but it's too long a trip both ways. I can catch the streetcar and be home well before dark."

"I'll walk with you to the car line then."

"Me, too," Eddie said.

"I want to go," Stella begged, jumping up and down.

"All right," Birdie said, "we'll all go."

So Claire ended her visit basking in the affection of good friends as they all walked together to the streetcar stop.

CHAPTER THIRTY

Farley Dodd arrived late at the office on Monday morning. "Tibby got here on Saturday," he told Claire, "and yesterday we went for a buggy ride to give her the feel of the place." He went to the window and gazed out over the city. "She loves Los Angeles! And she's very pleased about my plans to run for mayor. That's something I could never have hoped to do back in Chicago."

"I'm looking forward to meeting her."

"As a matter of fact, I'm giving a dinner party at the hotel on Saturday evening," Dodd said. "A welcoming party for my Tibby. We'd both be pleased if you'd come."

The invitation surprised Claire. She was, after all, merely an employee, hardly in the same social class with respectably married matrons like Tabitha Dodd. She would indeed like to go, but Saturday was Joanna's sixteenth birthday, and Claire hoped desperately to be celebrating with her daughter. Still, if Joanna hadn't returned by then . . . "I'd be delighted to come," she said.

"And I'm sure Tibby will need your advice on . . . well, womanly things," he continued, "the best dressmakers, appropriate charity organizations, cultural activities . . ."

Claire had never in her adult life enjoyed the luxury of time and means to pursue such things. "I'll be happy to help in any way I can," she assured him.

Then, taking advantage of his fine mood, she ventured, "Mr. Dodd, I've made a rather interesting investment that I'd like your opinion on." She told him about the brick house, receiving not only his enthusiastic approval, but also his regret that he hadn't seen it first. He suggested that if she wanted further information on the property, she should look up records of the Los Feliz area at the recorder's office.

Taking his advice, she used her lunchtime to walk to City Hall. In the recorder's office she discovered that the lot on which the brick house stood had once been part of the 7,000-acre Los Feliz Rancho, originally granted to Don Jose Vincente Feliz. Upon his death, the land was inherited by Maria Ybnacia, widow of one of his sons, who then married a man named Don Jose Maria Verdugo. But the property remained in Maria's hands, and when she died in 1861 her heirs sold it for one dollar per acre. In 1882 the tract came into the hands of Colonel Griffith J. Griffith. Fine residences were being built in the western and southern portions, and there was speculation, Claire learned from the clerk, that Griffith might offer the remaining wilderness of more than 3,000 acres to the City of Los Angeles for a public park. Claire was ecstatic. Such a location was well worth the price she would have to pay for the property.

She left the recorder's office feeling a certain pride in being able to play even a small part in the evolution of the historic Spanish ranchos. Her new sense of area history prompted her to take a short detour into the old part of town, to stroll through the heart of *El Pueblo de Nuestra Senora la Reina de Los Angeles*—The Town of Our Lady the Queen of Angels—that had stood since 1781, more than 100 years.

The Church of Our Lady still dominated the old square, and a hotel built after the Civil War, Pico House, the city's first three-story structure, stood next to the historic Merced Theater. She strolled around the dusty plaza where idlers sat in the sunshine on the rim of the old fountain watching the horse-drawn traffic around them. Others stretched out for a midday siesta in patches of shade from a row of tall cypress trees. A jail and several saloons, squat adobe structures, stood in various stages of dilapidation. Claire found it interesting that though the old adobe settlement had nearly crumbled away, the Spanish names remained, marking streets and landmarks all over the area.

Claire remembered that one of Farley Dodd's books was a history of California, so when she got back to the office, and he went out to lunch with a client, she took it from the shelf and, while eating her sandwich at her desk, she thumbed to the section on the pueblo of Los Angeles. In the early days, the text verified, the tiny settlement, built on mesa land in a sharp bend of the Los Angeles River (originally named the Portiuncula River, after the little church in Assisi where St. Francis prayed), was merely a stopping place on a crude, meandering trail through the cactus-covered hills, *cahuengas,* the Mexicans called them. Cahuenga Pass was the gateway to the deep sands of the San Fernando Valley and to *El Camino Real,* the principal passage up the coast. Travelers from the pueblo, herds of cattle, bands of sheep, or ox-drawn freight wagons starting out from the pueblo in the morning could cross the hills in less than a day's journey.

The Spanish, establishing a succession of missions along the California coast to encourage settlement, founded the Mission San Gabriel Archangel a few miles above the pueblo, then brought twelve reluctant families up from Sonora, Mexico, to inhabit the settlement. For many years the squalid El Pueblo de Los Angeles, dozing under the desert sun on that dry and disheartening terrain, was home to fewer than 150 souls.

Claire found this information fascinating. She learned that it had long been the custom of the Spanish government to grant large tracts of Spanish-owned land around the world to Spanish noblemen who would colonize those territories. As early as 1783, the king of Spain began bestowing huge California tracts on dozens of Spanish dons. At least one of these tracts, granted to Don Manuel Nietos, covered 350,000 acres. Among the many others receiving large grants were Don Jose Vincente Feliz, Don Jose Maria Verdugo, Don Antonio Yorba, Don Juan Jose Dominquez, and Don Francisco Reyes. When California passed from Spain to New Spain (Mexico) in 1822, the practice continued; large parcels of unoccupied land were offered at no charge to encourage further colonization, and a successful petitioner could claim ranchos as large as 44,000 acres merely by submitting a simple sketch showing recognizable natural landmarks to identify their lands.

Reading further, Claire determined that after California's 1846–47 revolt against Mexico, which consisted of only a few skirmishes, Mexican General Andres Pico signed a peace treaty that annexed the territory to the United States. The 1848 discovery of gold at Sutter's Mill in the Sacramento Valley followed immediately upon this annexation, and with this promise of riches the Territory of California was taken into the Union as a state in 1850.

Claire was intrigued with the huge ranchos. With so strong a presence in California, why had Mexico given over such a vast amount of land so easily?

When Farley Dodd returned from his luncheon meeting, Claire had to put the book aside to do the copy work on the client's new venture. It wasn't until the next day during her usual solitary lunch period that she again found time to pursue an answer to her looming question: How had the

United States acquired California so easily from Mexico?

She found the answer by going back to earlier accounts of the state's history. With the advent of sea trade along the coast, ships braving the dangerous mudflat in San Pedro Bay soon discovered some profitable cash crops: cowhides and tallow from the expansive ranchos, oil and whalebone from the whales that moved up and down the coast, and oil from the livers of sharks that infested the waters of the bay. A ship could often spear more than 100 sharks in one day, and as late as 1862, whaling vessels could count on harpooning and harvesting at least one whale every twenty-four hours.

While they were about it, the ships also delivered foreign goods and purchased supplies in the Los Angeles pueblo, and though Spanish law prohibited it, no one objected to this lucrative trade, since the great landowners and the padres at Angel Gabriel Mission were beneficiaries.

Into this milieu came Joe Chapman, member of a pirate crew captured while raiding the great Ortega rancho near Santa Barbara and taken to Angel Gabriel Mission to be executed. Chapman, a Nordic sailor from Massachusetts and master craftsman, managed to charm his Spanish captors out of killing him. In return, he built for the mission a water-run gristmill, the first in California, and a small schooner for sea otter hunting, then supervised completion of the pueblo's Church of Our Lady. On the basis of all this benevolence, Chapman was given a pardon, providing he would renounce his American citizenship, become a Catholic, and swear allegiance to the king of Spain. All of this he did. Immediately upon gaining his freedom, he returned to the splendid Ortega ranch where he wooed and married the don's beautiful daughter, Guadalupe. The newlyweds were given a rancho near the Angel Gabriel Mission, and outlaw

Joe Chapman became the first gringo grandee, Don Jose.

Upon hearing of Chapman's good fortune, another wanderer, Joe Pryor from Santa Fe, also joined the Holy Roman Church, took the Mexican oath of allegiance, and promptly married into the wealthy Sepulveda family, thereby also coming into the title Don Jose, plus ownership of a sizable orchard and vineyard.

The idea caught on like wildfire. Jack Temple, a Massachusetts merchant, married Senorita Rafael Cota and became Don Juan, owner of the Los Cerritos rancho, upon which Long Beach was later platted. Abel Sterns, a Massachusetts trader, wed Dona Arcadia Bandini and became Don Abel, owner of the great Los Alamitos rancho. Johann Groningen, a German, married into the Feliz family and assumed the title Don Domingo.

A Connecticut Yankee named Jonathan Warner married into the Pico family and became Don Juan Jose, owner of two great ranchos, one near Los Angeles, one near Santa Barbara. Hugo Reid, a Scotsman newly arrived in Los Angeles, surveyed his prospects and wed the daughter of the chief of the Gabrielino Indians and took over the entire reservation, the vast Santa Anita rancho, later made famous by its subsequent owner, Elias J. "Lucky" Baldwin, who planted long lines of eucalyptus trees and built a horse-racing empire on it, along with the towns of Arcadia and Monrovia. And a man named Ben Wilson won the lovely Senorita Ramona Yorba and the equally lovely San Pasqual ranch, which later became Pasadena, claiming the title Don Benito and the privilege of naming Mount Wilson for himself.

Claire was beginning to understand. By marrying eligible senoritas and the lands that went with them, these lucky—if not calculating—gringos wedded the land. And though each had sworn allegiance to Mexico, when the United States announced it was taking over California, all the gringo dons suddenly became American patriots. Though many pretended to support Mexican control of California, many served as spies against Mexico, fought on both sides, or simply got drunk together before a skirmish and watched from a safe distance.

So this was the legacy of the ranchos. Claire closed her eyes, visualizing the succession of California landowners: first the proud Spaniards, then the pious Mexicans, followed by the gringo dons and subsequent ranch land owners who, disappointed by cattle and sheep raising and impatient with agricultural difficulties, were carving up the gigantic tracts to sell to the hopeful newcomers now pouring into the state by the thousands. People like Claire herself.

Late in the day, Randy came by with the news that Harry Graham had approved his loan. "Imagine that, Claire. He's loaning me two thousand dollars!" He pulled a chair up next to hers and spread on the desk the note he had signed as well as the contracts on both properties. Then, raising one eyebrow in his appealing quizzical expression, "Have you ever stopped to think how handy it is, you workin' for Dodd?"

"I'm well aware of it." She was also aware of Randy Plank's growing stature. She couldn't help comparing the lanky youth who did odd jobs around Kohl's Café back in Westport with the broad-shouldered man responsible for building the Stanfield and Plank livery into a successful venture in such a short time. He also had cultivated a handlebar mustache, glossy auburn like his hair, which defined his face handsomely.

"Randy, do you have any relatives out here?" she asked. "There's a dancer at the Barbary Theater named Priscilla Plank. I saw her name on the marquee."

"Priscilla Plank?" He shrugged. "Maybe a long lost cousin." He thought for a moment, then said, "Might be interesting to find out. How about you and me taking in the show tonight?"

CHAPTER THIRTY-ONE

In front of the Barbary Theater, Claire and Randy checked the placard announcing comedienne Priscilla Plank's appearance. Randy purchased tickets, and they found seats close enough to see the performers clearly.

The lights dimmed, and the show opened with a slapstick comedy team, Keegan and O'Malley, who made Claire blush with their suggestive repartee.

> *O'Malley: Keegan, you been visitin' widow O'Shaughnessy every night for some time. Don't you think it's time you married the lady?*
>
> *Keegan: I would, but then where would I spend me evenin's?*

> *Keegan: O'Malley, do you understand French kissing?*
>
> *O'Malley: Only if it's translated into the Irish tongue.*

"Sorry, Claire," Randy whispered as the jokes became more risqué. "Do you want to leave?"

"Not until we see the dancers." Though she blushed at the coarse humor, they sat through Keegan and O'Malley, followed by an aging vaudeville couple's song-and-dance routine, a magic act featuring live birds, and a quartet of barbershop singers. Then the band struck up a lively cakewalk and a line of dancing girls in bright green Southern-belle costumes strutted onto the stage. As each girl appeared she turned her back, bent over from the waist, and to a syncopated boom from the bass drum flipped up her skirt, revealing her ruffled pantaloons. One of the girls wore no skirt at all, only abbreviated pantaloons, her thin legs encased in lavender and yellow polka-dot stockings.

The garish costumes, teased hairdos, and rouged cheeks caused Claire to doubt momentarily whether she would be able to recognize Joanna should she appear. Then there she was, the one on the end—her copper hair unmistakable.

"Joanna!" Claire rose from her seat, fingertips to her mouth to muffle her outcry, but Randy caught her arm and eased her back into her seat. It was Joanna all right, stepping and turning, fawning and simpering across the stage. "It's Joanna," she whispered, tears of relief springing to her eyes.

Randy nodded. "And look at the one in the polka-dot socks. That's Peach Oliver."

Suddenly Peach took an undignified fall, rolling her eyes suggestively as she sat facing the audience, elbows on her widespread knees. She gave the audience time to laugh, then got back in step with the other dancers. Claire could now easily recognize Peach's pretty face under the painted-on freckles, and soon the new comedienne's budding talent also became evident. Several times during the dance, she drew attention to herself by stumbling, mugging, and wise-cracking.

"She's pretty funny," Randy whispered.

But Claire saw only that Peach was making herself and the others look cheap and bawdy. Joanna pranced through the routine like a veteran. Several banjo players in blackface shuffled into view, strumming a lively tune as they comically ogled the Southern belles. When the embarrassingly suggestive number ended, wild applause, whistles, and cheers erupted from the audience.

Claire tugged Randy to his feet. "Quick," she said, "before the girls leave the theater." They hurried backstage where they watched as the last of the Southern belles clambered up a narrow staircase to a dressing room. Some were hastily stripping off parts of their costumes, and Randy discreetly waited near the door while Claire followed them up the stairs. Lining the walls of the long cramped room were dressing tables with mirrors that reflected the clutter of pomatum and rouge pots, powder dabbers, combs, and brushes. Joanna, standing at a dressing table, saw Claire's reflection in the looking glass.

"Mother!" She whirled around, her surprise revealing both dismay and delight. "What are you doing here?"

Claire clasped her daughter in her arms. "Oh, Joanna. Are you all right?"

"I'm fine." Joanna smiled happily as she stepped back to show off her costume. "Look, I'm a dancer now, Mother."

"Yes, I see."

"I'm getting paid, too. Mother, it's such fun."

"I'm sure it is. But, Joanna, how could you have left like you did? Without a word? Without getting in touch? I've been so worried."

"I was going to let you know as soon as I got settled enough so you wouldn't make me come home."

Her statement shocked Claire. "Don't you want to come home?"

"Are you and Randy still carrying on?" Joanna tossed her head haughtily.

"Carrying on? Randy and I are just friends. You know that."

"I don't know any such thing."

"Was it because of Randy that you left?"

"What did you expect me to do?" Joanna's voice rose

271

angrily. "Watch you make a fool of yourself?"

"Is that what you think?" Claire glanced around at the other dancers, who rushed about, changing into street clothes.

"Well, aren't you? You're too old for . . ." But she didn't finish, for at that moment Randy appeared in the doorway.

"Hello, Joanna." His casual tone did not reveal how much he had overheard. "You're quite a dancer."

"Thanks." Joanna flopped down on a chair.

"Are you through here?" Randy asked cheerfully. "I'd like to take you two ladies to the ice-cream parlor."

"What about Peach? She lives with me at the boarding-house."

"Peach can come, too," Randy said. "Where is she?"

"She'll be along. She's talking with Bernie." Joanna smiled at him then as if she had forgotten her harsh words with her mother.

"You get changed," Randy said. "I'll wait outside."

Peach, rushing into the room, bumped into him in the doorway.

"Easy there." He grabbed hold of her to help her regain her balance. "You've taken enough tumbles for one night."

"Well, Randy Plank." Peach's eyes lit up behind the freckles and circles of vermilion on her cheeks. "Did you see the show?"

Randy nodded. "You girls were real good."

"He wants to take us to the ice-cream parlor," Joanna said.

"Oh, piffle. We can't." Peach looked disappointed. "Bernie wants to talk to us about a new number."

Joanna groaned. "Now?"

"There's a choreographer down here from San Francisco just for tonight."

"Peach, Blanche is worried about you," Claire interjected. "She came to see me."

"She did?" the girls said in surprised unison.

"You two have been most inconsiderate. Not letting us know where you were."

Peach shrugged. "Maybe I'll go see Blanche tomorrow." Then she added, "But I'm not going back to Lorenzo's."

"Come and stay with Joanna and me for a while," Claire offered.

"But we have to work, Mother," Joanna protested.

"I'm not asking you to quit your jobs." Claire searched for a convincing argument. "You could save rent if you lived at home."

The girls looked at each other, then Joanna shook her head. "We have noon rehearsals every day. Three matinees a week and six evening performances. Going back and forth would take too much time."

Peach agreed. "The boardinghouse is a lot more convenient."

Claire sensed that forcing Joanna to come home was not the solution. She would only run away again if she didn't want to be there. But if she were allowed to keep dancing, just until school started, perhaps she would get it out of her system.

"Joanna, next Saturday is your birthday, and Mr. Dodd has invited us to a party. A very nice affair at the Overland Hotel. I'd like you to have a new dress as your birthday present."

"Can we afford a new dress?"

"I think so. I've made some extra money recently. We'll splurge with something new for me, too—if we can find a dressmaker who'll work on such short notice."

"Sophie can make me a dress," Joanna said. "She's our

wardrobe lady here at the theater, and she sews beautifully."

"Well, all right," Claire agreed. "I think a pale pink would be nice with your hair. Voile, maybe, it's so hot now. Something with little sleeves and a sash. I could go with you to pick out the material. And you'll need shoes."

"Mother, I can buy my own material and shoes." Joanna stopped short, the $100 she had taken from her mother suddenly looming large between them. "I mean from my wages. We got paid today."

"What about the money you took, Joanna? Do you have any of it left?"

"Some of it. I'll pay you back, Mother. Every cent."

Claire sighed. "Won't you come home with me now, just for tonight, so we can talk about all this?"

"I'm tired, Mother. Besides it's so late, and my things are at the boardinghouse."

"All right. All right. But when will I see you? I have to work except at noon and during the evenings, the very times *you* seem to be working. Do you think you can get off for the Dodds' party?" Claire hoped the Dodds wouldn't mind her bringing Joanna. It was essential that Joanna be made to feel a part of her mother's life, and soon.

"No, I can't miss a performance," Joanna said, "but I can come after the show. I'll stay overnight with you after the party, and we'll have all day Sunday together."

"That will be wonderful." Claire gave her another hug.

"By the way," Randy said, "who is Priscilla Plank? Was she in the show?"

Peach beamed. "It's me, silly. I needed a name that sounded good with Priscilla, so I borrowed yours."

"Well, I'll be . . ." Randy chuckled. "Joanna, don't tell me you're usin' a made-up name, too."

Joanna grinned impishly while Peach, with a slight bow, gestured toward her. "Folks, meet Josephine Carter."

Next morning, having gone to the district attorney's office to report that Joanna was no longer missing, Claire arrived a few minutes late for work. She found a tall, attractive woman in her office. Elegantly coiffed, with light brown hair and merry brown eyes, the woman wore a summer frock of white lawn, nipped at the waist to show off her shapely figure. She carried a matching parasol.

"Claire?" she said in a warm, cultivated voice. "I'm Tibby Dodd."

Claire held out her hand. "Welcome to California."

"Farley speaks highly of you, Claire."

"He's very happy you're here at last."

"Yes, I've kept him waiting rather a long time, but now I can see that all my worries about the place were silly. It's actually a rather civilized place."

Claire laughed easily. "We all come to that realization."

Tibby smiled. "He tells me you're dabbling in real estate, too."

"I guess dabbling is the word."

"I'm sorry, I didn't mean to diminish your expertise. I know he relies on you."

"I do my best to absorb as much as I can, but in this crazy market . . ."

"We started hunting for a house yesterday but didn't find anything suitable. I was hoping you might know of something that Farley has overlooked. We'd like to be out of the downtown congestion."

The brick house whose title Claire now had in her possession would be perfect for the Dodds, Claire thought, but she had listed it for double what she paid. Farley Dodd

knew the original price and might resent the inflated increase. She couldn't afford to reduce the price just for him
when she could get the full asking price from someone else.
"I'll keep my eyes open for something," she said.

"I do hope you're coming to our party Saturday night,"
Tibby continued in her lyrical voice. "I'm so very eager to
get acquainted with everyone."

"Yes. And I'd like to bring my daughter, Joanna, if I
may. It happens to be her sixteenth birthday."

"Oh, by all means. I'll order a cake for her."

"That's kind of you."

"Farley and I love children." Tibby's dark lashes swept
her cheeks. "Unfortunately we've never been blessed."

Tibby seemed to be everything her husband claimed.
Warm, intelligent, cultured, and devoted to him. Claire
hoped they could become friends.

Determined that Mrs. Farley Dodd would not be the
only well-dressed woman at the party, Claire used her lunch
break to purchase ten yards of plisse-tucked silk taffeta in a
lovely heliotrope shade, ten yards of two-inch-wide ribbon
in a deeper violet, and matching pearl buttons. Carrying the
large parcel, she went to the bank and transferred into
Vanda's new account repayment of the original $400 loan,
plus the $1,000 earnest money for the Los Feliz house.
Then, seeing Harry Graham through the open door of his
office, she went in to tell him that she had found Joanna at
the Barbary Theater after all.

"She's all right?"

"Yes, she's fine," Claire said. "She has the notion that
she wants to be a dancer. I'm not sure it's the right thing—
that theater is rather tawdry, to say the least—but I've
agreed to let her continue until school starts."

"Are you sure that's wise?" Harry said.

"No, not really." She had hoped to be reassured, but Harry seemed to disapprove of her daughter's employment. Perhaps allowing Joanna to try her wings *was* wrong. But then again, what did Harry Graham know about raising a child? Was Harry looking at her in a different light now that she had a "wayward" daughter? Did he think she might be lax in her own moral principles? "Now that I know where Joanna is," she assured him, "I'll keep a close eye on her."

"That's probably an excellent idea." He chuckled, apparently amused.

Back at the office, Claire made sketches of the party gown she envisioned, and after work, she took the sketches and materials to Vanda's dressmaker, Mrs. Ramirez, a pleasant Mexican woman who took her measurements and promised to have the garment ready for fitting on Thursday evening.

It had been so long since Claire had anything new, let alone a fancy evening dress, that she hardly knew what would be appropriate for accessories. Perhaps the teardrop pearl earrings that Carter had given her for a wedding present, with her mother's pearl-trimmed comb for her hair. And Joanna could wear the tiny garnet-and-pearl ear bobs Claire had worn to her own coming-out party.

If this was to be their social debut, they must make the most of it.

CHAPTER THIRTY-TWO

After making down payments on both the adobe warehouse and the Pico barn, Stanfield and Plank had enough left of the $2,000 to buy a team of dappled mares, Dolly and Dot; a pinto saddle horse, Patches; a used buckboard and surrey; plus additional smithing equipment, leaving some in the bank for operating capital.

The lumber tenant immediately vacated the warehouse, and Randy hired two carpenters to build several stalls with feed bunks along one side and a sturdy wooden fence around the small corral area in back to accommodate boarding horses. Warren hired a blacksmith, a fellow named Rogers, to work at the new location. Warren preferred to remain at the Pico barn, where he had a steady stream of customers and Birdie needed his help in lifting and transporting her signs. Daniel, just turned eleven, assisted her by filling in the outlines on some of the easier lettering and found he was quite good at it. Tucker had been the chief groom and stable boy throughout the summer months, while Eddie begrudgingly kept an eye on his little sister, who had a tendency to stray too far in her explorations of the neighborhood.

While carpenters' hammers echoed through the adobe building, Warren helped Rogers set up the new forge, explaining the standards to which the new blacksmith would be held in both his work and his dealings with customers. Randy arranged billing and bookkeeping supplies in the little office in a back corner of the building, which would also serve as his living quarters. Thus engaged, they received their first customer.

"Hey there, gents!" It was Swifty Lydick, unkempt hair, protruding teeth and all. "You open for business?"

Randy greeted him tentatively, fearing he could become a pest.

"I need to rent your surrey." Swifty's sharp eyes took in the new layout.

"Got the money?" Randy asked.

"No, but I got two old ladies at the depot ready for a tour of the town. I'll pay you when I get back. I can hit the main attractions—from the old pueblo to the snazzy houses out in Vernon—in a little over an hour and a half." He pulled a large pocket watch from his tattered vest, his wide grin emphasizing his prominent overbite. "If I dazzle 'em with a spiel and a smile, I figure I can charge enough to pay you, pay me, and have some left over for my expansion fund."

Randy chuckled. "Well, Swifty, I don't see any other customers linin' up here yet for Dolly and the surrey. But I'll expect you back before the afternoon train gets in. I want you to meet it with the buckboard."

"Righto, Mr. Randy." Swifty fumbled with the harnesses hanging on the side wall near the stalls, making it clear he didn't know how to proceed. Randy showed him the rudiments of hitching Dolly to the surrey, and the youth drove off to his waiting customers.

Randy grinned after him. The kid was a go-getter all right. But it was probably best if they hired him at a fixed wage. He was much too resourceful as an independent operator, and if there was profit to be made Randy wanted it to go to Stanfield and Plank, not to Swifty Lydick's "expansion fund."

★ ★ ★ ★ ★

That evening, after Claire's fitting at the dressmaker's, she stopped by backstage at the Barbary where the performers were preparing for the show. Joanna, startlingly immodest in a flimsy camisole and the ruffled pantaloons, sat at the dressing table applying lip rouge. She smiled happily at seeing her mother, but turned her face away from Claire's kiss to avoid smudging her makeup. "It's swell of you to come."

"I brought you something to wear to the party." Claire showed her the garnet-and-pearl ear bobs. "I wore them at my own coming-out party."

Joanna held them to her ears before the mirror. "They're beautiful."

"They'll be a nice touch with your new dress. Did you find some material?"

"Yes, a pretty rose color. Satin, I think. Sophie's making it for me."

"Satin may be a little warm for this weather."

"It has short sleeves, Mother. And I bought some white summer shoes with little heels like Mrs. Kolinski's. Oh, I can't wait till the party. Would it be all right if Peach came, too? She feels left out since it's my birthday and all."

"No, dear, not this time."

"Oh, piffle!" Joanna's smile faded. "What can I tell her?"

"Just say it's a private party, that we aren't free to invite others."

After Joanna's assurance that she had everything she needed, that she knew where the Overland Hotel was, and that she would take a hack to the party immediately after the Saturday show, Claire left her amid the backstage confusion. Joanna would be with her all day Sunday and that would be the time to broach the subject of going back to school for the fall term. Claire took a horsecar to her street, then trudged on home to her apartment for a quick supper and a much-needed night's sleep.

McKenzie Tate, a red carnation in the buttonhole of his white linen suit, stood out from most of the clients who came into the office. His matching fedora and ivory-handled walking stick bespoke his growing prosperity.

"My dear Mrs. Chadwick, I may have another opportunity for you. I trust you still have the money you made on our previous collaboration."

"No, Mr. Tate. It's already invested in another property."

"A pity. I've discovered there's a nice return to be made on rentals. Do you realize there are literally thousands of people pouring into Los Angeles every week? Five trains a day from the East. Where are those people going to live? In my buildings, that's where. I've decided to build apartment houses."

"That's a good idea," Claire said. "It was difficult to find a rental when I came five months ago, but I understand it's nearly impossible now."

"Most folks like to rent while they look around for a good place to buy. There's so much shady advertising. If a lot lies in a rocky river wash or a stony canyon, the place is advertised as handy to building materials. If it's in a swamp, it claims water privileges. If out on the desert, it's touted as a natural health resort. There's no reason, Mrs. Chadwick, why you and I can't come out ahead by providing some decent intermediate housing. I want to treat 'em, not cheat 'em."

"I'm afraid I haven't anything left to invest at the moment," she said, wondering why he seemed so eager to include her in his plans.

281

"Leverage. That's the secret. All it takes is a minimum down payment. In a market like this, you simply cannot lose." He glanced toward Farley Dodd's office. "Is our legal leviathan here?"

"He's out this morning." The fact was, since Tibby arrived he had hardly been in the office at all.

"Would you please give him these papers?" Tate took a document from the inside pocket of his jacket. "I've purchased a rental building under construction out on Washington Street." Then, almost as an afterthought, he added brightly, "Mrs. Chadwick, how would you like to come to work for *me?*"

"Why, Mr. Tate, I . . ."

"I need someone to manage the new property. I'll double your salary, and if you can manage some kind of down payment, I'll give you a proportionate part ownership in the project. I feel if your money is in it, your heart will be in your work."

"But I told you," she said, "I haven't that kind of capital."

"What about the property you bought?"

"It's a handsome brick house in the Los Feliz Tract, but I have no idea how long it will take to sell."

"You've listed it?"

"Yes. For double what I paid."

"Good. If it doesn't sell in a week, triple it." He tipped his fedora. "Meanwhile, give some thought to my offer. I'm sure the proceeds of this Los Feliz house would be more than enough to get you started in the rental business." Then he was gone.

Claire sat stunned. Go to work for McKenzie Tate? Who *was* he anyway? She knew little about him except that he seemed to be amassing considerable real-estate holdings.

He was such a strange man, yet he seemed to be offering her an outstanding opportunity.

But how could she leave Farley Dodd? He had been so good to her, had taught her so much. She loved her job, and with his mayoral campaign coming up in a few months he would need her more than ever.

Neither alternative seemed to offer her more time with Joanna.

When she left the office at six, Harry Graham was waiting for her out front in a shiny rented buggy. "I thought maybe we could have dinner . . . if you're not spoken for." His tender gaze made her heart leap.

"If you don't mind stopping by the dressmaker's," she said. "I must pick up the dress I'm wearing to the Dodds' tomorrow night."

Harry offered his hand to steady her as she climbed into the buggy. "I hope you'll allow me to escort you to the party." He took his seat and flicked the lines to the dappled horse.

"Yes, I'd like that." Claire gave him the address of the dressmaker.

Should she tell him about McKenzie Tate's offer? She needed to talk with someone about it, and Harry Graham seemed exactly the right person. When she had related the details as she understood them, Harry asked, "What do you know about this Tate?"

"I know he has developed a business block in Pasadena. He gave me the chance to get started in real estate with that two-flat deal. He seems honest. A bit eccentric."

"I'll check on him for you," Harry said. "Maybe I can find out if he has any warts."

"I'd appreciate that. But even if McKenzie Tate's reputation is impeccable, I'd hate to leave Mr. Dodd. I've learned so much from him and he's been very good to me. I feel disloyal even thinking about going to work for someone else."

"Claire, you must do what's best for *you*."

"I don't know how he would manage without me."

Harry chuckled. "Your loyalty is commendable, but if it's in your best interest to move on then you should do so."

Suddenly her spirits soared like released doves. "Harry, thank you." She had to resist the impulse to throw her arms around his neck and kiss him. "I needed some encouragement," she confessed. "I'm rather new in the business world, you know."

Harry grinned at her. "I'd say that for a newcomer you're doing just fine."

CHAPTER THIRTY-THREE

Harry called for Claire just after dark on the evening of the Dodds' party. When she answered the door, his expression showed his delight in her transformation from a primly dressed businesswoman to a radiant lady in a ball gown.

"You look wonderful!" His gaze lingered on her for a moment, finding her eyes an even deeper blue with the heliotrope of her dress, its off-the-shoulder neckline emphasizing her creamy throat and bosom. She had arranged her hair in a high stylish pouf, adorned with her mother's pearl-trimmed comb, the teardrop pearls at her ears.

She responded playfully, "You look quite wonderful yourself." In his white tie and tails, he was truly as handsome as any man she had ever seen. And his brown eyes, with their mysterious flecks of green, seemed to reflect his growing feelings for her.

They clasped hands. "I'm a lucky man to be escorting such a lovely woman," he murmured.

"Thank you, Harry." She stepped away, adjusting the ribbon sash defining her slender waist above the bustled skirt. "Joanna is coming to the party, too, after her performance," she said.

"Good. I was beginning to wonder if I'd ever meet this girl."

"I'm hoping that after tonight she'll be ready to come back home."

Claire couldn't remember when she'd felt so light-hearted.

★ ★ ★ ★ ★

A string quartet played Strauss waltzes at one end of the gaslit Overland Hotel ballroom; at the other stood three tables beautifully set to seat twenty-four. As the party guests arrived, Farley Dodd welcomed each one and introduced his wife. Tibby Dodd looked stunning in a flounced gown of apricot voile with an exquisite cameo at her bare throat, her hair elegantly arranged high on her head.

"This is my dear Tibby," Farley said to the many friends he had made since he arrived in Los Angeles: District Attorney Nelson Haycroft and two of his staff attorneys, Mayor William W. Wallace, Chief of Police Clarence Feeney, and real-estate broker Roscoe Longworth, with whom Claire had listed the brick house, all with their wives; McKenzie Tate, Colonel Mercer Albright, Judge Stanley Fairchild, and Farley's ward captain Joe Biggs, each of whom arrived alone; and P. B. Mossburg with his daughter Daisy.

The Dodds greeted Claire and Harry warmly. "Good evening, Harry," Tibby said. "Claire, how nice to see you again."

"Hello, Mrs. Dodd."

"Please call me Tibby. And where is your daughter?"

"She'll be along a bit later," Claire said.

McKenzie Tate arrived right behind them, and after the Dodds' preliminary introductions, Harry drew Tate aside, eager to assess his attributes as Claire's potential employer. "I understand you've developed a business block in Pasadena." He took a glass of sherry from a tray offered by a white-gloved waiter. "I'm with California Security Bank. We're looking to expand to a couple of outlying towns, and I'm considering Pasadena."

"Oh, yes, indeed." Tate's fingers fluttered towards his

silk cravat. "Pasadena is the most promising of any of the new towns."

Mayor Wallace, learning that Claire was associated with Farley Dodd, engaged her in conversation. Guests rotated smoothly around the room, and Claire found each person most interesting, chatting on topics ranging from real estate and the boom economy to law enforcement and politics.

"If you gentlemen will excuse us . . ." Tibby appeared at Claire's elbow and led her to an attractive, dark-haired young woman in a stunning gown of butterscotch silk trimmed in black Belgian lace. "I want you to meet my new friend, Daisy Mossburg. We met on the train from Chicago," Tibby explained. "Daisy, this is Claire Chadwick. She works with Farley."

It was kind of Tibby to say "works *with*" instead of "works *for*," Claire thought, thus elevating her above mere clerical status.

"Don't tell me you're a native Californian." Daisy's dark eyes were warm and friendly.

"Heavens, no," Claire said. "In the five months I've been here I've only met one native—my dressmaker, Mrs. Ramirez."

Tibby scrutinized Claire's dress. "You mean a Mexican woman made your gown?"

"Yes. She's quite good, I think."

"Indeed she is." Daisy, fingering the web of ebony beads filling in her own low-cut neckline, spoke with little conviction.

Claire regretted having invited comparison of her dress to their haute couture and changed the subject. "I'm beginning to feel I belong here. I lived in Westport, Missouri, for fifteen years, but I was raised in Chicago."

"What a small world," Daisy said. "All three of us from

287

Chicago and we haven't met before."

It was clear to Claire why this was so. Daisy appeared to be a few years younger than she, and Tibby was probably close to forty. "My late father was Elsworth Newell," Claire continued. "He was in securities." It wasn't in her nature to make such a statement, but standing there in her California-made dress with two such elegantly gowned women prompted the boast.

"Then I'm sure my father must have known him," Daisy purred. "And your husband?" She apparently had noticed the wedding ring Claire wore for Joanna's sake.

"I'm divorced."

"Oh." Daisy gave her the look she usually got from women when she revealed her marital state—a look entirely different from the one she got from men. She didn't know which she detested more.

"Farley says Claire is an absolute treasure," Tibby gushed. "And I think Harry Graham thinks so, too." She rolled her eyes toward Claire. "I saw the way he was looking at you when you came in together."

Daisy's smile faded. "You and Harry came together?"

"Why, yes. Do you know him?"

"I used to," Daisy murmured.

"I believe he worked with your father in Chicago," Tibby said, "didn't he, Daisy?"

"If you'll excuse me . . ." Daisy gave Claire a withering look and turned away abruptly.

Tibby stared after her. "That's odd. Did I say something wrong?"

"I think Daisy may know Harry Graham rather well," Claire said.

"Oh, dear me. I had no idea . . ." Tibby was interrupted by a waiter informing her they were ready to serve. "Please excuse me, Claire." She joined her husband and they led the way to the three round tables, each of which accommodated eight guests in candlelit splendor.

Harry appeared at Claire's side, offered his arm, and they followed the others, finding their place cards at one of the tables with P.B. and Mrs. Mossburg, Roscoe Longworth and his wife, and McKenzie Tate, who was seated next to an empty place reserved for Joanna.

Daisy, who had assumed a false gaiety, was seated at the Dodds' table with widower Judge Fairchild, District Attorney Haycroft and Mayor Wallace and their wives. Claire was glad the district attorney was not at her table, lest he recall who she was and be reminded that in the past few days she had reported her daughter missing, then found. Claire had hoped Joanna would arrive before they started dinner, but apparently that was not to be.

"What time is it?" she whispered to Harry, who checked his pocket watch and told her it was almost ten. Joanna should arrive soon. Claire regretted the awkward situation; she had so wanted her daughter to have a memorable birthday.

Sixteen years ago today, just about this time of night, she had given birth to Joanna in the "convalescent" home in Westport. Sixteen long years of struggle. But now, here she was in Los Angeles, California, an independent woman with a profession—yes, an actual profession—and a start toward financial independence. And she was seated here beside Harry Graham in the company of some of the city's most prominent citizens. Only a few months ago she would have thought such things impossible.

McKenzie Tate elaborated for P. B. Mossburg the probability that Los Angeles would grow to the south and west, while broker Longworth touted new opportunities on the east side of the city. "Mayor Wallace bought property in Boyle Heights twenty years ago for five and ten dollars an acre," Longworth commented. "Now he's getting a hundred an acre for it. Why, I hardly have time to advertise a place before the price at least doubles. Some of the better properties have tripled."

"Do you suppose the price I paid for my Los Feliz house could actually triple?" Claire asked.

"No question about it," Longworth said. "Do you want me to raise the asking price?"

"Why not?" She smiled at Longworth as if casual dealing in real estate were an everyday matter for her.

Harry leaned closer. "You know, Claire," he said quietly, "this is the first time I've actually enjoyed one of these dinners." She felt his breath on her bare shoulder. "Being with you makes it seem . . . perfect somehow."

She didn't dare look at him lest the others notice the exquisite glow he kindled in her. "It's lovely for me, too," she said, following Tibby's lead in picking up her soup spoon.

Suddenly a muffled shout was heard at the door. "You can't go in there, miss. It's a private party."

"But I'm invited." It was Joanna's voice. Claire turned to see a young woman lunge into the room, the uniformed doorman tugging her arm to restrain her. Claire's gasp echoed those of most of the ladies in the room. Joanna was dressed in a low-cut pink satin gown that barely covered her breasts and clung tightly around her hips, both areas crudely decorated with red-dyed ostrich feathers. Her face was powdered and a beauty mark had been applied to the corner of her rouged lips. Her hair, ratted into an exaggerated pompadour, was anchored with a single red ostrich feather.

"Come on, miss," the doorman coaxed. "Don't give me no trouble now."

"Is that Joanna?" Harry turned to Claire just long enough to see her mortification, then he was on his feet and hurrying to the door. "Just a moment, Charlie," he called to the doorman. "The young lady is my guest."

"What?" Charlie sheepishly released his grip on Joanna's arm. "But, Mr. Graham, she . . ."

"Joanna, I'm Harry Graham," he said quietly. "A friend of your mother." He took her arm and led her toward the tables. "I'd like all of you to meet Joanna Chadwick," he announced to the guests. "She took part in a theatrical program tonight and didn't have time to change her costume. For a moment there, I didn't recognize her myself." His explanation produced a round of relaxed laughter.

Tibby rose from her table and went to Joanna. "My dear, you are absolutely fabulous." She tweaked one of the feathers, then offered her hand. "I'm Tibby Dodd."

Joanna smiled then, a bright and winning smile that dispelled the impression created by the gaudy dress and makeup. "Good evening, Mrs. Dodd. I'm sorry to be late."

"Don't give it another thought. We're only on the first course." Tibby looped her arm through Joanna's and said to the crowd, "I insisted this young thespian join us this evening because it's her birthday."

A few friendly birthday wishes came from the diners as Harry led Joanna to her place at the table. A waiter placed a soup plate before her.

"Good evening, Mother," Joanna said, completely at ease now.

"Good evening, my darling."

Joanna heard the tangle of emotions in her mother's voice. "I guess maybe my new dress isn't quite right," she whispered, looking about at the other ladies, "for a fancy party like this. But I wore the ear bobs, see." She brushed back the plume in her hair to reveal her mother's gift. "And the locket Mrs. Kolinski gave me. Thanks, Mr. Graham, for coming to my rescue. That doorman would have thrown me out."

"You know, I believe he would have." Harry grinned, starting belatedly on his vichyssoise.

"So you're Claire Chadwick's daughter." McKenzie Tate regarded Joanna with amused interest, while Harry introduced her to the Mossburgs and the Longworths, all of whom offered birthday greetings.

"Was this a school production, my dear?" Mrs. Mossburg asked.

"Joanna's involved with a rehearsal group," Claire improvised.

"I always liked the theater," P.B. stated in his forceful baritone. "Always wanted to run away and become an actor when I was a lad."

"Why, Phineas," his wife reprimanded. "You never told me that."

"Guess I just remembered. Of course my father would have tanned my britches if he'd gotten wind of it." He allowed the waiter to place the fish course before him.

"Dancing's what I really love," Joanna said sweetly.

"Dancing?"

Again Claire interrupted. "Joanna studied ballet back in Westport."

"Did she now?" P.B. smiled at her in a grandfatherly way. "Well, she's a talented little lady."

CHAPTER THIRTY-FOUR

Claire and Joanna lingered over a late breakfast at the apartment, Joanna telling her mother all about her entry into the world of theater: how quickly she had picked up the dance steps, how Peach was becoming a comedienne, and how she had come to know Lottie and the other girls, Bernie, and Sophie. She chatted gaily as they prepared a picnic lunch for the afternoon outing they had arranged with Harry Graham. She seemed blithely unaware that Harry's quick action had saved them both considerable embarrassment at the Dodds' party.

"Mother," Joanna said, suddenly serious. "A man has asked me to have supper with him, but . . . well, I've never gone out with anyone alone before . . . without Peach along, I mean."

"Joanna, you shouldn't be having supper with strangers . . . with or without Peach."

"Now don't be a fuddy-duddy, Mother. It's just for supper. He came backstage after the show and he's really very nice, but . . . well, he's older."

"Older? How much older?"

"Oh, I don't know. About your age maybe."

"Joanna, that's much too old for you!"

"Well, you're a lot older than Randy." The steely comment was intended to wound.

"That's different," Claire murmured.

"I don't know what's so different." Joanna's casual tone changed to one of anger. "You were *kissing him on the lips!*"

Claire sighed. How could she ever make Joanna understand when she herself didn't understand her feelings for Randy. "Even mothers need a comforting shoulder once in a while."

"*Shoulder?* You were *sitting on his lap!*" Joanna was clearly upset by what she had seen that night. "You've been *throwing yourself* at him."

"No, dear, I haven't. And as for being too old for him, I think that would be up to Randy to decide—*if* I were interested in him."

"You mean you're not?" Joanna frowned as if the idea hadn't occurred to her.

"I'm far too busy to be interested in any man at the moment. So much is happening." And Claire told her all that had taken place—buying and selling the two-flat, buying the brick house, and McKenzie Tate's offer of a job. She wanted Joanna to know that she was determined to build a good life for them, a comfortable life with a promising future. She tried to explain the social implications of the Dodd invitation and making a good impression at the party, wanting Joanna to see how important it was for one to understand all kinds of people in order to better find one's own niche.

When she had finished, Joanna said stiffly, "I didn't realize I was an embarrassment to you, Mother."

"You're not, my darling. In fact I'm more proud of you than anything in my whole life, but . . ."

"But . . ." Tears welled in Joanna's eyes. "I suppose you're going to say I have to start school next week."

"Of course you must."

"No, Mother, I won't."

"You don't want to go to high school?"

"I want to dance, Mother. Bernie says I'm very good. I could even be famous."

"I'm glad you enjoy it," Claire said, "and I'd be proud if you became a fine dancer. But life on the stage is . . . well, you know how I feel about schooling. Without knowledge, life can be empty."

"Without dancing, life can be empty."

Claire studied her daughter's determined young face. "I'll make a bargain with you, Joanna. If you still feel this way after you graduate from high school, then I'll not say a word against it. But for the time being, I must insist that you give school first priority."

Joanna's lower lip jutted in her familiar pout. "I don't see how I can study during the day and dance at night."

"That's not what I mean. You'll have to give up your dancing entirely during the school term."

Joanna seemed stunned. "Why, I can't do that."

"But you must. Don't you see? Being a dancer will take you into an entirely different world, perhaps an unsavory one. You're too young to make such a decision. Didn't you like the party last night? Can't you see yourself fitting into that sort of life? If you become a dancer, you'll . . ."

"I'll never become a Tibby Dodd, you mean? Or a Mrs. Mossburg? I'd rather be dead than be like them."

"But you don't know them."

"Do you?" Joanna said defiantly.

Claire could not answer.

"I'll tell you what, Mother. I'll keep going to school, for your sake, but I won't stop dancing. If you try to make me, I'll run away where you won't find me."

A knock sounded.

"That's Mr. Graham, I suppose." Joanna rose from the table. "Mother, I'm not in the mood for a picnic. I'm going back to the boardinghouse."

"Joanna, please. I'm sorry if I've made you angry. Let's

just forget all this and have a nice day together."

But Joanna was already opening the door to Harry Graham.

"Good afternoon, Mr. Graham," she said pleasantly as she brushed past him, hurried on down the stairs, and was gone.

"I just don't know what to do about Joanna." Claire expressed her worries to Harry as they sat under a eucalyptus tree in the park, their faces dappled by sunlight filtering through the leaves. She had hoped that by attending the Dodds' party, then spending the day with them, Joanna might see a more desirable way of life than the one she was pursuing. But the plan seemed to have created only more defiance in her.

"Give her a little time," Harry said.

"But you saw what the Barbary Theater is like. Those girls. That's not what I want for Joanna."

Harry stretched his legs out across the blanket and leaned back on one elbow. "I have a friend in Chicago who's on the opera board, a bigwig in the arts. Do you think if we could get Joanna into a ballet company there, she might be willing to continue her academic studies as well?"

"Harry! That might be the very thing that would sway her. She's so determined."

"All right, I'll write some letters. She's strong–willed, all right. A little like her mother." He grinned.

"Maybe I've spoiled her."

"Isn't that what mothers are for?" The dappled shadows played across his face as he added pensively, "I've always wished I could have known my mother. She died when I was five."

"That must have been hard for you."

"My grandmother raised me. She was good to me but rather distant, maybe because she didn't want to come between me and my father, and the result was that I wasn't close to either of them. My father was always working. He and my grandfather built a good printing business in Chicago. When Dad died, my grandfather sold the plant." He shrugged. "Somehow I ended up working in a bank."

"You don't like banking?"

"It's all right, but I find myself looking at every printing job I see, picking out the flaws, wishing I had the chance to improve it. Lots of interesting innovations in printing now. Could be profitable out here."

"You mean you'd like to go into the printing business?"

"After my grandfather sold our presses, I used to get a twinge once in a while when I stumbled onto a well-printed book or some fine engraving. Guess it's in my blood. This town could use a better newspaper, too."

They sat in silence for a moment, considering the idea. "Harry, why have you never married?"

"Guess I just never found anyone who would put up with me."

"I can't believe that."

He grinned. "Well, there *were* one or two."

"Was Daisy Mossburg one of them?"

He glanced sharply at her. "How did you know?"

"She made it plain at the party that she had some claim on you."

"I regret that she still feels that way. I broke it off before I came west. Somehow my feelings for her just weren't enough to make it permanent."

Claire nodded, realizing that he could be describing her feelings for Randy—just not enough.

"Claire, I do feel something very special for you." He put his arm around her and drew her to him.

"Do you, Harry?" Her eyes searched his.

When he pressed his lips to hers, she gently touched his cheek as if to hold him there with her open palm.

The city continued its growth. Entrepreneurs looking for investments, businessmen seeking opportunity, immigrants wanting work, adventurers, invalids hoping for cures, retirees drawn to the warm climate, and countless other categories of settlers continued to pour into Los Angeles.

Randy and Warren, observing the increasing influx, kept their downtown livery open seven days a week, and the close proximity to the depot proved to be as advantageous as Randy had hoped. In the first few days of operation at the new location, with demand for service high, Randy purchased yet another buggy and a harness horse named Blackie. Stanfield and Plank now had seven horses to power their fleet of two buggies, a surrey, a buckboard, and a wagon if they put the pinto saddle pony, Patches, to pulling one of the buggies. The new blacksmith, Rogers, applied himself readily to the work, also dealing with livery customers when Randy had to be out. Swifty Lydick, who had accepted Randy's offer of a regular job, worked from early morning until late at night—as a driver when one was needed, a front man when the trains came in, and a stable hand when forced into his share of the chores.

The Pico location, which Warren continued to run with the help of his sons, also continued to do well, but Warren closed the shop on Sundays so he could spend a quiet day with his family. One Sunday Birdie made up some sandwiches for a picnic lunch, and the family drove the dappled

team with the surrey out Sunset Road, an unpaved thorough-
fare named for its heading into the setting sun.

The day was beautiful, the air so fresh it made them feel
good just to breathe it. They planned to see the Cahuenga
Valley where, Claire had told them, acres of land previously
considered barely fit for raising sheep had been reclaimed
from the coyotes and cacti for vegetable gardens, orchards,
and even small fields of wheat and barley.

The Stanfields saw vineyards and a few citrus groves, but
the fruit, they learned after purchasing some at a struggling
orange farm, was not of good quality. The oranges were
sour, pithy, and thick-skinned.

"I had hoped for better," the farmer told them, "but
that's the way they come out."

Warren scooped up a handful of the porous, sandy soil,
feeling its texture. "You'd think with enough water this
ground could grow about anything."

"That's just it," the farmer said. "Soil's fine and year-
round temperature's just right along these foothills, but water's scarce. Some are trying to irrigate where they've found
artesian sources, but without more water there's no hope
for this valley."

He offered the Stanfields some drinking water, and with
his permission they decided to have their picnic right there.
Stella and Eddie ran to play hide-and-seek among the
stunted orange trees growing in the field adjoining the road.
Warren and the two older boys relaxed in the shade beside
the surrey as Birdie got out the sandwiches.

"Someday, when they figure out how to get the water
out here, I'd sure like to get us a piece of this cheap land,"
Warren mused, reclining against the surrey wheel. "I can
just see this valley with fine fruit trees as far as the eye can
see."

"That would be a pretty sight in blossom time," Birdie agreed, smiling as she watched the two youngest children chase each other among the trees, beautiful dark-haired Stella and fair Eddie, whose blonde curls billowed in the sunlight like dandelion fluff.

"You know, Tucker," Warren said to his oldest son sitting beside him, "when you're through with school, you could get a job with one of those orange growers over in Pasadena, learn what we'd need to know to grow better fruit here. Learn irrigation . . ."

Tucker looked across the land but didn't seem to see the same dream. "I like workin' with horses, Pa. I don't see much in growin' oranges."

"You're only in the eighth grade," Birdie reminded. "You won't be through with school for a long time yet."

"Well," Warren mused, "it's somethin' to think about."

Eddie, coming near enough to hear the talk of orange trees, offered his opinion. "I bet we could grow 'em this big," he said, framing a good-sized space with his hands.

"Before we talk about growing anything," Birdie said, "I'd like to see us livin' in a house." She handed sandwiches to Warren and the boys, then called to her roving daughter, "Stella, come eat." But Stella had wandered to the far end of the orchard and didn't seem to hear. "Run and get her, will you, Eddie?"

Eddie dashed off in pursuit of his sister, his sturdy legs going as fast as he could make them. "Hey, Stella!" he yelled. "Ma's callin'!"

Stella heard his call, then turned and ran away again to coax her brother into a game of tag, the sound of her laughter floating through the orchard. As Eddie ran after her, he suddenly pitched forward onto the ground, gripping his ankle. Warren and Birdie watched for a moment, waiting for him to get up. When he didn't, they hurried to where the boy lay writhing in pain.

As they approached, both parents stopped stock-still. Something moved in the grass beside the boy's crumpled form. They heard a whirring sound.

"Rattlesnake!" Warren warned. The snake slithered off.

"Oh, my God, is he bit?" Birdie dropped to the ground beside her son, whose breath came in long gasping cries, his rosy cheeks already turning a ghastly gray, his eyes wild with panic.

Warren quickly found the double puncture on the child's ankle. In an instant, he whipped a jackknife from his pocket and struggled to open the blade, his hands shaking. "They say you got to get the poison out."

"A tourniquet! You have to do a tourniquet!" Birdie pulled Eddie onto her lap.

Warren tied his handkerchief tightly above the wound and, gritting his teeth, pressed his knife blade against the tender flesh of his son's bitten ankle, making an incision across the two punctures. Eddie screamed in pain. As the cut began to bleed, Warren, holding the leg firm, put his mouth over the wound and sucked deeply, spitting onto the ground the small amounts of bloody, bitter fluid he was able to draw out.

"It'll be all right," Birdie soothed, her voice trembling. "It'll be all right."

"We've got to get him to a doctor," Warren said. He helped Birdie, the wailing child clasped in her arms, into the front seat of the buggy, while Tucker and Daniel scooped the picnic things into the cloth and clamored into the backseat with it, making room for Stella. Warren picked up the lines and whipped the dappled team back toward town.

As they careened over the country roads, Eddie's cries quieted to occasional whimpers, his eyes closed, and his breathing became a spasmodic wheezing.

"Hurry, Warren! Hurry!"

Warren lashed the dappled team into the fastest pace he felt was safe for the light surrey and its precious cargo, while he tried to recall just where the nearest doctor might be located.

When little Eddie's breathing became almost imperceptible, Birdie frantically rubbed his chest and abdomen. Then, with a long shuddering sigh, the shallow breaths ceased.

"Warren!" Birdie screamed. "He's not breathing!" Guttural noises came from her throat as she placed her mouth over Eddie's and tried to force her own breath into the child. Warren pulled the team to a stop and began rubbing the small wrists to stimulate a pulse. But there was no response. In the terrifying stillness, Birdie pressed her ear to Eddie's chest, trying to detect a beat from the small stricken heart—the tiny sound she had taken for granted but that she now knew to be the most miraculous and precious sound in the universe.

Tucker, Daniel, and wide-eyed Stella watched in horrified silence as their parents' faces became masks too terrible to look at.

Eddie's heart was no longer beating, the wound no longer bleeding.

"It's no use, Birdie," Warren murmured.

"No! We got to keep tryin'!" Birdie struck out at Warren as he tried gently to restrain her from further efforts. Her eyes were glazed with anguish. "He has a chance if we get him to a doctor."

Warren picked up the lines.

★ ★ ★ ★ ★

On the day of the funeral, Randy drove Claire and Joanna to the little church, where the blacksmith Rogers, Swifty, and a few of Warren's customers and suppliers made up the small group of mourners. Birdie, who had collapsed when the doctor failed to revive her golden-haired boy, moved as if in a trance, seeing and hearing little of the service. Warren wept beside her. The three remaining Stanfield children clung to each other, bewildered by the loss and their parents' unspeakable grief as little Eddie was laid to rest in a far corner of the new cemetery.

CHAPTER THIRTY-FIVE

The following day, numb from the Stanfield tragedy, Claire had to tell Farley Dodd that she had been offered another job, and that she had decided to take it.

"What are you saying?" He seemed unable to comprehend.

"I'm indebted to you for all you've done for me," she went on. "But I feel this is in my best interest." She didn't mention that if Harry managed to get Joanna into a ballet school in Chicago, it would take a substantial amount to keep her there.

"May I ask just who has made you this irresistible offer?"

"McKenzie Tate."

"What? You want to work for a fly-by-night like McKenzie Tate?" The vertical furrow deepened over his nose. "I had thought . . . in fact I expected you to show a certain loyalty to your position here. When did all this happen?"

"He first mentioned the job last week," she said, "and he reminded me at your party that he was waiting for an answer. You see, he's giving me an investment opportunity along with a manager's position and a substantial increase in salary. I like my job here with you, Mr. Dodd, but I'm sure you can see that it makes good financial sense to accept his offer."

"But, my dear Mrs. Chadwick, by this time next year I'll be *mayor* of Los Angeles. Your future with me is every bit as promising—more so, I'd say—than it is with McKenzie

Tate. How much is he offering you?"

"Double my salary, and a chance to invest in a rental project he's developing."

Farley groaned. "Good God! So he's come up short on investment capital again."

"I did very well with him the first time. He seems—"

"He's clever all right, but I wouldn't touch one of his deals with a ten-foot pole."

Claire's heart sank. Why would Dodd deflate her so cruelly—unless what he said were true? Maybe the job would be risky, but . . . She remembered something she once heard her father say: The meek *do not* inherit the Earth.

Dodd's bluster mellowed somewhat. "What if I meet his salary offer?"

Claire was astonished. Even if he were serious, equaling McKenzie Tate's salary offer wouldn't give her the same advantage. There was a chance with Tate's investment opportunity for her to achieve the financial independence she sought. It was a chance she had to take. "I appreciate your consideration, Mr. Dodd, but my mind is made up."

"Very well," he said curtly, "write up a newspaper advertisement for your replacement. It must be a man this time. Women tend to be fickle and unreliable."

That settled it. His peevish attitude eased her misgivings about leaving.

"Incidentally, Mrs. Chadwick . . ." Dodd's tone suddenly changed to one of cordiality. "This brick house of yours. How much are you asking? Tibby and I looked at houses again yesterday, and we can't find anything that suits us."

"I've been advised to triple the price I paid."

"Maybe Tibby and I should take a look at it."

"But . . . I couldn't offer it to you for less, Mr. Dodd. I need the money for my new venture."

"I'm not asking you to. Roscoe Longworth tells me the price is in line with other houses of that quality, and he's promised to show it to us this afternoon." Then he added, "I won't be back in the office today. These papers are ready for McKenzie Tate to pick up this afternoon."

"Excellent!" Tate exclaimed when Claire told him she could start work for him in two weeks. "I'm calling the place the La Paloma Apartments. It's a two-story, stucco building, thirty apartments, U-shaped around a central court. And you'll set up your office in a charming little bungalow they've left on one corner of the property. Rose-covered fence around it. Nice palm tree in front. You'll like it."

Claire smiled, amused as always by his direct way of expressing himself.

"I'll keep a small office there, too," he continued, "but since I plan to be out in the field most of the time, you'll be dealing with workmen, builders, suppliers, and City Hall until the units are finished, then you'll be in charge of leasing apartments and running the place. We'll get you an assistant to handle the bookkeeping and secretarial, all the hocus-pocus."

"Mr. Tate, I—"

"Name's McKenzie. I'll call you Claire, if I may."

"All right . . . McKenzie. I assure you I won't let you down, but I'm surprised you have so much faith in my abilities."

"I see how you work for Farley, always there with whatever is required, always prompt, always competent, always handling things intelligently. You're also nice-looking and

306

gracious. Very important in any business." He grinned, eyes twinkling, his little sharp teeth peeping in neat rows between the orange muttonchops. "My only regret is that without you, Farley may not be able to handle my legal work as efficiently."

She laughed. "I guess we'll find out, won't we?"

"One other thing," he added. "As soon as the building is completed in about a month, I want you to move into one of the apartments. More convenient."

Was there no end to the surprises this man came up with? Living in a new apartment right next to her place of work, perhaps one with a separate bedroom for Joanna, would be heavenly. "Is there a high school nearby?" Claire asked. "I'll need to enroll my daughter."

"Don't know about that, but of course that's the sort of thing I want you to be on top of. You need to have all the answers for prospective tenants—school, pharmacy, doctor, grocer, livery, car lines, even railroad schedules—whatever they ask. And most important, you'll be standing in for me with information for tenants on all the latest subdivisions; they'll eventually be *buying* a home, of course, and I'll be brokering properties." He glanced toward Dodd's office. "Now where are those papers Farley was supposed to leave for me?"

When he was gone, Claire took a deep breath. Her new position would indeed be challenging. It was most unusual for a woman to have so much business responsibility, and she wondered how the men with whom she would be dealing—workmen, city officials, brokers, renters, buyers—would respond to her. She felt some reassurance in that she already had good legal and banking connections in Farley Dodd and Harry Graham. Yes, the rewards for the gamble far outweighed the risks.

★ ★ ★ ★ ★

Next morning, Farley Dodd brought startling news to the office. "Claire," he said, rubbing his palms together in delight. "Tibby's crazy about your brick house, and that rascal Longworth has convinced us we should buy it."

Claire caught her breath. If the Dodds bought the house, she would have the money to put down on McKenzie Tate's apartment building. Buoyed by the good news, Claire further learned there was a high school close to the Washington Street project. Now the question was: Would Joanna agree to live at home? Or, if she continued dancing and living at the boardinghouse with Peach, could she also manage her schoolwork?

Tucker and Daniel Stanfield came running when Claire and Randy drove up to the barn on Sunday afternoon. "We're gonna get a house," Tucker burst out. "A real house."

"And I'm gonna have a room by my own self," Stella chorused.

"It's an old farmhouse," Warren explained, as he and Birdie came to greet them. "Not far from here. We'll be movin' in next week."

Daniel held Sugar's bridle while Claire stepped from the buggy. "Ain't that swell? Now we won't have to live in a barn."

Birdie smiled at her son. "The farmland's been sold off—but there's a big yard for the kids." Except for the lines of sadness around her eyes, she seemed to have renewed her courage in the month since Eddie's death. Grief-stricken after the funeral, she had taken to her bed for three days. But with little Stella at her bedside, her innocent eyes full of worry, Birdie got up on the fourth day vowing to put her grief behind her. She had Warren and the other children to think about, and she still had much to be thankful for in this golden land.

"You're not giving up your sign business, are you?" Claire asked.

"I should say not!" Birdie replied. "I'm hirin' a sign painter to work with me. Once we move to our house, there'll be plenty of room here in the barn for another painter. Daniel won't have time now that school's startin'."

"It's Birdie's sign money that's payin' the rent on the house," Warren said proudly.

"Come on in," Birdie said. "I cooked up some dinner for us." She led the way into the makeshift kitchen. "How's Joanna?"

"We're moving, too, into a larger place where she'll have her own room." Claire related the changes that were taking place. "So I hope to have her with me."

"Sometimes, Claire, when I think about Eddie, I wish we'd never come here." Tears sprang to Birdie's eyes, but she quickly composed herself. "But bad things can happen anyplace, I guess." She sniffed, found a hankie, and blew her nose. "When I see how well Warren's doin'. The other kids. Then I'm real glad we came." She put her hand on Claire's arm. "Joanna will be just fine."

What good people they were. Warren and Birdie were solid as rocks, and it was easy to see that their children would be, too. And Randy. So full of ambition and the desire to better himself. The struggle of these decent people inspired her. They had welcomed her as a member of the family, and she was grateful. Yet something prevented her from accepting that comfortable niche. From returning the love Randy offered. Something continued to pull her in another direction, perhaps toward the life she had known as a child.

If circumstances hadn't caused my privileged world to disintegrate, Claire mused, would I be a Tibby Dodd, married to a successful man, wearing Paris fashions, and living in a big brick house? Would I be a Daisy Mossburg chasing Harry Graham all the way to California? Perhaps. But Harry doesn't want a Daisy Mossburg. He wants me. Am I willing to make the inevitable compromises that will come if I become his wife?

Perhaps I'm more like McKenzie Tate. Not sure where I belong.

PART FOUR

CHAPTER THIRTY-SIX

A tall, well-dressed woman wearing a stylish hat crossed the courtyard at her Washington Street residence in the La Paloma Apartments. Carrying herself with the confidence of one who has achieved a satisfying degree of success—which indeed she had, in the little more than a year that she had been managing the La Paloma—she walked along the rose-covered fence to the bungalow that housed the office of Tate & Chadwick Realty, her pace energized by the demands of her work.

The year 1887 had brought an influx of thousands more immigrants, opportunists, and tourists into the burgeoning city. The boom that until then had been based largely on outside capital began to attract the skeptical longtime residents and established businessmen who had thus far remained on the sidelines. Having finally become believers in the new economy and the possibility that the area's rampant growth offered still more opportunity, these new investors plunged in. Civic improvements attesting to the boom included a new City Hall, a new courthouse, improved sewers, pavements, and more schools.

Newspaper reports of increasing population and rising construction statistics kept the frenzy at a high pitch. The glowing accounts advertised the formation of land companies, irrigation enterprises, and real-estate firms, of which there were an estimated 2,300 within the city limits. The city seethed with promoters and prices soared. As business property became paramount, a fifty-four-acre tract on Main

Street, "fine for subdivision," was offered for $100,000. A two-story building and sixty-one-foot lot on Spring Street was offered for $87,000. Business frontage brought $700 to $2,000 a frontage foot. When prices for some city lots reached $25,000, bargain-hunting buyers turned to outlying areas where "rich, level, loamy land" could be had at $350 per acre. But one advertiser argued, "Why go forty miles away when you can purchase half-acre lots in South Los Angeles at $160 in installments?"

Newcomers, devouring the barrage of propaganda, wrote enthusiastic letters to relatives and friends urging them to come to Los Angeles, thus obligating the post office to handle more than 200,000 pieces of transients' mail during the last three months of 1887. Hotels and boardinghouses bulged, and the most talked about topic anywhere was land. Another building spurt recorded 260 new Los Angeles residences under construction, along with several newly platted business blocks. Streets were choked with traffic, and property was changing hands faster and for higher prices than ever.

McKenzie Tate stayed on top of it all. Waiting when Claire arrived at the office, he shared his excitement with her. "I'm thinking of investing in a development now being proposed out toward Santa Monica. Could be extremely lucrative if they go ahead with a harbor out there." Tate & Chadwick, which now owned several rental apartment buildings in addition to the La Paloma, was to him an almost inconsequential part of his holdings, a part he left entirely to Claire's management. His personal satisfaction came from putting together what he considered "important" deals.

"And did you hear about the fancy four-story hotel scheduled for Tenth and Main?" He continued his barrage of information through the open door of his tiny office, originally a bedroom just off the former parlor that served as Claire's office in the little bungalow. "The architecture will be Franco-English Renaissance."

"Sounds fancy," Claire said. "I swear Los Angeles will soon be as grand as San Francisco."

"Got to be cautious though. Remember the rumor that the post office would be moved to Broadway and Seventh? Nearby lots began selling for almost nine hundred a frontage foot." Tate chuckled at the recollection. "Just a false rumor started deliberately to sell those adjoining tracts. One poor sucker realized he'd made a mistake and sold out for little more than a hundred dollars a front foot. Considered himself lucky to have recouped as much as he did."

Claire browsed the morning *Times*. "The San Gabriel Valley Railroad plans to build a new station at the corner of Aliso and Los Angeles Streets," she said. "Should stimulate east-side sales."

McKenzie nodded. "And there's another new town platted out on the west side you might want to take a look at. It's called Hollywood."

"Hollywood," Claire mused. "Nice name. Is there holly growing there?"

"That's what they tell prospective buyers but . . ."—he bent forward in a posture of mock confidentiality—"truth is, the developer's wife heard the name back east somewhere. Big landowner named Wilcox. He bought the hundred-and-twenty-acre tract just north of Sunset last year. Paid a hundred and fifty an acre for it. He's squared off streets and planted pepper trees along them to make quite an attractive offering."

But Claire hadn't the time to follow up on every new

subdivision filed with the county recorder. She simply cata-
logued the information for future referral to clients. Now,
in mid-December of 1887, with the city of Los Angeles
alone boasting a population of 80,000, she determined to
make the most of the continuing demand for housing. The
passing months of bone-wearying work had been marked by
a number of successes: her part-ownership of the La
Paloma, her move into her own apartment in the building,
her profits from select real estate she managed to invest in
on her own, and a growing income from her partnership in
Tate & Chadwick.

McKenzie offered her the partnership after she had
worked for him only three months. He was much too preoccupied, he insisted, with sniffing out rancho parcels, city
tracts, and suburban subdivisions—often building on them
and improving them with bricked streets before reselling—
to spend time with the mundane details of operating the La
Paloma Apartments. Claire had done a fine job of overseeing completion of the construction, he observed, including landscaping the courtyard with azaleas and planting
four palm trees along the street, which when they grew
would match the one in front of the bungalow. He praised
her resourcefulness in getting the units rented, dealing with
the city and the jumble of hocus-pocus, his term for any
kind of detail, and said he felt certain that making her a
partner in that branch of his business ventures would be
profitable for both of them.

McKenzie's generosity baffled her, but she wasn't about
to question it. Always most respectful of her, he revealed
nothing of his private life. One day she asked him whether
he had a family.

"Not a soul," he responded merrily. "I'm a free spirit."

Reluctant to ask if he had ever been married for fear he

would think she had a personal interest, she let the matter drop, grateful for her good fortune in having such an ideal employer.

He allowed her to select one of the La Paloma Apartments for her residence, and she moved into the downstairs unit fronting the court. The attractive two-bedroom layout featured the latest plumbing fixtures, a built-in icebox, gas-lights, and a small gas range. She purchased a few pieces of furniture to furnish the place, including a bed, bureau, and desk for Joanna's room.

Neither Claire nor Joanna had much time for domesticity. On the job from dawn to dusk, Claire spent her evenings going over paperwork or writing instructions for her secretary-bookkeeper, Perry Rupert. Just out of the new Woodbury business school, the slender, somewhat awkward young man wore small round spectacles to correct his weak eyesight, but there was nothing weak about his capacity for details and figures, and Claire soon came to depend on him for nearly all of the bookkeeping and office detail.

Joanna rejected the idea of going to Chicago to study ballet. Harry's inquiry had gotten a reply offering her an audition for a Chicago ballet company, but Joanna wanted to stay on at the Barbary, and Claire preferred to keep her close by as long as possible. Joanna had settled into the routine of attending high school classes while performing six evenings a week, with two matinees. She and Peach continued to live at the theatrical boardinghouse, Joanna spending her free Sundays and Sunday nights with Claire. It was not an ideal arrangement, and Claire still worried about the life her daughter was leading, about her companions, and her future.

The Stanfields enjoyed a busy family life in their newly acquired farmhouse. The boys, doing well in their studies, helped out when they were not in school, giving Birdie more time for her sign painting. Thanks to the bank loan, the expansion of Stanfield and Plank brought in almost more livery business than Randy, Warren, Rogers, and Swifty could handle.

Of all the Westport emigrants, Randy perhaps changed the most. He purchased a dapper cinnamon-brown suit with matching fedora, a pocket watch on a gold chain, and a fancy walking stick, and began to frequent various cafés and saloons, his wry sense of humor and friendly manner impressing ladies and men alike. One of his favorite haunts was the Golden Goose, a popular gaming room and brothel opened during the previous holiday season by Blanche Oliver. Blanche encouraged Randy's flair for poker, giving him insight into strategies for the game, and he began taking home considerable winnings that, along with his growing income from the liveries, enabled him to take up residence at the Del Rio Hotel.

He escorted Claire to a café for supper when she could find the time, but she often seemed distant, preoccupied, and he suffered in silence. Waiting. Giving her time.

Claire also enjoyed the limited time she spent with Harry Graham. Harry was working long hours, too, having opened three California Security Banks over the past year, in Pasadena, Inglewood, and the little village of Hollywood. P. B. Mossburg was not convinced of the wisdom of the Hollywood location when he learned that the city fathers had passed a law that no more than 2,000 sheep could be driven through the main street at one time. But he accepted Harry's judgment, assigning him permanently to Southern California.

Daisy Mossburg had gone back to Chicago with her father, and Harry had not heard from her in more than a year.

The invitation to the Dodds' Christmas party caught Claire completely by surprise. She hadn't seen Farley Foster Dodd since leaving his employment, and, having bumped into him a few times at City Hall, she realized she missed his brusque conversation. The party would be held at the Dodds' Los Feliz home on Christmas Eve. Claire ordered a new gown of peacock-blue velveteen with a matching cloak, elegant and subdued, as befitting her new station in life. She still hoped to become friends with Tibby, perhaps to share remembrances of Chicago and their similar girlhoods. And she longed to once again take part in holiday social events as she had during the years she was growing up. So it was with happy anticipation that she accepted the invitation.

CHAPTER THIRTY-SEVEN

One early December morning McKenzie Tate dropped by the bungalow office. "I have something to show you, Claire," he announced. "Something most special." He spread some documents before her. "Remember I mentioned a residential development out toward Santa Monica? Fine homes, artesian water, paved streets, school, firehouse, stores, offices?" He waited for her reaction. "It's to be called Wonderburg."

"Wonderburg?" Claire chuckled at the name.

"I've got a chance to go into it in a big way, and I don't mind telling you, I stand to make a fortune. In fact I've already sold my Pasadena holdings to buy into it."

"You sold everything?"

"The problem is . . . I've come up a hundred thousand short." His eyes narrowed as he summarized. "Tate & Chadwick is doing well—I'm happy as a pup with the way you've been running it—but . . . well, for me there's not much excitement in it anymore. You know how I operate. On the edge. Double or nothing." He cleared his throat before continuing. "Claire, I think we should sell this company and put everything into the Wonderburg project."

His suggestion seemed preposterous to Claire.

"Your share of Tate & Chadwick will buy you a sizable piece of the pie." He pushed the documents toward her. "Look at this."

Claire read the proposal. He had itemized the properties owned by Tate & Chadwick, their value, and the gain they could expect if it were all invested in the new project.

"I'm sorry, McKenzie, but I'm quite comfortable with Tate & Chadwick." She hated to turn him down, but such a venture would put all their eggs in one basket—a mistake her father had made. "I have no desire to take such a risk."

"But it's the chance of a lifetime. We can have this thing locked up in one twitch of a cat's whisker."

"You've been very good to me, McKenzie. I appreciate all you've done. But I like what I have right now, and I want to protect it."

"Where's the risk? This is a prime location. Right on the rail line to Santa Monica. No one doubts that the city's moving west."

"Perhaps, but I think I'll stand pat."

His smile faded. "Claire, all my life I've dreamed of a really big one like this Wonderburg deal, but without your share of the cash, I won't be able to swing it."

"McKenzie . . ." Claire hesitated, scarcely daring to voice what she was thinking. "What if I buy you out of Tate & Chadwick? Your figures here show that your share is worth just over a hundred thousand. Would that give you enough to buy into the Wonderburg project?"

McKenzie's eyes opened wide. "Why, yes. But you . . . how would you get that much money?"

"By selling off my private investments and borrowing the rest."

"By Jove, Claire, you're the one who's built Tate & Chadwick. You deserve to keep it, if that's what you want."

"That's what I want, McKenzie."

"Then there's no time to dillydally," he said. "Have Farley draw up the papers as soon as possible, and I'll expect the money when we sign." He backed quickly out of her office and, with a playful wink, was gone before she could respond.

Claire studied his figures carefully, poring over her own records and comparing recent valuation of similar properties and current citywide sales records. McKenzie Tate's evaluation was perhaps a bit above his fair share, yet he was offering her sole ownership of a solid, established company—something she wanted with all her being.

Her mind made up, she took several property deeds from the safe and put them into a large sturdy envelope along with the company ledger. Leaving Perry to manage things, she put the envelope under her arm and took the streetcar to California Security Bank where she was ushered into Harry's office.

"Claire! What a fine surprise. I hope you've come to have lunch?"

"No, I'm here on business."

She explained her plan. Borrow half of the amount she needed to finance McKenzie's deal—a short-term loan to be repaid as soon as she could sell her miscellaneous properties. The balance of the amount required would be a long-term loan to be repaid from the operation of Tate & Chadwick, which she planned to rename Pacific Realty Company. She would keep the La Paloma Apartments, which alone would provide more than a good living.

"This time I have the collateral," she said, showing Harry the documents she had brought. "And each of these properties is an exceptional value. I handpicked them myself, and they're worth quite a bit more now than when I bought them."

Harry put on his serious business face. "Very well, madam. I'll go over all this documentation and have the properties appraised."

"Thank you, Harry." She could hardly resist throwing her arms around him right there in the bank. "I can't tell you how much I appreciate it."

"Good thing you're a close friend of the loan officer," he teased.

"Now, Harry, you know I don't expect special consideration. This is strictly business. I'm sure Roscoe Longworth can sell the properties quickly. And the bank will make a tidy profit on the loans."

"I wouldn't be at all surprised."

After signing the loan applications, she went directly to Farley Dodd's office to have him draw up the buyout papers. Three weeks later, they signed. Claire turned over to McKenzie Tate a bank draft in the amount of $100,000—proceeds from the sale of three of her properties plus two rather daunting loans from California Security Bank—and she became the sole owner of the La Paloma Apartments and the newly named Pacific Realty Company.

Christmas Eve was warm with the faint smell of the ocean in the air. How different the California holiday seemed from Christmas in the Midwest, where heavy snow or ice storms often hampered party plans. Harry called for Claire in the early twilight.

"You're fabulous, my dear," he said when he saw her in her new peacock-blue gown, her hair crimped halo-like around her glowing face, curls hanging at the back. She now could afford regular visits to a professional hairdresser. He embraced her for a long moment. "And I've brought you a present." He fished a slim velvet box from his vest pocket, and raised its top to reveal a square-cut ruby pendant set in filigreed Mexican silver with smaller matching rubies on each of the ear bobs.

"But I couldn't accept . . ."

"Of course you can." He lifted the pendant from the box and fastened it around her bare throat. "Please. Wear it tonight."

She looked into the small mirror in the corner whatnot. Prisms of the rubies catching the light enhanced the tones of her gown as she slipped the old pearl drops from her ears and put on the extravagant rubies. "Oh, Harry, they're perfect with this dress."

"*You're* perfect with that dress," he said. "Merry Christmas, Claire." They kissed tenderly. Then she slipped from his arms to retrieve a small package from the hall table.

"And this is for you, Harry. Merry Christmas."

He removed the wrapping. Inside was a gold stickpin, its medallion engraved with the initials H.G. "Say," he grinned as he inserted the pin into the center of his puff tie, "this is just like a real Christmas."

"It is," Claire said. "If only Joanna weren't working at that seedy theater—and on Christmas Eve. But she'll be with us for dinner tomorrow."

It did seem like a real Christmas riding through the twilight enjoying the azaleas, bougainvillea, poinsettia, and roses blooming everywhere along the way. Holly wreaths festooned front doors, gaslights winked on, and candlelit Christmas trees glowed through the windows of homes where families were gathered.

"I want you to know," Claire told Harry, "that Roscoe has sold two more of my properties, and I'll put the profit into repaying my loans as soon as I receive the settlements."

Harry held a finger to her lips. "No business talk tonight, Claire. Tonight we're going to enjoy the holiday."

"All right." She snuggled against him. "I promise not to

mention anything about business the rest of the evening."

Harry touched his lips to her forehead. "If you can manage that," he joked, "then this night will see a second Christmas miracle."

Tibby Dodd had done up the Los Feliz house in fine style with holiday decorations throughout, including a huge tree trimmed with sparkling ornaments in the sunroom. It was the first time Claire had seen the house since the Dodds moved in, and she found it even more attractive than she remembered.

"Claire, we simply love our home," Tibby confessed as she showed her and Harry through the first floor's two parlors, library, dining room, and sunroom, Tibby's expensive taste evident everywhere. "And how do you like *your* new place, Claire? I understand you bought a building."

"I like it very much," Claire said. "But I'm afraid my work leaves little time to really enjoy it."

"Farley told me you have your own business now, too." Tibby seemed genuinely interested. "I think it's about time we women took the bull by the horns, so to speak, and showed men what we can do."

The women laughed.

"I'd dearly love to work with Farley," Tibby continued, "but he says when we have children I'll need to be at home. *If* we have children."

"Taking care of a child can be a full-time job," Claire said.

Tibby laughed gaily. "Do come and meet some of our friends." She led Claire and Harry into the parlor where they were introduced to three couples chatting around a punch bowl filled with eggnog. They were prominent couples whose names Claire had seen in the social columns of the papers, friends Tibby had made: the Thomas Corgans, the Madison Burnses, and the Franklin Schroeders. Also among the guests were District Attorney Haycroft, Mayor Wallace, and Police Chief Feeney with their wives, as well as State Senator Myron Ferguson, and a few city councilmen, ward captains, and aldermen. Everyone was either socially prominent or politically expedient to Farley's coming campaign. McKenzie Tate had not been invited. Claire wondered why she had been included. Probably because of Harry.

"A public office is a public trust." Farley Dodd had adopted the slogan used by President Grover Cleveland during his '84 campaign and he repeated it as he talked with Thomas Corgan. "I favor a reform platform that will reduce graft and favoritism by breaking up excessive power in the city council." Though Farley had not yet officially announced his candidacy, it seemed understood, even by the ineffectual Mayor Wallace, that he would throw his hat into the ring in '88.

Corgan defended the status quo. "But you've *got* to have a strong council to run this town."

"You mean this haven for realty deals and rheumatism?" Chief Feeney quipped.

"A haven for railroads," Franklin Schroeder interjected. "If you ask me, we've made it too easy for those buzzards."

"Not necessarily," Mayor Wallace joined in. "All of us benefited from their phony rate war, didn't we?"

"Phony?" Claire was surprised by his remark. It hadn't occurred to her that the supposedly bitter competition might have been staged.

"Absolutely. They've never made it public to their stockholders, but I have it on good authority that the so-called rate war was a fake."

"Thousands of people took advantage of it," Claire said.

"That's just it," Senator Ferguson interjected. "The Southern Pacific and the Santa Fe *agreed* to the cut rates in order to open up Southern California for their own profit. They wanted the public to think they were bitterly competitive, but they had an *understanding*."

"Whether they did or didn't," Harry summed up, "it's accomplished what they wanted."

"It certainly has," the senator granted. "Before the gold rush, Los Angeles had a population of five thousand. Then it dropped down to only sixteen hundred in forty-nine when everyone went north looking for gold—a mere village. When the Southern Pacific got here in seventy-six, it was still only eleven thousand. Can you believe it's now topping *ninety thousand?*"

"And more immigrants descending on us every day," Mayor Wallace complained. "Don't know how we're going to absorb them all if it keeps on like this."

"It's the railroads and their advertising that keeps bringing them in." Franklin Schroeder obviously was uncomfortable with so much power in the hands of the railroads. "Every retired farmer and invalid in the country, not to mention all kinds of shysters and misfits, and it won't end till Huntington and his ilk have gotten their greedy hands on every dime they can squeeze out of these people."

"You're right about that," the senator agreed. "And what bothers me is that after they sell off the thousands of acres of land adjoining the rail lines, they'll still have control of freight prices."

"Can't see that it matters whether it's commercial rivalry that drives the two lines to such cutthroat tactics," Schroeder said, "or whether they're in cahoots. The fact remains, railroads *are* the patron saints of Los Angeles."

Farley Dodd held up his hands in a dismissive gesture. "What's important is that Los Angeles gets good passenger service and reasonable shipping rates. I intend to do my part to see that it does."

Talk centered around politics all through dinner, and when finally the men retired to the library for port and cigars, the women settled into the ladies' parlor to enjoy Mexican coffee with sweetened cream prepared by Tibby's cook.

"Tibby tells me you're in the real-estate business," Evelyn Schroeder said to Claire. "I understand you found this marvelous house for them." Evelyn's velvet gown set off an exquisite complexion and her alert personality enhanced her rather ordinary features. "I wish I had something to keep me occupied."

"Your work must be very satisfying, Claire," purred strawberry-blonde Cissy Corgan, fluffing the ruffles on her gown of olive taffeta.

"And liberating, too. To be self-supporting, I mean," Evelyn commented.

Julia Burns raised her lorgnette to better assess Claire's ruby pendant. "I can't imagine finding time to run a household . . . and a business, too."

Dora Ferguson, wife of the senator, clad in black silk with jewelry of onyx and Mexican silver, said, "I've always longed for a special talent. But we women seem to spend our lives pursuing our husbands' dreams." Dora, tall and graying, with a serious demeanor, actually resembled her handsome silver-haired husband, and they made an impressive couple.

"Well, why shouldn't we? You and Senator Ferguson have accomplished so much." There was a touch of envy in the comment of the mayor's wife.

"Myron has," Dora said. "For a long time, his goals were my goals, but now that the children are grown, it seems that all I do is go to teas and listen to political speeches. I admire you, Claire, for building something of your own. You're among the few who've managed to, you know."

Claire, flattered by the compliment, stopped herself from admitting that she had had little choice in the matter, that she had been forced to support herself and Joanna. "It *is* satisfying in many ways," she said. It was indeed satisfying to know that though some of these women might look down on her for having to dirty herself in the business world, at the same time they envied her.

"Claire, our League is having our spring luncheon in April," Evelyn said. "I wonder if you'd care to be on the committee. We're trying to raise money for the destitute immigrants stranded here. Some of them are greatly in need."

Evelyn Schroeder was making a gesture of friendship, of acceptance, but Claire had no time for charity luncheons, no matter how worthy the cause. Yet she didn't want to offend by refusing. "I'd like to, if I can squeeze it in."

"Good." Evelyn offered a sincere smile. "I'll drop you a note when we're ready for our planning meeting in February."

It was exactly midnight and the sound of church bells rang out across the city as the guests departed amid a clatter of carriages and buggies. Claire leaned back into the crook of Harry's arm, the rubies at her throat and ears catching the glow of an occasional streetlamp as their carriage passed.

"You were wonderful tonight," Harry said. "I could

hardly keep my eyes off you. And you charmed the others, too. Franklin Schroeder asked me if your business came from family money."

Claire smiled. "It's odd, isn't it, that one is considered more respectable with inherited wealth than with money earned."

"You certainly didn't want for respect there tonight."

"Nor you."

When she turned admiring eyes to his, he murmured, "Claire, you're such an elusive little carrot."

"Carrot?"

"Yes, like a carrot on a stick, you're always just a little out of reach."

"Not at all." But his comment gave her pause. *Was* she always just a little out of reach? Wasn't the passion she felt for him obvious? She couldn't go on pretending indifference while this chance to be loved passed her by. She tenderly touched his face with her fingertips. "I do love you, Harry. I'm sure you know that."

"I can't be positive," he teased. "Tell me again."

"You're the only man I've known who hasn't wanted to change me or tried to control me. You're the only one, Harry, who hasn't tried to convert me into a domestic manager."

"A domestic manager is not what I need," he murmured against her cheek.

His lips on hers dismissed any further conversation, and she melted into his arms, desperately wanting his love. Here was a fine man who could love her without feeling he owned her.

That night Harry Graham shared her bed.

CHAPTER THIRTY-EIGHT

January 1888 in Los Angeles saw a month of rare torrential rains that turned dry streambeds into rivers and lots into gullies, disrupting real-estate transactions. Promoters, ignoring drooping sales figures, loudly insisted that the lull was temporary, due to the rains, and that by summer the boom would surpass itself. But immigrants, sated with outlandish advertisements, were responding in fewer numbers. When the rains ended, those who had bought conservatively congratulated themselves and went about their business with faith that, in the long run, their investments were sound. Those who believed fervently that the boom would go on indefinitely continued to bolster the market, but the more prudent of them, instead of investing in risky tracts outside the city limits or in sky-high business properties, looked for bargains that would provide ongoing income rather than speculative profits.

Claire began to realize that her buyout of McKenzie Tate and the selling off of most of her properties had been well-timed, but McKenzie continued his defense of the boom.

"Traffic between Los Angeles and Pasadena is the heaviest it's ever been," he reported on one of his infrequent visits to her office. "Sales may be fluctuating a bit, but just look at the Wolfskill Orchard Tract."

Claire had been keeping an eye on this land in South Los Angeles near the river, owned by the Wolfskill family since the early part of the century. Covered with orange and walnut trees, the 120 acres, bounded by Third and Seventh, Alameda and San Pedro, recently had been platted into lots, with a strip of land donated to the Southern Pacific Railroad for a station.

"With that new depot the price of nearby lots is shooting up," he said.

"Maybe," Claire agreed, "but sales aren't going at all well for the Electric Railway Homestead Tract. The rains washed through there and caused a great deal of erosion, actually destroyed some of the houses."

"Just poor planning," McKenzie insisted. "The Homestead Tract management hasn't lived up to their agreements, hasn't supplied good drinking water, and even the electric railway is undependable."

"Just the same, I feel sorry for anyone who bought a home there."

"It's unfortunate, yes, but an isolated case," McKenzie continued. "Look at all the new towns going in. Melrose, Dayton Heights, Wilderson, Edna Park, Bettner, Rowena. Mark my words, this boom is in its infancy."

"I hope you're right," Claire mused. "I know Highland Park, in the hills west of the Arroyo Seco, claims it will be to Los Angeles what the Campagna is to Rome—the wonder of the artistic world. And there's a new avenue under construction in Hollywood. It's called Lincoln Drive. A hundred feet wide and five miles long. Imagine!"

McKenzie chuckled. "Yes, my dear, there's no end to the fabulous things we're yet to see here."

That evening Claire voiced her concern about the unsettled market to Harry over dinner in a restaurant near the La Paloma. She had spent the late afternoon at the recorder's office checking platting statistics and hadn't had time even to change her plumed hat—too overpowering at the dinner table, she thought—but Harry didn't seem to mind. As he held her chair for her, his admiring eyes swept from her cheeks, flushed from her day's activities, to her lithe body, smartly dressed in a high-collared dress of navy gabardine.

"I learned today," she said as she pulled off her gloves, "that just since the first of last year, a total of sixty new towns have been surveyed—eighty thousand acres of land and five hundred thousand lots—enough to accommodate nearly two million people." She emphasized each of the optimistic numbers. "But guess what the combined population of those sixty new towns is at present."

"Not too impressive, I'd say."

"Twenty-three hundred. And sales have fallen off almost to nothing."

"You can't expect to fill up that many towns in less than two years," Harry argued.

"No, but many of them have never been anything but wishful thinking. They never actually materialized. Of those that did, much of the land sold was on credit, and the buyers have disappeared."

The waiter came and they ordered the fresh swordfish with herbed lemon-butter sauce.

"In Los Angeles," she continued, "real-estate transfers peaked almost a year ago. They've been dropping ever since. Harry, I'm afraid I can't sell off the remaining Tate & Chadwick properties without taking a considerable loss."

Harry nodded. "I'm not too optimistic right now either. The Hollywood bank hasn't attracted nearly the depositors we had hoped."

"McKenzie pooh-poohs my concern," Claire said. "But

I'm not sure what I should do. If properties continue to devalue . . ."

"Let's hope it's only a temporary lull caused by the rains." Harry reached across the table and cupped her chin in his hand. "Now if you don't mind," he added, "my digestion would prefer that we talk about something other than financial ruin."

Her laughter came quickly, and they enjoyed a pleasant meal.

Downtown, at the adobe warehouse occupied by the Stanfield and Plank Livery, Randy sat in his office totaling the day's receipts. Warren, who had brought a new and bigger sign Birdie had painted, stood out front with Rogers conferring about the best way to position the sign over the door.

As Randy glanced out toward the two men, the big warehouse doors suddenly began to undulate. Just a slight shudder at first, then they swung on their hinges as if phantom hands had seized them. Randy blinked in astonishment as the adobe wall before him began to ripple. A frightening rumble rose from somewhere deep in the earth and the ground itself seemed to shift beneath him.

Randy jumped up from his desk. A sharp cracking sound over his head warned him that a heavy beam supporting that corner of the roof was falling. He dove for the door, but the roof gave way. With a deafening roar, the beam came down, pinning his right foot beneath it, and showering him with crumbling adobe. He cried out in agonizing pain, but his voice was lost in the chaotic noise, the choking dust and dirt.

At that exact moment, as Claire and Harry left the restaurant, Claire suddenly felt dizzy. The street seemed to be rolling in gentle waves, the eucalyptus trees on either side swayed hypnotically. A horse reared at the hitching post, overturning its buggy as it broke the reins and stampeded down the street, dragging the rig. Other horses, tied at the hitching post, sidestepped nervously, straining in their traces.

"Harry, I think I'm going to faint." As she turned toward him, she saw that he, too, was tottering as if he had lost his balance.

"I think it's an earthquake!" He reached for her and they clung together. Disoriented by the strange phenomenon, they stood frozen to the spot, staring at the diminishing undulation of the street and the swaying movements of unlatched doors and shutters as the seismic wave passed. A few bricks toppled from a chimney. Dogs set up a racket, and frightened people came running from buildings.

A man emerged from the restaurant, his eyes wide with bewilderment. "Haven't had a quake here for a while," he said. "You folks okay?" When assured that they were, he hurried to the hitching post to try to calm the panicked horses.

An earthquake. Claire felt as if her dizziness had come from within, but the fallen bricks and skittering animals were proof of the powerful force that had rocked the area.

Joanna! She was at the Barbary. "Harry, I have to be sure Joanna is all right."

"We'll drive past the La Paloma first," Harry said, "and I want to check on the bank, too." He led her to his buggy and drove her through the disordered streets to the La Paloma where they saw at once the narrow crack in the stucco on one wall of the building. Claire scanned the structure that had become more than just a business to her—it was home, and she had come to love its Spanish style, its earthy ochre and terra-cotta.

"It doesn't look too bad. That crack in the stucco can easily be repaired." Harry's cursory glance detected no broken or dislodged tiles on the roof. "I only hope the bank fared as well."

Continuing on downtown, they saw minor destruction everywhere—bricks fallen, a few porches collapsed, windows broken. People milled about assessing the damage. Though the quake had been relatively minor, downtown a few people had been injured by breaking glass, falling cornices, or stampeding horses. Two mild aftershocks produced further concern, but the worst seemed to have passed.

The theater, too, had escaped damage. They found Joanna backstage just ready to go on. "Oh, Mother, did you feel the earthquake?" She ran into her mother's embrace.

"Thank heavens you're safe," Claire murmured. "I guess we're lucky."

"I have to go on now, Mother," Joanna said. "I'll see you tomorrow after school. Thanks for coming, Mr. Graham."

After checking the bank and finding no serious damage, only a few books and papers shaken from shelves and scattered about the floor, they drove past the adobe livery of Stanfield and Plank, and saw immediately that a portion of the warehouse roof had fallen in. A man lay on the ground out front, tended by a graying man with shirtsleeves rolled, apparently a doctor, while Warren, Rogers, and a few passersby looked on.

"Randy's had quite a blow," Warren said, and Claire realized that was who lay on the ground. "We felt the tremor, then the roof gave way in that corner by his office. One of the beams fell on his leg."

Claire knelt beside her injured friend. His eyes, dull with

pain, searched hers as if begging her to stay with him. She held his hand, trying to offer comfort, but sweat beaded on his forehead as the doctor removed his right shoe and examined the foot and ankle.

"How bad is it, doctor?" she murmured.

The doctor indicated that she and Harry could help by holding the wooden splints in place as he tightly bound the lower leg and foot with a bandage. Randy writhed in agony.

"The knee seems intact, but his ankle and foot are broken up pretty bad," the doctor said. "And there are fractures of the tibia and fibula. I've set everything as good as I can, but he'll be off this leg for a good long while."

"He can stay at our place while he heals up," Warren said.

"Keep him as quiet as possible." The doctor wrote out a prescription and handed it to Warren. "I've given him an anodyne, but he'll have considerable pain and swelling for a while. You can get this sulphate of morphia and conserve of roses at a pharmacy. You mix them together and roll the mixture into pills; the pharmacist will tell you how. Have him take one whenever the pain gets too bad. Now tell me where you live, and I'll check on him tomorrow."

"We'll come with you," Claire murmured to Warren. Harry helped support Randy's injured leg as the men lifted him into the buckboard.

"No need," the doctor said, snapping shut his bag before starting off in search of others who might be injured. "That anodyne will put him to sleep for quite a while."

"We can at least help you and Birdie get him settled." Claire gently touched Randy's forehead. She wanted to tell him how much he meant to her, but this didn't seem like the proper time.

CHAPTER THIRTY-NINE

It was growing dark when Harry dropped Claire off at her apartment. She found the cupboard doors in the kitchen flung open and a few dishes lying broken on the floor. In the parlor, pictures on the wall hung askew, books had been shaken from their shelves, and the whatnot had toppled over, smashing a vase. She lit the gas lamp and began putting things in order.

Was this part of living in California? First torrential rains, now an earthquake. Neither would do much to attract new settlers or lure real-estate buyers. When word filtered back east, would people be afraid to settle in Los Angeles? Would those already here pack up and leave? Might the tremor be only the first, with more to come?

Worst of all, Randy certainly didn't deserve such a cruel blow. Tears filled Claire's eyes. Her head ached. She wanted to focus on happiness and success, not destruction and pain.

In the weeks that followed, the city of Los Angeles felt the effect of the rains, the earthquake, and the oversold real-estate market. A few early investors claimed profits, but far more were lamenting the sagging market. Claire's business continued to decline. Twice she had to ask the bank to wait for payment on her loans while Roscoe Longworth scurried to unload another of her properties at a loss.

By early summer, having waited too long for things to

pick up and fearful that values would go even lower, Claire had sold off all of Pacific Realty's holdings, sustaining a significant loss, and she was still not able to clear up all of her outstanding obligation. Only the La Paloma remained, and she applied her efforts to replacing departing tenants while assuring the bank that overdue payments would soon be forthcoming.

On the Fourth of July, Claire and Harry took a picnic supper to the park to watch the fireworks display sponsored in part by City Councilman Farley Foster Dodd. But their mood was far from festive. Preoccupied with her failing business, Claire nibbled a fried chicken leg while they awaited the darkness that would show off the star shells and Roman candles.

Harry had been unusually quiet, but finally he broke the silence. "P.B.'s decided to close the Hollywood bank."

"Oh, Harry." Claire hadn't considered that the bank could be in serious jeopardy. She put aside the chicken leg, wiping her fingers on her napkin. "Is it bad loans?"

He nodded. "Some of the early ones are already in default, and most of the new applications are just too risky to approve. Too few deposits, too."

"I'm sorry, Harry. You worked so hard to establish that location."

"Harder than with either of the other two—luckily both are still sound—but this one just didn't take hold. There was nothing I could do to pull it through, and P.B. insists that we cut our losses."

Claire understood. "I've cut expenses to the bone at Pacific Realty, too, but I may have to let Perry go."

"Who would have thought things could get this bad so fast? Just too many disappointed folks leaving town."

The explosion of the first star shell lit up the sky, and they watched as the fiery fragments fell to earth. Harry turned to her, his expression desolate. "But that's not the worst of it, Claire." His bleak tone alarmed her. "There's no easy way to tell you this." For a moment he seemed to be studying the dying embers drifting on the night air, then, mustering his resolve, he turned to her. "I'm afraid the bank has to call in your loans."

"What!" She searched his face for some sign that he was joking. She saw none. "But you know I'll make up my late payments . . . as soon as possible."

"I know you'll do your best, but P.B. thinks I've been lax in some of my loan approvals, and . . . well, he's foreclosing on any loans in default over sixty days."

Panic gripped her. "But I've explained that I don't have the money just yet. Too many of my tenants have run out on their leases."

"You'll need to come up with the full balance by the end of the month or forfeit the La Paloma."

She couldn't believe her ears. "Harry, I can't lease all those vacant units in such a short time. And I have nothing more to sell . . . even if I could get a decent price. Surely the bank can give me another extension."

"P.B. isn't permitting any more extensions." His mouth pressed into a grim line. "And I haven't any influence over him now. I've resigned from California Security."

"Resigned? But why?"

"P.B. never liked the idea of the Hollywood bank."

"But you've proved yourself many times over."

"I thought I had . . . but there's Daisy. I've disappointed him there, too."

"Harry, there must be other banks that will jump at the chance to hire you."

"The point is, I don't want to kowtow to P. B. Mossburg—or anyone like him—for the rest of my life. As a matter of fact I've just learned about a small printing business that's up for sale. The owner came to the bank asking for operating capital, but his plant is so poorly run and ill-equipped that I couldn't approve the loan. Claire," he turned to her with a level gaze, "my grandfather left me a modest nest egg that I've managed to hang onto. I'm thinking of making an offer to buy that printing plant."

In the flare from a Roman candle, Claire saw something new in Harry's eyes.

"The old ink is still in my veins, I guess," he continued. "It'd be risky, but with one of the new Mergenthaler Linotype machines and a webfed press, I believe I could turn it around. It's putting out a newspaper called *The Nickelodeon* that nobody with any sense reads."

"Isn't *The Nickelodeon* mostly just cheap advertising?"

"It is, but I'd put out a whole new paper. I have an editor friend on the *Chicago Tribune,* a fella named Norwood Phelps, who wrote me that he wants to come out here if he can find a job. A crusty old curmudgeon, but he knows the newspaper business backwards and forwards. God, Claire, just think of the satisfaction of creating a top-notch paper that could grow right along with Los Angeles, become a leading source for progressive ideas."

A series of rapid explosions sent showers of colorful stars into the dark sky, and spectator applause postponed further discussion for a few minutes.

Claire sat thoughtfully during the shower of cascading sparks. What would she do without Harry at the bank? She had counted on him approving any borrowing she might find necessary to sustain her own enterprise.

"I'm not sure what I want to do," he continued as if he

had picked up her thought. "With *your* business failing, I could use that money to bail you out. It may be foolish to want to get into printing again anyway."

"No, it isn't," she said earnestly. "It's a wonderful idea, and starting a newspaper would be an incredibly exciting challenge."

"But what about you, Claire? If you lose the La Paloma, how will you live? Even if you manage to pull it through, you're too fine a woman to be satisfied with our . . . our *arrangement*."

"Harry . . ."

"I mean it, Claire. We could throw in together, use my nest egg to pay off your loans, then put both our energies into rebuilding Pacific Realty."

She studied the man seated beside her, a man most women would be thrilled just to be with, a man who was offering to take care of her. And yet, she knew she could never give up her independence, her ambition and dreams—perhaps her very soul—simply to guarantee her security. "Marriage would change things, Harry."

"You could continue with your business interests," he assured her. "Nothing needs to change."

"That's easy to say. But things would be different."

His expression held a special poignancy. "Claire, I have no quarrel with the way things are. I'm offering to make an honest woman of you."

"I appreciate that," she said softly. Her refusal was understood.

But what could she do? The thought of losing everything was almost more than she could bear. And how could she possibly come up with the $20,000 she needed to save the La Paloma and her realty business? McKenzie couldn't help her; he had sold or mortgaged everything he had to get into the Wonderburg project. Vanda had taken Claire's advice and invested the balance of her money in a nice little two-flat rental property that would pay her a modest income.

"Harry, you're dearer to me than you'll ever know, but I wouldn't dream of interfering in any way with your plans for that newspaper."

"I'm thinking of calling it *The Sentinel*." His eyes showed both relief and gratitude. "And I figure I can come out with the first issue early in September."

The deafening boom of skyrockets bursting red, white, and blue across the dark sky did little to ease Claire's anxiety.

CHAPTER FORTY

Claire slept little that night. It wasn't just the $20,000 it would take to pay her debt in full. She had to have immediate income; her dwindling La Paloma rentals would barely cover her overhead on the property. If she let Perry go, she could save his modest salary, but then she would have no one to run Pacific Realty while she took a paying job to put food on the table. She had to keep Perry on, at least for now. She would begin at once looking for work.

But only a few days of job hunting convinced her that her search was in vain. Businesses were closing. Realtors' offices stood vacant. Cafés had few customers. The railway station teemed with people wanting to leave. The boom had indeed gone bust. She explained her experience and skills to so many of the remaining proprietors that her words began to sound hollow. Well-qualified men were desperate for employment, she was told over and over, their families were going hungry, and hiring them would certainly take priority over employing a single woman—if there was any work to be had, which there wasn't.

One night while soaking her feet to ease the ache of her futile search, she forced herself to face the truth. There was one person who might hire her. Still, she immediately dismissed the idea, vowing she would never go back to work for Axel Kohl.

But a few more fruitless days of job hunting wilted her resolve. Perry's salary was due and, knowing her dilemma, he offered to wait. But he couldn't do that for long. Claire's cash reserve had shrunk to just a few dollars.

The July sun boiled down on her as she trudged the downtown streets, then rode the horsecars to outlying communities in search of work. Grasses on the foothills had browned in the arid season, and palm trees trailed their parched petticoats like cornhusks after shucking. Window boxes and flower beds still overflowed with colorful sweet-scented blossoms and the deep blue of the distant mountains still framed the cloudless sky, but Claire began to doubt her destiny in this City of Angels. Had it all been a cruel hoax? A false promise that had allowed her to test her wings, only to dash her to pieces on the rocks of reality.

Swallowing her pride, she took a train to Pasadena. Near the depot she immediately spotted Kohl's Kafeteria. But she passed on by. There had to be someplace else that would hire her. Perhaps among the realty offices—of which there seemed to be considerably fewer than McKenzie Tate had boasted when they first arrived. Most of those shook their heads at her audacity to apply.

She spent most of her remaining cash on a room at a boardinghouse that night, and continued her canvassing the next morning. The sun beat down relentlessly, and by mid-afternoon, she knew it was hopeless. Thoroughly disheartened, she made her way back toward the depot and, before she could fully prepare herself, Kohl's Kafeteria again loomed before her. Still she hesitated, looking both ways along the street, hoping for another solution. Seeing none, she opened the door and stepped inside.

The restaurant, several degrees cooler than the street, had a simple but pleasant interior that had beckoned several customers in out of the heat to enjoy cool lemonades or sarsaparillas. Perhaps she could tolerate a job as manager for Axel in a place like this, which certainly would pay more in wages than waiting tables in just any café.

"Claire! Jehoshaphat!" Axel, wearing a spotless white apron, came to greet her, his ruddy cheeks flushed as if he were embarrassed to see her. "I was hopin' you'd come by."

"I was in Pasadena and I . . . I just stopped to say hello."

"Good. I been wantin' to talk to you," he said, signaling the waitress to seat other customers. "Come with me." Leading the way to his office in the back, the big, gruff man, his pale eyes bulging, held a chair for her with both his reddened paws. "Claire, I been worried about you. Hope the earthquake over your way didn't do you no damage."

"Almost none. But poor Randy was injured."

"I heard. Guess he and Stanfield have built quite a business. I see their rigs way over here once in a while."

Claire nodded.

"What about you?" He took out a handkerchief and mopped sweat from his face. "Still workin' for Farley Dodd?"

"I have my own business now. I call it Pacific Realty."

"But this real-estate stuff. Ain't it kind of risky? I mean, with things slowin' down like they are."

"I'm doing just fine, Axel." She shifted uncomfortably in her chair, wishing she hadn't come, hadn't given him another opportunity to inveigle his way into her life.

"That's real good, Claire, 'cause . . ."—he twisted the edge of his apron—"Claire, I'm afraid I have some disappointing news. I hope you won't take it too hard."

She waited for him to come to the point—if there was one.

"Claire . . ." He cleared his throat. "I'm afraid I can't marry you." He averted his eyes. "I . . . well, truth is . . . I met somebody else."

"You did?" A surge of relief rose in her and she suppressed a smile.

"Her name's Emma. Fine little waitress and a good manager, too. We're gonna tie the knot."

Claire's response was a mix of compassion for his distress in telling her and despair in knowing that her only lifeline of employment had vanished. "I'm happy for you, Axel."

"Then you're not too disappointed? I mean . . . I did promise you."

"I appreciate your telling me."

"And you're not mad?"

"These things happen," she said, standing and extending her hand. "Good luck with everything, Axel."

"Gosh, Claire, I wasn't wrong about you. Not many women would take this kind of thing so good. But I s'pose you're in with Dodd and his crowd now."

"Not really," she said. "He's running for mayor of Los Angeles, you know."

"He is? Jehoshaphat! I never heard that." His eyes opened wide with the realization that he had actually made the acquaintance of the mayoral candidate.

"Don't you read the papers?"

"Sure, but I never saw nothin' about Farley Dodd. Papers are full of Mayor Wallace and what a good job he's doin' for the city."

"Newspapers can be biased."

"They make a pretty good case for Wallace. I figure they know what they're talkin' about."

Axel's lack of discernment prompted a sudden inspiration that struck her like a thunderbolt. If Axel hadn't heard, perhaps Farley Dodd's message wasn't getting out. A change in city government was the only hope of adopting policies adequate to cope with the boom. And its aftermath. To lay sufficient groundwork for the city that was to come. Mayor Wallace, who was totally lacking in ideas and planning and whose agenda was controlled by self-interested politicians, had to be defeated—and Farley Dodd elected.

Yes! There might be a way that voters could be made aware of the importance of this mayoral election, a way that also would save Claire's business.

"Good-bye, Axel," she said abruptly, renewed energy surging through her. "I'm afraid I must catch my train."

"So soon? How about a glass of cool lemonade? It's awful hot out."

But she was out the door, leaving the restaurateur gaping after her.

Early the next morning Claire was ushered into Farley Dodd's office by his primly efficient secretary, a rotund, middle-aged man whose pudgy neck bulged over a high starched collar.

"Mrs. Chadwick!" Dodd jumped to his feet. "What a fine surprise." He hurried to pull up a chair for her, dismissing the secretary with an impatient, "Everett, shut the door on your way out." When the man had complied, Dodd shook his head, muttering, "Competent, but sour as a grape. And just when I'm ready to start my campaign." He sighed heavily as he reseated himself. "It's going to be a difficult one, you know, with the papers supporting that scalawag Wallace."

"That's what I've come to talk to you about," Claire said. "Not only are the newspapers supporting Mayor Wallace's reelection, but I'm sure you're aware that information on your candidacy is hardly getting out."

"That's what worries me. There's big money behind

Wallace, and I guess the newspapers know which side their bread is buttered on."

Claire nodded. "You need a newspaper solidly behind *you*."

"Easier said than done. I've talked with the editors and publishers but they turn a deaf ear to any kind of reform; even the reporters give me short shrift." Then he added, skeptically, "Don't tell me you have an idea how this can be turned around."

"I do. You see, Harry Graham is thinking of buying a printing business. One that has been putting out a small newspaper called *The Nickelodeon*."

"That flea-bitten rag?"

"Yes, that's the one. But it won't remain so for long. Harry comes from a printing background, and he has some wonderful ideas for an all-new newspaper. He's going to hire an editor from Chicago, a man named Norwood Phelps."

"I know Phelps," Dodd said. "Fine journalist."

"Harry supports your ideas for city government, and he wants to make his own journalistic contribution to Los Angeles."

"From what I know of Harry Graham, he should do all right in the newspaper business."

"I'm sure he will." Claire paused while she considered how to phrase her proposition. "The problem is with me," she said. "I've had some difficulty recently, losing tenants, having to sell off properties at a loss to meet my payments."

He pulled off his spectacles, fixing his myopic gaze on her while he nervously polished the lenses with the edge of his cravat. "I was afraid of that . . . when you tied up with McKenzie Tate."

"I was able to buy McKenzie out," she explained, "but

now California Security is threatening to foreclose on my loans."

Dodd frowned as he returned his glasses to his nose. "Isn't Harry Graham the chief loan officer?"

"He was, but he's left the bank. The part that concerns you, Mr. Dodd, is that Harry is eager to use his newspaper to promote your campaign."

"That's generous of him. But I'm not sure the endorsement of a paper like *The Nickelodeon* would be good for any candidate."

"Harry will give it a fine new look and a new name—he's calling it *The Sentinel*. It'll be a paper you'll be proud to have supporting you. In fact, its very newness will attract attention to your campaign."

Dodd stared at her as one would at a suddenly materializing genie. "Can Harry put all that together in time to support me?"

"With my help, he can. While he sets up the printing end and oversees the plant, *I'll* be managing the paper."

"But what about your realty business?"

"I have a young man working for me. I'm sure he can keep up with things at Pacific Realty through this slow period. As for *The Sentinel*, Harry and I intend to put everything we have into promoting your campaign and supporting your agenda for the city."

"Mrs. Chadwick, you certainly are full of surprises."

"Harry plans to have the presses up and rolling by early September. That will allow enough time for comprehensive coverage of your campaign before the November election."

Satisfied that he saw the advantages in what she had presented thus far, Claire steadied her nerves and took the final plunge. "But I need something from you in return, Mr. Dodd. I want you to loan me the money to pay off my loans. Twenty thousand dollars."

"Twenty thou . . ." He grimaced. "That's a . . . a considerable sum."

"And I need it on terms I can handle until the market turns around."

"But I'm in no position to take such a gamble," he argued. "Money is tight these days. It may be some time before things improve."

"I'll put the La Paloma in escrow as collateral. It's worth twice that."

Dodd sat for a moment regarding her. Finally he cleared his throat as if to push out his consent. "Very well then. I'll talk to Tibby. It may be possible to get you the money by . . . when did you say you need it?"

"By the end of this month. With your help, Mr. Dodd," she said, "I can save my business, Harry's paper will get off to a flying start, and you'll be elected mayor of Los Angeles."

"You're an astonishing woman, Mrs. Chadwick. Astonishing." He stroked his goatee thoughtfully, then mused to himself, "Not too bad a bargain, when you get right down to it."

Claire found Harry in the dining room at the Overland Hotel, and she quickly seated herself across from him. "Harry, I have something to tell you."

"I hope it's not that you've found work in Pasadena. I don't want you so faraway."

"My job will be right here in Los Angeles. Very close to you, indeed." She would have hugged him had it not been for the other diners who were already staring at her unconventional arrival. "As a matter of fact, I'll be working for you—if you'll have me."

He looked puzzled. "Working for me? What do you mean?"

"Harry, I want you to make me manager of *The Sentinel*. I hope you haven't hired one yet."

"No, but . . ."

"I have no experience in newspaper work, but I have business sense, I'm knowledgeable about the workings of City Hall, I get along well with people, and what I don't know, I can learn. I'm sure Norwood Phelps can help me get off on the right foot."

"Claire, this is no solution to the foreclosure on your property. I'm sure you'd make a fine managing editor, but your salary at the paper would be little more than enough to live on, for a while at least."

"Harry, Farley Dodd will loan me the money to pay off my bank loans in return for *The Sentinel*'s endorsement of his candidacy for mayor. You do plan to endorse him, don't you?"

"Well, yes, but . . . I mean, if you're scrambling to save your own business, how can you be working as my managing editor? I don't doubt your abilities, Claire, but you can't be in two places at once."

"Perry can handle the everyday things with minimal supervision, and nothing much is happening right now." She took a folded paper from her pocket. "Harry, I've got all kinds of ideas for the paper. I've made a list. You need me so you can give your attention to the printing operation. You know you do."

"Well, yes. But it never occurred to me . . ." After savoring this new ingredient in the stew, he seemed to like its flavor.

"And you'll give full support to Farley Dodd?" She had to be sure.

"Who else? Our current mayor is hopeless." He gazed at her with amused appreciation. "You know, Claire, creating some excitement in the campaign, increasing emphasis on controversial issues—this could be just the kind of splash we need to launch *The Sentinel* in an important way."

His enthusiasm fueled her own eagerness. "When can we get started?"

"I've done considerable groundwork this past week," he said. "Your timing is perfect."

Claire smiled warmly at the man she loved.

CHAPTER FORTY-ONE

Throughout the long weeks while Randy's leg healed, he continued to manage the liveries as best he could; at first from his cot at the Stanfields' farmhouse, then, after the warehouse roof was rebuilt and he was able to get around with the aid of a cane, from his office there. His foot and ankle still gave him considerable pain, but the doctor had long ago forbidden the continued use of the morphia sulphate, and Randy knew now that he would never walk without the cane, possibly never without the pain.

Claire had visited him several times during his convalescence at the Stanfields', but the meetings were awkward with the shadow of Harry Graham looming between them. Because she was constantly in his thoughts, he decided to pay her a call, to tell her how he felt, perhaps to settle things once and for all between them. Taking the pinto and buggy and driving to the La Paloma, he found her outside her bungalow office, a hammer in her hand, hanging a Pacific Realty sign amid the climbing roses on the picket fence.

"Randy, it's good to see you." She wiped her sleeve across her moist forehead. "Birdie painted this sign for me."

He was struck by the radiance of her face, the happiness in her eyes, which seemed even lovelier than he remembered.

"So much has happened, Randy." She shed her work gloves and looped her arm through his. "Come in and I'll tell you all about it."

Limping along beside her, leaning on his cane, he greeted the industrious Perry Rupert, then followed Claire into her office where they sat down on the divan.

"How's the foot doing?" she asked. She knew that the bones in Randy's foot and ankle hadn't knit properly and that he might never be able to support his full weight on it.

"Can't complain," Randy said. "Gives me a chance to get the hang of this cane."

"I do hope it heals completely, Randy."

"It may," he murmured, looking pointedly at her. "But some things just never heal." He moved closer and took her hand. "I'm glad things have worked out for you. You know how much I care for you, Claire."

"Randy, you mustn't." The reflex was automatic. "You are one of the dearest friends I have," she said, "but that's where it must remain."

The wounded look on his face tore at her heart. She wished desperately that she could take back her words, that she had said it a different way, a gentler way. "Randy, I wouldn't hurt you for the world, but I . . . well, Harry and I . . ."

Randy shrank back, wanting to save them both further embarrassment. So she loved Harry Graham. No wonder her recommendation had carried so much weight in the matter of the loan. Graham was obviously in love with her, too, even then.

"I guess that's about as plain as you can make it," he said. He wanted to ram his fist into Graham's aristocratic nose, anything to relieve the awful realization that she was no longer his, perhaps never had been, and never would be. But what good would it do? A cripple with a cane was no match for a man like Harry Graham.

"Randy, I'm so very sorry."

355

"No need to apologize." He got to his feet, limped toward the door, and left the office.

Claire watched him release the lines looped over the hitching post, hook his cane over the buggy dash, and struggle aboard. The little spotted horse started off at a walk, head bowed much like that of his driver.

At that moment Joanna, coming from school, saw Randy leaving the apartment. "Randy, I'm late. Could you give me a ride down to the Barbary?" Not waiting for an answer, she climbed into the buggy beside him.

"Hello, Joanna."

"I never see you any more." She chatted merrily. "Why don't you ever come to see me dance?"

"No time, I guess."

Noticing he seemed downhearted, unusual for Randy, she asked, "Do you like it here in Los Angeles, Randy?"

"I've built a good business here."

"I suppose I'll like it, too. When I'm through with school." She gave him an adoring glance. "Now that Mother and Mr. Graham seem to be . . . well, you know. For a while I thought maybe you and she . . ."

"Joanna . . ."

"Don't deny it. I know you liked Mother a lot. I can't tell you how glad I am to see her with Mr. Graham. Now maybe you and I . . ."

"No, Joanna." Randy had been avoiding Joanna's infatuation, but now he knew he had to disappoint her, tell her the truth once and for all. As lovely as Joanna was, he could never care for her the way he cared for Claire. "Joanna, I like you . . . as a friend. But there can never be more than that between us." He had heard almost those exact words from Claire just minutes ago.

Joanna's lower lip jutted out in the familiar pout. "Why

not? Randy, I've been thinking of no one but you for two whole years."

"You're young, Joanna. You're a dancer. You have all kinds of people admiring you."

"But I don't want all kinds of people. I want you to admire me, Randy."

"No, Joanna. You've got to forget all this."

"Forget?" Joanna seemed stricken. "But I can't." Tears threatened to spill over. "I . . . I love you, Randy."

"You have a lot to learn about love, Joanna. Maybe we both do."

They rode in silence until he pulled up in front of the theater. Leaning on his cane, he took her hand to steady her while she stepped down to the curb. "Now go in there and be the best little dancer in town."

"But when will I see you?"

"We won't be seein' each other, Joanna." He climbed back onto the driver's seat, snapped the lines and drove off, leaving her standing at the curb.

Claire spent each day from dawn till dusk preparing for the first edition of *The Sentinel*, scheduled to hit the streets on the tenth of September, coinciding with the grand opening of Harry's new printing company, Graham Press. Farley Dodd had come through with the $20,000 Claire needed, Tibby generously offering some of her personal funds. Claire placed the La Paloma in escrow to secure Dodd's loan and paid off the bank in time to avoid foreclosure.

Shifting much of Pacific Realty's office work to Perry, she handled organizational tasks at *The Sentinel*, while the crusty, white-haired Norwood Phelps took over the paper's editorial content, demonstrating within days that at age

sixty he was still fearless and brilliant. He enticed two type-
setters, a copy editor, and a reporter to come from Chicago,
while Harry hired a press crew, set up the new plant, and
made contacts to sell both printing and advertising. "In the
banking business," he assured Phelps, who was at first skeptical about Harry's journalistic aplomb, "one learns a lot
about a town and those in it."

At Claire's insistence, Swifty Lydick was given a job as
distribution assistant and roving part-time reporter. She remembered the trained typist Meta Triffen, desk clerk at the
Angeleno Boarding House, and offered her a job on the
paper. She also invited Evelyn Schroeder to tea at the Del
Rio and enlisted her services as society reporter.

Joanna sometimes helped her mother with various tasks
at the newspaper, and her imaginative spirit delighted
Claire, just as it had during her growing up years. Except
that now her girlish dreams focused on engagements on the
Orpheum circuit, and performances in New York and
London. Her crush on Randy Plank faded, and she had
long since forgiven her mother's relationship with him,
since Harry Graham was obviously Claire's choice. Joanna
liked Harry, and he often showed up at precisely the right
time to take Claire and Joanna to dinner.

A blue haze of cigar smoke hung about the noisy main
room at the Golden Goose, which echoed with the laughter
of men drinking at the ornately carved bar or cozying up to
seductively clad ladies in the shadowy booths. A curving
stairway led to a second floor, and crowded gaming tables
were visible through a wide doorway at the back.

Randy, arriving for his regular poker game, ran into
Peach who had come to see Blanche. For once, Peach
seemed shy and flustered, and it was obvious to Randy that

she didn't belong there. He stared at her, taking in her soft, pale skin, her eyes that were round and blue as cornflowers. On impulse, he said, "Let's go and get some supper somewhere."

Peach nodded. She sensed sadness behind his words. And she knew what had put it there. She had seen Claire and Mr. Graham together.

"That would be nice," she murmured.

Her soft response touched him and, as they stood for a moment looking into each other's eyes, he saw something more than her exquisite face, a part of her she usually covered with her wisecracks.

Blanche appeared from the back room, striding regally toward them in a gown of purple satin, its décolleté filled in with a necklace of amethyst beads. "Peach, honey!" Her husky voice penetrated the noise of the barroom as she hurried toward them, arms extended, her multicolor rings flashing in the lamplight.

Peach smiled happily. "Hello, Blanche." They puckered their lips to kiss lightly.

"Now don't you look fine." Blanche held her at arm's length, savoring the infrequent visit. Then to Randy, "Hello, handsome. Thanks for bringing her to see me."

"I came on my own," Peach said. "We just bumped into each other at the door."

"We're going to have some supper," Randy added. "Would you like to join us?"

"Can't right now." Blanche looked from one to the other. "But can't you stick around here a while?"

"We'll be back," Randy said.

The first week in September, with everything in place for *The Sentinel*'s launching, Harry invited Claire and Joanna on a weekend excursion to Santa Monica where, at long last, they would get their first look at the Pacific Ocean. To fulfill this long-held dream, Joanna arranged to get off on Saturday night, her first such request since she had started dancing.

Taking the Los Angeles and Santa Monica Railroad, they checked into rooms at the Hotel Arcadia, a splendid resort near the beach named for Arcadia Bandini, daughter of the early Spanish settler. Claire knew there would be talk if she vacationed in the company of Harry Graham, even with Joanna along to chaperone, but she didn't care. Life was too wonderful at the moment to worry about busybodies. Besides, they had respectably reserved two rooms, one for Harry, one for Joanna and her, and of course everything would be entirely proper while Joanna was with them.

The surf lay calm the day they arrived, and the breathtaking Pacific spread before them more vast and awe-inspiring than Claire had imagined. Gulls sailed overhead and laughing children played in the warm sand as Claire and Joanna stepped into the gently lapping waves in their new bathing dresses—navy blue middy tops with big sailor collars, and knee-length skirts, below-the-knee bloomers, and navy stockings. "I don't know why I let you talk me into this scandalous outfit," Claire said.

"Don't be a fuddy-duddy, Mother," Joanna chided. "I may even roll down my stockings."

Claire smiled. Her modern daughter had a remarkable sense of humor. She stretched out her arms to the azure water as if to experience its infinite horizon. Was it an omen that she had arrived at this point on this particular day when new possibility seemed limitless?

Harry, preparing to set up the big sun umbrella, took a deep breath of ocean air, reveling in the refreshing coolness of the breeze. "Ah, the smell of the sea. Intoxicating."

"Smells fishy to me." Joanna giggled at Harry's red-and-black-striped bathing suit, which ended immodestly at his shoulders and knees, leaving his arms and his hairy calves stark naked.

Claire, pleased by the easy rapport between the two, felt a glowing contentment, a happy confidence she hadn't felt in a long time. How fine of Harry to arrange this pleasant weekend for them, the first such vacation Claire had had in all of Joanna's growing up years. How wonderful to be spending it in the company of the two people she loved most in all the world—and at the luxurious Hotel Arcadia on the Pacific Ocean in beautiful Santa Monica.

The success of the Hotel Arcadia over the past two years had stimulated construction in Santa Monica to include several business blocks and a number of fine residences. Other impressive structures were St. Augustine's Episcopal Church and Steere's Opera House, where Joanna insisted on seeing each evening's performance. Harry invited the president of Santa Monica's new First National Bank to dine with them one evening, and he verified that, though attempts to finance a wharf there had fallen through, the ocean-resort town was holding its own better than some other communities with fewer natural attractions.

One such community was the highly publicized town of The Palms on the Rancho La Ballona, which their train had passed through on the way. Planned as a center for the grain-growing area between Los Angeles and Santa Monica, The Palms touted its grain warehouse and a provision in the deeds to exclude saloons. According to its promoters, soft water had been found in abundance twenty-seven feet below ground, eight miles of streets had been graded, and parks planted with 6,000 shade trees. But Claire noted that the developers were now offering a free lunch to anyone who would come to look at the lots for sale—a discouraging sign for a project of this quality. The Palms lay directly adjacent to Wonderburg, the town site that had swallowed McKenzie Tate's fortune, but which, Claire noted from the train, showed little development as yet, and she felt some concern about McKenzie's investment.

But this was no time to be dwelling on business concerns. She wanted to make the most of the precious days she had with Joanna. "Better stay out of the sun," she cautioned. "A *headliner* must take care of her delicate skin."

"Oh, piffle. A girl can't have any fun." Joanna flopped down beside her under the big umbrella, envying Harry, who sat in full sun, enjoying its warmth on his face, his bare arms and legs.

Claire sat with her arms clasping her knees, enchanted by the rhythmic surge of the waves rolling endlessly into shore. "Isn't California just heavenly?"

"It's swell," Joanna agreed, jumping up. "And I'm not going to let this ocean go to waste." She ran along the beach splashing in the shallow surf, her dancer's grace evident in every move, and soon she had joined a group of young people playing beach ball.

Claire leaned back on her elbows, feeling the cooling breeze on her face. "Have you ever seen anything as lovely, as mysterious, as the ocean?" she mused.

"Yes," Harry said. "You." He reached for her hand and laced his fingers through hers. "It's good being here together, isn't it, Claire?"

Claire smiled, grateful for the brief interlude of tranquillity after the hectic weeks of setting up Graham Press and preparing for the *The Sentinel*'s debut, and before the final frantic days of getting out the first issue, which would plunge them into the arduous routine of publishing a daily newspaper. The daunting task would be facilitated by an abundance of campaign news that would fill pages until the election, then, if Farley Foster Dodd were elected, by strong support pieces for his reform of city government.

She watched the gulls swooping over the tidal pools, their flashing wings echoing the triangular sails of a few small boats. The warm sand beneath her and the cool ocean zephyrs lulled her anxieties about the newspaper venture, the survival of her real estate enterprise, and her daughter's future. From such a serene vantage point, she saw only smooth sailing ahead.

CHAPTER FORTY-TWO

"Things aren't looking too good, Mrs. Chadwick," Perry Rupert lamented on Claire's first morning back from the beach. "The papers say land sales and building starts are at their lowest in two years. The Los Angeles area had more than one hundred fifty thousand population at its peak a year ago, but they're saying there may be less than fifty thousand when it all settles out. The railroads have put on extra trains to handle all the people leaving."

"I guess I'm not surprised," Claire admitted. "People don't want to sleep three and four to a bed in those boarding-houses forever."

"But if they're leaving by the thousands, what will happen to all those undeveloped town sites and unsold lots?"

"They'll remain undeveloped and unsold. People will lose their money," she said, "especially on more speculative investments—unless those who bought can afford to wait till prices come back up."

"That could take years."

"I'm sure it *will* take years." What Claire wasn't sure of was whether *she* would be able to weather those years.

"Perry, I'm having a party on the tenth to celebrate the grand opening of Graham Press. I hope you can come."

"Thanks, Mrs. Chadwick. I wouldn't miss it."

"Perhaps you can help Joanna with some of the details." Claire hoped to somehow organize the event despite her overwhelming work schedule.

"Be glad to." Each time Joanna came into the office, Perry remained buried in his ledgers, occasionally casting a shy glance at the vibrant dancer.

To Claire's delight, Joanna took over much of the preparation, addressing the special engraved invitations produced by Graham Press, contacting a bakery to provide breads and pastries, organizing the buffet table, the coffee and lemonade. Vanda Kolinski insisted on bringing her delicious *golabkis*. Perry offered to procure an excellent port for the gentlemen.

When *The Sentinel* hit the streets at five o'clock on the morning of September 10, the ubiquitous Swifty Lydick was on the job determining where more copies were needed and overseeing supply of that demand. Around ten, he burst into Harry's office to report the issue completely sold out.

Harry, hosting an open house for potential Graham Press customers, instructed the press manager to run an additional printing for the afternoon trade and to double the next day's print run. Claire chatted cordially with guests at the open house about the objectives of *The Sentinel*, and provided them with information on the new printing company. Meta Triffen, a whirlwind of efficiency, kept the refreshment table supplied in addition to batting out copy for the next edition on her Remington.

At six o'clock, leaving Harry still talking with lingering customers, Claire took a hack to the apartment, where she found that Joanna and Perry had everything ready for the guests. Joanna had gone to the theater but would return after her performance.

Vanda was first to arrive, carrying a towel-wrapped roasting pan. "Hallo, hallo." Flushed with party excitement, she proceeded to the kitchen where she put the pan into the oven to stay warm. "Did you know I got two little Mexican girls living at my house now?" she said. "Sisters. They go to the high school. I give them room and cook for them like their mama would. Nice Catholic girls. They make me laugh with their jokes." The mention of her new boarders evoked an affectionate chuckle. "They sing beautiful, too? 'La Golindrina.' Ah, so pretty." Claire was delighted to see Vanda so happy. Her kindness and generosity had been an important factor in Claire's success, and she had become a dear friend.

The arrival of the five Stanfields seemed to fill the parlor to overflowing. Tucker and Daniel, their hair slicked down, had grown taller, and even little Stella, her dark curls anchored with a red bow, seemed very much a little lady in the ruffled gingham dress her mother had made for her.

Birdie embraced Claire warmly. "I brought you a basket of fresh tomatoes and peppers from my garden," she said. "Sure is good to be where I can put in another crop this time of year—that is, if I can find time away from my painting." Glowing with health, Birdie seemed to have been restored, body and soul. Still she blushed when Claire exclaimed over how beautifully her dress of ochre taffeta complemented her amber eyes and sun-streaked hair.

Warren, decked out in a new suit, took the basket of vegetables to the kitchen. "Nice place you got here, Claire," he commented, noting the woodwork and moldings.

Amid the happy confusion, Farley and Tibby Dodd appeared at the door. Claire gaped when she saw Tibby, tall, elegant . . . and large with child.

Tibby's face glowed with the fullness of her pregnancy, as she quipped, "It must be the climate."

"I'm delighted for you both." Claire clasped their hands

affectionately while giving Farley a why-didn't-you-tell-me look.

"I know it's brazen of me to be attending parties in my condition," Tibby said. "But why not? I'm feeling fine, and I did so want to see you."

"Where's that talented daughter of yours?" Farley said.

"She'll be along later." Claire felt tremendous affection for these two who had been so kind to her. "I want to thank you both again," she said. "That loan saved my life."

"Who's to say who's saving whose life?" Farley said. "I sure had no trouble getting a copy of *The Sentinel* this morning. Those newsboys were everywhere. And I must say, Claire, I'm pleased with the coverage you gave me in this first issue. Had people stopping by the office all day."

"That's wonderful. Will you be taking part in the campaign, Tibby?"

"I had intended to, but now . . ." Tibby laid her hand on her belly. "In my condition I'm afraid such audacity would outrage more voters than it would attract. And the baby's due around Election Day. Isn't that an amazing coincidence?"

"He'll be a little Los Angeleno," Farley said proudly. "A native Californian who'll grow up with the state. We're not just having a baby here, Claire, we're founding a dynasty."

Tibby blushed at her husband's immodesty.

"However the election goes," Claire said, "you two will be winners."

The room was humming with conversation and laughter when McKenzie Tate arrived, looking as droopy as the bouquet of wilting poppies he carried. "Hello, Claire," he said without a hint of cheer. "Guess maybe you heard. The Wonderburg project went broke."

She nodded. "I'm sorry, McKenzie. Were you able to recoup your investment?"

Dee Marvine

"Well, actually, no. Seems I'm in a bit of a pickle. Just a trifle overextended." The usual twinkle was gone from his cat-like eyes. He followed her about the kitchen as she found a vase and arranged the scarlet blossoms in water. "I was hoping . . ." he ventured. "I hate to ask but . . . Is there any chance you could see your way clear to giving me a small loan?"

Claire was stunned. Had he lost *all* his holdings? "You know I would if I could, McKenzie, but I've nothing left except the La Paloma, and it's in escrow. Have you talked to California Security and the other banks?"

"They won't help me. I'm wiped out."

"There must be something you can do," Claire said.

He shrugged. "Move on somewhere, I guess. Arizona maybe."

"But you can't just walk away . . . Can you?"

He sighed. "My creditors will sweep up the crumbs."

"Must you make such a drastic move? Maybe in a few months . . ."

"Too many folks leaving the area." He shrugged. "I suppose I should have been more prudent but . . . well, I thought I had something in that project. Wonderburg could have been my crowning achievement. Who'd have dreamed the whole thing could go belly-up so fast?"

Claire shuddered at the thought of her own narrow escape. If she had gone along with his suggestion to invest everything in the Wonderburg project, she would now be as destitute as he apparently was. "I'll always be grateful for all you've done for me, McKenzie."

He smiled wistfully. "Your gratitude is my reward, my dear."

McKenzie carried the poppies into the dining room for her and placed them on the buffet table. Then, with a

368

flourish of his fingers across his orange whiskers, he dismissed his doleful mood as if brushing away an annoying gnat, and soon he was talking with Tibby about Spanish architecture.

A welcoming cheer went up from some of the guests as Harry appeared in the doorway carrying a stack of newspapers that he proudly dispensed to those gathered around. "Completely sold out," he announced. "Both printings. Not a shred left. And subscriptions are already coming in." He winked at Claire. "Meta stayed to help Norwood and the others with tomorrow morning's edition. They'll be along later."

"The Schroeders will probably be fashionably late, too," she told him.

"Harry, sorry I didn't get over to your opening," Farley apologized, "but I had so many people in my office after they read about me in your paper that I couldn't break away."

Harry returned his hearty handshake. "If that's any indication, Farley, you'll be our next mayor for sure. And if half the commercial business comes in that we've been promised, we'll keep the new press hot. Swifty's out right now recruiting a couple more newsboys."

The evening proceeded with food and merriment. Joanna arrived, looking astonishingly mature in a simple gown of pale green silk that modestly exposed her creamy arms and shoulders and set off an exquisite cameo on a black ribbon at her throat. "A gift," she explained breezily, unable to recall the giver.

McKenzie Tate went to greet her, exclaiming loudly, "Don't tell me this is Joanna." She looked very different from the frowsy girl in the red ostrich feathers who was nearly thrown out of the Dodds' party that night. Soon he had engaged her in a conversation about the cultural advantages in Chicago.

Claire hurried to answer the knock of still another latecomer, and Randy greeted her with his familiar grin. He looked especially dapper in a new black suit and ascot tie with a pearl stickpin, an ivory-handled cane over his arm. Beside him stood Peach, radiant in a white traveling suit and large plumed hat. Claire stared in astonishment as she grasped the significance of their arriving together, dressed as they were.

A momentary hush swept over the room as the other guests, too, caught sight of the beaming couple. Randy gazed lovingly at Peach, who clung to his arm, smiling happily.

"I want all of you to meet my wife," Randy said.

Claire found her voice. "What! Why, that's wonderful! When did all this happen?"

"Yesterday. We been keepin' company for almost two weeks now and thought it was high time. We're leavin' tonight for a honeymoon in San-Fran-cis-co." Randy playfully sailed his sleek new derby toward Tucker Stanfield, who caught it as if reaching for a fly ball and tipped it onto his own head.

Joanna recovered her composure. "Oh, Peach, I'm happy for you. Really I am. And, Randy, you couldn't have made a better choice. I love you both." She encircled them in her arms.

"Thanks, Joanna." Peach returned the hug. "We love you, too." Peach smiled up at her new husband. "We're going to get us a house, a real house, now that prices are down. And we want to start a family right away. Neither of us ever had much of a family life, you know."

"You mean you're not going back to the Barbary?"

Joanna's incredulity was obscured by Harry stepping forward to offer congratulations, followed by others expressing their good wishes. Warren said they could have knocked him over with a feather, and Birdie, her eyes shining with tears, said she hoped they would have a long and happy life with many beautiful children.

Vanda clucked, "So much good things happening."

"Yes," Joanna murmured pensively, "but I don't see how Peach can give up her career. Why, she's practically a headliner."

Claire, who had stepped back near the door to make room for others to gather around the newlyweds, felt Harry's arm around her shoulders.

"This seems to be a day of memorable events," he said, inclining his head toward the bride and groom. "Maybe that should have been us."

She flushed. The past few weeks she had felt entirely content in her relationship with Harry. Working together, they made an excellent team and they would undoubtedly build a fine business together. They had become creative partners, supportive of each other, their strengths complementary. Would he press her now for something more? She hoped not. Not when everything was so perfect. While she knew that Harry respected her independence, she still felt that if they were to marry he might change. He might expect, even demand, the conventional female subordination. Instead of being his partner in every sense of the word, she might become merely his helpmate, always standing behind him, as the capable Dora Ferguson stood behind the senator.

What if, in legalizing their union, they lost the camaraderie they now enjoyed, destroyed the love and mutual respect they now shared? Marriage, however appealing the idea, would present that risk.

It was a risk she didn't intend to take.

"Harry, you're going to be an important man in this town someday."

"Maybe. And I want you there beside me, Claire."

"I'm beside you now."

"What I mean is, without you, Claire, things wouldn't be happening as they are. I thought it was just my being in love with you that made you so essential in my life, but now I doubt that my business could survive without you."

"Of course it could."

"My God, Claire!" he flared. "Here I am shouting my love for you from the housetops, and you're all business?"

She regretted her flippant response. Perhaps revealing her passion for him only in intimate moments was not enough. Wanting to reassure him, she led him out into the courtyard.

The beautiful September night held a faint scent of the ocean in the air, and as they stepped away from the flickering gas lamps and into the shadows among the azaleas, they could see a bright sliver of moon in a sky hung with stars.

She loved him even more for his insistence on clarifying what was between them. "You know I have very deep feelings for you, Harry. I think I would die if I ever lost you. But . . ."

"But what? If we love each other . . ."

"Let's not rock the boat, Harry." Then, searching for a rationale, "We have *The Sentinel* to think of."

"What are you saying?"

She had to tell the truth. If only to admit it to herself. "Harry, I'm afraid."

"Of what?" he asked incredulously.

"Of you. Of myself, maybe. Everything is so perfect the way it is. I guess I'm terrified it might change. That we might become emotionally distant from each other."

"Claire, I can't believe that you, of all people, are afraid of risk. What about the chances you took coming out here? You've learned. You've grown. You're part of Los Angeles now. And if I know you, Claire, you can survive anywhere."

"That's different. Harry, can you promise me you'll never change? That things will always be the way they are now with us?"

He took her in his arms. "I love you now, Claire. I can't imagine my feelings for you ever changing. But that's all I can say for sure. Life offers no guarantees." It was an honest answer.

"Harry, we have something rare." Her eyes searched his in the darkness. "I want it to stay just as it is."

"Tongues will wag if we don't marry."

"Wagging tongues keep women in their place," she said, "and I've too much to do to accept such limitations. Harry, Los Angeles is like a child needing nourishment to grow. Our child. Needing direction. Social. Political. Intellectual. With *The Sentinel*, we have the chance to help this town become a fine city. That's more important than the trivial concerns marriage would bring to distract us."

"All right, my little visionary, I'll get up off my bended knee and stand beside you."

"I'd be honored," she murmured.

Their lips touched, sealing the bargain. "How did I ever find you, Claire? You're one in a million."

"More like one in a hundred thousand," she teased. "A hundred thousand California immigrants. But it was *I* who found *you*. Remember? When I came into the bank for my first loan."

"The one I refused to grant."

"Yes, the one you refused to grant."

"That non-loan has paid me some remarkable dividends." He gazed for a moment at the wide arc of starlit sky. "Remember those early pamphlets? 'Come to Los Angeles and find paradise.' I must confess that . . . until this very moment . . . I never believed them."

"I did," she murmured. "Oh, Harry, I *did*."

ABOUT THE AUTHOR

Following a career as a Chicago editor, **Dee Marvine** moved west and began writing historical novels. A member of Western Writers of America, and a founding member of Women Writing the West, she lives in Big Timber, Montana, with her artist husband Don Marvine.